DEADLY
BUSINESS

By Quintin Jardine and available from Headline

Bob Skinner series:
Skinner's Rules
Skinner's Festival
Skinner's Trail
Skinner's Round
Skinner's Ordeal
Skinner's Mission
Skinner's Ghosts
Murmuring the Judges
Gallery Whispers
Thursday Legends
Autographs in the Rain
Head Shot
Fallen Gods
Stay of Execution
Lethal Intent
Dead and Buried
Death's Door
Aftershock
Fatal Last Words
A Rush of Blood
Grievous Angel

Oz Blackstone series:
Blackstone's Pursuits
A Coffin for Two
Wearing Purple
Screen Savers
On Honeymoon with Death
Poisoned Cherries
Unnatural Justice
Alarm Call
For the Death of Me

Primavera Blackstone series:
Inhuman Remains
Blood Red
As Easy as Murder
Deadly Business

The Loner

Quintin Jardine

DEADLY BUSINESS

headline

First published in 2013 by
HEADLINE PUBLISHING GROUP

1

Cataloguing in Publication Data is available from the British Library

978 0 7553 5708 6 (Hardback)
978 0 7553 5709 3 (Trade paperback)

Typeset in Electra by Avon DataSet Ltd, Bidford-on-Avon, Warwickshire

Printed and bound by CPI Group (UK) Ltd, Croydon, CR0 4YY

Headline's policy is to use papers that are natural, renewable and
recyclable products and made from wood grown in sustainable forests.
The logging and manufacturing processes are expected to conform
to the environmental regulations of the country of origin.

HEADLINE PUBLISHING GROUP
An Hachette UK Company
338 Euston Road
London NW1 3BH

www.headline.co.uk
www.hachette.co.uk

In memory of my lovely sister-in-law, Fiona McGrane,
who left us on June 30th, 2012

One

'Woof woof.'

That's little Lily Simmers' war cry. They were the first proper words she ever uttered, and on the day of her third birthday party they were still her favourites, even though she had amassed a much larger vocabulary by then, a mixture of the Catalan and Castellano spoken to her by her mum, Tunè Miralles, and her dad, Ben Simmers, and the English which she uses with her paternal grandparents, all three of them.

All the kids in Catalunya grow up bilingual, with two native languages, and around St Martí d'Empúries many are like Lily, picking up English or French as they grow up in the cosmopolitan community that it has become. My son speaks four, having learned French while living with his father in Monaco, then picking up the local lingos when we settled here, after his father's death and my rebirth. He's literate in all of them, more so than I am. I'm very proud of that because he's . . . I almost said 'only twelve', but Tom Blackstone isn't 'only' anything. I still think of him as my child, but he isn't any more, not really. He's a big boy, one metre sixty-two (around five feet four) already, mature for his years, and has taken the first steps into adolescence.

Lily's toddler barks were directed at her parents' two Labradors, Cher and Mustard, as they patrolled the perimeter of the party site, a grassy area enclosed by the remaining walls of what was, a couple of hundred years ago, the first house in the village as you approach up the hill that leads from the beach, on the other side of the church from our place. Tunè and Ben had chosen it because it's shaded even in June, when the sun was at its highest. They'd held her first two parties at home, but they had been as much for adults as children, maybe even more so, since Ben's father told me after the second that the last of the guests didn't leave until after midnight.

Tom and I were invited to all of them because, as Tunè put it, we're almost family. I'm 'Tia' to Lily; that's 'Auntie' in English ('Primavera' has at least two syllables too many for her at the moment), and I am her number one babysitter. I volunteered as soon as she was born. When Tom was an infant, I was in a big mess personally and emotionally, and I didn't get the most out of that time. Oz . . . that's his father . . . and I were in the terminal stages of a very short marriage when I discovered I was pregnant, and I was so antagonistic towards him that I left him the same week that my Clearblue kits both showed positive. Yes, I did it twice, to be sure, to be sure.

Oz: my strength and my weakness, the guy I met when he was a nobody, without the merest twinkle of a film actor showing in his eye, then loved and battled with alternately as his star gained luminescence, until those people who suggested snidely that he was cast in his first movie only because of a passing resemblance to Keanu Reeves came to refer to Keanu as 'Oz Blackstone lookalike'.

I let him think that I had run off with someone, but I hadn't; in fact I cut myself off from everyone I knew, family and friends, although I had very few of the latter at that time, and one of those wouldn't have been interested in helping me out as she was in a similar situation herself.

I didn't know it at the time, and didn't find out until I made the mistake of attempting to front him up just after Tom was born, that my fecund spouse had managed to knock up both me and my erstwhile best pal within a few weeks of each other, and that she had filled the vacancy I'd created. When I found out, I beat another hasty retreat, and it was another three years before he discovered that little Janet wasn't his first child after all.

Things got even more complicated after that, and I lost my precious Tom for a while. I don't know what would have happened if Oz had lived, but I'm certain of one thing. I would have fought tooth, nail and very sharp claw to get my boy back, for every day that I spent without him caused me pain that I cannot bear to recall and, if I did, wouldn't be able to describe.

But he didn't live, damn him. I re-emerged from my

shadows, and did a deal with Susie, the official widow, who was my friend again by that time, to regain custody. I couldn't think of moving anywhere else but St Martí. I'd lived here before, with Oz and without him. Tom doesn't know it, but he was conceived in a house not far from where we live now; some day soon I'll tell him, for a person has a right to know every scrap of the truth about himself. I may refrain, though, from telling him that his half-sister was also conceived there, a very few weeks later. Once he learns a little more about human gestation he will work out the timing for himself, but I'll deal with that when it happens.

The two young people in question were both on party parade as I sat on the wall watching the fun, acting as toddler wardens, handing out drinks and wiping off smeared chocolate cake before it did too much damage to clothing. Janet looked completely at home, and in command. She's bilingual in English and French, but she sees enough of her half-brother . . . Susie and I tried from the start to ensure that they, and wee Jonathan, her younger child with Oz, spend at least six weeks together each year . . . to have picked up plenty of Catalan and Spanish from him, even if she doesn't really know which is which. She's growing fast too, only a few centimetres shorter than Tom. She's a pretty girl, taking after Susie in looks as much as Tom takes after Oz, but in a year or so she'll have reached her mother's height, while he'll be eye to eye with my one metre seventy. Wee Jonathan, I reckon, will always be just that; he's a small broody child, with his father's dark hair, like Tom, his mum's oval face and eyes that never give any hint of what's going on behind them. He'd opted out of the celebrations; instead he was on the beach with Conrad Kent.

Conrad Kent? Susie's minder. His official title was logistics manager, but make no mistake, that's what he was employed to be, back when Oz was alive, so that she could run her property and construction group from Monaco, with a managing director in charge in Scotland. The idea was that he would keep the family home secure, well maintained and running smoothly, with his wife Audrey as Susie's personal assistant, but that he would also be driver and bodyguard, and his number one priority would be keeping the children safe.

Oz employed both Kents some years ago, and they were even more needed after he died. Conrad isn't a big bloke, and he dresses like a hotel manager, or the principal in a very expensive car dealership. He's half Welsh, half Jamaican, and he has a degree that he's never used, in some obscure subject. He's very neat, always precise and immaculate, but he has a military background and there is something about him that tells you he is not a man you should ever mess with.

He'd come with the children, and would stay until it was time for them to go home, in a few days. We'd been a three-kid (and one minder) household for a month, for a reason that still concerned me. A year before, Susie had told me that she had 'a wee health issue'. As it turned out, it was bigger than she'd suspected. She'd been investigated for anaemia but leukaemia had been diagnosed. She'd undergone a course of chemotherapy during the autumn, another a few months later, and, as scheduled, was just completing a third.

On each occasion the children, and Conrad, had stayed with me. Audrey had stayed by Susie's side, to help her in any way she needed. She'd told the kids that she had to go away on business, and neither of them had questioned that, but the last time I'd seen her, when I took Tom along to hers for Easter and saw the effects of the chemo, I couldn't imagine that she could fool them for much longer.

If it came to that: her consultant was absolutely sure, she said, that the third course of treatment would see her in remission. I wasn't as bullish; I'd paid a visit to the man myself and used my nursing experience to interrogate him. I reckoned he wasn't even absolutely sure that the sun would rise next morning. Now I'm not an oncologist, and although I have worked in that area, I only have a little knowledge . . . and you know what they say about that. Nonetheless I was worried, for Janet and Jonathan, but also, cravenly, as I will admit, for myself and my lifestyle. Those two kids don't have a close relative in the world other than their mother and Tom, and my thinking was if anything did happen to Susie, well, I could hardly let them go into an orphanage, could I?

'Are you all right, Auntie Primavera?'

Janet's question startled me. 'What? Yes, of course. When am I ever not all right, kid?'

She smiled. 'Never, but . . .' she hesitated for a second or two before blurting out, 'I can tell when Mum's thinking about my father. You looked the same way just now.'

That cut the feet from under me; Tom had said much the same thing to me a couple of years before, when he'd caught me off guard.

I dealt with it as casually as I could. 'Did I indeed? And who do you imagine I might have been thinking about?'

Wrong move, Primavera. Janet's face fell; she frowned and bit her lip. 'I'm sorry,' she murmured. 'I thought you might have been . . .'

'Thinking about him too?' I said, smiling to ease her embarrassment. 'As it happens, I wasn't, but you're right, I might have been. I do think about him, for the very same reason your mum does, and you do, and Tom does, and wee Jonathan does. Because we all loved him and we all miss him.'

'You loved him too?' There was a hint of a challenge in her voice.

'Of course I did,' I replied. Janet and I had never shared a 'big girl' conversation. I decided that the time had come. 'I take it that by now you understand the reproductive process,' I continued, making it into a question with a raised eyebrow.

She flushed a little. 'How babies are made? Yes, we did that at school a long time ago.'

'Yeah well . . . Love has, or should have, a lot to do with that. I've had one baby, that's Tom. I made him with your father. That's why he's your half-brother, and I will tell you this, I wouldn't have wanted to make him with anyone else in the world. So yes, I might not have been very good at showing it sometimes, but I loved him. I'm proud of it too, just as your mum is.'

'Did he love you?'

I nodded. 'Yes. He said he did and I believed him. Your father had a great capacity for love, and I don't mean that sarcastically. He loved me, and he loved your mother and he loved his first wife.'

Her eyes widened, and she gasped. 'His . . .' she began, then fell silent.

Christ on a bike, Primavera! Right off the cliff. Susie hadn't told her. 'Yes.' I looked her in the eye. 'You father was married three times. The first time was to a girl he grew up with.'

'What happened to her? He never talked about her, and Mum never has either.'

'It hurt him too much to talk about her. It hurt him very, very badly.'

I could see her feel his pain. 'What happened to her?'

'She died, Janet. There was a simple, one in a million, household accident and she died. It broke his heart.'

She frowned again, a little wince. 'Once when I was young, I saw him crying. He was sitting in his chair, on his own, and he was crying. He didn't see me, but it frightened me, so much that I couldn't ask him why. Do you think that was why? Was he thinking of her?'

I nodded. 'Probably. He wouldn't have been thinking of me, that's for sure.'

She didn't pursue that. Instead she asked, 'Did you know her?'

I nodded. 'Yes I did; she was around when I met your dad. He and I were together for a while, but she was the one.'

'Did Mum know her?'

'Yes, they met.'

'So why has she never mentioned her?'

That was a good question and I reckoned that I knew the answer. If she had, then given her daughter's perspicacity, it would have opened a whole barrel of worms about that time in her life. Susie had been right to keep the lid on it, and I was going to have to apologise to her for taking it off.

'I don't know,' I lied. 'You'd have to ask her yourself.'

'Maybe I won't.'

'Your decision, but I think you have to, now that careless old Auntie Primavera's spilled the beans. There shouldn't be any secrets between mothers and daughters.'

'She kept it a secret from me,' she retorted, resentfully. 'It involved my father, and she didn't tell me.'

'No,' I countered. 'The way I see it, she hasn't told you yet, that's all. I'll bet she was only waiting till she judged you were old enough.'

'Do you really think so?'

'I wouldn't say it if I didn't.'

She gave me an appraising look, then nodded. I thought we were done, but no.

'What was her name?' she asked.

I'd started, so I had to finish. 'Jan,' I told her, 'short for Janet.'

Her mouth dropped open again. 'I was named after her?'

'I wasn't around when you were named,' I pointed out, 'so I can't say that for certain.'

'But I was, wasn't I?'

I smiled, and gave in. 'For sure, kid, for sure,' I admitted. 'How do you feel about that?'

She thought about it for a few seconds, then a slow grin spread across her face. 'My father named me after his lost love, his childhood sweetheart. I think that's pretty cool.'

To you, no doubt, I thought, *but I wonder what Susie thought about it. Could it be why she's never spoken a word to you about Janet the First?*

She jumped up on to the wall beside me, all arms and legs and red hair. Out of the shaded area, I could see that her face was pink; given her hair colouring and her complexion, her mother had always insisted that she uses fifty-factor sun protection, and leaves nothing uncovered. I did not intend to send her back home sunburned or I'd hear about it.

'Do you have any Nivea with you?' I asked.

She shook her head.

'Then do me a favour. Even though it's evening now, there's still power in that there sun. Go back to the house and put some cream on, everywhere that isn't covered.' She was wearing shorts and a cap-sleeved T-shirt so that meant most of her. I gave her the key and she headed off, obediently, knowing, no doubt, that whatever her mother chucked at me, she'd get it first. I wondered if Janet ever had rebellious moments at home, for she's never shown any when she's stayed with me, not one. I guessed that she must have inherited that virtue from her grandparents, for it hadn't been evident in either of her parents.

'Hey, Primavera.' I looked around, to see Tunè heading towards me with a plate held out before her. 'You want some?' she asked me, in Catalan. 'I didn't think it was possible that we could make too many sandwiches for Lily and her friends, but it seems that we have. The Nutella ones are all finished, but there's tomato and cheese spread.'

'Oh damn,' I laughed. 'I was looking forward to a Nutella sandwich.' I helped myself to a handful from the plate. She smiled with me, as if she thought I'd been kidding, but I wasn't; they're my weakness. In Vaive, our beach bar of choice, they have Nutella toasties on the menu now, and I'm the cause.

'Ben still working?' I asked her. I'd noted his absence.

'Yes. He closed the shop for Lily's birthday, but one of his restaurant customers needed an urgent delivery, so he had to go. He'll be back soon, though.'

Ben runs our local wine shop at the foot of the narrow street that leads up to St Martí's main square, extravagantly named Plaça Major. It's taken up entirely in summer by café restaurants, of which all but one are big on pizzas. It was quarter to seven, on Friday, June the twenty-third. It was quiet at that moment in time, but in a couple of hours it would not be, for on that auspicious date the Festa de San Juan, the national celebration of the summer solstice, takes place.

Once I heard a Brit expat describe San Juan as 'like Guy Fawkes night. You know.' That's akin to describing the Spanish Civil War as 'a little local dispute'. San Juan has fireworks too, but it's much, much more. It's more like the bombing and rocket campaign that preceded the invasion of Iraq at the start of the second Gulf War. If it's explosive and they can get their hands on it, the locals will set it off, and by that I mean locals all across Spain. L'Escala, the municipality of which St Martí is a part, is a big enough community to make some serious noise, and we were about an hour away from the usual kick-off time. They don't wait for dark; thunderflashes make their point twenty-four hours a day.

That was why the party was starting to break up, and why Tunè was trying to offload the sandwiches. I scoffed mine and jumped down off the wall ready to help with the clear-up. In fact there was little to clear; Cher and Mustard are very effective in that respect, with anything that's edible.

We were finished, the party guests and their parents had all gone home, and Tom was fitting a reluctant Lily into her pushchair . . . if I'd tried that there would have been trouble, but she's his girl . . . when Janet reappeared. She looked at her half-brother. 'Did you ask?' I heard her say.

'Ask what?' I said.

Tom replied. 'Can Janet and I go to the concert?' His voice had begun to deepen over the winter; I've noticed that the more serious he is, the lower the register.

I frowned at him, as if I meant it. 'Which one?' I retorted.

He gave me his exasperated sigh; I'm told that's something else that comes with puberty. 'You know which one, Mum. The one tonight, on the beach, for San Juan.'

I kept my frosty face on. 'Do you know when it starts?'

'Yes, round about midnight.'

'Remind me. How old are you two?'

'You know how old; twelve.'

'Then I rest my case.'

'Oh, come on, Mum,' he protested. 'It's happening three hundred metres away from our house. Do you think we're going to sleep through it? Never mind the concert, the rockets and the bangers will go on till one o'clock, earliest. Please, Mum. We won't be drinking, or smoking dope or anything like that. You can send Conrad to look after us, if you like.'

As he spoke, I saw the man in question, and his sandy charge, crest the hill behind him.

'I don't send Conrad anywhere,' I pointed out. 'He's responsible to Susie Mum for Janet and Jonathan; he decides where they go.'

'So I can go, but not Janet?'

'Did I come close to saying that?' I exclaimed. 'Conrad,' I called out, 'these two want to go to the reggae concert on the beach tonight. What do you think of that?'

He pursed his lips. 'Definitely not without a minder,' he said. 'And that's a problem 'cos for all my West Indian heritage, I can't stand reggae.'

'Then it's just as well for everybody,' I told him, grinning, 'that I've been waiting for a few years for Tom to be old enough for us to go.' I pointed at him, and his half-sister. 'There'll be a curfew, mind,' I warned them. 'Two o'clock, latest.'

'Three o'clock?' my boy shot back.

'Two thirty. You'll have had enough by then, trust me. Janet, it'll probably be cool during the night, so make sure you dress warm enough.'

'I will do, Auntie Primavera,' she promised. 'But what about Jonathan?'

I was about to tell her that he was just too young, when he beat me to the punch. 'No,' he snapped. 'I don't like loud music and I don't like big crowds.' He spoke French, as if he was trying to cut the rest of us out of an argument between him and his sister, but I knew by that time that it went deeper. Wee Jonathan made a point of speaking French almost exclusively in Monaco, and would do the same when he's at mine if I let him get away with it. I will only speak English to him there, and won't acknowledge his reply unless it's in the same language. I have no idea what goes on inside the kid's head, but I can only guess that he's rejecting something, possibly his entire family.

'That's okay,' Tom said to him, in the same language. 'I hadn't thought about you. I'm sorry. I'll stay with you if you want, Jonathan.'

'You will not!' Janet snapped. 'He's the baby of this family and he's not going to decide what we do.'

'No more are you,' Tom murmured, in Catalan.

'I don't want anyone to stay in with me!' Jonathan shouted, exploding into English. 'Go to your fucking concert and enjoy yourselves!'

'Hey,' Conrad barked, grasping the child by the shoulder. 'That settles it. You are grounded, boy. You don't leave the house till Monday, earliest.' He glanced at me. 'I'm sorry about that, Primavera. I don't know where he picked that up.'

I laughed. 'You don't? His father and I used to have conversations just like that. For all that Oz and Susie were happy, I'm sure they had their moments too.' I went over to the kid. His eyes had more life in them than I'd ever seen before, but it was the wrong sort. I took his hand; he tried to pull it away but I didn't let him. 'Come on, Jonathan, let's you and I go home. Would you like to phone your mum? You haven't spoken to her for a couple of days.'

'No.'

'Send her an email, then?'

'No.'

'She'll be missing you,' I ventured as we started to walk towards the house.

His bottom lip trembled. 'She won't, or she'd have taken me with her.'

'Mum,' Tom called, from behind me, 'can Janet and I go down to the beach bar for a Fanta?'

'Okay, but be home before eight, so you can get cleaned up for dinner.'

'I'll go with them,' Conrad said. 'I fancy a beer.' And he didn't fancy letting Janet out of the sight of an adult. Oz was rich and famous, and he had been obsessive about his kids' security. He and his minder had been very close, and Conrad still heard and obeyed his master's voice, even from beyond the grave.

They went on their way, and wee Jonathan and I continued on ours. There's a simple cold shower at the side of the house. I made him stand under it for a minute or so, not as a penance, but to wash the sand off: standard practice. When it was done, I towelled him half dry and then we went inside. He would have headed straight for the room he was sharing with Tom, but I wouldn't let him. Instead, I took him into the kitchen, gave him a glass of Activia pouring yoghurt, vanilla flavour, and sat him at the table. I'd seen enough of him by that time to know that always gets his attention.

'Now,' I began, 'now that everyone's tempers have cooled, tell me again why you think your mother won't be missing you.'

'Because she didn't take me,' he repeated, quietly, but stubbornly.

'She couldn't. Your mother's a businesswoman. Sometimes she has to be away.'

'She's never left me before, only this last year. Any time she's had to go to Scotland before she's always taken Janet and me.'

'And Conrad and Audrey.'

'Yes.'

'And those times I'll bet she worked a lot and you didn't see much of her.'

'Yes,' he conceded, grudgingly.

'In that case, do you think she might have decided that now you're old enough for her to leave you for a while, that's best for you?'

He avoided the question by attacking his glass.

'Jonathan,' I continued, 'I know how I feel when Tom visits you and I'm not there. I promise you, I miss him every day he's away, but still I let him go, because it's good for all you kids that you spend time together when you're growing up. Your mum feels the same way.'

'She can't.'

'Why not?'

'Because I saw her plane ticket in her office. She's gone to America.'

He was right about that. Susie's consultant had sent her to the Mayo Clinic in Scottsdale, Arizona, for her treatments.

'I think she's gone with Duncan,' he whispered.

Two

Duncan. That was a name that I thought had been consigned to the past. There's a significant difference between Susie and me in the way we've dealt with life after Oz. It may have had something to do with the fact that while I was around halfway through the journey between forty and fifty, Susie had seven years fewer on the clock than I did, but as single women, I've always found that I managed perfectly well without a man in my bed, while Susie usually had an 'escort' somewhere or other in her vicinity.

I'm still fertile, although the menopause can't be far away, but I was having trouble remembering the last time I looked at a bloke and thought, *'I'd really like to fuck you.'* No, sorry, I lie. It was eight years in the past, the man in question was Oz, and I did, regardless of the small detail that he was married to Susie at the time. Biter bit, and all that.

Susie's Duncan had been around for longer than most of her consorts, almost two years from start to what she had told me was the finish. His surname was Culshaw, and he was the nephew of her managing director. They were introduced at a company meeting in Glasgow, and before long, he was making regular visits to Monaco. He was a few years younger than her, but not so many that he could be classed as a toy boy. I'd met him a couple of times on visits to Monaco during his 'tenure of office', so to speak.

He was a good-looking bastard, I'll give him that, not tall for a man, about my height when I'm in high heels, taller than Susie without towering over her, with fairish hair that wasn't quite blond, pale blue eyes and a narrow waist. He scrubbed up well enough, and I'll admit he looked not bad in swim gear around the pool, although he was a bit on the bony side and had unsightly clumps of hair on his back. When Susie asked me what I thought of him, I pointed this out. She couldn't argue otherwise, but she assured me that his best feature was hidden from view. I didn't ask for specifics, but I wasn't sure I believed that; my scepticism was based on several years' nursing experience, when I saw a lot of skinny guys . . . or a little, as was mostly the case.

I did ask about his profession, though, over dinner one night at her place when the kids had gone to bed and Duncan wasn't in residence. 'He's a writer,' she told me.

'What does he write?'

'Newspaper articles, magazine articles, that sort of stuff.'

There was a vagueness about her answer that was very un-Susie-like. 'Who pays him to do this?' I murmured.

She raised an eyebrow. 'Were you born cynical?'

'I'm not cynical,' I insisted. 'But I don't take a single fucking thing for granted either, least of all when it comes to men.'

'That's why you don't have one,' she chuckled.

'Maybe . . . but I prefer to believe that since my boy's going to start shaving in a couple of years, I don't want him to have to compete for the bathroom mirror. So,' I went on, 'who does your guy work for?'

She laughed. 'Your boy has an en-suite bathroom, so don't give me that one. Duncan's freelance,' she continued. 'He gets stuff in the Scottish papers, mostly their weekend magazines, but he says that his best clients are airlines. You know, those flight mags that you read then forget as soon as you step on to the air bridge.'

'Your wild weekend in Shagaluf? Great European stag night venues? That sort of stuff?'

She nodded. 'You've got it. Pays well, he says. He does other stuff, though; corporate. For example he's going to write the text for the Gantry Group's next annual report.'

'How about books?'

'He says he's working on a manuscript. He won't let me read it yet, but he says it's a thriller. He's looking for an agent just now. He says you can't get published without one.'

'How about Oz's old agent? What was his name again?'

'Roscoe Brown?' She shook her head. 'No, Primavera, he's Hollywood; that's not what he does.'

'I could always send it to my brother-in-law,' I suggested. 'He'd read it if I asked him.'

'Miles Grayson? I thought he'd retired.'

'From acting, yes, but he still produces and directs. Although he has so many business interests these days, he insists that films are still his main focus. Everything else is just a sideline.'

'Including the wine business?'

'Very much so. It's only a small part of his portfolio.'

A couple of years ago Miles and my sister visited me in St Martí. I introduced him to some of the better wines from our region and he was so impressed that he bought one of the producers. I've been a director for the last two years and it's doing all right.

'Well,' Susie ventured, cautiously, 'if you think he would read it, I'll tell Duncan, and ask him to give you a call.'

Tom and I went back home next morning, and I thought no more about it, until last autumn, over a year later, my phone rang, and it was Duncan Culshaw, calling out of the blue. He'd booked himself into the Nieves Mar Hotel, in L'Escala, and he told me that he'd like to see me.

'You came all this way on spec?' I asked.

'Susie said you'd be here,' he said. 'She told me that you might be prepared to show my book to your brother-in-law.'

'I might, that's true, but you don't need to throw yourself at my feet for it to happen. If I do it, it'll be as a favour to Susie, pure and simple.'

'I appreciate that,' he said, 'but I wouldn't want you to embarrass yourself with him by sending something blind.' He paused. 'Have dinner with me tonight, and I'll give you a copy.'

'I can't do that,' I replied, 'unless you fancy feeding my son as well. But lunch tomorrow would be okay.'

He had his manuscript with him when we met in the hotel restaurant, not in printed form but on a four gigabyte memory stick. 'It's not quite finished,' he told me. 'I have a couple of rough edges that I need to smooth out.' He handed it to me. 'Read it please, and we'll meet again, possibly for coffee tomorrow morning. I'll call you to arrange something.'

'That's a tight timescale,' I observed, 'for a whole manuscript.'

'You'll finish it, I promise you. It's a page-turner.'

I took the stick from him. 'Obviously not literally,' I pointed out, 'but I'll do it.'

We had a pleasant enough lunch; most of our conversation was about the Emporda region, its front-line tourist pitches and some of the spots off the beaten track. 'That was very useful,' he told me as he signed the bill. 'I have a piece to write for one of my airline clients; you've given me just about everything I need.'

'That's handy,' I remarked. 'You'll be able to put me down as a business expense.'

I had a flash of concern that I might have sounded waspish, or been 'a nippy sweetie', as my Glaswegian Granny Phillips would have put it, but far from being wounded, Duncan nodded, beamed, and replied, 'Yes, indeed, Primavera; the whole damn trip in fact, with free air travel and car hire.'

My only reaction was a smile, but I felt that for the first time I'd had a flash of the real Duncan Culshaw.

I drove straight home, dug out the rarely used MacBook laptop that I keep as a back-up for my computer, took it out on to the terrace, with Charlie, our Labrador, for company, and plugged the stick into one of the USB sockets. There was only one document on it, a large PDF file, titled *The Mask*. When I clicked on it, a box came up on the screen advising me that it was read only and that I would not be able to copy or edit it. 'Fine,' I muttered, and clicked the button to proceed.

There was no foreword, only the title, author's name and a copyright declaration. I turned to the first page and started to read.

'My wee brother?' she began, then paused, as if she was framing every word in her eventual reply.

'He was like a loch on a fine summer's day. Not a mark, not a ripple on his surface. You looked at him and you thought, he's one of the fairest things I've ever seen. And he was, the boy I grew up with.

'But then life took a hold of him and the water was disturbed, choppy at first, and then rougher, till it was storm-tossed, white-crested. He was still beautiful, but in a different way, darker, ominous, and you knew that not far below that surface there was another man, someone different, someone dangerous, like the monsters of legend given form.'

As she spoke, Lady Doreen March's plain but strong face seemed to change, to weaken, to crumple, and her voice began to crack. And as she finished, there were tears running down her cheeks, cutting ravines in her make-up.

I sat bolt upright in my chair. 'What the fuck is this?' I shouted, loud enough for Charlie to bark, his fur rippling, readying himself to defend me from attack, even though he couldn't see the threat.

'Doreen March?' I said, more quietly. 'Ellie?'

He'd changed a name, but only by a couple of months. 'My wee brother' was always how Lady Ellen January referred to Oz. Lady January, wife of a Scottish Supreme Court judge, formerly Ellen Sinclair, born Ellen Blackstone, is my Tom's aunt, and she remains my good friend.

That surname surely had to be an alias for her, but as for the rest, Ellie is the most down-to-earth woman I've ever met. She's never spoken like that in all the time I've known her; moreover, she never wears any make-up to speak of, and the Stone of Destiny is more likely to shed a tear than she is.

I realised that I was shaking, and that my heart and respiration rates were way above normal. I closed my eyes, took a deep breath and waited until I had restored myself to a state of calm. When I opened them again, I saw Charlie, looking up at me. If a dog can frown and show concern, that's what he was doing.

I had slammed the MacBook closed, as if I was running away from its contents, putting it to sleep in the process. I waited for it to come back to life, then read the second chapter.

'My son?' Frail old Michael Greystock sighed. 'He broke my fucking heart. All I ever wanted was for him to be a teacher like me, but no, not him.'

If Doreen was Ellie, then Michael Greystock had to equal Macintosh Blackstone, a dentist, not a teacher, who had threatened both his kids with fire and brimstone if they ever entertained the idea of following him into his profession. As for frail, the guy's had a heart-valve replacement but he's still capable of two rounds of golf a day.

'No, he had to go off to be something he never really was. First to Edinburgh, with his silly country notions of fame and fortune on gold-paved streets, then to bloody Spain, then to Glasgow, chasing that stupid dream. And him being him, eventually he caught up with it. He did have a gold star set in some fucking pavement in Los Angeles. As far as I know it's still there, but he isn't. It turned out to be a shooting star and, like they all do, it burned itself out.'

I laughed out loud. This was supposed to be Mac, Tom's rock-solid Grandpa Mac coming out with all this fanciful shite?

'But it wasn't his fault,' I read on, aloud. 'It was that woman. She came into his life and she beguiled him. She cast her spell on him, like a witch, and the poor guy

hadn't a fucking chance after that. It was that Phyllis woman; the first time he ever brought her to my house, I had a premonition not just that she would take him from me, and from all the other people who loved him, but that she would be the end of him. If I could play that scene again, that first meeting, I'd stab her through the heart, and take the consequences. They'd be worth it.'

'Phyllis?' I yelled. 'Fucking Phyllis?'

'Gobsmacked' didn't come close to how I felt. No, it didn't. I tried to define my reaction at that moment, and could only come up with one analogy. I felt raped.

My mobile was in my hand without any conscious thought, and I was about to hit the button on Mac's speed dial entry, when I stopped myself. 'No,' I told myself 'let's read it all.'

And I did. Chapter three quoted someone called Sheila.

'He was damaged when I met him,' the widow said. 'He was still bereaved, but she hadn't given him time or space to grieve properly over the loss of his precious soul mate. Some people, and by that I mean the odd obsessive fan, but mostly Phyllis's famous politician sister and brother-in-law, still blame me for taking him from her, but I don't give a shit about them, for what I was really doing was trying to save his life. She had her claws in him, as deep as she could sink them. I tried, but to be honest I never really could prise them loose.

'I don't know what happened to his first wife. "A tragic accident in the home"; that was how the papers described it, but I'm not so sure. There was a continuing state of warfare between his two women. At that time, Maureen was on top, but she'd only won a battle. The war ended with her death, the only way it ever could have. Accident? If that's what "they" say, I'll have to accept it, but really, "they" have no idea what Phyllis is capable of: she's done time, for Christ's sake. That's why we retreated to Italy, to a house that I insisted should be made as secure as possible. I wasn't afraid for my children while I had him, although that's what I let him think. Truth is, I was afraid for myself, afraid of her.

'When they told me he was dead, the first thing I felt wasn't shock. Before that there was an instant when I felt relief, because finally I'd be free of Phyllis. Afterwards . . .

'I was furious when I heard that he'd been cremated. They told me it had been necessary because of the heat in Guatemala, where he'd been making a video for his new album when it happened. The unit had a doctor with it; he certified that a congenital heart defect had been the cause of death, and I have no grounds to doubt that, and yet . . .'

I had to break off then; I was so angry that I could barely see the words on the screen, far less concentrate on them. I closed the laptop and kept it shut, until our evening had run its course, and Tom had gone to bed. Not for the first time, no, not by a long way, I was glad my boy was there to keep me on an even keel, and possibly to keep me from taking Charlie along to the Nieves Mar and setting him on the son-of-a-bitch Culshaw, although my distraction must have shown through, for he asked me a couple of times whether everything was okay. Although I assured him it was, I reckon he knew it wasn't, but trusted me to tell him if and when I needed to.

I rarely drink spirits, but I mixed myself a gin and tonic and took it up to the terrace, back to the manuscript. I scrolled through it before getting down to the detail, and I saw quickly that after the three opening 'testimonials', the book became more conventional. When I did start to read again, it was clear that it was a mock biography, the life and times of someone called 'Al Greystock', rock star and tragic hero . . . or rather, anti-hero.

The book wasn't warts and all; it was plain fucking warts, pure and simple. Culshaw had done his research on Oz, that was for sure. The story proper began with what purported to be a news article in the *Saltire*, a fictitious Scottish daily newspaper. It said that workmen dismantling an outbuilding on the Perthshire property that Al and Sheila Greystock had owned had found a shotgun encased in the foundations. To the police its origins were a mystery, and they could trace no record of its registration anywhere in Britain.

That got my attention, for Oz and Susie had lived beside Loch Lomond, and indeed a shotgun had been found there when the next owner had demolished the playground they'd built for the kids. I knew this because Susie had told me about it, after the police asked her, politely, if she had any idea where it had come from. She hadn't, but Oz had. I knew because he told me.

Culshaw offered no theories in the early part of his story; instead he went back and gave a brief account of the so-called Al's early life in Newport on Tay, highlighted by a story told by one of his classmates, about him going mental and beating the shit out of two guys in his year because of a casual schoolboy remark about Maureen, his childhood sweetheart. That wasn't fantasy either; that happened, not in Newport, but in Anstruther, where Oz was raised. He told me about that too, very early in our relationship; eventually he told me everything.

The scene changed to Edinburgh and Al's early life there, first as a trainee fireman, and later as a self-employed journalist, as he was said to style himself, who made extra money singing with an up-and-coming rock band.

That was the point at which I made my first appearance. 'Phyllis' turned up at one of his gigs, and sank her hooks in him straight away.

'The boy Al was okay until he met her,' a guy called Saeed Nawaz was quoted as saying. Saeed had to equal Ali Patel, the neighbourhood grocer in Edinburgh, and Oz's pal.

'Him and Maureen, his bird from when he was a kid in Fife, they were fine, an item, although they didnae live together. Then she turned up, that Phyllis. She was in

bother of some sort or other, he helped her out, and she helped herself. They went off together on some business trip that she'd lined up, only for a week like, but when they came back everything was different. They went off again, but for a while this time, then just when I thought he was gone for good, he came back, out the blue, and things were all right wi' him and Maureen again. They got married, he selt me the flat and they moved tae Glasgow.'

True, all of it, and he'd got Ali's accent right as well; but then it drifted into pure fiction.

'Al made it big in the music business; he got lucky, ken, became a big star overnight. A wee bit later, Phyllis came back. Ah don't know how, but she'd missed all that. I was in one night, there was a ring at the doorbell and it was her. She looked at me, surprised like, and asked where Al was. Ah telt her he didnae live there any more, that him and Maureen had got married and moved tae the Wild West. The look she gave me scared me shitless. Then she turned on her heel and went off. A wee bit later, Ah heard that Maureen was dead, that she'd been electrocuted by a dodgy washing machine or something. Accident? Maybe so, but the timing was a bit funny.'

Another outright lie soldered on to some truth; that doorstep exchange never happened. The truth was that when

Jan died, I was in Spain, and Oz was with me. We'd met up completely by accident, and there were people around who could prove it.

I read on, into the night as the story moved on. In some ways it was a pretty accurate account of Oz's life, with only the names, geography and occupations changed. There was a chapter that was based on an incident when Oz was making a movie, and a real-life drama developed, involving the kidnapping of my sister Dawn . . . an actress, of course, not a politician. He had some of that story right on the button, but not all of it; my guess was that his source had been Susie, and that she'd held back a part that related to her. But 'Sheila' came into the narrative, right on cue, paying a visit to Al and Phyllis in St Tropez, where they had bought a mansion and were starting out on married life.

> 'Al *was pathetic then,*' her 'account' read. '*I think he realised that he'd been drawn into something that he didn't really want, a relationship in which he had no control. He made a pass at me, one night when Phyllis was away . . . fucking up somebody else's head, no doubt. It seemed to me like a plea for help more than anything else. In normal circumstances, I'd have told him to get lost, but he was so wasted . . . I suppose I took pity on him.*'

'Hah!' I snorted when I'd finished that section. 'The poor little innocent had her knickers in her handbag from the moment she stepped through our door.' For Al and Phyllis, read Oz and me and for St Tropez, read L'Escala, in the house where Tom was made . . . and Janet too, as it happened.

The last time Oz and I were alone together, in the Algonquin Hotel in New York, he spent a good chunk of the night filling in all of those parts of his life to which I hadn't actually been a witness. His confession: that's all I could call it, made to the only person he knew would keep all his secrets, since some of them were mine too. His account of that get-together was rather different from the fictionalised version in Culshaw's manuscript, and much later Susie had pretty much confirmed it to me.

I went back to the 'book' and continued until, as I knew it would, it came back to that shotgun. Then it really did go into wonderland. The premise of the story was that Sheila's family steel stockholding business was under attack by Glasgow gangsters, who were looking to drive down the share price so they could take it over, and that with Phyllis urging him on in the background, no longer part of his family, but still part of the scene, Al had taken matters into his own hands . . . with the shotgun.

Of course, that was nonsense. Culshaw had missed the point. 'Al' might have done that, but no way Oz would. No, he'd have paid someone else to take the guys out. As for my alleged involvement . . . I was too busy living on my own in London and looking after a two-year-old at the time.

I pushed a keyboard button to move on, but there was no more. The story came to an abrupt end; nothing about Al's life after that, or his death, or even about Phyllis, the Wicked Witch of the West.

I checked my watch; it showed 2.30 a.m. I was on the point of calling Susie regardless, but her illness had manifested itself by that time, and she was on medication. It would have been cruel to waken her, and probably pointless, as her head would have been like mush.

But I wanted to be cruel to Culshaw, as cruel as I could; waking him in the middle of the night was pretty tame, I know, but it was a start. I called the hotel. The night porter must have been catnapping, for it took him a minute or so to answer. I recognised his sleepy voice as one of the long-term staff members who'd drawn the short straw.

'Hello, Andoni,' I said, in Castellano, for he's from Asturia and doesn't speak the local tongue. 'It's Primavera. I'd like you to put me through to Mr Culshaw's room, please.'

'But Madam,' he exclaimed, 'Primavera, it's very late. He'll be asleep. He was in the bar till midnight; he'd had a few drinks by the time he asked for his key.'

'Nevertheless, he'll be expecting me to call. Connect me, please.'

I had another wait, but not so long this time. 'Mmmm.' The voice that came on the line could only grunt, at first. 'I thought you'd wait till morning.'

'Duncan,' I told him, 'if the version of me that you portray was real, you wouldn't have had a morning. My friend the night porter downstairs would have gone conveniently absent, leaving me free to come up and cut your throat while you slept. By the way,' I added, after a pause, 'don't be too sure that won't happen. Enjoy the rest of the night, and if you do waken up, I'll see you for coffee in L'Escala, at ten, in a café called El Centre, next to the church.'

In the morning, I kept him waiting. I had some sleep to catch up on. My lovely son helped me do that; even at eleven, as he was then, he could be a self-starter, and he wakened me with a mug of tea and a bowl of cereal around eight, having fed himself properly, taken Charlie for a trot and got ready for school. Slut of a mother, you're thinking, but it's wonderfully liberating when your child gets to that stage. It gives you just a little extra freedom, and takes a little of the constant pressure away.

I had another call to make before I met Culshaw, and that delayed me for a few minutes, and so it was pushing quarter past ten when I arrived at the café. He was seated at one of the outside tables, almost in the shade of the huge palm tree that stands between the church and the town hall, as if it's keeping them apart.

I'd hardly sat down before a waiter appeared. I ordered a *cortado*, a short coffee with milk, and a bottle of Vichy Catalan sparkling water.

I put my bag on the table, and laid my phone beside it as I settled carefully into my plastic chair: sometimes their legs can be a little wobbly, and it would have spoiled the moment if I'd landed on my arse. I looked at Duncan; he was neatly dressed in white trousers, a pale blue T-shirt and a tan cotton jacket, but his eyes were a little baggy, and I guessed that he hadn't slept too well after my call. First points to Primavera.

That said, he didn't seem nervous; the opposite, in fact. He had a faint smile on his face, and those baggy eyes said that he was rather pleased with himself.

He gazed at me, as if he was waiting for me to open the batting, but I wasn't going to play his game. I waited him out, until finally he said, 'Well? What did you think of it?'

'It's not going to win the Booker Prize,' I replied drily.

'That won't worry me,' he laughed. 'They're famous for not selling. My book will be a blockbuster.'

'It's a heap of shit, Duncan. It's a hatchet job on Oz, thinly disguised as a novel. Most of it's fabricated into the bargain.'

'Hey,' he chuckled, 'it's a work of fiction, so by definition it's fabricated. How big an advance do you reckon I'll get for it?'

'Fuck all,' I snapped.

'That's not what my new literary agent says. He has three publishers fighting for it, and that's just on the basis of a synopsis. We're up to six figures and the bids are still rising.'

'Then you're going to have a major delivery problem,' I pointed out. 'It's not finished.'

'It could be if I wanted it to be. I could wrap it up where it is now, go straight to Al's death and have Phyllis in the vicinity, only for Sheila to join all the dots, and kill her in a big bloody finale.' He paused. 'But you are right. It could be better than that, and that's why I need your help.'

'You what?' I gasped. 'You need my help? Are you completely out of your tree?'

'No,' he said smoothly. 'There's a gap in my knowledge, and only you can fill it. Susie certainly can't.'

'Susie doesn't know about this travesty, does she?'

'No, not at all.'

'But you have been pumping her for information.'

He had the nerve to wink at me. 'I've been pumping her in all sorts of ways, my dear,' he murmured. I wanted to punch his lights out, as I think I could have, given our relative sizes, but I mastered my anger as he continued. 'But I haven't been interrogating her, if that's what you mean. I've simply encouraged her to talk about her past and made notes as she's gone along.'

'What about Mac and Ellie, and Ali Patel? Did you talk to them or was that pure imagination too?'

'Oh yes, I spoke to them all, and to Oz's school chum, one of the two he beat up. I told them I was a journalist researching a magazine feature about Oz. None of them were very helpful, apart from the victim of his violence.'

'Jesus,' I said, 'you're lucky he's not around, because I hate to think what he'd do to you.'

'That is rather the point of the novel. It's about the decline of the central character into darkness, even as he grew rich and famous. And through it all there's this character in the background, this duplicitous manipulative woman, Phyllis, dragging him down. And that's not all that far from the truth, is it, Primavera? Go on, be honest, admit it.'

I looked him in the eye. 'Do you even understand honesty, you little shit? You understand duplicity, that's for sure, but do you have a straight bone in your body?'

'This discussion isn't about my morals, Primavera, it's

about yours. Go on, do you recognise the people I've described?'

He leaned back in his chair, drawing me a challenging look. I decided to answer him. 'To an extent, yes I do. Oz changed over the years, there's no doubt about that, but the trigger for it had nothing to do with me. He never got over Jan's death, and that's the real truth of it, that's the point you've missed by a mile in your concoction of nonsense. As for suggesting that I had something to do with it, I wasn't even in the same country when it happened.'

'No, that's true,' he agreed. 'You were here in Spain, with him. And wasn't that convenient for both of you.'

'How the hell did you know that?'

'Susie let it slip, and a friend of Oz's, Everett Davis, confirmed it.'

That made sense, but I was conceding nothing. 'So what?'

'It's interesting, that's all, the fact that you were both clear of the scene when the . . . accident . . . happened. But what about you anyway? Did my description hit the spot?'

'Was I angry with Oz? Yes. Twice in my life; first when he chose Jan over me, and then when he two-timed me with Susie. Did I hit back at him? Yes, but I regret it now. Duplicitous, manipulative? Hurt and betrayed sums it up.'

'Which leads us to that plane crash in the US,' Culshaw said, 'the private plane that Oz was supposed to be on. That's a matter of record, for he was listed as missing, presumed dead, until he showed up in New York. You, on the other hand, were listed as missing too, and you didn't surface again until after Oz was dead.'

'That's true,' I admitted, 'but I had my reasons.'

'I'm sure. But what if I suggest that your "reasons",' he smirked, 'for staying underground were to plot and bring about his death? What if I suggest that you were never on that plane either, that you slipped away first, and that Oz realised this, smelled a rat and got off himself?'

'Then I would suggest to you that you are crazy.'

The smirk became a beam, a great self-satisfied beam. 'That's not how the publishers will see it when I use it as the basis for the completion of my novel, as I intend to do, now that we've had this conversation. They'll buy it and you know it. As I said, I could do a deal today, even without that ending.'

'And I'll sue.'

'On what basis?'

'That it's a thinly disguised defamation.'

'Of whom? Oz is dead, and remember, you can't libel the dead.'

'Of me, you idiot. And your book will only be bankable if you can throw out the hint that it's about Oz and me, without saying as much.'

He shrugged. 'So go ahead and sue. I'll defend, and the case will go to trial, with ensuing publicity that will be truly global. Is that what you really want, Primavera?'

'Fuck you, boy,' I barked.

'Come on,' he persisted. 'Is that what you really want, your name dragged through the courts, for everyone to read, including your son, your precious boy?'

'And what if I don't?' I asked, tentatively. 'How can I avoid that?'

He leaned across the table. 'You could buy the manuscript yourself. Then all your problems would disappear.'

We'd finally got to where I'd known from the start that we were heading. 'Mmm,' I murmured. 'And how much is it going to cost me?'

'Two million,' Culshaw answered. 'Sterling. I know that the time you spent with Oz has left you a wealthy woman, even if you're not in Susie's class. You can come up with that; if you're short, I'm sure your wealthy brother-in-law would chip in. That's why I thought you might like to show him the manuscript. Otherwise . . .'

He left the alternative hanging in the air, but he didn't have to spell it out: otherwise, we'd go to trial in a libel suit and Oz's real life story, and mine, would be laid out before a jury. Undoubtedly, investigators would be employed to go digging, and there were things that I did not want them to uncover, not least the real story behind that shotgun. If I went to court, that would happen. If I didn't, the book would publish, I'd be smeared for certain, and my privacy in the nice wee world that I'd built for Tom and me would be shattered for good.

'Why are you putting the bite on me?' I asked him. 'As you say, Susie's a lot wealthier than I am, in her own right.'

'Susie's a peripheral figure in this story.' He paused. 'Besides, I have other plans for her.'

'Such as marriage?' I guessed.

'We've discussed it.'

'You publish, she'll blow you out.'

'I publish I make a fortune, so I'd get over that.'

I nodded. 'You've got all bases loaded, eh Duncan?'

'And a pitcher on the mound with a very weak arm.'

'So it would seem,' I agreed. 'But let's forget the baseball analogies. What you're really doing is extorting two million pounds from me.'

He laughed, the insolent bastard. 'No, I'm selling you global rights to a work of fiction. Once you've bought it it'll be up to you whether you exploit it or not.'

'I'd still call it extortion.'

He held up his hands, palms outwards, as if in surrender. 'Okay,' he said. 'I concede, it's extortion. You pay, and you keep your reputation and Oz's unblemished. So, are you going to come up with the two million or not?'

'I don't think I'll have to.' I picked up my phone, put it to my ear, and said, in Catalan, 'Have you got all of that?'

'Yes,' a voice replied. 'It's all recorded.'

For the first time since I'd joined him, a frown of uncertainty furrowed Duncan Culshaw's forehead. As he peered at me, he didn't see two men come out of the café through the door behind him and walk towards us. In fact he didn't notice them at all until they took the two vacant seats at our table.

'What the . . .' he began.

'People I asked to join us,' I explained. 'This is Alex,' I

nodded sideways, towards the man on my left, then forward towards the other, 'and this is Marc.'

'Oh. Really? You've brought heavies along? Come on, Primavera, this is a public place, and unless I read it wrong when I arrived here, that's the police station right behind us.'

Alex nodded. 'Yes it is,' he conceded in accented but assured English, 'but it's only the town police, and they look in the other direction when they see us.'

Culshaw looked around him, as if he was counting the number of potential witnesses to what might happen next.

'Senora Blackstone didn't introduce us properly,' Alex continued. 'I am Intendant Guinart and this is Sergeant Sierra. We are officers in the criminal investigation division of the Mossos d'Esquadra, the Catalan police force. You have just described what you have just tried to do as extortion. We agree with you, and for that we are arresting you.' As he spoke, Marc Sierra took Culshaw by the arm, stood, and drew him with him.

'Senora,' Alex said, formally, as he rose, 'you will also need to come with us to make the *denuncio . . .*' he looked at their prisoner, as he had become, and added, in explanation, '. . . the official complaint.'

I nodded. 'If you say so, Intendant.'

They took him away in the Mossos car that was parked round the corner on Carrer Enric Serra (I've no idea who Enric was but he must have been important to have a street named after him, especially the one that runs in front of the church) and I followed in mine.

Traffic flow in L'Escala is quirky and so I arrived at the nick before they did, and was climbing out of my jeep when Marc Sierra pulled in and parked two bays along.

Culshaw was as white as a sheet when Alex helped him out of the car; he had to, because they'd handcuffed him. He glared at me; I looked back at him, my eyes trying to say, 'You try to do me over in my own town, idiot, and this is what happens.'

I followed as he was led into the building, past the reception counter and through a door behind it. The duty officer made a move as if to stop me, but Alex stopped her instead, with a glance and a brief shake of his head.

We went upstairs, and into a room that was the polar opposite of those drab dirty interview boxes beloved of TV drama, the kind where you can almost smell the sweat. Yes, it had a table with two seats on either side, and a recorder, but it was bright and air-conditioned with a big window looking over the medical centre on the next plot and on to the Mediterranean beyond.

I stood to the side as they sat Duncan on a chair facing the door, then removed the cuffs. He seemed to relax a little in the surroundings, until Sergeant Sierra dropped the venetian blind and shut out the sun and the view, making us completely private.

'Empty your pockets, please,' Alex requested.

'I want a lawyer,' his guest exclaimed. 'I want to phone the British Consulate.'

'I'm sure you do, and in time we may allow that, but first, please put what's in your pockets on the table.'

'If you insist.' He reached into his jacket and produced, from various pockets, a set of Oakley sunglasses, a mobile phone, a wallet, a few coins, a car key with a Hertz fob on the ring, and a British passport.

Alex picked it up, and opened it, turning to the identification page. 'Señor Duncan William Culshaw,' he read. 'Age, let me work it out, thirty-four, born in Kil . . . Kilmack . . . I don't know how to say that.' He glanced at me. 'Where is it, Primavera?'

I completed the place name, with correct pronunciation. 'Kilmacolm; it's in Scotland.'

'Mmm. More Scottish, eh. Let's see where else you've been.' He flicked through the passport, checking the pages. 'Singapore,' he read, 'USA, Ecuador.' He smiled. 'You've been to Ecuador? That's unusual. Why did you go there?'

'I had an airline magazine assignment. All those trips were for airline magazine articles.'

'So it's a coincidence that Ecuador is where Senor Oz Blackstone died?'

Culshaw nodded. 'That's right; a complete coincidence.'

Alex tossed the passport on the table and picked up the wallet. 'Money,' he murmured, 'Mastercard, American Express, Priority Pass, driving licence . . .' he stopped, squeezed a finger into a compartment behind the card slots, and drew something out, something I couldn't see.

He looked up at his colleague, and smiled. '*Preservativos,*' he chuckled. '*Con sabor y aroma manzana verde.* Condoms,' he repeated, his eyes returning to their owner, 'green apple flavour.' He shrugged. 'You're not married, senor, are you?'

'No.'

'Girlfriend?'

'I'm in a relationship.'

'And your lady is in L'Escala?'

'No, of course not.' He looked across at me, and smirked. 'But one takes one's opportunities as they arise, so it pays to go prepared. And after all, this morning, I was meeting a single mother,' he drawled, 'a popular lady by all acc—'

He was stopped in mid-sentence by the back of the cop's hand, cracking him in the side of the mouth. I'd never seen Alex move so fast; nor had I ever seen him hit anyone before.

'You're in enough trouble, mister,' he growled, 'without making it worse. Yes, Primavera is a popular lady here, but not in the way that you infer. She is an important member of our community and she is also the godmother of my daughter.'

Alex's clout had left a vivid red mark on Culshaw's cheek.

'Okay,' the intendant snapped, 'we get down to business.' He tapped the recorder on the table. 'Everything you said this morning, your entire conversation with Senora Blackstone, was transmitted to us through her phone, which was active all the time. It was recorded and we have it here, all of it, including your admission to your attempt at extortion. We're not here to negotiate, or even to interrogate. The evidence of our ears and of this tape shows that you have committed a serious crime. Under Spanish law that will earn you a minimum of three years in prison, but given the amount of money involved here, it is likely to be much more. What will happen now? Primavera will make a formal complaint against you and you will be held in jail while I report to the public prosecutor. From then on it'll be in her hands, but I warn you, she's a very tough lady.' He looked round at me. 'Primavera, will you write the *denuncio*, in Catalan of course, or would you prefer to dictate it?'

'I'm literate enough to write it myself, Intendant,' I replied. 'If you give me a form, I'll complete it.' I stepped towards the table.

'That's good,' he said. 'The spelling doesn't have to be one hundred per cent; the meaning has to be clear, that's all. Marc, would you fetch a *denuncio* paper, please.'

Finally, as the sergeant left the room, Culshaw seemed to realise that he wasn't involved in any sort of a game, that the cops were not bluffing and that I wasn't either. He looked up at me. 'Primavera, can we talk about this?'

'We're done talking, chum,' I told him.

'I was joking, only joking,' he protested, but so weakly that he didn't even fool himself, for his voice faded as he spoke.

'Well, we ain't.'

'Please.' He was begging, pure and simple.

As I looked at him, the anger that I'd been nurturing since I'd read the first few pages of his manuscript began to subside. I paused and began to think rationally. Duncan's entire pitch had been based on the premise that there are things in my past and in Oz's that might not stand up to detailed examination and that I would not want exposed to the full glare of publicity. He'd been right about that; he'd been a complete bloody idiot in the way he'd tried to exploit it, that's all.

If I went ahead with a complaint, and it entered the Spanish judicial system, I wouldn't be able to claw it back. Their courts might work very slowly, but eventually they do work. If Duncan got himself a decent lawyer and sought to defend himself in a trial, then everything would come out. More than that, even if he was locked up in Spain pending trial, bail denied, he'd still be able to do a book deal through his agent. Indeed the thing might become even more valuable.

Shit, the guy was on a winner either way, but he hadn't realised it. I frowned at him, severely, but I asked Alex, 'Would you leave us alone for a couple of minutes?'

He agreed; he was reluctant, but he agreed.

'Okay,' I said, when we were alone, 'this is what it will take. You give me a document, which Alex will witness, transferring copyright ownership of your book to me. You do that now. Then you give me the device that holds the original . . . a laptop? . . .' he nodded, 'so that I can erase the entire hard disk. Then you disappear; you get out of Susie's life and stay out. It's that or you spend the next ten years being rogered up the arse by the cellmate of your choice, and I can promise you he won't be using apple-flavoured condoms. Deal?'

He considered it for all of two seconds, and croaked, 'Deal.'

'One other thing,' I added. 'Should you stash away a copy and try to use it in the future, or should you even stick your head above the parapet, I can still make the complaint and Alex will still have that recording. That would be if you were lucky. The alternative would be that I would send Conrad Kent after you, with a free hand to do whatever he deems necessary. That's where your thinking was flawed, Duncan. You should have realised that when you threaten my well-being, you threaten my son. If anybody does that, there are no limits to what I would do to protect him. You got that much right about Phyllis, and me.'

We were out of there in fifteen minutes, and he was out of town within an hour, taking with him a laptop with a completely blank hard disk.

Three

'Duncan?' I repeated. 'What makes you think she's gone anywhere with Duncan? She doesn't see him any more, Jonathan.'

'He went away on business, Mummy said. But I think he's come back.'

'What makes you think that, son?'

'I saw him in Monaco, before Mummy went away; one day Conrad was driving Janet and me back from school and I saw him sitting in Casino Square. Janet didn't see him, though, and I haven't said anything to Conrad. She'd be upset if he came back.'

'Are you sure it was him? When you're travelling in a car and you only get a glimpse of somebody, it's easy to make a mistake.'

His mouth set in a hard line. 'It was him,' he muttered. 'Why don't you believe me, Auntie Primavera?' There were tears in his eyes.

I ruffled his hair, and took his hand. 'I do believe you, wee man,' I said, gently. 'If you're certain, that's good enough for me. Was he with anyone?'

'No, but there had been somebody else at his table, because there were two glasses on it.'

'Maybe they were both his?'

'No. One was a beer and the other was a long pink drink, with straws and things in it. And there was a bag on the table, a lady's bag not a man's bag, and it was red, like one that Mummy's got. And when we got home, she wasn't there, and she'd said she would be. Auntie Primavera, I don't like Duncan. He's not a nice man. When Mummy and Conrad aren't there he's rude to us, and shouty. And he hit Tom once.'

'He did what!' I exclaimed. If I'd known that when he was in Alex's custody . . .

'When?'

'One day last summer when Tom was with us. He and Janet were playing scrabble, in Catalan . . . Tom was teaching her . . . and Duncan told Janet to get him a beer. He didn't say please or anything; he'd had lots of beers before that. Tom said that he was nearer the fridge so couldn't he get his own, and Duncan pulled him to his feet, and said that just for that he could get it. And he swore, he used that rude word that Conrad got angry at me for using. Tom said no and Duncan hit him, on the side of the head, quite hard.'

'Did anybody see this?' I murmured.

'Only Janet and me. Janet shouted at Duncan, but he told her to shut up or she'd get the same.'

'Didn't either of you tell your mother, or Conrad?' I asked him.

'No, because Tom said we shouldn't.'

'He did?' *Poor kid*, I thought, *he must have felt shamed.* He'd never been hit in his life before. Oh, what I would do to Duncan Culshaw if our paths ever crossed again.

'Yes, because . . .' He looked up at me and a small precious smile lit up his face. 'After he'd hit him, Duncan asked Tom if he'd get him his beer now. Tom said, "No chance," and Duncan tried to hit him again, but Tom made him miss and kicked him in the stomach.'

'In the stomach,' I repeated.

Jonathan pointed to his groin. 'Yes, there; he kicked him like Jean Claude van Damme does. Duncan fell down, making funny noises. It was a long time before he could get up again. I was scared. I thought that when he got up he would really hurt Tom. I was going to go for Conrad, but Tom wouldn't let me. He said he had used wing chun, and his teacher had told him he should never use it against anyone who isn't trained in it himself.'

I smiled; that's my boy. An adult attacked him, he decked him and he felt guilty about it. 'What happened when Duncan did get up?'

'Nothing. Duncan didn't go near him again. Janet got him a beer, and he sat down and drank it.'

'Did neither of you tell your mum what had happened?'

'No. Tom wouldn't let us. He said Duncan wouldn't bother any of us again, and he didn't. I was glad when he went away,

Auntie Primavera; I didn't want him to come back. I don't want Mummy to see him.' His eyes filled with tears again, and finally, they flowed. 'I just want my daddy back,' he cried.

I hugged him to me. 'I know, wee man,' I whispered, 'I know. You're far too young to have learned how tough the world can be.'

I thought of Susie as I spoke, Susie and her precarious future. I hoped that wee Jonathan had been wrong about what he said he'd seen in Casino Square, but he's a very bright wee chap and not given to flights of imagination or extravagant statements.

'Auntie Primavera,' he murmured, as he wiped his eyes with the back of his hand, 'am I really grounded till Monday?'

'I can't overrule Conrad,' I told him. 'He's your guardian while you're here. But I can tell him what's worrying you, and if you tell him that you're very sorry for using that word and promise not to use it again, you might find that he gives you a suspended sentence.'

'What's that?' His eyes widened. 'You mean he'll hang me?'

I couldn't stop myself from laughing. 'No, love, I mean he might let you off. Now, go on with you, get yourself out of that beach stuff and into clean clothes before they all get back.'

As I spoke, there was a loud bang or small explosion, from somewhere not too far away. Wee Jonathan jumped. 'What was that?' he gasped.

'That was the start of the San Juan celebrations. Fireworks don't scare you, do they?'

'No!' He said the word as if I'd insulted him.

'Good, in that case we can all watch them from my bedroom terrace. Go on, now, get yourself ready.'

I shooed him upstairs then went along to the sitting room. I checked the time and worked out that it would be around midday in Arizona, then picked up the landline phone and punched in Susie's mobile number.

'Primavera,' she answered . . . number recognition is a very useful tool, 'how are you? Is everything okay? Are the kids okay?'

'The kids are fine, Susie; the two older ones and I are all going to a reggae concert tonight.' As I spoke, another firework exploded.

'What was that?' Susie asked, sounding as anxious as had her son. She sounded tired, too, wearier than I'd ever heard her; I knew that the treatment had been tough, but I'd hoped against hope that she was on an upward curve.

'Relax,' I laughed, 'it's a fiesta tonight. Big celebration in Spain. There's music on the beach from around midnight; I'm taking the two older ones.'

'Sounds like fun. How's my daughter?' I guessed what was behind the question. Janet's periods had started in the month before Susie went for her third treatment.

'Timely,' I advised her, 'and perfectly normal. She's coping fine.' I smiled. 'I had to take her for some new bras last week, and a couple of bikinis.'

'My God, she's growing fast. I hope she knows when to stop.'

'Like mother like daughter, I reckon.' Susie's not very tall, but she's a big girl.

'And Tom?'

'Next time you call, and he picks up, you will get a shock.'

'Oh dear,' she sighed. 'Does he sound like . . .'

'Put it this way, the vocal register's still a little bit higher, but he's on the way there. He said something to me the other day when I had my back to him. He sounded so like his dad it made me shiver.'

'Primavera, they're so young. Or is it us that's old?'

'Hell no! It's life; it's what happens to your kids. What did you think, that they were Peter Pan and Tinkerbell?'

'Maybe,' she giggled, 'with wee Jonathan as one of the Lost Boys. How's he behaving?'

'He's as good as gold,' I fibbed, slightly. 'He doesn't fancy the reggae concert.' I paused. I'd been wondering how to get round to the reason for my call, and she'd given me an opening. 'He and I have just been having a chat. You know what he told me? He thinks he saw Duncan Culshaw a few weeks ago, sitting at a table in Casino Square.'

There was a silence, just a couple of seconds, but it registered with me. 'Oh,' Susie exclaimed, breaking it, 'that wee scamp. What an imagination he's got.'

'Yes, indeed. I doubt that even Duncan would have been stupid enough to go back to Monaco after you'd ended the relationship.'

'I didn't end it, Primavera,' she said. 'He left me, remember.'

'I meant you, plural.'

'Of course. Sorry.' Her tone had changed. She was definitely shifty, where before, she'd been upfront.

I changed tack. 'Have you finished your treatments?'

'Yes. The last one was four days ago, but they gave me a platelet infusion after that. They said my count was low.' She sounded matter-of-fact, but I didn't like the sound of that. It meant that her blood was thin and that its essential ability to clot had been compromised, leaving her open to potential risks. 'They've finished now, though,' she continued. 'My supervising clinician wants me to stay here to recuperate for another couple of weeks, but I'm not so sure about that. We'd like to get home sooner.'

'We?' I repeated.

'Audrey and me,' she replied, quickly.

'Mmm. I tell you, Susie,' I said, 'I'm so glad wee Jonathan was wrong. You are well shot of that Duncan character. When I heard about him hitting Tom . . . I go cold with anger thinking about it.'

'He did what? Who told you that?'

'Wee Jonathan did, just now.'

'Why the little . . . He never did like Duncan, Primavera.'

'Come on,' I protested. 'You're not calling your own son a liar, are you?'

'No, but . . .' She hesitated. 'Has Tom said anything to you about it.'

'No, he hasn't,' I admitted. 'Possibly to stop me from thrashing the bastard.'

'When's this supposed to have happened?'

54

'Last year, at your place. Duncan tried to use Janet as a servant and Tom took exception to it.'

'And Duncan hit him?'

'That's what wee Jonathan said.'

'But Tom never complained to me. Honestly, Primavera, he didn't. This is the first I've heard of it. Why didn't he say anything?'

I chuckled. 'From what I gather, he felt that when he kung fu-ed Duncan in the balls after he tried to hit him a second time, it put an end to the matter.'

'He did what?' At the other end of the line I heard a sound that was half gasp, half chortle. 'Last year? He was only eleven then.'

'Tom's been going to his martial arts class since he was six, Susie. He was one grade off his black belt when this happened, and he got it a few weeks later. It's lucky for Duncan that he was only eleven. He's grown over the winter; if he did it now the guy would be looking for his nuts behind his ears. And it would serve him right.' I took a deep breath. 'That man is a nasty piece of work. From the start of your relationship he was using you.'

'Using me? How?'

Suddenly she sounded even more tired and deeply anxious. I hesitated. I was concerned that I was about to go over the top with her. After all, this was a woman who had undergone rigorous treatment for a life-threatening condition. She did not need undue stress or disturbance in her life. 'Forget it, Susie,' I sighed. 'I've said enough. You don't need to hear this story right now. Since the guy's history, you don't need to hear it at all.'

'But I do need to,' she insisted, sounding as if she'd dredged up renewed strength from somewhere. 'If it involves Duncan and it affects me, I want to know about it. So come on, girl, out with it.'

Oh Primavera; your hot head and your big mouth. 'All right,' I said, 'if you insist.' I launched into the tale of Culshaw's unannounced visit to L'Escala, his exploitative 'novel', his attempt to screw two million out of me to protect Oz's reputation and my own, and to the way I had seen off both him and his threat.

She heard me out without interruption. When I was finished I heard her blow out a huge sigh. 'Did you keep a copy of the book?' she asked.

'I destroyed the original. As for the copy he gave me, that had a bloody virus on it that crashed my laptop a couple of days later. Trust me, Susie, you wouldn't want to have read it.'

Another sigh, a very tired one at that. 'Ah, Primavera, why didn't you tell me all this at the time?'

'I was going to, and then you were diagnosed, so I didn't. Culshaw was gone, so I decided it wasn't necessary.'

'Ah, but as it's turned out it was. I didn't tell you the truth earlier. Wee Jonathan was right in what he saw. Duncan is back; and what have I done? I've only gone and married the guy, that's all.'

'You've married him?' I repeated. 'Duncan bloody Culshaw? Are you out of your mind?'

'Given the circumstances,' she said sadly, 'that's possible.'

Four

I had to end the call with Susie's sensational announcement still hanging in the air, as the front door burst open and the house was invaded by the wave of energy that is Tom and his half-sister.

'How's foul-mouth?' Conrad asked me after they had headed off to their rooms to smarten themselves up for dinner and the night ahead.

'Contrite,' I told him. 'He's going to apologise to you, and ask for mercy. Your shout, though,' I added. 'I'm not involved . . . even though it is my roof you'll be imprisoning him under over the weekend.'

The minder smiled. 'I might give him a reprieve, if he's sincere.'

'I think he is,' I said. 'The wee chap's had something on his mind. Has he said anything to you about Duncan Culshaw?'

'Him?' One word, but it carried a volume of contempt. 'No, nothing at all. Why should he have?'

'Because he thought he saw him, in Monaco, before you all came here.'

'Slim chance, I reckon,' he murmured. 'That man's a gold-digging waster if ever I saw one. I was glad when the boss got shot of him. So were the kids. He scared Jonathan. If he'd been around much longer I'd have had to do something about him, but thankfully, Susie saw the light, although she's never said anything about it, not even to Audrey.'

My face must have been sending out signals, for suddenly, his eyes narrowed. 'Little Jonathan was wrong, wasn't he?' he asked. 'That wasn't really Culshaw he saw, was it?'

'I'm afraid so,' I replied. 'He's back.'

'Oh shit.'

'And there's worse.' I dropped Susie's bombshell on him.

'What?' he gasped. 'She's . . . ? But Audrey's with her, I've spoken to her just about every day and she's never said a word about it.'

He pulled his mobile from his pocket and hit a speed dial button. Cellphone reception can be dodgy in St Martí, because of the thickness of the stone walls of its buildings, and so he stepped out on to the front terrace to maximise the signal and probably also for privacy while he interrogated his wife. I left him to get on with it, and I went down to the kitchen to warm up the seafood pasta sauce that I'd knocked up earlier in the day. I was weighing enough linguine for five . . . yes five; wee Jonathan may be a shrimp, but he can eat with the hungriest of us . . . when Conrad joined me again.

'It's true,' he announced, not that I'd been in any doubt. 'Audrey told me that Culshaw turned up in Scottsdale just after they did, "to be with her and comfort her" he said, and moved into their hotel. Susie told her to keep it secret, even from me. He wasn't with her for the hard yards of the treatment though; it was still Audrey who went to the clinic with her when she had her chemo. He just hung around the hotel and fawned over her when she got back. Two days ago, the day after the course was finished, Susie told Audrey to charter a plane. Audrey wasn't sure about it, for the chemo had knocked ten bells out of her, but Susie insisted, and yesterday morning the three of them flew to Las Vegas and did the whole Elvis Presley impersonator wedding bit. Audrey thinks that Culshaw had arranged it all last week.'

'And she didn't tell you even then?'

'She hasn't had a chance. They only flew back to Scottsdale late last night. She had to do her own insisting this morning: she called a doctor this morning to check over Susie, over her objections, because she was so knackered from the trip. He'd to give her a multi-vitamin injection, just to get her out of bed.'

'Bloody hell.'

'Indeed,' Conrad said, hesitating before going on. 'I don't know what this means for me, Primavera. I can't stand the man, and I've never hidden it from him. He's going to want to get rid of me, that's for sure.'

'And Audrey?'

'No, I don't see Susie ever letting her go. They're too close.'

'Then don't you worry about it. I have a feeling you'll be okay. Susie didn't employ you originally, Oz did, and for a very specific reason, one that's still valid. Do you have a contract?'

He nodded. 'Yes, twelve month rolling, with the company, but effectively it's Susie who employs me, and if this guy's her husband . . .'

'If he is. It all sounds as fishy as this here sauce.'

'He is, Primavera. Audrey was there, remember. She was their witness.'

'Vegas marriages are as easy to dissolve as they are to do,' I said. 'I lived there for a while; I know how the place works.'

'Maybe they are,' he countered, 'but only if Susie wants to do that, and from what Audrey said, she won't. She says she's besotted with the guy.'

'She may have been yesterday, but I'm not so sure about today, not after I filled her in on some background she didn't know about.' I gave him a potted version of the previous year's blackmail attempt and of how it was thwarted. 'I had my reasons for not proceeding with a criminal complaint,' I told him, 'some of which you can probably guess, but if I have to, I can still fill out a *denuncio*. The tape of our conversation is pretty damning and I suppose the cops will still have it. In fact, tomorrow morning I will do that very thing.'

He frowned. 'That would be risky. You were right to hold off last year. Oz wasn't exactly whiter than white, but the truth is, he was blacker than even you know.'

'Do I want to know how black?' I murmured, although I wasn't sure he'd kept any secrets from me.

'No, you don't, but understand this, a full investigation into his past wouldn't just be tricky; it could be calamitous.'

His firmness made me pause. 'I'll sleep on it,' I conceded, 'and decide in the morning.'

'Okay, but think really carefully before you do anything.'

I made him that promise and set about the evening meal. The sauce was simmering, the linguine was boiling, and I was making some tomato bread when the phone on the counter rang. I snatched it up, hoping that it was Susie calling to tell me that she'd just terminated the shortest marriage on record, but it wasn't. No, it was Duncan fucking Culshaw.

'Ah, the happy bridegroom,' I said after he'd announced himself.

'Ecstatic,' he agreed. 'Tough luck, Primavera. Your attempt to shaft me with Susie fell flat, I'm afraid. I heard her talking to you . . . I'm never far from her now. I'd assumed that you'd go nuclear the moment you found out about us, so I've been prepared for a while. There are two sides to every story, and I've just told her mine. If you're interested, I explained that I'd gone to you to ask for your cooperation in preparing an authorised biography of Oz Blackstone, and in selling the idea to Susie. Your reaction, I told her, was to twist everything around and set me up with your friendly local cops. I added that they scared me so badly that I made myself scarce . . . which is pretty much true . . . until I decided that I really couldn't live without her, and came back. Naturally, Susie takes her husband's word over yours, so get used to the idea of her being Mrs Culshaw, and not the widow Blackstone any longer. Naturally also, I take her safety and that of her kids as seriously as she does. To emphasise that I've persuaded her to give Conrad Kent a fifty per cent salary increase, with a bonus for every incident-free year.'

'And what about my kid's security?' I hissed.

'Your Tom can look after himself very well,' he chuckled, 'a lesson I learned very painfully. You had best keep him close, to look after you.'

'Are you threatening me, you idiot?'

He laughed, mocking me. 'Of course not; I've got no need to threaten you. Primavera, you aren't even a faint blot on my landscape, not any more.'

He paused for a few seconds. 'But here's something you should consider; think of it as a promise though, not a threat. As Susie's husband I've now got free access to her considerable resources. I intend to use them. I may not be able to touch you, or your son, not physically, but I'm going to get you both back, you for what you did to me with those cops, and him for that kick in the family jewels. I'm going to investigate everything that your beloved Oz Blackstone ever did. If there are secrets hidden, as I suspect, I'm going to uncover them. If there aren't, then what the hell, I'll make them up. Either way, the memory of the blessed man, which Tom seems to hold so dear, that'll be something you and he will want to hide from rather than worship.'

Five

Culshaw's threat was pure bluster, I was certain, but still it rattled me, so badly that I forgot about what I'd been doing and let the linguine boil over. By the time I'd taken it off the hob so that I could wipe off the spillage with a tea towel, an unwelcome smell told me that the sauce had burned itself into the base of its pan. 'Bugger!' I shouted, just as Tom came into the kitchen.

'What's wrong, Mum?' he asked.

'Dinner's wrong. I think I've ruined it. Smell that sauce.'

Without a word, he took another pan from its place in the rack, lifted the original off the heat and emptied its contents into the replacement. Then he turned down the ring from level three, where I'd mistakenly set it, to one, and set the meal back to cooking. He looked at the rest of it and murmured, 'We haven't lost very much. It'll be okay.'

I looked at him and thought of one of my favourite movies, *Con Air*, and the part where Agent Larkin asks Cameron Poe what he's going to do for him and Cameron replies, '*What do you think I'm gonna do? I'm gonna save the fuckin' day!*'

'Thank you, Cameron,' I said, and Tom laughed. It's his *absolute* favourite movie, the one we watch together on shit weather nights in the winter. We know it so well that we can recite some of the dialogue ourselves, although he omits the F-words.

'Put the bunny back in the box,' he countered, with pauses, just like Nicolas Cage. (Real name Nicholas Coppola, but he changed it because he didn't want to be known simply as the *Godfather* director Francis Ford Coppola's nephew: that's how much of a movie anorak I am, and why I am in constant demand for L'Escala quiz night teams.)

If it hadn't been for Tom I'd probably have freaked out when the sauce caught, and run screaming for the inevitable takeaway pizzas, but as it turned out, dinner went fine, and if anyone else noticed that it was well done and that the linguine was a little beyond *al dente* they had the very good sense to keep quiet about it.

Tom and Janet took on the waiting duties, with wee Jonathan, cheered up after apologising for swearing and being reprieved, helping out by setting the table. That left me free to have a drink with Conrad on the terrace, and to update him on Duncan's triumphant phone call.

'He thinks he can buy me, does he?' he mused, when I told him about his pay rise. 'He can stick that up his fundament. I'm very well paid as it is, and Audrey and I already have a bonus in place, in the form of share options in the Gantry

Group. Susie's thinking is if we help her run the company profitably, we should share in it. Don't worry, though, I'll stay, for her sake and the kids, but also to make sure he doesn't try to make good on that threat.'

'But what can you do about it if he does?'

He took a swig of his Saaz beer, straight from the bottle. 'Whatever I reckon is necessary.' His eyes went somewhere, but just when I thought he was lost in thought, he started humming an old Rod Stewart tune. (Sorry, let me rephrase that in case you thought I was being ageist; an old song by Rod Stewart.)

All the way through dinner we could hear fireworks exploding, but since San Juan is the summer solstice celebration, I knew that the real action wouldn't begin until it began to grow properly dark, and so we didn't have to rush. The sun was pretty much down by the time we were finished, and when I led everyone, including our Charlie, who is a brave, if slightly dim-witted, dog, upstairs to the top floor and through my bedroom to the terrace. It was something of a treat for the crew; my suite is the only part of the house that really is mine alone. The days when Tom could come crashing in are over. Now, he and I have an agreement that he knocks on my door and I knock on his.

The terrace offers a panoramic view of the entire bay, from L'Escala all the way round to Ampuriabrava, Santa Margarita and Rosas, so we were able to watch four firework displays, simultaneously, most of them far enough away for the sound to reach us a few seconds after we'd seen the multi-coloured lights.

The kids loved it all. I'd have enjoyed it more if I hadn't been preoccupied with the shock of Susie's new husband, and I'm sure that Conrad felt the same. By that time my greatest worry wasn't Culshaw, or Susie; as far as I was concerned she'd made the mistake and she'd have to live with it. No, I was worried about how Janet and wee Jonathan were going to take it, and how it might affect my son's relationship with them. With that guy as the official consort in Monaco, and him having history with Tom, I would worry about him every minute he was there. As for the others, I knew already that wee Jonathan hated his new stepfather, and as for Janet . . . in the brief time I'd spent at Susie's when he was there, I'd picked up vibes from him that I didn't like, the sort that would make me careful not to leave any adolescent daughter of mine alone with the man.

The pyrotechnics carried on unabated past eleven o'clock, as Tom had said they would. I called a halt around the half-hour. It was curfew time for the youngest member, and also I could see that they were getting ready for action under the floodlights that lit up the concert platform near the old Greek wall. Wee Jonathan didn't protest; he was tired and, also, he knew he'd used up all that day's leeway.

I stuck a metaphorical finger up to assess the weather, and decided that the temperature would not drop much during the night. Tom and Janet had both donned T-shirt and jeans for dinner and I decided that they'd be fine like that. 'Come on,' I told them when we were back downstairs, and after Tom had fed Charlie, 'let's go . . . unless you've changed your minds, that is.' They both looked at me as if I was dafter than the dog.

As we left the house, I decided that if I was going to introduce them to adulthood, I might as well go all the way. Also, I'd skipped coffee after dinner and I felt like a fix, and so, instead of heading straight for the beach, I took us down instead to the square. The four café restaurants there can seat over three hundred people at their outside tables, and I knew that earlier, punters would have had to queue until one became free. As midnight approached, they were all still busy, but the frenzy was over and we found a vacant spot in Can Coll. I asked for an Americano with a little cold milk on the side, and a glass of the decent house white. The kids each copied my coffee order, but didn't push their luck by asking for wine as well.

'I liked the linguine sauce, Auntie Primavera,' Janet ventured as the waiter returned with a laden tray.

'Yeah, Mum,' Tom chipped in. 'Top form.' He paused. 'Can we cook tomorrow night, Janet and me?'

'Tomorrow's Saturday,' I pointed out. Our norm is to eat out on weekend evenings, and I'd kept up the habit while the Monaco Three had been with us. 'Do it one night next week, if you like.'

'We might not be here then,' Janet said. 'I'd a call on my mobile from Mum, just before dinner. She said she's coming back early and that she's going to ask Conrad to take us home, on Monday or Tuesday.' She frowned. 'She said she wasn't sure when their flight would land, since it was a long way, but that she'd let me know as soon as she did, and she knew for sure when we could come. I don't understand that. It's not a long flight from Scotland to Nice Airport. Has she really been in Scotland?'

'Isn't that what she told you? That she had to go there to run her business for a month?'

'Yes,' she conceded. 'It's just funny, that's all.'

'Maybe something came up in the business,' I suggested, 'and she had to go somewhere else. Life isn't always predictable.'

'Ours is,' Tom commented, as he added some milk to his coffee.

I laughed. 'Does that concern you?' I asked, changing the subject swiftly. 'If it does we could always do unpredictable things.'

'Could we go to America to see Jonny play on the tour next week?' he shot back.

Jonny Sinclair (Big Jonathan) is his cousin, his Aunt Ellie's older son from her first marriage. He's a promising young pro golfer, and he'd lived with us for a while a couple of years earlier, while he was starting out on tour. He'd won his first tournament, made some very decent money in Europe since then, some of it from a second win, in Italy, played all four rounds in the US Open, finishing in the top fifteen, and was teeing up again in a week's time in Pennsylvania, on a sponsor's invitation secured for him by Brush Donnelly, his reclusive but very effective agent.

'No,' I said firmly. 'It would be a lot of cost and a lot of hassle, and if we did go there, Jonny would be too busy to spend any time with us. Maybe next year we'll go to the Masters, if he gets an invitation, and if it fits with the school holidays.'

'Auntie Primavera.' Janet's voice wasn't much more than a whisper. 'There's a man at a table in the next restaurant and he's looking at you.'

'Should I be pleased?' I asked. 'Does he look like a rock star?'

Tom covered his mouth with his hand. 'Yes, but think Steven Tyler,' he muttered. We'd watched a DVD of *Be Cool* a few weeks before, and Tom had been amazed that anyone could look like the Demon of Screamin' and still be alive. 'Next time they film a Terry Pratchett book,' he'd suggested, 'he should play Death.'

Casually, I looked around the square, then over my left shoulder. Yes, there was a dude not far away and he had been looking at me. I knew this by the intensity with which he was examining the façade of the church. It happens if you're a woman on her own, or even with a couple of kids. Men sometimes eye you up and down; when you catch them at it, almost invariably they look away and pretend that they hadn't been. When they're bold and persist, you frost them until they desist . . . unless, of course, you don't want them to desist, but I hadn't come across one of them in many a year.

He didn't look a bit like the Aerosmith front man, apart maybe in the size of his chin, and yes, he had high cheekbones too, accentuated by the glasses he wore, round like John Lennon's but bigger and with blue-tinted lenses. He was a lot younger too, probably around my age, but from Tom's perspective, within the human species that fits comfortably into the box labelled 'old' . . . for everyone other than me. His close-cropped hair was fairish with only a few streaks of grey, and he wasn't skeletal like Mr Tyler, not in the slightest. In fact he looked as if he might have been something of an athlete once, and still kept in shape.

I turned away from him as casually as I'd glanced in his direction, and back to my young companions.

'Do you know him?' Janet asked, switching into French.

'No,' I replied, in the same tongue, 'not at all.' And yet, even as I spoke I realised that there was something there, the merest hint of a possibility that, in fact, I did. But if that was the case, I couldn't place him and I wasn't about to spend any time trying. Thousands of people pass through our village, year after year, and come back, so it was entirely possible that I'd seen him before. Instead I devoted myself to the coffee, and the white wine, which was actually rather better than decent.

The fireworks were still blazing away as my watch passed midnight, although they were more sporadic than they had been, and sounds of music had started to drift up from the beach. Tom and Janet were fidgeting in their seats, having finished their coffee, and I'd paid the bill, but I was not about to rush my wine. Not being a wholly irresponsible mother and guardian, I did check them for signs of tiredness, but they looked more awake than I felt. The stress of earlier in the evening had left its mark on me, and I had a feeling that it wasn't going to get better any time soon. There were going to be ructions when the Monaco youngsters learned what their mother had been and gone and done, and while I wouldn't be there to see them, I expected to hear about them very soon, as Janet and I had taken to exchanging emails on a regular basis.

'Come on, then,' I said. 'Let's go and hear how Bob Marley's torch-bearers sound. But first, I will make a pit stop. I suggest that you two do the same.' In recent years, the agency that manages all the beaches in Catalunya has installed a few portaloos for the summer months, but they're not places I choose to visit when there's another option.

They took my advice, then we headed off. I glanced to my left as we did so and saw that the guy who'd been appraising me earlier had gone before us. I felt a strange pang of disappointment, as if I'd wanted him to give me a wink, so I could blow him out, but it seemed that I hadn't come up to scratch. *God, Primavera*, I sighed inwardly, *when Steven fucking Tyler doesn't fancy you, it has to be all downhill after that.*

I cheered up, though, when we met Ben and Tunè at the top of the hill, heading in the same direction as us. 'Mum's babysitting,' he explained at once, adding, 'and dog-sitting. Cher and Mustard hate the noise.' He ruffled Tom's hair, and slung an arm round Janet's shoulders. 'Hey, you two, all grown up and heading for a night on the beach.'

'Not all night,' I told him, quickly.

Tunè grinned at me mischievously. 'They can stay with us, Primavera, if you want to go home early.' She was only pulling my chain, but it felt like another kick in the morale.

'What's early for you is late for us,' I countered.

'I know, really,' she said, 'but for us it's a change to have a whole night to ourselves. You must remember that, from when Tom was three.'

I smiled and nodded. I couldn't tell her that I didn't, because I had no such memory. When Tom was three, I was raising him unhappily on my own and plotting my irrational revenge on his father, having cut myself off from all my friends and family, even from my beloved old dad and mum, missing the last years of her life in the selfish process.

Nine years on, I'm a different woman, and I roundly dislike the other one. Most of the time she was an absolute bitch.

As always, I had my phone in my bag, but the last thing I expected was that it should ring at that time of night. I took it out and looked at the display, which shone brightly and told me that the caller was 'Susie mobile'. I almost sent it to Voicemail, but relented and accepted it, slowing my pace a little as the kids walked on with Ben and Tunè. A few seconds later I wished I'd just rejected it.

'Can't come between me and my man, girlfriend,' she growled. 'You tried it once before and it didn't work.'

'Excuse me,' I hissed, 'I'm not having that from the woman who came to visit and fucked my husband, in my bed, the minute my back was turned.'

'I took him from you, though,' she chuckled, slurring her words, 'and don' tell me you didn't try for a comeback.'

She sounded drunk and venomous and I reacted badly. 'If I had done,' I'm afraid I sneered . . . an ugly word for an ugly sound, 'I'd have had him, honey. He only ever saw one thing in you and you're sitting on it right now.' She'd flipped my switch. But for the music from the beach, I'm sure the kids would have heard me. 'You waved your child in his face. That's why he married you; it wasn't you he was in love with, it was her that he'd put inside you. Like an idiot, I hid mine. If I hadn't . . .' I stopped myself from yelling at her.

'Sour fucking grapes, Primavera,' she mumbled. 'You just can't stand to see me happy, can you?'

'Listen,' I retorted, 'you're pissed as a rat, and you'll probably have forgotten all about this in the morning, but what I actually cannot stand is to see you unhappy, and that's what you're going to be if you don't get rid of that arsehole right now. Even worse, your children will be miserable, because they can't stand him either.'

'Another black lie, you fucking tart.'

'Yeah, well, you phone wee Jonathan tomorrow and tell him who his new daddy is and see what sort of a reaction you get. He was in tears tonight when he told me he thought Duncan was back, and they weren't tears of joy.'

' 'Cos you've poisoned him against him.'

'Bollocks!' I wasn't at my most articulate. 'Speaking of poison, who poured you the drink you've just had too much of? No,' I said before she could reply, 'that was a rhetorical question. I know bloody hell who did. In case you've forgotten in your euphoric state, you are recovering from chemotherapy for a form of cancer that is quite likely to damage your liver. The last thing that clown should be doing is giving you any alcohol, and as for getting you bloody trousered . . . Jesus Christ, Susie, you'd better employ a food-taster from now on.'

'God,' she said, contemptuously. 'You really hate him, don't you?'

'I won't deny that. I detest the man, I loathe him, and okay, hate will cover it as well. I know he's spun you a story, Suse, because he phoned me a few hours ago, to tell me what it was, and to rub my nose in it . . . or so he thought. Everything I told you about his attempt to blackmail me is true, and I can even prove it.'

'You might have to, girl, for Duncan says that if you repeat it,' she hiccuped, 'Duncan says we're going to sue you for slander, or libel or whatever. He says we'll put you in the fucking poorhouse, girl.'

'Is that so?' I laughed. 'He thinks he can use your money to intimidate me? In that case, Mrs Culshaw, you tell your precious husband to bear this in mind. The version of me that he invented in his pathetic pseudo-novel might be a hell of a lot closer to the mark than he realises.'

'What the fu . . . does that mean?'

'It means,' I told her, 'that he has no idea who he's taking on, or what could happen to him if he threatens my boy and me. Now, I've had enough of this shit. Call me tomorrow, Susie, when your headache subsides and you can think like the intelligent, rational woman that I know you are underneath all this nonsense. And please, for your children's sake if nobody else's, do not drink any more.'

Just as I ended the call, I heard her say, 'Fuck off!'

Janet and Tom were waiting for me at the foot of the slope at the start of the boardwalk that runs behind the beach. Ben and Tunè were in the distance, heading for the music with another couple. 'Who was that?' my son asked.

I was still blazing mad, but sensible enough to realise that 'Nobody' would not cut it as an answer, so I told him the truth. 'We were just having some girl talk,' I added.

'Did you ask where she is?' Janet enquired. She hadn't forgotten our earlier discussion.

Maybe my state of mind influenced me, but I'd like to think that I simply decided it would be plain wrong to deceive her further. 'She's in America,' I told her. 'Something came up and she had to go there.'

'When she went away last winter and before that in the autumn, was she in America then too?'

There was something in her question, in its intonation, that told me she wasn't buying any cover stories, not any more.

'Yes, she was,' I admitted, then went further. I owed Susie nothing and I wasn't going to jeopardise my relationship with Tom's highly intelligent half-sister, or him for that matter, by insulting them with any more attempted wool-pulling. 'Your mother's had a health problem,' I told her. 'She's being looked after by a consultant in Monaco and he's referred her to a clinic in America for treatment.'

She stood tall and looked me in the eye, directly, giving me no wiggle room. 'She's not going to die, like Dad, is she?'

'Your father died from a heart condition that wasn't detected until it was too late. Your mother's illness has been diagnosed, and it's being treated appropriately. Her doctors are very happy with her.'

I was dreading the next question: *is it cancer?* Thankfully, Janet seemed to decide that she had enough information and didn't ask it. Instead she digested the news for a few seconds. 'I won't say anything to Jonathan,' she said. 'He worries about too many things as it is.' Good kid; perceptive kid; caring kid.

I nodded. 'He doesn't need to know.'

'No. Thanks for telling me, Auntie Primavera. Mum'll tell me too, eventually. When she does, I won't let on that I knew already.'

'I don't mind if you do. My roof, my rules, like we say. If it was me, I'd have told Tom, but we all have to make our own judgements on the big issues in life. So don't go blaming her, will you?'

She frowned. 'I don't know. That's two secrets in one day.' She looked at her semi-sibling. 'Did you know that our dad had been married before he married either of our mums?'

He nodded. 'Yes, Mum told me, after he died and we came to live here. Grandpa Mac talks about her too. Hasn't he ever mentioned her to you?'

'I haven't seen Grandpa Mac since I was seven,' Janet murmured, 'the summer we came here and he was here too. I'd like to go and see him in Scotland, but Mum won't take me.'

That didn't surprise me. While I get on with the entire Blackstone clan, I know that they don't have a lot of time for Susie. I got over, more or less, the way she and Oz got together, but they never did, Ellie especially. I wouldn't want to be in the same room as the two of them.

'In that case,' I promised, 'next time you're here with us, I'll make sure that Grandpa Mac's here too.'

'And Grandma Mary?' Tom asked.

'If she wants.' I wasn't sure that she would. Mac hadn't said anything specific, but I wasn't sure that he and his second wife were doing too well.

As I spoke, I realised that the crowds were gathering, and that I was way above their median age. 'Enough of all that stuff,' I declared, firmly. 'Do you guys want to go to this gig or don'cha?'

They beamed, both of them, and Janet jumped up and down like a one-woman football team that had just won the cup.

'Well, let's go,' I shouted, 'before the band gets tired and the bar gets emptied.'

Not that there was any chance of either eventuality.

We headed along the boardwalk, towards the old Greek wall, and the bandstand. It might have been billed as a reggae night but the musicians were all Catalan, mostly local, and they were pretty damn good. We were all wearing flip-flops, but I removed mine and stowed them in my bag, making damn sure it was zipped. Ours is a peaceable place but there were bound to be strangers around. Spain is a lovely country, but be under no illusion, it has its fair share of casual, opportunist crime and then some, if you're casual and careless enough to provide opportunities.

The beach bar was still well provisioned when we reached it but it was thronged, and selling out fast. Sensibly, they weren't dispensing anything in glass, but I wasn't fussy. I caught the owner's eye and asked for three bottles of still water. I gave the kids one each and we wandered closer to the action. I recognised the bass player and one of the guitarists, and the girl with the mike was familiar too. They'd switched from reggae into a set of gipsy-style music; it was earthy, to say the least, and the singer knew all the actions. For a moment I wondered whether it was suitable for twelve-year-olds, then Tom laughed at one of the lines and I realised that a frontier had been crossed somewhere without my noticing.

But I did notice something else, or rather someone. The bloke from the square had made his way to the concert too, or maybe he'd just been curious and followed the noise . . . or maybe he'd followed us. *Nonsense, Primavera*, I scolded myself mentally, *all that crap with Culshaw's making you paranoid.*

The one certainty was that the man was as smitten by the singer as every other guy with a pulse in the audience, even my son by the looks of it. With his attention elsewhere I was able to study him more closely than in the restaurant. Yes, he was probably early to mid-forties, quite tall, a little over six feet, with a fairly muscular build under his striped short-sleeved shirt, and he hadn't been in the area for very long, for he was still a bit of a paleface. Plus he was British; I've lived in the village for long enough to make an educated guess at individual nationalities. Sometimes the clue is in height, with the Dutch for example; others, it's how their kids are dressed, for example if a boy's wearing a blue football shirt with a rooster crest and the name 'Ribery' on the back, then he's either French or confused. With the Brits, it's their pasty or pink faces and their general deportment. That falls into two categories. There are those who think that everywhere is a colony and that therefore they have first dibs on tables, waiters, etc., and who assume that if they speak English very slowly and very loudly they will be understood. Then there are those who are diffident to the point of nervousness, and completely out of their comfort zone in any country that doesn't serve warm dark beer or tea in large earthenware pots. The man I was looking at was harder to place than most, but I decided that he belonged in the former category, if only because he didn't look as if he had ever been nervous in his life.

Therefore, summed up, mystery man was a middle-aged British citizen, a stranger on his own in a place that almost without exception attracts families or older couples. A widower, perhaps, or a divorcee, but certainly not gay from the way he was admiring the vocalist. Profession? You can't tell a book by the cover. I have seen men shuffling along the beach in the sort of swim shorts that should never have left the factory, unshaven and with at least three over-spilling bellies, and learned later that they were corporate lawyers, hedge fund managers, surgeons or whatever. But Mr Brit was well dressed in his expensive tourist shirt and trousers with a discreet Lacoste alligator just below the waistband, and he had the air about him of someone who had no need or desire to dress down from his day job. *Simple, Primavera, he's a rep.*

I nodded at that verdict, at the very moment when the singer took a break and he glanced across and caught me looking at him. He smiled, and started to move in my direction. *Oh shit*, I thought, and harboured the notion of using the kids as a human shield but they'd drifted a couple of metres away from me, closer to the stage. All I could do, other than grab them and beat an undignified, not to mention cowardly, retreat, was to stand there and wait, pretending that I was ignoring his approach.

'Primavera?' Ben Simmers' call took me unawares. I turned towards him and realised from his expression that he had taken in the whole thing. His raised eyebrows, and his concern, asked, quite clearly, whether I wanted him to intervene, but I shook my head briefly.

The guy drew closer; he was smiling and didn't pose any threat in such a throng, but still, I felt a pang of something that might have been alarm, if not outright fear. Rarely do I feel vulnerable, but I did then, because I had this continuous nagging feeling that I was missing something.

He stopped, standing in front of me, no closer than the kids were, sorry, kid, because Tom had left Janet's side and was standing in front of me, a five foot four inch, fifty-nine kilo bundle of something serious.

As I put a hand on his shoulder, the newcomer spoke. 'You don't remember me, do you?' Slightly Irish accent, but I still couldn't pin him down.

'If that's a pub quiz starter,' I replied, 'the answer is, it's a line from *It Started with a Kiss*, by Hot Chocolate, early nineteen eighties. If it's a chat-up line, it's crap and you'd be well advised to desist, because quite apart from my son here, there are at least three guys watching you right now who would be happy to take you to the top of the old Greek wall and chuck you in the sea if they thought you were annoying me.' I paused. 'If, on the other hand, it's a straight question, then no, I don't have a clue.'

'You're Liam Matthews!' Janet's exclamation cut in out of the blue. 'You were a friend of our father's. You were in some films with him and you came to visit us once when we lived in Scotland, beside Loch Lomond. I wasn't very old at the time, but I remember you. Don't you, Tom? It was just after you came to live with us.'

'Got it in one,' the former stranger laughed, as Tom shook his head. 'You can only have been about . . . what . . . four, then. I didn't meet your brother that day, though, just you. You wandered in when your dad and I were talking and he introduced me, and made you shake my hand, like a little lady. By God, but you've grown up. You're a proper lady now, no mistake; he'd have been very proud of you, as I'm sure Susie is.'

Liam Matthews! Liam bloody Matthews. A name from way, way, in my past; it must have been almost fifteen years back. Finally I remembered him, and the first time I'd ever seen him. It was in Barcelona, and I was covered in blood.

After Oz left me for Jan, and went back to Scotland, I stayed on in our apartment in St Martí and took a job as a nurse in the Trueta hospital in Girona. A few months later, I was in the near-legendary JoJo's Bar in L'Escala one night when the telly ran an ad for a wrestling show in Barcelona, and who was doing the promo but Oz. The shock knocked me off my bar stool.

The nutter had got himself involved with a Glasgow-based outfit called the Global Wrestling Alliance. Ostensibly he was their ring announcer, but as it turned out he was really working on an undercover investigation into a series of attempts at sabotage. Whatever, I couldn't let the circus leave town without seeing for myself; I booked a ticket and drove down.

It wasn't my intention to meet him . . . well, that's what I told myself and still do . . . but there was another serious incident that very night. One of the wrestlers was shot, yards away from me, in the middle of the ring, and I wound up in there doing some battlefield first aid. The man's name was Jerry Gradi, and happily it still is, because they reckon I saved his life. I'm still on Jerry's Christmas card list and he's on mine, but he's the only one of that crew I kept in touch with.

Liam was there too, although I didn't pay too much attention to him, or give him any thought, considering everything that was going on, then and afterwards.

It's an evening I'll never forget, for a reason that Duncan Culshaw touched on in his scurrilous book. After the shooting, Oz and I crossed paths at the hospital where Jerry was taken, when he came to check that he was going to be all right. The two of us had dinner together and that's where he was when he had the phone call that told him that Jan had been electrocuted by the faulty washing machine in their flat in Glasgow.

Fast forward a little. I kept in touch with him, this time to check that he was going to be all right. Eventually, one thing led to the other, I moved back to Scotland, and we became a couple again. Odd? No, I'd never stopped loving the boy, and he didn't hate me too much either.

He was still involved with the GWA; indeed, that's how he got into the acting business. As a ring announcer, he fell well short of being Michael Buffer, but nonetheless he made an impression. As a result, he landed some voice-over work on TV commercials. Eventually Miles Grayson, my brother-in-law, was brave enough to cast him in a movie, and it all took off from there. Before it did, though, Oz and I had socialised with some of the wrestling crew and Liam had been among them.

He'd looked a hell of a lot different then, hence my failure to recognise him. Apart from the specs, which were new, and the fact that he'd carried at least ten kilos more muscle in those days, he'd lost the big hair. Liam had been famous . . . some said notorious . . . for his ponytail, which hung on the end of one of the worst mullets I've ever seen. He'd looked like a holdover from a seventies pop band, but at some point since then he'd turned into a New Age man.

My brother-in-law may have had something to do with that too; at Oz's suggestion he'd cast Liam as a cop in one of his movies. The Showaddywaddy look would not have worked for that.

When my reverie was over and I rejoined the moment, I saw that Liam was gazing down on Tom, who still hadn't relaxed from his defensive posture. 'Wow,' he murmured. 'Even if I didn't know who you were, son, I'd have picked you out of a line-up of five hundred as Oz's kid.' He grinned. 'You think you could take me, slugger? Your dad could have, that's for sure.'

'I'm not a slugger,' Tom replied, quietly. 'What's your wing chun belt?' he asked.

Matthews put his thumb in his waistband. 'About thirty-four just now. What's wang shine anyway?'

'Wing chun is the martial art I study. It's Chinese, something like karate.'

'I'm only kidding,' Liam said. 'I know what it is and I can guess what it means: it means, "Don't mess with me," right?'

'No; actually it means "Forever springtime". It's close to what my mother's name means in English.'

'Whatever, young man,' the ex-grappler chuckled. 'I am more pleased to meet you than you could ever imagine.' He extended his hand and Tom shook it. Then he looked at me. 'And I'm just as pleased to meet you again, Mrs Blackstone.'

'Stop kidding around,' I told him. 'It was Primavera back then and it still is. So, Mr Matthews,' I continued, as the singer reappeared to finish her set, 'what brings you here? Are you a tourist, and if so is Mrs Matthews back at the hotel? Her name was Erin, wasn't it?'

'Don't you give me the "mister" either,' he replied then shook his head. 'Erin was never officially sanctioned, so to speak, nor has anyone else ever been. If you remember, she was an air hostess. She wound up marrying a pilot she thought was a safer bet than me.'

'Maybe the Specsavers look put her off. I didn't mark you down to wear those ever.'

He shrugged. 'I don't like contacts, and I won't let anyone burn my eyes with lasers. These are the best I can do. You're still twenty-twenty, yes?'

'So far,' I said. 'So, Liam, what are you doing here?'

'It isn't a long story,' he replied, glancing up at the stage, 'but this is probably not the place to tell it. If you'd like to meet for lunch tomorrow, today rather,' he corrected himself, 'I'll tell you then.'

Given the Susie situation, I wasn't sure how the day would pan out. 'Lunch might be a problem,' I said. 'Coffee would be better. Same place you were earlier, eleven thirty?'

'That's good for me. I'll say goodnight then.'

'Aren't you staying for the music?'

He looked up at the singer once again. 'Better not,' he chuckled. 'I can't understand a word she's singing; I can only guess at it, and it's driving me crazy.'

Six

We called it a morning at one thirty. Just being there had been enough for Janet and Tom. Sheer excitement – and that coffee – kept them going for a while, but eventually they both showed signs of flagging, and didn't protest when I suggested that we head for home.

I was as tired as they were but I didn't sleep very well. My head was still buzzing with jumbled visions of Susie, her new husband, and a younger version of Liam Matthews, complete with big hair, drifting in and out of mental focus.

I got up at the usual time, showered and dressed, maybe a little further upmarket than usual, with my coffee date in mind. I did flirt with the idea of dialling Susie's mobile in what would have been for her the very early hours of the morning, to get even for her drunken, abusive phone call, but Culshaw would probably have answered, and the only thing I wanted to hear of him was his eulogy.

But I did call Alex Guinart, as soon as I reckoned he'd be

at his desk in Girona. 'How was San Juan for you?' I asked him when he answered. 'Quiet?'

He laughed. 'Quiet is not a word I'd apply to it, but in police terms it was peaceful, as it usually is. The firefighters were busy as always, but most people were too happy or drunk to make trouble. How was yours?'

'Mixed. Tom and Janet took me to the beach concert for a while. I needed the diversion because I'd had a difficult day. Alex,' I asked, 'do you remember that man you helped me get rid of last year, the would-be extortionist?'

'Hah,' he barked, 'I remember him very well. Mr Duncan Culshaw. I didn't simply let it go, you know. I opened a file on him, and entered it into our database. He is now officially a person of interest in Spain.'

'So you still have the recording?'

'Oh yes.'

'I don't suppose you could give me a copy?' I ventured.

'That would be correct, Primavera, I couldn't. But I could give it to any criminal authority that is investigating him. He's not trying to con you again, is he?' he asked.

'It's worse than that.' I told him about Susie's nuptials. 'He's persuaded her that black is white, and that it was us who tried to set him up.'

'To hell with that!' he exclaimed. 'Make that *denuncio*. It'll still be valid and I'll act on it. Where do they live?'

'Monaco, but—'

'Fine. He may think he can thumb his nose at us from there, but he's wrong. Spain has an extradition treaty in place with that country, and if we have a criminal action against him we can get him.' My friend was seriously pumped up.

'Slow down, Alex,' I pleaded. 'I didn't make an official complaint against him last year because I didn't want the publicity that would flow from it. That still applies. But if there's some way I can prove to Susie that she's married a crook . . . That's what I'm after, you see.'

He was silent for a few seconds. 'Let me think about it,' he murmured, eventually. 'Let me talk to my boss in Barcelona. Maybe he would authorise me giving you a transcript of the recording, since your voice is on it. But I'm not confident,' he warned.

I didn't press him. I knew that if he could make it work, he would. But even if he did, and I laid a notarised transcript in front of Susie, I had a foreboding that the loathsome Culshaw would be able talk his way out from under it.

I spent the morning tidying the house and catching up on the laundry. To his eternal credit Conrad always insisted on doing his own, and he would have done Janet and wee Jonathan's as well if I hadn't drawn the line at that.

Janet was on edge, waiting for her next call from her mother, and maybe brooding over her illness. In the bright light of morning I regretted having told her about it, but I knew that if I'd lied I'd have been regretting it more. To get her out of her preoccupation, I proposed that Conrad take all three kids off for a morning at the water park in Ampuriabrava. The youngsters jumped at it, although I'm not sure he did.

I was at a table in La Terrassa d'Empuries, with an

unusually placid Charlie at my feet, when Liam came up the slope and into the square. He was less immaculately dressed than the night before, but stood out more. It wasn't the shorts, they sported Mr Tommy Hilfiger's discreet badge; not the Croc flip-flops. No, it was the T-shirt. The GWA corporate logo was all over his chest and at its centre was his own image in wrestling gear, white sequinned tights and boots to match, with a shamrock logo on each one . . . not that anyone in the square, apart from me, would have linked the pouting poster beefcake to the guy who was sporting him.

I laughed as he approached. 'Did you wear that in my honour,' I asked, 'or are you always so understated?'

He smiled. 'No, this is for a special occasion. I stuck a couple in my bag for the trip . . . and yes, I admit it, in case you and I did meet up.'

There was a camera slung over his shoulder, a big, heavy Nikon digital SLR, with a zoom lens. As he seated himself, he placed it on the table.

'That looks like a serious piece of kit,' I remarked, as he asked the waiter for an orange juice, freshly squeezed. 'Are you into photography now?'

'Yeah, it's become quite a serious hobby. More than a hobby, actually; I write the occasional magazine piece and if there's a photograph needed, yes, I'm good enough to supply it myself.' He glanced down at Charlie. 'Nice dog. Is he your other minder?'

'Him? He has enough trouble minding his manners,' I retorted. 'As a guard dog he's all sound and no substance, I'm afraid. As for the minder-in-chief, this is one of his mornings for just being an ordinary kid.'

'Rather than following his mother everywhere,' he murmured, 'like the kid in a poem I learned when I was one myself?'

'I stared at him, genuinely surprised. 'You're full of surprises. You didn't strike me as a man who would know his A.A. Milne.'

'Some things stay with you for life.'

'In that case you might recall that the poem those lines come from is called "Disobedience". I wouldn't dream of disobeying my boy.'

'Not with him being a wing chun black belt.'

I frowned. 'Are you making fun of him?'

'Hell, no,' Liam replied, hurriedly. 'Nor am I underestimating him. I can't imagine anything worse than getting my arse kicked by a thirteen-year-old.'

'Twelve,' I corrected him.

'Bloody hell, Primavera, then he really is a big lad for his age.'

'How about you?' I asked. I knew hardly anything about the man. 'No wives, okay, but any kids?'

'None that have ever come looking for me.' He chuckled. 'If any do, they'll probably be half Japanese. I did some time on the Bushido circuit when I was young, and I was a popular boy there. That's where I really learned the business. Most of that stuff wasn't worked.' I peered at him, not understanding. 'I mean it was for real,' he explained. 'Not rehearsed and staged.'

'As in "fixed", like the GWA and the rest?'

'Sure,' he agreed. 'It has to be or the audiences would walk. In amateur Greco-Roman wrestling, the guys spend most of the time on the floor looking for submission holds, or trying to manoeuvre pins. Sports entertainment has to be more the latter than the former. Television demands it. That's why there are more body-builders and second or third tier footballers on the rosters today than there are pure wrestlers or martial artists. And because so many of those guys have no skills or subtlety, it can be a dangerous business. If Tom ever gets romantic ideas about being a GWA superstar, talk him out of it.'

'Don't worry,' I promised, 'I will. Not that it's likely. Tom's a very gentle boy.'

Liam chuckled. 'He didn't look very gentle on the beach last night when he thought I was going to come on to you. Christ, Primavera, that took me back to the last century and a night in Newcastle.'

'Why?'

'Because I had a run-in with Tom's father.'

Oz had told me that his and Liam's relationship had a rocky beginning but he'd never gone into detail. 'Oh yes?' I murmured, intrigued.

'I was a young arrogant son-of-a-bitch then, with a lot of the Belfast cockiness still in me. You probably won't remember; they billed me as being from Dublin, but actually I'm Northern Irish. Oz had just joined the company, so we'd met, but just casually, at home base. I thought he was just another suit. Jeez, was I wrong.'

'How did you find out?'

'I made a pass at his wife.'

'Ouch! What did he do?'

Liam reached up and pinched his nose, just below the big tinted specs. 'He broke this. I'd never been hit so hard in my life, and I'd been hit plenty. That was the closest Everett Davis . . . remember, the great big boss man . . . ever came to firing me, and believe me, I gave him plenty of reasons. He made me apologise to Oz and to Jan, but he didn't have to because I would have anyway. Oz taught me the error of my ways in that one encounter. I was full of myself, I thought I could do anything to anyone and get away with it. He showed me how wrong I was. He didn't have any martial arts skills, but wow, upset anyone he cared about, and he was unstoppable.' He frowned. 'I'm glad your lad's gentle, but I'll tell you this; he'll do whatever he has to, if it's to protect you.'

'Don't say that,' I murmured, 'you're scaring me.'

'It's nothing to be scared about. You must want him to be able to look after himself if you let him study wing chun.'

'Yes,' I conceded, 'but it's more for self-discipline than anything else.'

'Yes, and turning the other cheek is fine in principle, but not when it's someone else's. How is he at cheek-turning, by the way?'

Immediately I thought of Duncan Culshaw, writhing on the deck beside Susie's pool, moaning and clutching his nuts. 'It's maybe not what he does best,' I chuckled.

'What's his belt grade?' Liam asked.

'Black, first dan.'

He whistled. 'And he's twelve? I didn't get mine in karate till I was fourteen. Now, I'm sixth dan; I would love to train with him, while I'm here.'

I looked at hm. 'Which brings me to . . . why are you here?'

'I am genuinely on holiday,' he replied, 'properly, for the first time in years.'

'Are you still in the business?'

'Sports entertainment? No, my body took me out of that, finally, about seven years ago. That and your brother-in-law Miles, when he cast me in that film with Oz. I did a few more movies after that. The last one was two years ago. Since them I've done mostly TV, but not acting; a couple of documentaries, colour commentator on mixed martial arts events. I've even been on *Celebrity Big Brother*, in Ireland. When they ask you to do that, the subliminal message is that you should look for another line of work. That's what I've been doing with the magazine articles, and I suppose the photography, if I can ever make myself good enough. Oh yeah,' he added, 'and I'm writing a book.'

I shuddered. *Oh hell*, I thought, *not again*. 'An auto-biography?' I asked, quietly.

'Absolutely not,' he declared, putting me at ease instantly. 'I respect the business I was in too much to take any liberties with it. Also I value my own privacy too much to tell stories about my friends,' he paused, 'alive or dead. That's important to me, Primavera; there's something in my personal history that I never want to revisit. So you see, if you tell me to fuck off and leave you alone, I'll understand you completely.'

I recalled Oz telling me, back in the Glasgow days, that when Liam was a boy in Belfast, his father had been killed by Loyalist paramilitaries; and so I understood him completely.

'I'm not going to do that,' I told him. 'You were one of Oz's close friends, so how could I? But you're right, I keep my profile as low as I can, so how did you know where to find us?'

'Miles told me. I met him in Ireland a few months ago. He offered me a small acting gig in a TV series he's co-producing, but I'd just escaped from the *Big Brother* slammer, and decided it was time to take a serious look at the rest of my life, so I declined with thanks. I told him I needed a break, some chill-out time. He suggested that I head out to Spain and look you up.' He smiled. 'He said you'd turned into the coolest person he'd ever met. I was glad to hear it, because the last time we met, out in Vegas, you were very fucked-up indeed.'

Jesus, yes! The very worst time of my life, and I had blanked out the fact that Liam had been a witness to it. I'd forgotten, completely.

'So,' he went on, 'when I was ready I took him up on the first part of his suggestion, to come here. I wasn't so sure about the second, though. I thought you might have decided to cut yourself off from the past and the likes of me. As a first step, I booked myself into that hotel at the end of the beach there, the Riomar, and went for a wander last night. And what do you do but wander into the place next door.' He laughed, quietly. 'I repeat, that is one considerable boy you've got there.'

'Oh, I know it. And before you say it again, I will; he's looking more like his dad with every year's growth.'

'How does that make you feel?'

'Proud. I can't think of a better model. But . . . there are some things I don't want him to replicate.'

'I think I know what you mean.'

I said nothing; I didn't have to. In the silence a firework exploded, not far away. The San Juan festivities usually carry on into a second day, and sometimes beyond. Liam twitched in his seat, then shifted in it, casually; he'd been startled but wasn't for letting it show.

'You guard Tom's privacy then?' he continued.

'Too right.' I paused, recalling the principal threat to it. 'If you've been doing magazine work, have you ever heard of a man called Duncan Culshaw?'

He frowned. 'The surname's familiar, but I don't know why.'

'Remember Susie Gantry, Oz's third wife? Janet and wee Jonathan's mother?'

'Sure. To tell you the truth I've followed her business career since Oz died. I've even got a very small sentimental shareholding in her company. And of course,' he exclaimed as he made the connection in his head, 'her managing director's a man named Culshaw.'

'That's right: Phil. Duncan's his nephew, and, God help us, as of a couple of days ago, he's Susie's new husband.'

'And you don't approve?' he murmured, with a small smile.

'No, I bloody don't. Liam, can I tell you something, in the strictest confidence, because it relates directly to Tom's privacy.'

'Of course you can.'

Looking back now, I'm not sure how I knew that I could trust the man on the basis of such a fragmented acquaintance, but I did. I told him the Duncan story from the start, from our first brief meeting when Susie had taken him on as her man about the house, through his surprise visit to me the year before, and its thwarting, finally bringing it up to date with Duncan's reappearance in Monaco, and the Elvis Presley impersonator wedding ceremony.

'The guy's a blackmailer,' he summarised, when I was finished, 'and Susie's married him?'

'Yes, and now he's threatening to use his new status to get even with me, and with Tom in the process. He's out to blacken Oz's name, Liam.'

'The vicious bastard,' he murmured, evenly.

'Indeed.'

'Are you worried about him and his threat?'

'Yes, for lots of reasons. If he does start spreading stories about Oz, it won't just be Tom who's hurt. So will Janet and wee Jonathan. And the damage won't just be emotional either. You've got to know that Oz has become a bit of a cult since he died, like James Dean, or John Lennon or Amy Winehouse. His DVD sales are massive, and the income from them goes into his estate. That belongs to the three kids. If that was affected they'd feel it most.'

'Who manages the estate?' he asked.

'Susie and I do, between us.'

'Amicably?'

'Completely, until now. The last conversation she and I had probably put an end to that.'

'There could be a further complication,' Liam murmured, 'if the new stepdaddy gets himself involved in running the kids' affairs.'

I hadn't thought about that one.

He grinned. 'You could always marry someone,' he suggested. 'Somebody who would scare the shit out of him.'

I glared at him for an instant, then chuckled when I saw he'd been joking. 'That would be a step too far. I'm like you; I'm not in the marrying game.'

'Your sister is, though. That might be another way of scaring him off.'

'Run that past me?'

'Come on, Primavera, you must realise how much of a player your brother-in-law is. Miles Grayson isn't just another guy who made films. When I first worked for him, in Edinburgh on that movie Oz was in . . . What was it called again?'

'*Skinner's Rules*,' I reminded him. 'Film of the book.'

'That's the one. Even then, I thought he was a fairly ordinary bloke. You know, there were no airs about him, didn't push himself. I didn't realise he'd been the guest of the last three presidents at White House dinners, and of two prime ministers at Number Ten, or that he's got business interests worth several times as much as Susie's construction group. And he's Tom's uncle . . . He still is, isn't he? They haven't got divorced or anything?'

'No. He and Dawn are very happy; they'll stay the course.'

'In that case, if you appointed him as a trustee of the estate, to look after Tom's interests . . .' He raised an eyebrow. 'You get my drift? He would fucking eat Mr Culshaw.'

'Mmm.' The possibility of involving Miles was one that had occurred to me during the listless night, but I had rejected it. 'That would be a last resort, Liam,' I told him. Another super-banger went off close to the village, but he ignored it. 'I'm taking this personally,' I added. 'I've got teeth too.'

'But you'll have to be careful how you use them,' he said, then frowned. 'Listen,' he went on, 'if this guy's a professional conman, as it seems he is, my guess is that you are not this man's first target. I have an ex-girlfriend in London, a cop who's now a fairly senior officer in the Met. I could tell her about this, and ask her to have a look at Mr Duncan Culshaw. If he has indeed done this before and he's been caught, he'll have a record. If he has, you could tip off Susie. And even if he hasn't, my lady might turn up something about him, given time.'

'There may not be too much of that,' I said. His glasses had slipped a little; he peered at me over the top. 'There's something I didn't tell you about Susie.' I filled him in on her illness. 'She's finished her final round of therapy, and they're making all the right noises.'

'But?'

'Yes, but: Liam, this is something I haven't told a soul, and I'm only telling you because you have history with Susie and Oz, and I think you care about her. When I went to see her consultant in Monaco, he was more forthcoming than I expected, but he let something slip that I don't think he meant to. He told me the type of leukaemia that she has, and he used its long name, thinking probably that it would mean nothing to me. But it did, because twenty years ago and more, I nursed someone with that condition. It's one of the rarest and most aggressive forms of the disease that there is. Even with the very latest treatments, the kind that Susie's been having in America, her chances of five-year survival are not good at all. Worse, there's a real possibility that she might not see the end of this year. So you see, we may not have a lot of time to deal with Culshaw.'

'Ouch,' he whispered. 'If she dies and they're married . . .'

'Then regardless of any will she leaves, he'd inherit a large chunk of her estate, and he'd be bound to be the children's legal guardian.'

'That does make it urgent.' He took off the glasses, revealing warm blue eyes. 'Tell me, Primavera,' he asked, 'apart from you, who knows about Susie's illness?'

'The Kents do, obviously.' He looked at me, blankly; I had to explain who they were. 'And there's one other,' I added. 'When Susie was diagnosed, and she knew she'd be taking extended periods away from the business, she felt she had to tell her managing director . . . Phil Culshaw.'

'Duncan's uncle,' Liam said.

'That's right. Now I know nothing about the man. For example, is he straight?'

'He's running a listed company,' Liam pointed out. 'That means he's subject to audit and public scrutiny, not to mention

Susie having oversight of everything he does. She's executive chair, remember. Is he indiscreet? That's the real question. Did he let slip to his nephew that she was ill?'

'It needn't have been that way,' I pointed out. 'Let's assume that uncle knew about Susie and Duncan when the relationship began. When nephew disappeared, after my cop friend Alex Guinart . . . and he's no more than that,' I interjected, '. . . and I sorted him out, if Susie decided that she wanted to get in touch with him again, who else would she use as a messenger but Uncle Phil?'

'True.' He nodded.

'But leave him aside, let's assume he's honest. There's one thing I can do, and I might well. I've spoken to Alex and I can still make a criminal complaint against Duncan in Spain. I was hesitant, but talking this through with you has changed my mind. I think I'll do it. That'll shake things up.'

'Christ.' Liam laughed. 'Miles told me you were living the quiet life out here. That's what he calls it, is it?' But suddenly, he frowned. 'Primavera,' he murmured, 'I'm no lawyer, I only watch the telly, but from what you've told me, I've got a worry about any complaint you make. If this was *Law and Order: UK*, or similar, wouldn't any half-decent barrister have the recording you made thrown out as evidence, on grounds of entrapment?'

That hadn't occurred to me, but he had a point. 'Maybe,' I conceded, 'but I'm still going to do it. I'm up for anything that will sort this character out.'

'Then you go for it.' He killed what was left of his orange

juice, checked the bill that the waiter had left, clipped on to a little tray, and laid a ten-euro note on top. 'That enough of a tip around here?' he asked.

'Thirty per cent? It'll get you remembered.'

'Good, because I'll be back. Soon, I hope. Have dinner with me tonight, say eight o'clock, here in St Martí? You choose which restaurant. You must know them all.'

'I do, but dinner? Cut to the chase, Liam. On what basis?' I asked, bluntly.

He understood what I was asking. 'Two old friends across the table, and that's it, I promise. I won't even hold your hand . . . although if you try to hold mine I won't tear it away.'

'On that basis, I'd like that, because . . . Liam, I just don't: hold hands or anything else. Understand?'

'That's okay.' He grinned. 'Primavera, I expect to meet Oz again one day, in hell or maybe in heaven if they've relaxed the entrance requirements. I don't want him punching my fucking lights out again!'

'Over me?' I laughed.

'Over you: I wouldn't chance it. Which is your house?' he asked, suddenly.

I nodded, eastwards. 'That's it, jammed up against the church.'

'Wooo!' he exclaimed. 'That's quite a palace. Stone-built?'

'Absolutely. It's not a palace, though; that's an exaggeration. But it is big, I'll grant you, bigger than it looks from here; the garage is three floors below where we're standing.'

I left Charlie in our small garden, where his kennel is, then walked with Liam down the slope, towards the beach, to put him on the path back to his hotel. He told me he'd come via the road, and hadn't known about the shorter route.

'I can understand why you settled here,' he said, as we turned past the Foresters' house. 'In fact, I'm having trouble understanding why you and Oz ever left.'

'That's several long stories,' I replied. 'Yes, this is an ideal place for a forty-something single mother who doesn't need to worry about money ever again to raise her kid, but for the volatile couple that he and I were, there was no paradise. We were mixed up when we were here, both of us. Neither of us had any sense of purpose. Now I do, and that makes all the difference.' I looked at him, into those blue tinted lenses. 'But I don't have him, and that's the only cloud in my sky.'

'That's sad,' he murmured. 'You know, the whole world thinks that you and he were a two-person disaster area, but that's not really true, is it?'

'Oh, we probably were, but what's also true is that once we met, I was never very good at living without him, not until Tom came along. As for him, though, that's another matter. We couldn't keep our hands off each other when we were together, but when we weren't the sod got along without me perfectly well.'

'Don't be so sure.'

I stared at him. 'What makes you say that?'

'Probably nothing more than the way he was when he spoke about you. Even when he was calling you all the names under the sun, there was a something in his eyes, as if another part of him was saying, "Okay, but she's my scheming manipulative little bitch!" There's an old story about an English footballer who was being kicked all around the park by his Scottish marker. After the tenth or eleventh time, the Englishman got up and shouted at the guy, "You're just a big Scots bastard!" and the Jock gave him a toothless grin and said, "Aye, and don't you forget it." That's the sort of look Oz had in his eye when he talked about you; pride of a sort.'

I felt myself go squidgy inside. 'Did he indeed?' We stopped at the foot of the hill. The path to the Riomar Hotel went off to the left.

'Yes,' Liam said. 'Something else too. After you disappeared, when everybody thought you'd been killed in that plane with all the rest, Oz went completely schizo. He kept up the front, sure, made his movies, did the personal appearances and all that stuff, but behind the scenes he had detectives looking for you all over the bloody world. We got drunk together one night, after a chat show we did in London, and he told me. He said that after he did the eulogy at your memorial service, he realised that he'd been playing a part like any other, because inside, he refused to believe that you were dead. Ironic, isn't it; you weren't, but now he is.'

'Ironic,' I repeated. 'Yes, that's a word.'

'You know what else I think?' he said.

'Do tell.'

'I think that part of Oz, maybe the bit that was his mother's son, I don't know, thought he should have a nice, quiet, well-ordered domestic life, and went for it with Jan, and with Susie, because that's what they offered. But the real guy, he didn't want that at all. The real guy wanted you all along, because you weren't like that; you were the opposite.'

'I'm like that now; nice and well-ordered.'

'Are you? Are you really?'

'What do you mean?'

'I mean that you've still got it, that air of the devil about you, whatever your brother-in-law thinks.' He grinned. 'Not that you ain't cool with it, mind.'

'No, I don't,' I protested. 'I'm a middle-aged mum.'

His laugh boomed out. 'So was Maggie Thatcher, once. I'm telling you, Primavera, you've still got the spark about you that made you and Oz a couple. I'm not saying that you haven't changed a thousand per cent from the last time we met, but still, I wouldn't be in this Culshaw guy's shoes for all the Guinness in Dublin.'

'Ach, away with you, man,' I said, scornfully. 'Whatever you think, my wayward days are over.'

'Maybe that makes you even more formidable.'

I laughed at his insistence. 'Go on, Liam,' I chuckled. 'Bugger off and let me get in touch with my cop friend. My friend Susie needs saving from herself, and there's nobody else who can do it.'

He beamed at me. 'See what I mean?'

Seven

'Hi, Mum.'

My body was in the kitchen, but my mind was years away, thinking of times past, of Liam Matthews, but mostly about Oz and what Liam had said, about him searching for me, all the time I was hiding out, hiding from him, because I'd believed he was behind that plane going down, and that I'd been his number one target. He'd refused to accept I was dead, but was he really wanting to make sure of it? Once I'd have believed that, but not any more.

I looked at Tom and at the other two as they reached the top of the stairs from the garage. Their hair was tousled, their faces were flushed and their clothes were crumpled, just as you'd expect from three kids who'd just been taken to a water park by a guy.

'Are we late for lunch?' he asked.

'No, you're not,' I declared. 'But you ain't having any till you've got yourselves tidied up.' I grinned at Conrad, who'd just appeared in the doorway, in much the same state of disrepair as they were. 'And that goes for you too,' I told him, although in truth I was pleased that he'd been able to relax a little himself. He takes his job as seriously as anyone I've ever met, and so he's a very wound-up man.

Given the interesting morning I'd had, you might think it was a minor miracle that I'd been able to put anything on the table at all, but it's as easy to order takeaway pizza for five as it is for one, and just as easy to serve when you cut them into slices and tell everyone to eat with their fingers. Kids don't have a problem with that, and if Conrad did, he kept it to himself. They were done, and I'd just given them money to buy ice-cream desserts on the beach, when the phone rang.

'Hello,' a distant, very diffident, rather weak voice began. 'It's me.'

'How's your head?' I asked.

'Bloody awful,' Susie replied. 'Please tell me you've got Freddy Mercury singing "Barcelona!" full blast at your place, otherwise the bugger's trying to split my skull from the inside.'

'Sorry, kid,' I told her, 'it's only dear old Julio Iglesias at this end, crooning softly and adjusting his balls in that fetching way of his. Drink lots of water and take a couple of codeine and Freddy might lower the volume. Could be worse though; it might have been Pavarotti.'

'Don't.' I heard a heavy sigh. 'Primavera . . .' I waited for her to continue, 'if I say sorry about last night, can we forget it ever happened?'

'Susie,' I said, 'I'm surprised you can remember what never happened last night.'

'I wish I couldn't. I was horrible to you. I should just have ignored the whole thing, but I got drunk, and yes, I know I shouldn't drink, I know that my treatment doctors warned me about it, but for fuck's sake, I'm a realist and I know that it probably isn't my liver that's going to kill me but something else, so what the hell.'

She was right about that, but I couldn't say so. Instead, 'Ach, Susie, I said some stuff I shouldn't have too.' I paused. 'Not about Duncan, though. I'm sorry, but I meant that; the story I told you, about the book, that's true, whatever his version is. The police here still want me to make a formal complaint. They have him on tape, Susie, on tape.'

'Oh God,' she moaned. 'Please, Primavera, don't do that. I just couldn't deal with it right now. You say one thing, he says another; I just don't know.'

'Which of us have you known longer?' I asked.

'You, of course. But I'm married to Duncan now . . .'

'What's that got to do with it?'

'A lot,' she sighed.

'Susie, tell me something: when he came back, did you send for him, or did he just show up.'

'He came back; said he had missed me too much. When I told him I was ill he was really shocked, Primavera.' Her tone was pleading; she really did want me to believe her, but I'd seen the real man, so I couldn't.

'Whose idea was it that he go with you to Arizona?'

'He asked if I wanted him to come. I told him I did. Primavera, Audrey's great, but even so, you have no idea how lonely I've felt going through this thing, having to isolate myself from the kids, having to keep it a secret from them.'

'That's blown, I'm afraid.' I felt I had to admit it, even if it enraged her again. 'You underestimated your daughter. She's smart, she did some guessing and she put me in a position where I couldn't lie to her any longer. So I'm sorry, Susie, but I had to tell her that you had a serious illness, that it had been detected early, and that you were having the appropriate treatment in America.'

She was silent for a few seconds. 'You didn't use the C word, did you?' she asked.

'No; what I've just said, that's as far as I went. Nor did Janet. She knows as much as I reckon she wants to.'

'But not wee Jonathan.'

'I certainly didn't tell him,' I assured her, 'and neither will Janet . . . but to be honest, Susie, I really don't know what's going on in that boy's head.'

'Did you mean what you said about him and Duncan? That he was worrying about him being back?'

'Yes, and he is. The wee chap's going to need careful handling when you come home. So's Janet, for that matter,' I added, 'but she's a strong character already, like you are.'

Her sigh was so long drawn out that I thought it might evolve into tears. 'Not any more,' she moaned, 'not any more. I've been running the Gantry Group since my dad gave me the reins when I was twenty-four. I've always been in control, always been sure of my decisions, never had a moment of self-doubt. But now, I don't know what to do, I don't know where I am. Without Phil Culshaw in Glasgow, and Audrey, who's much more an executive than a secretary now, the business might have collapsed through my dithering. I'm lost. The only thing I know with any degree of certainty is that I'm going to die.'

'Susie . . .' I exclaimed, ready to tell her she was talking nonsense, but . . .

'Primavera, you couldn't lie to my daughter, nor can you to me; you know it. I'm not dumb, or in denial. I know the type of leukaemia I have and I know what the survival stats are. I know my own prognosis too; doctors here never want to be specific in case they get it wrong and you sue them for malpractice or causing emotional distress or anything else that a smart lawyer can come up with. But I asked mine, if he was a gambling man, how many Christmases would he put his own money on me seeing. He wouldn't go beyond one. When I asked him if he'd bet his house on that many, he looked away and shook his head. I asked him if that meant I got a discount off the bill.'

'Christ, what did he say to that?'

'He smiled and said the odds against that are far longer.'

'Are you still smiling?'

'As best I can,' she replied, 'because I'm well looked after. I don't have to worry about the kids, thanks to you, and Audrey and Conrad are bricks. But that doesn't cover everything. I still need shoring up, and that's where Duncan comes in. I don't have a single adult relative, girl, not one. He's all I have in the way of emotional support and I couldn't do without him, now I know what I'm facing.'

'I understand,' I told her. 'I'm not so insensitive I can't see that. It's just—'

'Look, I know you don't like him,' she interrupted, 'and I know you've got reason, with him hitting Tom. His story is that Tom was cheeky to him, but worry not, I don't believe that, 'cos I know the lad too well. Anyway, he's promised me he'll never lay a hand on any of them again.'

Especially Tom, in case he gets another kicking, I thought, but I let it lie.

'Thing is, Primavera, I need Duncan.'

'I understand,' I said, and I did. 'But tell me. Who did the proposing?'

'Mmm.' She mused for a few seconds. 'Nobody did, really. When the treatments were over and I'd begun the recuperation programme, Duncan suggested that we should get out of the hotel, for a break. He said that Vegas wasn't that far away, and that we could go there if I was up to the flight. The doc said I was, for that short a trip, so I had Audrey book a private plane. When we got there, the place was full of bloody brides. We laughed about it, then I think Duncan looked at me, and I said, "Why the hell not?" and before I knew it we were taking vows before some fat eedjit in a white cat suit. And I still think, "Why the hell not?" Where's the harm in it?'

'For you, none,' I agreed. 'One thing you never told me

before,' I continued, quickly, 'other than very loosely, was how you and he met up.'

'Phil introduced us,' she explained. 'I was over in Glasgow for a board meeting. Before it started he took me into his office and Duncan was there. Phil told me who he was, and what, and asked if I was all right with him doing some freelance stuff for the company, things like a newsletter and maybe even the text for our glossy annual report. I said it was, and gave him my phone numbers if he needed to talk to me about anything. He called me next day and asked if he could buy me lunch at Rogano, to talk over some ideas. One of them was for a newsletter feature about my modest home life, in my Scottish house, to distract attention from where the kids and I really live. I liked that and I went for it. Then I found that I liked him too, and me being without a man at the time, one thing led to . . . well, you know where it led to. That's how it kicked off. I was really gutted when he left, you know. How do I put it, Primavera? He's the devil I know, I suppose. Don't worry about me, please; he'll look after me.'

I sighed. 'Can I be brutal, Susie?' I asked.

'Go on then,' she chuckled, 'stick the boot in.'

'It's not you I'm worried about,' I confessed. 'Well, I am, but not as far as he's concerned. It's your kids.'

'Then don't. I've made it clear to him that we are not into physical punishment.'

'I don't mean that. Look, from what you've told me about the wedding, clearly you haven't done any sort of pre-nupital agreement.'

'No,' she agreed, warily, 'but I don't plan to divorce him.'

'That wasn't what I was thinking about.'

'Then . . .' she read my meaning 'Oh, I see. You mean when I pop off?'

'Yes, exactly. If that happens, God forbid, he would be their stepfather.'

'But you'd still be around to have an influence,' she said.

'Only at his discretion, and how do you think that would play out?' I didn't give her time to come up with an answer. 'Not just that, though. Where is your will lodged? Scotland or Monaco?'

'Scotland.'

'Then surely, he'd be entitled to a share of your estate, even if you don't mention him in it. You're still the majority shareholder in the company. I don't know if he would be, but what if he was legally entitled to some of those shares as a surviving spouse? If he was, it wouldn't affect Tom, but what about Janet and wee Jonathan's interests?'

'But my will puts all my shareholding in trust for them,' she countered. 'Only . . .' she hesitated, '. . . you're wrong about Tom. He does have an interest. He's Oz's kid, so my view always was that he should benefit as the others do; after all, Oz's personal shareholding was divided among the three of them. So you see, they're all in the trust.'

'And who's the named trustee?'

'Oz. I've never changed it since he died.'

'Then the court would probably replace him with his successor, wouldn't it?'

'Well, yes, I suppose.'

'Susie, can I ask you something else. Do you love this guy? It's just that I've never heard you use the word.'

'Love him?' she exclaimed. 'Don't be daft. You know who I . . .' Her voice tailed off. 'I've walked blindfold into something here, haven't I?'

'I don't think you've walked anywhere, Susie. I think you've been led.' Too frank, perhaps, Primavera. 'But,' I said, trying to retreat a little, 'maybe I'm wrong about the man.'

'Maybe you are, I hope you are. But you may have a point, and I'm not chancing my children's future to the fucked-up state my head is in at the moment. What should I do?'

'Change your will to appoint independent trustees to look after their interests, that's what I would do first.'

'How about you being one?' she asked.

'Only if you can't shift Duncan legally from the trustee list. I'm not independent, honey, remember.' Something obvious occurred to me, very late. 'Where is he, right now? He can't hear you, can he?'

'No. He and Audrey have gone to make arrangements for the flight back. He wouldn't give her his passport, so they both went.'

Why the hell not? I wondered. 'When are you coming home?' I asked.

'Tomorrow,' she replied, 'if everything's confirmed. We should get to Monaco on Monday morning. Audrey's going to ask Conrad to bring Janet and wee Jonathan home then.'

'How about holding off for a day or so?' I suggested.

'I want to see them,' she moaned.

'Then rest up for a bit before you do. Be at your best for them.'

'I'll think about it,' she agreed. 'I should speak to Janet. Is she there?' I filled her in on their day, and on where they were at that moment. 'That's nice,' she said. 'All kids together. When I do get to talk to her, after that she isn't going to be a wee girl any more, not ever.'

'She hasn't been for the last few months, Susie. You haven't been ready to see it, that's all.'

'No,' she whispered. 'Primavera,' she continued, after a while, 'about Duncan. You understand, don't you? I needed somebody and he was the only one around.'

'Sure, I understand.'

'Then watch out for me, love; watch my back. I realise now I'm way exposed. I need to get in touch with my lawyer quietly when I'm back, but meantime is there one you could talk to for me? Just to get some thoughts on the will and everything?'

I thought about that. 'There is one,' I told her. 'Although it would only be as a first step. Leave it with me.'

'Okay,' Susie said. 'But only for the kids' sake, Primavera, only for them. I've made my bed with Duncan, and I'll lie in it.' She giggled, an old-style Susie giggle that perked me up a little. 'Mind you,' she added, 'that's all I'll be doing there, for a while at least.'

'Good. Rest is what you need.'

I was far more shaken when we ended that conversation than I had been on the beach the night before. I should have known that Susie was likely to have researched her own condition. I tried to imagine what it had been like inside her head since her cross-examination of her doctor, but I couldn't. We all know that we're going to die, but the 'when' being added makes all the difference.

I thought for a while before making my next call, but I'd told Susie I would, so I didn't have a choice. My only qualm about calling Harvey January was that he's a judge and so might have felt himself unable to give any sort of legal advice, but that was overridden pretty quickly by the fact that he's the kids' uncle by virtue of his marriage to Oz's sister. He's also a pretty nice guy.

I didn't want to involve Ellie if I could avoid it, given the way she feels about Susie, so I called him on his mobile, hoping that they weren't side by side on the family sofa watching *Lawyers in Love*, or some other telly soap. I struck it lucky; he and his father-in-law were having lunch in the Golf Tavern in Elie, after Harvey's latest eighteen-hole arse-kicking by Mac the Dentist.

'You should know by now,' I told him, once he'd explained the circumstances. 'Mac spent several years peering into the distance after Jonny's tee shots, and now he's taking it all out on you.'

'I think of it as making an old man very happy,' he chuckled. 'Now, what's up? We're at the coffee stage so I can talk.'

I filled him in on the Susie story. He's neutral as far as she's concerned, having not been around when it all kicked off, so he was more concerned about her health issue than I guessed

Mac might have been. As for her legal situation, he sparked right away.

'Yes,' he murmured, 'that is potentially huge. As widower he'd be entitled to a percentage of her estate, even if he wasn't named in her will. That would not include any shareholdings, but that might not matter. In the event of her demise, do you know what percentage of the company's share capital would be held in the children's trust?'

I had to think about that. 'Something approaching seventy per cent,' I told him. 'Sixty-eight, sixty-nine.'

'And the new husband's uncle; does he have a personal holding?'

That one I knew, as I'd made a mental note of it the last time I'd read the Gantry Annual Report. 'Yes, nine and a half per cent.'

'In that case, if the children did inherit and the trust was under the control of Susie's widower, as he would be . . . tell you later, Mac,' he murmured, '. . . then he and his uncle could do anything they liked. They could sell the company out from under the minority shareholders, they could take it off the Stock Exchange, they could change its constitution.'

'But there's no reason to think they would do that.'

'Of course not,' he agreed. 'I'm talking worst-case scenario, that's all.'

'In those circumstances what could I do to stop that?'

'Mmm.' He did some legal pondering. 'Well, as Tom's mother I suppose you could go to the Court of Session and seek an interdict preventing any sale, as being against his interests. The problem with that would be that you might not win. If such a case came before me, and the proposed deal had the approval of the board, I would need strong evidence before I could go against them.'

'What can Susie do?'

'Step one, change her will pronto. Step two, actually set up the trust now so that she can set its constitution and prevent the children's vulnerability from being exploited. Step three, appoint a reputable non-executive chair, and put non-exec directors into a voting majority on the board. Who's her lawyer?'

'I don't know, but she won't be in a position to instruct him personally for few days.'

'Then she could give you, or someone else she trusts, a specific power of attorney to do that for her.' He paused. 'But listen, Primavera, none of this may be necessary; it would assume ill-will, by more than one person. What do you know of Mr Culshaw senior?'

'I've never met him, so not a lot, only what I've been told by Oz and Susie. He's in his mid to late sixties, he was a big-time accountant till he retired early. He was brought into the company as a non-exec director initially, and became managing director after Janet was born and Susie backed off a little. Oz liked him; he told me that once he helped see off a threat to the business, a potential takeover by a predator company.'

'Yes, Ellen told me about that,' Harvey said. 'It was called Torrent PLC, an office supplies business. It was a major company once, but it's changed its focus, since the photocopier leasing that generated a lot of its income was upstaged by computers. That's the area it's in now, as I understand it. There was a *Scotsman* magazine piece on it lately. When Ellen read it she said that Oz had dealings with it, and with its present owner.'

'Yes.' I confirmed that. I recalled the story, although he'd never mentioned the name of the company. 'Her name was Natalie Morgan. He told me about her. But those dealings were fairly confrontational, from what he said. As a successful businesswoman around the same age, she and Susie were seen by the media as rivals. It was true as far as Morgan was concerned: she hated Susie. That was the main reason why she tried to stage a buyout of the Gantry Group, with the support of the guy who was chairman at that time, and of a few other people who were less than clean. She nearly managed it, but Oz and Culshaw put paid to it. The old chairman fell on his sword after that and Susie's chaired the company pretty much ever since, apart from a short period when Oz did the job.'

'That's more than Ellen knew,' he remarked.

'What's Morgan doing now?' I asked.

'Same as most other people, from what I hear. Trying to see her business through some difficult marketplace conditions.'

'I wasn't really talking about business,' I laughed. 'I don't suppose you do gossip, Harvey.'

'I try to avoid it, but I recall Ellen mentioning something about her and Oz's actor friend, Ewan Capperauld. That was some time ago, though.'

'Yes, Oz did say she put it about . . . but never in his direction, he promised.'

I called Susie back straight away, and gave her a rundown on what Harvey had said . . . although I left out his worst-case scenario. She didn't need to be thinking along those lines.

'A non-executive chairman,' she murmured. 'In my darker moments, I've come to realise that I may have to step down soon. But . . . The Gantry Group might be a public company, Primavera, but I still think of it as the family firm, as it is in terms of majority control, and I don't want to hand over to an outsider. At the moment, the board is me, Phil, Gerry Meek, the finance director, and a lady named Gillian Harvey. She's the only non-exec just now. The company secretary's Wylie Smith, from our law firm, but he's not on the board. That's his preference, not mine; apparently most solicitors don't like to be directors of client companies. My dream was that one day, maybe another twenty years on, I'd step back and hand over to one of the kids, as my dad did with me. Now . . . twelve's a bit young, eh.'

'Just a bit,' I conceded, grimly.

'So I can only see one option, my dear,' she continued, her voice firmer than it had been. 'I want you to become non-executive chair of the Gantry Group.'

'Me?' I exclaimed, more loudly than was necessary. 'I couldn't chair a fucking whist drive.'

'Nonsense,' she retorted. 'You're a director of your brother-in-law's wine company. And look at that job you had in the consulate; I know about some of the deals you did there. For

FlyEuro, for example, and that Jack Weighley character . . . a journalist described him as a Scottish cult figure a couple of months back; I dropped a note saying he'd spelt it wrong.'

'But I'm not family, Susie.'

'You're the nearest thing I've got to family, girl. You're my stepson's mother. And we both loved the same guy. You know he's looking down on us, nodding approval at the idea.'

'If he's looking in any direction, it's up,' I countered. 'That's what Liam Matthews said.'

'Liam Matthews? Oz's wrestler pal? When did you see him?'

'This morning. He's here on holiday. I'm having dinner with him tonight.'

'Is he still single?'

'Yes, but forget it.'

Susie laughed. 'Come on, woman. Do you like him?'

'He seems like a nice guy,' I conceded.

'Not bad-looking either.'

'True.'

'Then do yourself a favour. There is absolutely no harm in getting yourself laid. The clock's ticking, you . . .' Her voice tailed away as she realised how ominous that was for her.

'Please do it, Primavera,' she whispered. 'Take the chair, for me and for him, and for Tom as well. You'll be looking after him.'

'Can I think about it?' I asked

'No. It needs doing now. I've thought it through. We'll make a formal announcement to the Stock Exchange on Monday that I'm stepping down from the chair on health grounds and that you're succeeding me on a non-exec basis. Also, Audrey Kent will be appointed a director.'

'Does she know?'

'No, she's not back yet.'

'Do you have the authority to do this? Won't the other three directors have to agree?'

'I have the power as chairman, and as majority share-holder. Okay?'

I sighed. 'Okay.'

'Good. Now, the kids' trust. I like what Harvey says. I want to do it quietly and quickly. Is there any chance of you going to Scotland next week?'

'Once Janet and wee Jonathan are back with you, yes, I could.'

'Fine,' she declared. 'In that case your first act as chair should be to set up a meeting in Glasgow, soon as you can, Tuesday if possible. While you're there I want you to go to see my personal lawyer. You know him. Remember Greg McPhillips, Oz's pal?'

'Yes of course. Flash bastard, bit of a womaniser.'

'Both of the above, but a great lawyer. I'm going to give you power of attorney to act for me in putting the trust together, and to appoint trustees. I'd like Greg to be one himself, and Mac Blackstone, if he's prepared.'

'For his grandchildren? Susie, if you didn't ask him he'd never speak to you again.'

'So you ask him for me. Then there's my will. I want you to ask Greg to draw it up so that my surviving husband gets what he'd have if he had to go to court for it, but no shares in the business, if that can be avoided.'

'I'll do all that, but you'll have to sign it.'

'I know.' I could hear her growing more tired by the minute. 'Tell Greg he'll need to bring it over to Monaco.'

'Will do. I'm sure he'll fancy the trip.'

'He always does,' she said. 'But Primavera, tell him not to hang about. I need to get this done soon. Just in case, girl, just in case.'

I searched for a reassuring counter, but I couldn't find one.

Eight

I promised Susie that I'd make sure Janet called her, and I did as soon as she came back from the beach. I took her up to my room, telling the boys that we were having some 'girlie time', placed the call on the landline, then went out on to the terrace while they spoke.

I stripped down to my pants, lay on my sunbed and closed my eyes, contemplating the day I was having. It was one of the most unexpected and most solemn of my life, and it was only a little more than halfway through. I thought over Susie's advice, but decided against taking it. Yes, I liked Liam, but I'd made myself a solemn vow that for me, there had to be more than liking involved, and I wasn't about to break it.

I'm not sure how long I lay there before I became aware of a fleeting shadow, a momentary change in the light as Janet passed between me and the sun and sat in the chair alongside.

I propped myself up on my elbows and looked at her. She

met my gaze and I saw that her eyes were moist. 'Did you have a good talk?' I murmured.

She nodded. 'Yes, she told me what's wrong with her and about the treatment she's had. And she said she was sorry for not telling me before, but she didn't want to worry me. She said that it's all finished now and that she's going to be fine. She sounded good.' Nonetheless the kid frowned. 'She told me something else, Auntie Primavera. She and Duncan; they're married. He's in America with her and Audrey.'

'How do you feel about that?' I asked her.

'I don't know. I don't like him, especially when he drinks. Wee Jonathan hates him; he's scared of him. He said he told you about him hitting Tom.'

I nodded. 'And about what happened afterwards. You won't have any more trouble with him, not that kind anyway. Duncan's not a fool; he knows that Tom's getting bigger and stronger every day, and that he'd protect you two.'

'But Tom's not always there,' she pointed out. 'If Duncan ever hits Jonathan . . .' I caught a flash of her father in her eyes.

'I'm sure he wouldn't. But if he ever does, or threatens to, you should tell your mother or you should tell Conrad. Okay?'

'Okay,' she whispered, then paused. 'Auntie Primavera,' she ventured, 'what is leukaemia?'

'It's a disease of the blood or bone marrow,' I replied. 'It can affect your immune system, make you susceptible to infections and so on.'

She frowned. 'You mean like AIDS?'

In spite of everything, I smiled. 'No, nothing like that. AIDS is a sexually transmitted disease. Leukaemia's ... different. It's just bad luck, really.'

'Can people die from it?'

Deep breath time, Auntie P. 'Yes, they can,' I admitted, 'but many, many people survive. And new treatments are being developed all the time. Your mum's been looked after at one of the finest clinics in the world. She couldn't be in better hands.' I reached across and touched her knee. 'She's had her therapy,' I said, 'and now it's up to her to get better. We've all got to help in that. Me, by looking out for you lot when I have to, and by doing some business stuff she's asked me to take on. Duncan, by making her home life as easy as possible. You, by being as strong for her as you can be and by getting on with Duncan, even if it goes against the grain. You up for that?'

'Of course I am,' she replied, instantly.

I swung myself upright and stood, reaching for my shirt and shorts. 'You've got a lot to take in,' I told her. 'It's not fair that you should have to at your age, but life isn't fair. As my old dad is very fond of saying, you will find no warranty or guarantees anywhere on your birth certificate.' I nodded downwards at the lounger as I finished dressing. 'D'you want some time on your own? Do some thinking and top up your tan?'

'That would be nice.'

'Okay then, but mind you use my sunscreen. Don't stint yourself either.' I tossed her the bottle and left her to it.

The door of Tom's room was open as I passed. He was in full big brother mode, giving wee Jonathan a drubbing at a computer football game. I left them to it and went down to the kitchen, to fetch myself a bottle of water from the fridge. Conrad was there, his mobile held to his ear.

'Okay,' I heard him say. 'Call me when you're wheels down at Nice.' He ended the call and put the phone back in his pocket.

'Audrey?' I asked.

He nodded. 'They leave Arizona tomorrow. She's worried; she doesn't think that Susie's fit to fly, and neither does her doctor. He's advising that she stay in his care for another week at the very least, but Susie's having none of it and Duncan's agreeing with her. He's an idiot, Primavera. Audrey said he gave her a whole bottle of champagne last night. She can hardly eat and he's pouring bloody Veuve Cliquot down her neck.'

'Yes,' I said, 'I know. But she's not giving him complete control of her life, and no sight of the business at all.'

'Yes, Audrey did say that she's just sent a statement to the group's financial PR firm for issue to the Stock Exchange on Monday morning. She said it'll surprise a few people, not least the new husband.'

And Audrey's husband, I thought, but if she hadn't filled him in on the detail, I couldn't either.

'She asked me to tell you that she's sending you a document by email. She wants you to sign it and fax it back to her. She was very specific about that. You have to fax it.'

'I can do that. I still have a fax, although it's ages since I used it.'

'She said also that Susie was speaking to Janet,' Conrad went on. 'I take it that's what you and she were doing upstairs.'

'Yes. Susie came clean with her.'

'How clean? Did she tell her how sick she really is?'

I shook my head 'No, she kept it positive. But you: do you know how sick she really is, Conrad?'

'I fear so,' he sighed. 'Audrey's with her every day. She says she's skin and bone. It's not going to end well, Primavera, is it?'

'No, it isn't. And Susie knows it. That's why she's asked me to do certain things for her. But there's one thing I want you to do for her that she might not ask. Keep an eye on Mr Culshaw.'

'Oh, I will,' he assured me, 'as close an eye as I can. He might say I'm his new best friend, but I don't believe him. I'm sure that he'd get rid of me tomorrow if he could, and Audrey for that matter.'

'Well, he can't,' I told him firmly. 'You said it yourself; you have contracts of employment with the Gantry Group, not with Susie personally and certainly not with him.'

'Yes, but . . .' He didn't have to spell out what he was thinking.

'But nothing. He will never get a toehold in that business.'

'I wish I was as sure as you.'

'Come Monday, you might be . . . and don't ask me to explain that.'

I left him to ponder and went to the office to check my email. Sure enough there was one from Audrey, covering three documents. One was the announcement of my appointment and hers, and another was a letter for my signature confirming that I was prepared to accept appointment as chairperson of the Gantry Group PLC, with a space for a second signature, that of a witness. The third attachment was a power of attorney giving me authority to instruct her solicitor in setting up a trust to administer the shareholdings and other bequeathed assets of Tom Blackstone, Janet Blackstone and Jonathan Blackstone. It was signed by Susie and witnessed and notarised by an American attorney. Thorough, Susie, I thought.

I printed off all three documents, signed the confirmation letter, then took it through to the front terrace, where Conrad was sitting. 'I'd like you to read and witness that, please,' I asked.

His eyes widened as he scanned it, but that was his only reaction, until he'd added his signature and passport number. Then he looked up and nodded. 'Congratulations, boss,' he murmured.

'Don't,' I said. 'That's probably the saddest piece of paper I've ever had to sign.'

Nine

I was so consumed by what had happened in the afternoon that I almost forgot I had a dinner date.

Audrey called me as soon as she'd received the fax. 'Susie says she wants you to call a board meeting in Glasgow on Tuesday; if you can make that, she says I have to get in touch with Wylie Smith and have him set it up. Can you?'

'If I can take Tom with me, yes. His school term's over. But can you make it? It's Saturday and you're still in Arizona.'

'Sure,' she replied, as confident and assertive as ever. 'I'll see Susie safely home on Monday morning, then catch a direct flight from Nice to Edinburgh in the afternoon. I can get you and Tom into the same airport at around the same time. We can meet up, take a taxi or hire a car and check into a hotel in Glasgow for the night. Sound okay?'

'Sounds brilliant,' I told her. 'Go ahead. But book a car, in my name, for I'll have other stuff to do in Scotland and part of it will involve seeing Oz's dad . . . and mine, while I'm there.'

'Will do. When do you want to come back?'

'Make it Saturday, to be on the safe side.'

'Fine. Primavera,' she added, after a few seconds, 'are you all right about this? The business side, I mean.'

The uncertainty of her tone took me by surprise. 'Let me put it this way,' I replied, buying a very little time to consider exactly how I should put it, 'it's not something I want to do. But if Susie needs me to do it, for her sake and for the sake of the kids, to maintain investor confidence in what she calls the family firm during her illness and recuperation: if she wants that, I'm fine with it. Why?' I asked. 'Aren't you?'

'I'm a secretary, Primavera; that's what I'm trained to be, those are my skills.'

'Can you read a set of accounts? Do you understand a balance sheet?'

'Yes,' she conceded.

'Then you're more qualified for the job than many a director I've met. You typed the stock market announcement, so you know what it says. It describes you as the outgoing chairperson's executive assistant, with an intimate knowledge of the working of the business. It describes me as a director of a Spanish wine producer and as a former consular official who played a part in negotiating several multi-million pound deals in Catalunya for Scottish companies. What it doesn't say is that I'm Miles Grayson's sister-in-law, but it doesn't have to. The PR people will make sure that everyone knows that. We are not a couple of bimbo figureheads and we won't be seen as such.'

'No,' she murmured, 'I suppose not.'

'So what's your concern?'

'It's Duncan,' she admitted. 'He doesn't know anything about this, but he's going to find out pretty damn soon. I don't know for certain, but my gut tells me that when he learns what Susie's done he's not going to like it. He hates you; I can tell you that.'

'You don't have to; I know he does. But anyone who lays a hand on my son should also be afraid of me.'

'Duncan did that?' she gasped.

'Yes. He paid for it at the time, but I'm not done with him. Let's make sure that everything is cut and dried when he does find out. The Stock Exchange opens at eight on Monday morning. You'll still be travelling when the news goes public, but to be sure, instruct the PR people that there's to be no advance briefing on this. I don't want bloody Culshaw reading about it on his iPhone in Charles de Gaulle Airport, at least not before eight o'clock BST. And one other thing,' I added. 'How much notice of a board meeting does the chair have to give to directors?'

'None, if it's an emergency. Otherwise company rules, twenty-four hours minimum. Normally, Susie gives a month.'

'Fine, this time it's by the rules. I want you to instruct the company secretary to fix the time as ten a.m. on Tuesday, with minimum notice. That way Duncan won't be getting a text from Uncle Phil at the airport either.'

'Do you think Phil would do that?'

'I don't know, but let's cover all possibilities.'

'Christ, Primavera,' Audrey laughed, 'are you sure you shouldn't be executive chair?'

'I will be whatever Susie wants me to be,' I replied, seriously. 'Although I'd rather be neither, and that she was still up to the job.'

'She will be,' her right-hand woman said firmly. 'It'll take a little while, but she'll be back in charge before you know it.'

How I hope that's true, I thought. 'Absolutely,' I said. 'Our job is to make sure that the ship's still afloat when she's ready to take the wheel again. That's me metaphored out for the day, Audrey.' I laughed. 'Send me flight arrangements and e-tickets and I'll see you in Edinburgh on Monday.'

It was only when I hung up that I remembered dinner with Liam Matthews. He'd left the choice of restaurant to me, so I hit on Meson del Conde, because the food's good, and because it has a nice, covered, air-conditioned terrace restaurant, away from the square, which can become a little frantic on a June Saturday evening. I called them and reserved a table, then sent a text to the mobile number on the card that Liam had given me when we'd parted ways earlier. 'Table booked; pick me up from home.'

Okay, Primavera, that's you sorted, now how about the kids? The realisation hit me as soon as my message whooshed on its way. I'd fed them a takeaway for lunch; no way could I allow myself to do that again. I charged into the kitchen, looked at what I had in the fridge: some gazpacho that I'd made the morning before, five tuna steaks and salad. I looked at my watch: six thirty-five. If I knocked up the salad, got myself ready, then grilled the fish, I could have them at the table by eight.

'Wassup?' Conrad asked me, from the doorway.

'I've got a date,' I confessed. 'And a very small window to get everything ready, including me.'

'Then I'll do dinner,' he said.

'You had them all morning.'

'So what? You've had Tom twenty-four seven for twelve years.' *Not quite all of them*, I thought, but didn't dwell on it. 'What do you need doing?' I set out my proposed menu. 'No worries,' he insisted. 'I do the best salad in our house, and I know how to flip a tuna steak on the grill.'

'If you're sure.'

He put his hands on my shoulders. 'Primavera, Audrey and I don't have, won't have any kids of our own. So any chance I get to play Dad, I take it. Who is the guy?'

'Liam Matthews.'

'I thought it might be. Janet told me about him this morning.'

'Did you ever meet him?'

'No, but Oz talked about him often enough. He liked him a lot, I could tell.'

'Did Tom say anything about him?' I asked.

Conrad frowned. 'No. But it was the way he didn't say it. I reckon that Culshaw's made him very wary of new men coming into mothers' lives.'

'Well, he needn't worry about Liam. It's a friendly dinner, that's all.'

'Then why are you so flustered? It's not like you.'

'Because friendly or not,' I exclaimed, 'it's the first proper date of any sort I've had with a man for four years, and even then . . . fuck me, he was the parish priest!'

'In that case, I don't imagine he did.'

I stared at him, then we both dissolved into laughter. 'Nor will this guy,' I said, as we subsided. 'Poor old Gerard, though. At first I was slightly insulted that he chose God over me, but now . . .'

'Now what?'

'Now I'm glad, because it wouldn't have worked. Mostly I saw him as a proper father figure for Tom. But as it happens, Tom doesn't want one. He's made that pretty clear.'

Conrad shook his head. 'Don't underestimate him, Primavera. Ultimately he wants what you want. But you wouldn't want anyone he doesn't fancy, or anyone who doesn't fancy him. He's your gatekeeper; to get to you, any man will have to get past him.' I recalled his stance on the beach the night before, as Liam approached. What Conrad was saying was the literal truth. 'But there's one big problem for that potential suitor,' he continued. 'He either has to make Tom accept one thing, or wait for him to be ready to accept it.'

'What's that?' I asked.

'That his father is really dead.'

'That's not Tom's problem alone,' I confessed. 'I have to make myself believe it as well.' I felt myself frown. 'Conrad,' I continued, 'if he wasn't, and you knew it, you would tell me, wouldn't you?'

He held up a hand. 'Stop it,' he said. 'Don't wander into fantasy land.'

I don't know what made me press him, other than the strangest feeling that our conversation had become very important. 'No,' I insisted, 'a straight answer, please.'

'Okay, if you must have it. If he wasn't dead and I knew it, I wouldn't tell you, for there would be a reason for him not having told you himself, and my first loyalty would be to him, always.' He paused, holding my gaze. 'But I don't know that, Primavera, I don't. Understood?'

His eyes were intense, more compelling than I'd ever seen them. I felt mine mist as I nodded. 'Understood,' I whispered.

'Good.' He smiled. 'Now go get yourself dolled up for Mr Matthews. I hope he knows how lucky he is.'

I did as I was told. I'm not big on make-up on a daily basis. Living in the sun as I do, I spend a small fortune on screens, body lotions and moisturisers, but mostly all I use of an evening is a little eyeliner, and, if I'm feeling racy, some mascara. That night, though, after I'd showered and fixed my hair, which I always keep manageably cut, I gave myself the full works, blusher, eyeshadow, lustrous lipgloss, all the stuff that my sister's rarely seen in public without. Thinking about it, the only thing I've ever learned from our Dawn is how to glam myself up properly.

To go with it all, I chose a dark blue dress that she persuaded me to buy the last time I'd visited her in Los Angeles. It's by Versace, close-fitting and beautifully cut, with two straps and a plunging V that absolutely precludes the wearing of a bra. I rummaged in my shoe cupboard . . . one day I must get round to cataloguing them and putting them in some sort of order . . . for the pair I'd bought to match, sprinkled some golden sparkly stuff between my tits, and I was done. Almost. I opened my safe and took out a pair of diamond earrings and a matching ring that Oz bought for me on a weekend in London that Susie never knew about. I put them on and then I really was ready for the evening. Had I forgotten something? No, I decided against wearing any, that's all.

When I went downstairs, at two minutes before eight, the kids were at the table in the kitchen, and Conrad was hard at work creating his legendary salad. Heads turned.

'Mum?' Tom murmured, as if he wasn't sure.

'Auntie Primavera!' Janet exclaimed, eyeing me from top to toe and back again.

Even wee Jonathan smiled.

Conrad said nothing, but the look in his eyes told me I'd got it right.

'I'm going out for the evening,' I explained. I'd have shrugged, but I wasn't sure it was safe. Instead I sashayed across to the wine fridge, took out a bottle of pretty decent cava, and looked at my son. 'Wine waiter wanted,' I said, haughtily. 'Front terrace.'

He and Janet rose from the table at the same time, just as the bell chimed, beating those in the church tower by about two seconds. He looked curious, she looked fascinated. I handed him the bottle; he knew what to do.

I went to the door and opened it. Liam had done some

dressing up of his own; tan razor-creased trousers, a buckskin jacket and a white silk shirt with a granddad collar, that wore no designer logo and fitted so well that it might have been tailor-made.

'So where are the fucking flowers?' I asked, breaking the silence in which we had inspected each other.

He laughed and held his hands up, as if to ward me off. 'I tried to get some, honest. I asked at the hotel where I could find a bouquet of roses. The receptionist gave me a funny look and said that Sant Jordi's Day was two months ago. What the hell's that?'

'It's the local version of Valentine's Day,' I explained as I led him inside, and up to the first floor. 'Tom and I observe it. The deal is that he gives her a rose and she gives him a book. I have to tell you that there are a hell of a lot more roses sold around here than there are books.'

I led him out on to the terrace, with its view of the square. 'This is like Buckingham Palace,' he said. 'Do you stand up here and wave to the multitudes?'

'Only on Christmas Day. Sit down,' I told him. 'I thought we'd have a drink before we go down to the restaurant.' As I spoke, Janet stepped out of the living room, carrying a tray with two champagne flutes. Tom followed, with the cava in an ice bucket. 'In fact, here are my staff now.'

'I knew it would be you,' Janet murmured, quietly triumphant, as she put the tray on the table.

'Me too,' Tom added. I'd heard him sound more welcoming. He was still weighing Liam up.

Suddenly, I realised that I'd been discourteous. 'Tom,' I said. 'Go and ask Conrad if he'd like to join us, if he's done with the salad. And Janet, fetch an extra glass, there's a love.'

'Actually,' Liam intervened, 'you don't need that, Primavera. I don't drink alcohol.' I must have looked sceptical, for he went on. 'Honest, I don't. I'm your atypical Irishman. I gave it up a few years ago, when I was wrestling. Like most of the guys, I had to take painkillers sometimes, and I found the two don't mix. When you start using booze to dumb the pain, there's only one way you go after that. So I stopped, and I found that I felt better for it, even when I quit the game and didn't need the super ibuprofen any longer.'

'Good for you,' I told him. 'What do you drink?'

'Sparkling water will be fine.'

'In that case you can have it in a champagne glass.'

Conrad joined us a couple of minutes later, after he'd shed his apron and replaced it with a blazer. 'I'm pleased to meet you,' Liam said as they shook hands, and glasses were filled. 'Oz spoke about you a lot. He said that there was nobody else in the world that he'd rather have watching his back . . . not even Everett Davis.'

'Who's Everett Davis?' Conrad asked.

'My old boss in the Global Wrestling Alliance. In billing they usually add a few inches to the performer's real height, but Everett really is seven feet two inches tall and built like a brick shithouse. He scared me witless even when I knew he wasn't really going to hurt me. So for Oz to say that about you, my friend, you must be one serious geezer.'

I'd never seen Conrad look even close to being flustered before, but he was then. 'No, no,' he murmured. 'I'm just a glorified caretaker.'

'Funnily enough,' Liam said, 'that's pretty close to how Oz put it. "There is nothing in the whole fucking world that I wouldn't trust Conrad to take care of." That's a direct quote.'

'In that case, he flattered me. Would you like to know what he said to me about you?'

'I can almost guess, but go on.'

'He said, and I'm quoting now, "Once Liam Matthews decided to stop being an arsehole, he turned into a very reasonable human being, one of the few people in the world I trust." Again, his exact words, which is why I'm not at all worried about you turning up out of the blue. Anyone else wouldn't have got over the door without me checking him out, even if this is my boss's house. The children in my charge live in it, which makes me very responsible.'

Liam tipped his glass to Conrad. 'In which case, I'm glad we're on the same side.'

We sipped and chatted, but not for long, as the kids still had to be fed and I didn't want to be too late for my table reservation. When our glasses were empty, I gave Conrad the ice bucket, so that Tom could put a stopper in the cava and return it to the fridge, then led Liam towards the stairs.

My son was waiting at the top. Something was coming off him in waves; I wasn't sure what it was, but it touched me. 'Have a nice evening, Mum,' he said. But he said it in Catalan. I thought that was rude and I almost made him repeat it in

English, but decided against. If anything was festering it wouldn't have been helped by a public correction.

'What did he say?' Liam asked, as soon as we were outside.

'He told me to send him a text if things get out of hand, and he'll be straight across.'

For a second he thought I was serious, so I gave him the authentic translation. He laughed. 'You know what, Primavera? That's what he might have said, but your version is what he really meant.'

Heads turned once more as we walked through the square. Given what I spent on Ms Versace's creation, I'd have been disappointed if they hadn't, although I found myself worrying that it was so close-fitting that the world, including Liam, would know that a mid-forties woman was out on the town with no knickers on. But I realised very quickly that they weren't only looking at me. My companion was a charismatic guy, something that had passed me by until then.

One of the turning heads belonged to Alex Guinart. He and Gloria, and Marte, my goddaughter, are regulars in the square on Saturday evenings; they were at a table in Esculapi. He said, 'Hello.' What he really meant was, 'Oh yeah, and who's this good-looking stranger?'

I introduced Liam to the family; of course he knew what Alex was from our earlier conversation. 'Nice to meet you all,' he murmured, making a point of shaking Marte's hand too. She put her hand over her eyes and giggled.

'That thing we were talking about,' Alex digressed, in Catalan again. 'Are you going to go ahead with a complaint?'

'I was,' I replied, 'but things have changed in the last few hours. I could be fighting the guy on another front very soon. I need to focus my attention on that.'

'Well, don't wait too long,' he warned. 'The opportunity won't be there for ever.'

'I know.'

He called after us as we left, 'Have a nice evening.'

Liam caught the greeting, understood and laughed. 'Him too, eh?'

'You better believe it. What I said last night on the beach about at least three guys watching you? I wasn't kidding. I know at least half the people in this square.'

'I'll bet,' he said. 'About those three people. Please regard this as comforting, for I am very firmly among your admirers, but they wouldn't have been enough.'

We reached Meson del Conde as he spoke. Jose Luis, the head waiter, greeted us and escorted us into the terrace restaurant, and to our table. He wouldn't have done that for me alone: he was as curious as the rest of them.

'If you don't mind me saying so,' Liam murmured as he left, 'that is quite a dress. It's been a while since I saw so many men drool simultaneously.'

I smiled. 'Thank you, kind sir. Funny, innit? Go to the beach beyond the Riomar when I'm on it, and they'd find a hell of a lot more of me on show. They might be impressed, they might not, but cover it up in the right way . . .'

'Cover most of it,' he countered, his eyes falling from mine. I tracked them downwards.

'Do you like the gold sparkles?' I asked. 'I do.'

'I like all of it. But why, given that it was you who set the ground rules?'

'Why am I wearing a "fuck me" dress? Because I paid two thousand dollars for it, thanks to my bloody sister, and I've never had an opportunity since to strut my stuff in it. You're the first man I've encountered in years with whom I've been able to wear something like this. I feel comfortable with you, Liam; I don't feel as if I'm being ogled across the table. Does it make you feel uncomfortable?'

'No.' He chuckled quietly. 'It makes me feel honoured. And it produces the vestigial memory of a very sore nose.'

I shot a question at him. 'Are you afraid of the dark?'

'No, of course not.'

'Then why are you afraid of the dead?'

He looked into my eyes once again. 'There's a difference between fear and respect. What Conrad said that Oz said about me: it wasn't what I expected. I thought he'd have said, "Good guy, but I wouldn't trust him with a water melon, let alone my woman." But he didn't. I can't tell you how touched I was to hear that.'

'Why did you come here? Was it just because of what Miles said?'

'Pretty much. I didn't tell you all of it. After he'd said how cool you'd become, he added something else. He said that often he worries that you'll become so cool you'll turn to ice, and then you'll break, or just melt. That worried me too when he said it.'

'Then he's wrong. Steel can be cool when you touch it, as cold as ice. So, how long are you staying?' I asked, as Jose Luis returned with the menus.

'I have no idea,' he confessed. 'I've booked into the hotel for a week with an option on another. I was hoping that you'd be my tour guide, and show me the best of this area. I've been to Barcelona . . . you know that; Christ, you were there . . . but you know how my life was then, a maximum of three days in any location, so I know next to nothing about it or about this part of Spain. And I need to, for my book.'

'Yes, your book,' I repeated. 'You never did tell me what it's about.'

'Travel,' he replied. 'It's about the places I've been in my wrestling career, and the places I've seen, however briefly. I'm writing about them, about the different cultures and mentalities of their people, and about what makes them special.'

'And you're doing all the photography?' I guessed.

'You got it.'

'You must have seen a fair few places with the GWA,' I said. 'How's the organisation going these days? The sports entertainment industry isn't something I keep up with. Nor does Tom. He's not barred from watching it,' I added, 'he doesn't, that's all.'

'He's a purist,' Liam replied. 'Any kid who knows what wing chun is is unlikely to be too impressed by the likes of Jerry The Behemoth Gradi.'

'Hey,' I protested, 'Jerry's a lovely guy. His was a life really worth saving.'

'I agree, I agree, and I'm not knocking him. I was talking about his type, the giants, the musclemen. The level of skill that Tom must have, with his belt, he'll see through everything they do, straight away. As for the GWA, it's doing fine. Everett's probably the biggest name in the industry now, in every way, performer and promoter. Starting in Europe and building a brand there was a brilliant idea. When he relocated to the US he was able to take his TV deals with him and ramp them up a notch.'

'And you have no connection at all?'

'Only my shareholding. That's considerable, and thanks to the big man it pays me a very nice dividend every year. It's helped to make me a free man. I haven't really thought about it, but I suppose you could describe me as semi-retired, which is not bad at forty-three years old. You should know; you're in the same position.'

I smiled across the table. 'Won't see forty-three again, though.'

'You're kidding. You don't look a day over forty.'

'Liam,' I laughed, 'if you've found the courage to try to get into my pants, you're wasting your time.' I almost added, 'Not least because . . .' but stopped myself just in time.

'No,' he said, 'but it's a matter of respect, not of courage. Anybody who didn't want to would be crazy, but I understand how you feel about it, and I'd much rather have you as a friend than a conquest. So, take the compliment for what it is, an honest opinion.'

'Then thank you once again, very much. You are good for

a middle-aged lady's morale. I'd be very happy to show you Barcelona, and even the whole of Catalunya. You may think this place is nice, but there are plenty to challenge it. Only problem being . . . it can't be next week. Tom and I have to go to Scotland on Monday. Something's come up, and I have to do it.'

'How long will you be gone?' he asked.

'Until next Saturday. I have some business to do, and some family to catch up on while I'm over there. Honestly, when I saw you this morning I didn't know about it, that's how suddenly it developed.'

'Nobody's ill, are they? Nobody close.'

'Apart from Susie, no. But . . .' I stopped as Jose Luis appeared beside us, order pad in hand.

'You choose for me,' my companion said. 'I'm lousy with menus.'

'Okay.' I looked up at the waiter. 'We'll have the fish soup and baked monkfish, twice. And to drink, sparkling water will be fine. You don't mind going all pescatarian, do you, Liam?'

'Not a bit. To tell you the truth, these days that's what I am, mostly. I'm not religious about it, but eating mammals makes me uncomfortable. You were saying,' he continued. 'You stopped on a "but" . . .'

'But the business I have to do is for Susie and involves Susie.'

'Can you tell me?'

I looked at him. 'This morning you said you were a shareholder in the Gantry Group, didn't you?' He nodded. 'In that case I don't think I can. I've got insider knowledge of the company, and I'm pretty sure that sharing it would be illegal.'

He laughed. 'That sounds intriguing. Are you joining the board?'

I looked at the table, feeling a flush spread down from my face to fill in the V of my seriously plunging neckline.

'Oh Jesus,' Liam exclaimed. 'I'm sorry. I won't ask you anything else.'

'Thanks,' I said, then added, 'but feel free to speculate all you like.'

'Mmm,' he murmured, at my invitation. 'You told me Susie's very ill, so if I was to make a guess it would be that whatever your business is with her . . .'

'For her,' I corrected him.

'Sorry. Whatever it is, it suggests that she's having second thoughts about this hasty marriage of hers.'

'Not one hundred per cent, but certain aspects of it, yes.'

'So she's looking to someone she can trust to help her out.'

I nodded. 'Two people. Audrey Kent as well.'

'In which case she's in good hands,' he said. 'You'll take care of her.'

'We'll do our best. It may all be plain sailing, but the unpredictable factor is the new Mr Gantry. He knows nothing of this, and he's decided that he's my sworn enemy.'

'What can he do to you?'

I told him about his threat to attack Oz's memory.

'That's his plan, is it?' Liam murmured. 'Look, Primavera, an enemy of yours is an enemy of mine; he might find that's a bad place to be. Not to mention being an enemy of Oz . . . if anyone can reach out from beyond the grave, it's him.'

I shivered as he said that, thinking back to my conversation with Conrad a few hours before. *Put that back in the box, woman.*

'Do you feel uncomfortable,' he continued 'about . . . whatever it is you have to do? Because if you need some back-up, you only have to ask, and I'll be there.'

I smiled at him, the shiver replaced by a lovely warm feeling. 'You'd be my knight in shining armour?' I murmured. 'Oh, Liam, that's nice, it really is.'

'There was a time in my life when I'd have been a shite in whining armour,' he chuckled. 'But no more, I hope. I mean it, if you need me, say the word.'

'I promise you, if I think that I do, I will. But it would have to be serious; you don't need to be bodyguarding the likes of me.'

He winked. 'Hey, babe, I'd guard your body any time.'

'I'll bet you say that to all the ladies.'

'Yup, I sure do. Usually it doesn't get me very far, though . . . and when it does, invariably I find it wasn't worth it.'

'Anybody serious since you and Erin split?'

'No. I got burned there; don't fancy repeating the experience. Maybe I should find myself a nice nun as a companion. Follow your example with the parish priest.'

I shook my head. 'I don't recommend it.'

'What was his name?'

'Gerard. He was a very good friend, and Tom liked him.

For a while I thought he might become more than a good friend, but he was a deep and complex man, with a past I learned about from someone else, not from him. Still, there was a time when we might have got together.'

'Any regrets that you didn't?' Liam asked.

'None,' I answered immediately. 'Relief, more like. He was too bloody serious. I can see now, he was too bloody serious. I like men who make me laugh, but since Oz . . . died, I haven't come across a single one of those. I think I felt sorry for Gerard more than anything else. Never fuck anyone out of sympathy or compassion, Liam.'

'You didn't, did you?'

'Not him, no. Somebody else, though, but he was conning me. I won't make that mistake again.'

'Me neither,' he said. 'By that I mean invest emotionally in the wrong person. Solitude is better than a miserable togetherness. I learned that lesson at home.' He hesitated, as if he thought that continuing was a serious step; and then he did. 'My parents hated each other. My dad was a bully who knocked the shit out of me when I was a kid, until he couldn't any more. He knocked my mother about as well, but she was capable of beating him up with her tongue. And me; I was never spared that, and she kept that up till she died, five years ago.'

'Some upbringing,' I murmured. 'Do you have any brothers or sisters?'

'No, it was just me; nobody to share the pain with.'

'Poor kid.'

'Not really; it made me a horrible little bastard as a young man, before Oz straightened me out. You'd have thought it would get better with my mother after my old man died. I hoped it would, but it didn't. All her venom was for me alone after that.'

'Your father,' I ventured, 'he was . . .'

'Shot by the Proddies? The UVF? That's what the cops, the RUC assumed, since he was a Catholic, but it's not true. My uncle killed him.'

'What?' I gasped.

'My mother's brother, Bobby McBride: he was an officer in the local Provo brigade. My dad was never involved with the IRA, not because he was anti, purely because he didn't have the bottle for it. Anyway, one time he gave my mother a particularly bad going over and Uncle Bobby found out about it. She didn't go to him, he called at our house and she didn't have time to cover up the bruises. He told my father that if it happened again he was a dead man. A year or so later it did. Uncle Bobby denounced him to his brigade as an informant, and they took his word for it. No trial, no nothing, they just took him into the countryside and shot him, then they dumped his body in a Loyalist area.'

'Rough justice. Had your uncle called in unexpectedly again?'

Liam's gaze dropped to somewhere in the middle of the table. I could see behind the spectacles, and his eyes were hard. 'No,' he replied. 'I told him. How about that, Primavera? I called a death sentence down on my own father. And you know what? If Uncle Bobby would have been up for shooting his sister, I'd probably have told him to do that too.'

I didn't know what to say. I just sat there and looked at him, until once again he was ready to go on.

'I don't know why the hell I just told you that,' he whispered, when he was. 'The only other person who knew the truth was my uncle, and the UDA put a bullet in his head a couple of years later. I've never shared that with another living soul, not even Oz, and he was my best friend latterly; Christ, my only friend. If you want to leave now, I'll understand.'

I looked at him, making him return my gaze. 'If Gerard was still here I might tell you to go to confession. You'd probably get off lightly; he'd a similar background, and it messed him up big time. Just you promise me you won't try and atone by taking holy orders and I'll stay right here.'

He smiled. 'That's a promise I can make, no problem.'

'Fine, duly noted. You did what you did. I've done stuff too that I wouldn't want to see the light of day, but it's firmly in the past.' I smiled at him. 'You know what I think?'

'No,' he chuckled, 'but I do know you're going to tell me.'

'Damn right. I think you should have kept a connection with the GWA, even after you weren't fit enough to perform. The thing I remember most about that crowd is that they were a family, and probably the only real one you've ever had.' I did what I'd said I wouldn't. I reached across the table and took his hand in mine. 'Miles said I was cool; well, so are you. You're a cool guy, but you're also very lonely. You don't have anybody in the whole damn world, do you?'

He shook his head. 'I'm pretty short,' he murmured, 'I admit it.'

'Then I'm glad you've come here. You were Oz's friend and this is his place, and mine. You'll never be alone here . . . apart from through the night,' I added, 'for I'm still not going to sleep with you. Take your past down to the beach, or somewhere else suitable and bury it there. Then get on with the future.' I paused. 'And with the fish soup,' I said as Jose Luis appeared with two bowls and a large tureen.

We changed the subject over dinner, having confessed as much as either of us wanted to for one evening. Liam told me stories of his wrestling career, from its pretty brutal early days in Japan, to the showbiz of the later years. I told him some, but not all, of what I'd done since I settled in St Martí with Tom.

The food was brilliant, as it always is in Meson del Conde (indeed in every restaurant in the square), and as the evening wore on I found that the Vichy Catalan was having the same effect on me as a bottle of decent white.

'So,' I said, once we were at the coffee stage, 'I'm willing to be your tour guide, as soon as I can. Meantime, do you want some ideas for filling in the next week?'

'I have some plans already. Mainly they involve lying on the beach, and not letting myself get too badly out of shape . . . and of course being on the end of a telephone just in case you do need some back-up in Scotland. Where are you going?'

'We head for Glasgow initially. Then I have to take Tom to see both of his grandfathers.'

'This thing you're doing for Susie,' he asked, 'is it going to be full-time?'

'Hell, no! Tom is what I do full-time. This, and the job I do for Miles in his wine business, are strictly sidelines. Hopefully, Susie won't need my help for long.'

He raised his glass. 'To Susie.'

'God bless her and keep her.'

His eyebrows rose. 'Are you religious?'

I laughed. 'I live next door to a thousand-year-old church, and I came close to shagging the priest. How much closer to religion can you be? Seriously? I don't know, which makes me an agnostic. I suspect it comes with age; hedging your bets and all that. Tom isn't though. His dad died therefore there cannot be a God. That's how he sees it, and I can't find a decent counter-argument.'

'Can I get to know him better?' Liam asked.

'I'd like you to. It might be good for both of you. You can start tomorrow, if you like; I'll have some stuff to do in the morning to get ready for our trip, but I plan to take the kids to the beach in the afternoon. Come with us?'

'Sure, which beach?'

'The one beyond your hotel, over the iron bridge. Dogs are allowed on it, and we take Charlie. On the way, we'll have a sandwich lunch at the beach bar; you can meet us there, at one o'clock. You can't miss it; it's called Vaive and there's a surfboard stuck in the sand outside.'

It was eleven thirty when we left the restaurant. There were still a few people around, a few more heads to turn. I allowed my date to walk me to my door under their gaze, and kissed him chastely on the cheek before stepping inside. Charlie surveyed us with his usual slightly bewildered expression.

The house was locked up and shuttered, and in darkness, apart from one small light in the hall that had been left on for me. I went straight upstairs, kicked off my shoes, slipped out of my only garment and hung it carefully in its wardrobe. I was tingling. For a while I thought I might be having a hot flush, until I realised that, no, the Change wasn't upon me. No, I was simply as horny as hell. It had been so long since that had happened that I'd almost forgotten the feeling.

I put my jewellery back in the safe and took something else out, a flexible and versatile friend that I'd picked up one day in Barcelona, on a very wild impulse. It had been in the safe ever since, unused, me having been overcome by matronly embarrassment when I took it out of the box, and saw all the things its makers claimed that it could do, with some careful placement and four working AA batteries.

They were right about its capabilities; in fact, they may have been understanding them.

Ten

Did I feel guilty next morning? No. I may have felt a little intimate tenderness, but no guilt. Why the hell should I have? I'd come like an express train, and I could recall nothing in the bible to say that was a sin. Okay, there is something in the Old Testament about a bloke called Onan, but I didn't believe that his case was at all pertinent.

That's what I tried to persuade myself, but I couldn't quite cut it. What I actually felt was confusion. When I analysed it, I realised that I'd believed that I was in complete control of my life, and that included my sexual appetite, which, I'd assured myself, had become non-existent. I'd been wrong. One night out in a posh dress with an attractive man had thrown all that on its head. As I put my friend back in its box and back into the safe, I wondered what I would have done if Liam had made a move on me.

I still hadn't answered that question by the time I'd dressed and gone down for breakfast. The three guys were up before me; I knocked on Janet's door, but heard her shower going and left her to it . . . courtesy of her gallant half-brother who gives up his en suite when she's with us.

'You were out late,' Tom remarked, as I dropped a couple of slices of bread into the toaster.

'With respect, young man,' I replied, 'I was out later the night before, with you and your sister.'

'But . . .' he began, then realised he wasn't going to get any further, and abandoned his interrogation. I hid my smile, as I recalled my father making exactly the same comment on another Sunday morning almost thirty years before. He hadn't pursued it either; just as well, as I'd just had my cherry cracked by my first serious boyfriend . . . a poor second, I must say, to my Duracell bunny from Barcelona.

Conrad said nothing. He was at the table, reading, or making a show of reading, the online *Daily Telegraph* on his laptop.

'Did you hear any more from Audrey?' I asked him, as I took a seat beside him, with my toast and a mug of tea.

He nodded. 'She called just after you and Liam left. You'll find an email in your box with your tickets attached. You're booked into the Glasgow Malmaison for two nights. She asked me if she should book a twin for you and Tom or separate rooms; I said separate. Okay?'

'Definitely. We need our own space now.'

'What rooms?' Tom asked from across the kitchen.

'We're going to Scotland tomorrow, you and me. For a week.'

'Why?'

'I've got things to do, and I'm taking you with me, so you can see your grandpas.'

He shrugged. 'Okay, but what about Charlie?'

Good question, boy; I'd forgotten about him. 'I'll ask Ben if he'll look after him with his two; otherwise we'll have to put him in the slammer for a week.' I knew it wouldn't come to that, and so did Tom: he and Ben run an informal Labrador retriever collective, taking care of each other's dogs as required.

'And what about Janet and Jonathan?'

'We're going home tomorrow,' Conrad chipped in. 'Susie Mum will be back by the time we get there.'

'Will Duncan be there?' wee Jonathan asked, nervously.

'So what if he is?' I replied. 'You'll be back with your mum and that's the most important thing, isn't it?'

'Yes,' he conceded, but it was grudging.

'Okay,' I announced, as Janet came into the room, her hair still damp from the shower, 'that's tomorrow. This afternoon we're going to the beach, all of us, and Charlie . . . well, not you, Conrad, if you don't want to.'

'Well,' he said, 'I do have things to take care of. I reckon they'll be safe with you.'

'And Liam,' I added. 'He's coming.'

'In that case, they'll be even safer.'

I had things to take care of also; first of those was to retrieve our e-tickets, and print them out. It seemed that company chairs and their companions fly business class. I'd have been happy to fly budget air, but in the circumstances I wasn't complaining. I was just under an hour short of being able to check in online, and so I spent it jamming the washing machine full of everyone's cast-off clothes, apart from Conrad's which he insisted were his business alone, then sorting out clothes for the trip for both Tom and me. There was no point in asking him to choose his own. He has no clue about the vagaries of the Scottish climate and would probably have packed half a dozen T-shirts and no socks.

When finally I'd checked us in I had to take a quick trip into L'Escala to buy cosmetics and other personal gear for the trip, top up the food stocks so that I could make packed lunches for Janet and wee Jonathan's road trip home, and fuel the jeep for the drive down to Barcelona Airport, to save time in the morning. Back home again I had to load the tumble dryer . . .

I could go on, but I won't; suffice it to say that when it was all done I was knackered and sweaty, and had to take another shower, to make myself fresh enough to go to the beach. Yeah, work that one out; I took a shower in preparation for covering myself in lotion and lying on a sunbed. Would I have done that if it had just been Tom and I? No, but it wasn't, was it? We had company, company who was making me feel more than a little confused, and who had shaken up all my certainties like a kaleidoscope by doing nothing at all, other than being nice, and gentlemanly, and pretty damn attractive.

Once I'd fixed my hair for the second time that morning. I chose a bikini . . . nothing skimpy, mind, a nice blue one with a halter top . . . with a pair of cut-off denim shorts worn over.

The kids were ready to go when I got downstairs, with my towels, lotions and change clothes in my beach bag. Tom had dragooned them into shape, although wee Jonathan looked less than ecstatic about the whole venture. For a moment I thought about letting him stay with Conrad, but decided against it. The boy needed taking out of himself, dammit.

'You got the tent?' I asked my son. It's a pop-up windbreak really, but it has a zip-up front that gives privacy for changing. We were going to a beach with a nudie option, but I was taking it with Janet in mind.

'Yes, Mum,' he said, wearily. 'It's in the hall with the rest of our stuff. Now can we go? Vaive will be busy today and we want to get a table.'

I let him lead the way. He wasn't wrong about it being busy. As we passed the car park, I saw that it was jammed full, and opportunists were squeezed into anything that looked like a space. We arrived at the beach bar ten minutes late but Liam was there already, in swim shorts and a white V-necked T, waiting for us at a table which otherwise we wouldn't have had. They don't do reservations.

'Hi,' he said, rising.

I sensed that he was unsure how to greet us, so I put him at his ease by kissing him on the cheek as I'd parted from him the night before. 'You didn't meet wee Jonathan yesterday,' I remarked. 'This is him, Oz and Susie's younger. We only call him wee Jonathan to distinguish him from his cousin, Jonny.'

'The golfer?' he asked.

'Yes.'

'He's doing very well for himself. Rookie of the Year in Europe in his first season.'

'He lived with us for a while,' Tom told him. 'Now he has a house of his own, quite near here. Mum,' he continued, 'I want a chicken pig.'

Chicken pig? That's Vaive's most celebrated sandwich, half a baguette stuffed with chicken, bacon, salsa and lots of other stuff.

'Fine,' I replied. 'Mine's a sobrasada. See what everyone else wants then go and order.'

Liam seemed to give the specialty some serious thought, but stuck to his principles and settled for a salad in a bowl. He looked around as Tom went up to the counter. The beach was crowded, but not as much as the one by the Greek wall would have been. There was a light wind coming off the sea, enough for novice windsurfers but boring for the experts. 'This is terrific,' he said. 'Do you guys come here a lot?'

'In the holidays, yes. Weekends when school's in.'

'Does Tom windsurf?' he asked.

'He does, but he prefers free surfing. He's pretty good. That's not Mum getting carried away either. His Uncle Miles says so too, and he should know. He was a lifeguard when he was young, in Australia and California. Have you ever done any?'

'A little, but only the kind with the sail. We don't have big waves where I live.'

'Where do you live, Liam?' We'd got through the whole of the previous day without me asking that or him volunteering.

'I have an apartment in Dublin,' he replied, 'but my main base is in Toronto. It's the city I liked best when I was on the road with the crew, so I made it home. Ever been there?'

'Yes, I have, but very briefly, only for one night, in fact. Not long enough to form a view about the place.'

'Then you must give it another try.' For a moment I thought a definite invitation was coming, but he left it at that.

'Hey,' I said quietly, as Tom returned with bottles of still water for all of us, 'about last night. I enjoyed it very much. We'll do it again before you leave, but on me next time.'

He peered at me over the glasses (someone told me once, firmly, 'One drinks from glasses, one wears spectacles,' but she doesn't speak Scottish, so I disregarded her advice) and murmured, 'Likewise and okay.'

As we waited for lunch he asked me about the history of the region . . . 'Preliminary research for the book,' he said . . . and I gave him a quick rundown, the standard stuff about the Greeks arriving first and establishing a colony, then being succeeded by the Romans, and in the modern era by just about every other nation in Europe and a few beyond, most recently the Chinese who probably do a bigger retail turnover than anyone else in L'Escala these days.

'Sounds just like Toronto,' he laughed. 'We've got everyone and everything there.'

'I'll bet you don't have chicken pigs,' Tom chipped in, with a smile. He seemed to be losing his initial wariness of Liam, and that pleased me.

'You may well be right, young man,' he replied, 'but we've got loads of other stuff. And our own wine too. Ontario's becoming a pretty big producer; they're quite proud of some of it too.'

'Why don't we see more of it in Europe?' I asked.

'Because the Canadians drink it all. They have a strange attitude to alcohol, but they're pretty damn good at brewing and now wine-making. Not that I would know any more,' he added.

'Mum makes wine,' Tom said.

'I don't,' I protested. 'I'm a director of a company that does, that's all.'

'So you make wine.'

I sighed. 'If you insist. When it comes to arguing a point, you're as determined as your father . . . even when you're wrong.'

He looked at our companion. 'Is that true, Mr Matthews?'

'First, chum,' he replied, 'you call me Liam. Second, yes, your old man was a pretty determined guy . . . but I don't recall him ever being wrong, not in his eyes anyway. Once he made up his mind about something, he wasn't for changing it.'

I realised that Tom was pleased to be able to talk about his father with someone other than Susie and me, with an impartial witness as he probably saw it; the flaw in that was that Oz was never a guy to inspire objectivity. You either loved him or the opposite; at times I did both.

The discussion was ended by the arrival of lunch, Liam's salad, bikini toasties for Janet and wee Jonathan and massive sandwiches for Tom and me. We ate in silence, for they demanded concentration. When we were finished, we were full and it was definitely time for the beach.

I gave my son a fifty to pay for what we'd had then led the way over the iron bridge that crosses the little river from which the beach beyond takes its name. As soon as we were on the other side, Janet, who'd been leading Charlie, let him loose, and he went scampering down to the water, riding the small waves that were breaking on the shore. The rest of us walked on, for fifty metres or so, until Tom decreed that there was enough free space for him to pitch the windbreak.

'Who wants to swim now?' he asked, after he'd erected the structure. The question was directed at his younger brother more than anyone else. I'm not sure the kid wanted to go into the water, but Tom had become an authority figure, so he took it as a command. He and his little bag disappeared into the tent-ette, and he zipped the front up while he changed.

The rest of us weren't so fussy. I unbuttoned my shorts, letting them fall to the ground, then spread my beach mat and sat on it, cross-legged, reaching for my sun lotion.

Janet did the same, then popped her bikini top off, in an instant, as always, regardless of our new companion. She might have been stepping into womanhood, but her mind and attitudes hadn't quite caught up with her body. Liam wasn't a man, he was an adult, and she hadn't been brought up to be prudishly modest.

So what could I do but follow her example, as I would have done on any other day?

I tossed my top into my beach bag and stretched out beside her, oiling myself from top to ankles. When I was done, I rolled over and looked around for the nearest man. Tom was busy rubbing his sister's back with her high factor cream, so I tossed my bottle to Liam, who had spread his beach towel beside my mat.

'You got the job, beach boy,' I told him. 'Do the rest, will you? Sorry if the informality bothers you,' I murmured, 'but that's the way it is here.'

He grinned. 'If this was Toronto, you'd be in jail.' He took the lotion from me and massaged it into my back, gently, with hands that were strong but surprisingly soft.

'I'll bet you're glad it isn't,' I whispered, but there was nobody close by to hear me anyway. Tom and Janet were escorting a hesitant wee Jonathan towards the Mediterranean. His little bag was slung over his shoulder, as usual. I couldn't imagine what he carried in it; his pet frog, for all I knew.

'You could be right,' he said. 'Hand-holding's still forbidden, I take it?'

'Absolutely,' I said firmly. 'So's this.' I rolled on to my side, propped myself up on an elbow, took hold of his shirt, drawing him to me, and kissed him, properly, none of that on-the-cheek stuff, but long and slow, feeling my nipples harden as my breasts pressed against him. 'Sorry,' I murmured as I came up for breath, 'but I felt an overwhelming need to do that. Let's just call it a reward for you being so Goddamned nice.' I smiled at him. 'But I warn you, if you suggest that you could be even nicer I'll have to put my top back on.'

'Don't worry,' he chuckled. 'My nose is hurting already.'

'I can cure that,' I said. 'I'm a nurse.' I kissed him again, for longer than before, slipping my hand inside his shirt and running my palm over his chest, feeling his heart beat fast against it.

'People will talk,' he whispered, when he could.

'People are talking already.' I laughed. 'After last night, I promise you, people are talking all over L'Escala. It's the way this place is. Gossip moves faster here than a fire through pine needles. Fuck them all. It's a while since they've had me to feed off. Let them choke on me.'

He drew a deep breath. 'Primavera, I'm having trouble working out when you're serious and when you're not.'

I rolled on to my back, felt for my Maui Jim sunshades and slipped them on. 'Right at this moment, Liam,' I confessed, taking his hand in mine, 'so am I. But I promise you this; I might be cautious but I'm not a tease. We're both going to find out quite soon.'

'Likely I'm as cautious as you are,' he said. 'I promise you something too. I really didn't come here with anything like this in mind. But I'm not going to run away from it either. Whatever else happens between us, it'll be at your pace. And suppose nothing else does, the last couple of days are the best I've had in years.'

I squeezed his hand. 'Apart from all the great things that come from being a mum,' I replied, 'the same's true for me.'

Liam slipped off his shirt, folded it neatly, and used it as a pillow. We lay side by side and looked at the cloudless sky for a while, counting the condensation trails of the aircraft passing five or six miles above us.

'We'll be on one of them tomorrow,' I murmured. 'Tom and me. I'd rather not be, but maybe it's come at the right time.'

'Are you sure you'll be all right?' he asked. 'If my speculation last night is anywhere near the mark, will you be welcome?'

'I hope so, but it won't matter. I'll be holding the reins, driving the bus, pick your own analogy. I have to go, Liam, regardless. If you don't feel like waiting around here, I'll understand.'

He rolled on to his side and put his hand on my belly, between my navel and my breasts. 'I'll be here when you go, Primavera, and I'll be here when you get back. My word on that as an Irishman,' he chuckled, 'and a kung fu master. I'm looking forward to working out with your lad, remember.'

'I think he is too,' I told him. 'You know he's been weighing you up, don't you?'

'Sure. I wouldn't expect anything else of him. How am I doing?'

'Okay. I'd say you're passing his test, whatever that is.'

'He doesn't discuss?'

'Not unless I ask him. He had a slight go at provoking me this morning, but he realised I wasn't ready to talk, so he dropped it. It's bound to happen, though, probably while we're away.'

'Then tell him that what I want more than anything else is to be his friend and yours.'

I propped myself up on my elbows. 'Tell him yourself,' I suggested. 'He's coming.'

He was, with Charlie on his lead, and he wasn't smiling. My instant thought was that he'd seen me snogging Liam's face off and was about to give us a rollicking for public indecency. If he had, it wasn't at the top of his worry list.

'Where's wee Jonathan?' he asked.

A small cold spasm of concern grabbed at the pit of my stomach. 'What do you mean?' I spluttered. 'He went off with you and Janet.'

'Yes,' he agreed, 'but he was being a miserable wee sod, so Janet told him to go back up to you. He did.'

'If he did, then he was quiet about it. We haven't seen him.' *Or we were otherwise occupied and missed him.*

'You must have seen him!' Tom snapped. He hadn't raised his voice to me since he was five and I'd said he couldn't have a third Cadbury's cream egg.

I jumped to my feet. 'Well, we didn't, okay!' I stepped across to the shelter and looked inside, hoping that he'd be lurking there, but he wasn't.

Janet had joined us. 'Maybe he needed the toilet,' she suggested, as anxious as the rest of us. There's a chemical loo on the far side of the bridge, parked there for the summer like the others along the beachfront. We'd passed it and wee Jonathan had asked what it was for. He'd made a face when I told him.

'Maybe,' Liam agreed. 'I'll go and check.'

'No,' Tom said, grimly. 'I will. If he's there I'll have a serious word with him. Janet, you look after Charlie.'

I didn't want that to happen. This was a new version of my son; I didn't think for a second that he'd thump his brother, but in that mood he was likely to scare the living crap out of him. 'We'll both go,' I declared. 'Meanwhile, Liam and Janet, you two have a look around here for him. He may just have settled down to play somewhere.' Janet gave me an *Are you kidding?* look but didn't argue. I put my bikini top back on and headed after Tom.

There was a queue of three outside the toilet cabin when we got there. A second later the door opened and a lady emerged, so large that she couldn't have smuggled a Chihuahua in there with her. I asked her, in Spanish, whether a small boy had been in before her. She looked at me blankly. I tried French and we touched base. She shook her head. 'No,' she replied. 'A very smelly German man.'

As I was having that conversation, Tom headed to check out Vaive but neither Theresa nor Philippe had seen him since we'd all left. We asked their customers as well but nobody recalled seeing anyone who fitted our description, not even the windsurfers, and that was bad news, for they don't miss much.

We returned to the other two, hoping to see him there, retrieved and chastened. I was even prepared to see his sister's palm print on his ear, indeed I'd probably have sanctioned it, but no palm print, no ear, no wee Jonathan.

I was in a panic, and so was Janet. Even Liam seemed at a loss. Fortunately Tom had his wits about him and took charge. 'Mum, one more place to try,' he said. 'Home. He may just have gone back to Conrad. He's upset about his mum being away, and about that . . .' he paused, then continued, leaving the epithet unsaid, '. . . Duncan, because he thinks he's come back and he's terrified of him.'

I looked at Janet. 'Does he know Susie's ill?' I asked.

'No,' she insisted. 'Not from me, Auntie Primavera; I didn't say a word to him. But I suppose . . . he's such a sneaky little sod, and he's good with computers, maybe he could have found out some other way.'

'He's not sneaky,' Tom said, firmly. 'He's unhappy. He just wants to be back in Monaco and for everything to be okay but it isn't. And if he's right about Duncan, then it won't be.' He looked at Janet. 'What about Susie Mum?' he demanded. 'Is she ill?'

I didn't want the poor kid being interrogated, so I answered for her. 'Yes, she is, Tom. I had to tell Janet eventually, because I couldn't keep the secret any longer. I should have told you at the same time.'

He frowned at me. 'I thought we didn't have secrets, Mum,' he said, the equivalent of a sharp jab to the solar plexus.

I wanted to hug him and tell him that we didn't, but if I'd tried that I knew damn well he'd just have shaken me off. So I did a girlie thing: I gave him the big doe eyes, bit my lip and murmured, 'I'm sorry.'

He shrugged. 'You thought it was best.' An acceptance of sorts. 'Come on, Mum,' he said, more gently, 'let's you and I go back home. We'll probably find him hiding behind Conrad; that's what he usually does when he's in a mood.

Janet, you should wait here with Liam, just in case he's off sulking some place we haven't checked and decides to come back eventually. If he does, don't be angry with him; that won't help.'

Twelve years old and he was firing out orders like an adult; and none of us even thought of questioning them. Instead, I pulled my shorts on, picked up my shoes and set off after him as before. Charlie made his own choice and followed, his lead trailing behind him.

We kept our eyes open as we crossed the beach and passed the dodgy toilet, but saw no lone child, not even any accompanied, that gave us a moment's pause. Once we reached the path, Tom broke into a jog, with Charlie on a short lead, and I followed suit, keeping pace with him, my flip-flops still in my hand, for they would have been worse than useless. If he'd wanted, he and the dog could have run away from me, but he bore my years in mind, another sign that he was well in control of himself.

I had to put my flip-flops on when we reached St Martí. It was only then I realised that I'd left my keys in my bag on the beach. If Conrad had gone out . . . and wee Jonathan had come home, we'd probably find him on the front step, or, him being him, holed up in Charlie's kennel.

But we didn't. There was no dark-haired kid moping at the door, and the doghouse was unoccupied. Conrad hadn't gone out either. We found him in the kitchen, seated at the table, working at his laptop. 'Hi,' he greeted us. 'I'm emailing the housekeeper in Monaco, telling her to get the place ready for a full invasion tomorrow morning. Audrey asked me to phone her, but she's out.' Then he looked at us properly. 'What's up?'

'Has wee Jonathan come back here?' I asked him.

'No,' he replied, his tone turning the negative into a question.

'He's vanished,' I told him, then explained what had happened.

'Jesus!' Conrad exploded. 'Primavera! He's been snatched. Primavera, you know how careful we have to be. I only let you go without me because Matthews was with you. Matthews! Bloody showbiz wrestler! I will kill him.' I believe that he meant it. I stared at him, not knowing what to say when . . .

'No, Conrad!'

The voice that came from behind me could only have belonged to one person, and yet it wasn't him. It was deep, it was full, it was unmistakable and it was impossible. It was Oz's voice. In the crisis, Tom had metamorphosed into his father, and if there was a single person in the world who could command the very formidable Conrad Kent, it was him.

'It wasn't Mum's fault,' he continued, in a tone that was more like his own, but not quite, with a serious edge to it. 'It wasn't Liam's fault. It was mine. He told me he was going back to them and I didn't take him, I let him go on his own, only he didn't. So don't be angry with Liam . . . and don't ever shout at my mum again!'

Wow! I couldn't love him any more than I do, but that put the cherry on it. He'd just nailed Conrad's balls to the wall, and calmed him down in the process. 'I'm sorry, Primavera,' he murmured. 'Tom's right; that was uncalled for.'

'And it's forgotten, but tell me, why did you think automatically that he's been taken?'

Conrad frowned and glanced at Tom, as if he was trying to give me a message.

I shook my head. 'I don't think there's anything you can say to me that I have to hide from my son, so shoot.'

'There is,' he countered, 'but I'll go this far. Two years ago I was warned that a group of English chancers were in Monaco, ostensibly on holiday, but in fact planning to snatch one of Oz and Susie's kids and hold them for ransom. I was able to head it off.'

'Well done the police,' I said.

'It had nothing to do with them. The tip came from a mafia kingpin; he approached me and told me about it. He said that the English team had approached a couple of his friends for help. It was a big mistake on their part. The mafia don't approve of things like that, for two reasons: one, they have respect for children; and two, they wouldn't do anything that would draw the kind of heat on them that a high-profile kidnap would bring. So they dealt with the problem.'

I didn't ask how; Conrad was right in that Tom didn't need to hear what I knew would be the answer. Instead, I asked him, 'Why did he tell you about it?'

'It was probably his way of letting Susie know that she was in their debt, but I didn't tell her about it. I don't plan to either.'

'So these could be the same people?' Tom suggested. He hadn't picked up on the fact that the mafia don't let people do encores.

'Or similar,' Conrad replied.

'In which case, I don't have any links to the local underworld,' I told him, 'but I am well in with the cops.'

I didn't waste any time. I called Alex Guinart on his mobile, straight away. 'Hey,' he said as he answered, a smile in his voice, 'sexy lady. How did your evening go, or shouldn't I ask?'

'No, you shouldn't because this is serious.'

'You want to make that complaint now? Couldn't it—'

'Bugger that! This is different.' I told him what had happened and about Conrad's suspicions.

He was all business, straight away. 'Kidnapping would be unusual in this part of Spain. In the south, and around the Mediterranean, much less so. The first thing to do is set up roadblocks, and search the immediate area. Do you have a recent photograph of the child?'

'Yes, on my computer. Tom and his sister are in it, but it's only a week old.'

'Then email it to me, and I'll circulate it right away. Where are you?'

'I'm at home, with Tom and Conrad. Liam and Janet are still on the beach, in case he shows up.'

'Liam?'

'The man you saw me with last night. If he had turned up, he or Janet would have called me.'

There followed a few seconds of silence. 'This Liam, when did he arrive here?'

'A couple of days ago.'

'And now the child has disappeared. And you've left him on the beach with the other one?'

The enormity of what he was suggesting made me gasp. I turned my back on Conrad so that he couldn't see my face and pick anything up from it. We were speaking Catalan, and he'd get nothing from that. 'Forget that,' I hissed. 'He was one of Oz's best friends, and I've known him for years myself.'

'But you haven't seen him for years either?'

'No, but what you're suggesting—'

'I'm not suggesting anything,' Alex said. 'I'm only establishing facts. Send me that email, Primavera. There are two routes from where the boy was last seen; I'll put blocks on those straight away and get his likeness to the people who are manning them. But we'll need more than that; we have to search the surrounding area.'

'In case he's hiding there?' I asked naively. 'He wouldn't do that.'

I heard an intake of breath. 'No, Primavera; not in case he's hiding.'

'Oh,' I murmured.

'I would like you and Tom to go back along there. Your man Conrad, the children's guardian, have him remain at your house. Tell him he's manning the phones or any other pretext. I know what he is, and I know what he's capable of. If the boy has been taken and we find him with someone, I don't want him around.'

'Understood.'

'I suggest that you bring the child Janet back from the beach. She and Tom should stay with Mr Kent. If you can vouch for your boyfriend—'

'He isn't!' I snapped.

'You fooled me, if that's so. He should stay where he is and you should join him there. We'll need volunteers for the search.'

That's how it panned out. Tom wasn't happy at first; he wanted to join the search, but when I insisted that he'd be of most use looking after Janet and keeping her as calm as he could, he accepted that.

I took my jeep along to collect Janet, and all the stuff I'd left along there. I'd have been almost as quick on foot, but I was taking Conrad's story seriously. I knew she'd be safe with Liam, and in the house, but with me, on an open pathway, maybe not.

I left the car at home once I'd delivered her and ran back. By the time I got there, Alex had arrived; he was in uniform, and in charge. Liam was waiting for me where he'd said he would when I picked up Janet, at the foot of the iron bridge. He looked as distraught as I felt; I hoped that it registered with Alex and that he'd apologise later for 'establishing the facts'.

I have to record here my appreciation for the way the beach people rallied around. As far as I could see, everyone who didn't have children of their own to look after had volunteered to join the search. The Mossos had an inflatable, crewed by divers; their job was to probe the little green river with poles, and investigate anything solid they detected. The rest of us were split into teams to cover the ground behind the beach, and to trawl through the adjoining campsites. Liam and I stayed together, searching the fields. They were un-cultivated and that made it worse, for the grass was waist high and tangled, hampering our progress. There was one very scary moment when a woman, no more than twenty metres away from us, screamed and put her hands over her face. We rushed across, to find her standing over the rotting carcass of what had been a large dog. We spent an hour combing our assigned area then another retracing out steps, but in the end it was all fruitless.

Finally a whistle was blown, and we all gathered back at the starting point, where Alex thanked us for our efforts, and stood us down.

'What do we do?' Liam asked.

'I don't know,' I confessed.

Alex came across to us. He shook Liam's hand, and gave me a quick hug. 'Keep your phone charged and switched on,' he told me. 'When I know something, you will too.'

'Thanks,' I said. 'What do you think?'

'I think,' he replied instantly, 'that the fact that we haven't found him makes it likely that Mr Kent was right, that the child has been taken. Has anyone been in touch with his mother? She's in America, you told me, Primavera, yes?'

'Yes, but she's probably started the journey home by now. I could probably get in touch with her, but what would be the point, with nothing positive to tell her? She's a very sick woman, Alex.'

'Then I leave that judgement to you. For now, you go home, you wait and you pray, if that will help.'

I nodded, and he left. I looked at Liam, and he looked at me; we must have made a distinctly uncool pair, in our crushed and sweaty beach gear. Suddenly I felt exhausted. 'I need some time,' I murmured. 'Let's go to your hotel.'

'Yeah.' He slipped his arm around my waist and half carried me there. It wasn't far, only a few metres along the path. He picked up his key from reception and led the way up to his room. As soon as he closed the door behind us, I collapsed into his only chair, and did something very un-Primavera-like. I burst into tears. He knelt beside me and hugged me as I cried it out, and I loved him for it. I couldn't have done that in front of Tom and certainly not with Janet around.

When I'd composed myself, I patted his arm, to let him know I was all right. 'I need to get back,' I said, 'but God, I'm filthy. Can I have a shower?'

'Of course.'

I pushed myself out of the chair and stripped naked where I stood. He'd seen everything else, so there was no point in being coy about the rest. I went into the bathroom and stood under a barely warm spray for five minutes, flushing the grime, sand and sweat off me and shampooing it from my hair. When I was done, I wrapped myself in one of the robes that hung behind the door, and let Liam take my place. I was still wearing it when he came out in the other one, but I'd put my shorts back on. My bikini was definitely done for the day, maybe for ever. 'Do you have a top I can borrow?' I asked.

He smiled. 'Sure.' He opened a drawer and took out another of those GWA merchandise shirts from way back. 'I brought this along with Tom in mind,' he said as he handed it to me. 'You can give it to him when you're done with it.'

I raised myself up on my toes and kissed him again, running my fingers through his damp hair. 'You're a lovely man,' I told him. 'When we've got wee Jonathan back safe . . .'

'Let's just concentrate on that part,' he whispered.

'I need to get back home now,' I said. 'Come with me. I want you near me while this plays out. Bring your toothbrush.' I rubbed his chin, and grinned. 'And your razor too. And your pyjamas, if you're bashful.'

'You sure?'

'Yes. I'm getting more sure by the minute.'

He put some stuff in a small bag and we walked back to the village. When we got there I didn't go up into the square, because I didn't want to run into anyone I knew and face the inevitable quiz; instead I let us in through the garage. It's alarmed all the time and there's a buzzer that sounds upstairs whenever someone comes in that way, until they cancel it.

Conrad was waiting for us at the top of the stairs when we reached them. If he was surprised to see Liam with me he didn't show it, but his eyebrows did rise a little when he clocked my replacement T-shirt. I left him to draw his own conclusions.

'Any news?' I asked him. He shook his head. 'Me neither. Where are Tom and Janet?'

'In the TV room. They're watching the local station. It's been running live coverage of the search.'

'They haven't named him, have they?' I didn't want that, no way.

'No, but they did run the photograph that you sent Alex.'

'Could he be recognised from that?' Liam asked.

'By a local, he probably could,' Conrad replied. 'We've been here long enough for him to become known as Tom's half-brother. Let's hope no reporter has the wit to ask.'

'I'd like to think,' I observed, 'that my friends would realise that we don't need that.'

'I thought you said this place runs on gossip,' Liam murmured.

He had a point, and I conceded it. 'As soon as his identity becomes known,' I said, 'this will stop being a local story and go international.'

I remembered how I'd heard that Oz had died; I was in Jimmy Buffett's bar in Las Vegas, when his face popped up on the big screen telly and I knew instantly that he hadn't won an Oscar. 'I hadn't wanted to tell Susie, not until we had some good news, and then maybe not ever, but now, I'm thinking we have to, just in case.'

Conrad glanced at his watch. 'Not for a while, we can't.

They were scheduled to take off from Phoenix ten minutes ago for Charlotte. That's a long flight.'

'Is it on time? Could they still be sitting in the airport?'

'No. Audrey called me an hour ago to say they were boarding.' He held up a hand. 'And before you ask, I didn't say anything to her.'

'How's Susie, physically? Did she say?'

'Not much, but I don't think she could. She said she was okay, but I wasn't convinced. I don't think she could speak freely; I reckon Duncan was too close.'

I walked through to the office where the second television is, and found the kids there. Janet looked up at me; her face was drawn beneath the tan and her eyes were anxious. 'They haven't found him, Auntie Primavera,' she said.

'I know, love,' I replied. 'Liam and I were among the people looking. That isn't bad news, you know.'

'But there were men looking in the river.' She was on the edge of tears

'Just in case,' Tom told her. 'Wee Jonathan wouldn't go near the river; it's green and smelly. He doesn't even like the sea much.'

'Well, where is he?' she wailed, and the tears did come.

Tom put an arm around her shoulders. 'I don't know,' he murmured. He didn't look too sound himself emotionally, a worried little guy in contrast to the strong kid who had taken charge earlier.

I might have cracked too, but Liam appeared in the doorway just in time. He read the situation, took me in his arms and held me fast, making me feel protected, for the first time in longer than I could remember. 'It'll be all right,' he said, to all of us.

Tom looked him in the eye, via the mirror on the wall. 'How do you know?' he challenged.

'I do, that's all; I have faith. Do you know what that is?'

'Religion,' my son replied.

'Yes, but it's more than that; it's when you have an absolute belief, even when there's absolutely no evidence to support it. I have faith that the little boy is all right.'

'But why?'

'If I didn't, what else would there be? Only despair. Come here,' he said, 'both of you.'

They did and we had a hug-in, feeling Liam's certainty spread to us all, making us all feel warm and safe.

That's not to say that we switched on the party music. No, we sat there and waited. As soon as I left that room, nagging doubts and awful visions came back to me. I joined Conrad in the kitchen and had a beer with him.

'If you're right,' I asked him, 'what will happen?'

'We'll have a message, once they feel secure; there'll be a ransom demand.'

'What do we do then?'

He stared at me. 'Pay it. Whatever the cops say.'

'But will they let him go then?'

'We can only hope they do.'

'No,' I contradicted him. 'First and foremost we can hope you're wrong.'

'There is that. But if I'm not, I promise you, Primavera, I will find whoever's responsible, and that will be that for them.'

'Don't say that.'

'This is Oz's son we're talking about. He'd demand it of me.'

'But he isn't here to do any demanding, so, who owns your loyalty now? Tom and Janet, I'd suggest. If you try to make them murderers by association, you'll cross me.'

The phone rang an hour later, ten minutes before the time at which I'd determined that I'd call Susie to let her know what had happened. Tom had tracked her flight on the internet and had given me its scheduled arrival time. Fifteen minutes later, I reckoned, she was bound to be in the transit lounge, and if her mobile wasn't switched on, Audrey's would be for sure.

We were all in the living room when the call came in. I'd made the kids switch off the news, and given Janet her choice of replacement. She'd opted for Spanish MTV which seemed entirely harmless, so I'd let them watch it on the big set.

Conrad sprang out of his chair, but I forestalled him. 'I'm taking this,' I told him, inviting no protest as I rose from the couch I'd been sharing with Liam. I picked it up, fearful that the next words I heard would change my life, but with no idea what they would be or even in what language they'd be put.

'He's safe,' Alex Guinart said, in Catalan.

All the breath rushed from me in a great sigh, and I slumped back on to the sofa. 'Oh, thank God, Alex,' I exclaimed, in English, so that everyone in the room could share the good news. 'Now tell me what happened,' I continued, switching back to his language.

'He ran away, Primavera, simple as that. There was a pick-up, parked down the road beside the river; windsurfers. The child climbed into the back and hid under a tarpaulin. When the owners, two gay men,' he didn't actually say gay men, but that's how I choose to translate it, 'came back, they put their boards in there and didn't notice him at all. They drove away, and went straight home, all the way to Badalona. Why they come north to surf, God alone knows, but they do.'

'Go on,' I said, impatiently. I wasn't in the mood for a discourse on the merits of beaches.

'Sorry, of course. The boy was in the back of the truck all the time; they only found him when they unloaded it. By then he was cold, and he was terrified. Neither of the men speaks English, but fortunately one of them is fluent in French. They're good guys; they fed him soup to warm him while they worked out what to do. Then one of them switched on the television, they saw the news and it was their turn to be scared. They phoned my colleagues straight away, and told them what had happened. Our guys went there, and the boy confirmed their story. They're bringing him home now, blue lights. He should be with you in an hour, no more. I'm about to release a statement that he's been found alive and well.'

'Will there be consequences?'

'For the two men?' he exclaimed. 'I can't see why.'

'Of course not, Alex; for wee Jonathan?'

'Good God, no. He's nine years old, and he's a sad, frightened child; if it was anyone else, I'd be holding him until I knew why. I'm only returning him because I trust you to make whatever it is right. What is happening in his family?'

I couldn't explain in any detail, for Tom would have understood everything I said and Janet would probably have picked up most of it too. I stalled him by telling him that I would explain everything next time I saw him, and that the problem would be leaving his patch next morning.

'It won't stop me worrying about the kid,' he said.

'I know, me neither, but his mother will make it right, I'm sure. He's worried about her; that's the heart of it.'

'So why run away?'

'As I said, I'll tell you later. Thanks, Alex.'

I hung up. Everyone else in the room, Tom, Janet, Liam, Conrad, even bloody Charlie was gazing at me intently. I told them what had happened, just as Alex had explained it. I hadn't got far before I saw that Janet was furious, but I hushed her until I was finished.

She had her say as soon as I was through. 'He did that to us, Auntie Primavera,' she snapped. 'It was cruel. I was terrified; so was Tom, so was Conrad even. I thought he was dead. If Mum had known about it . . . Wait till I see him.'

'What will you do, Janet?' Liam asked her quietly.

'What's it got to do with you?' she shouted at him.

'Nothing,' he replied, with a smile. 'You hardly know me. But I was here when it happened, and I helped look for him, and I was just as scared as the rest of you. So I'm asking you, what are you going to do when he comes back?'

'I'm going to . . .' She struggled for the words, but couldn't find them.

'We're going to ask him why he did it,' Tom told her. 'He's our brother, and he wouldn't do anything to hurt you and me. He's sad, Janet, and he's lonely. He didn't do that just to be bad. He isn't bad; he isn't like that. So we're going to ask him what's wrong, you and me, and whatever it is, we're going to make it better.' He looked at Liam. 'Isn't that right?' he asked. 'Isn't that what we should do?'

He nodded. 'It's what I would do, for what that's worth. I think Tom's right, Janet, that he's sad and he's lonely, but I believe he's angry as well, and you don't take someone's anger away by throwing more of the same at it. That's what your other brother's learned from his wing chun, and what I've come to understand from my own studies.'

'Don't get mad. Get even,' Conrad muttered.

'You're only half right. Usually there's nothing to get even for.'

'Mmm.' The kids' minder stood and walked from the room, without a backward look.

'He's old school,' I told Liam.

'So would I be if something had actually happened to wee Jonathan. There's nothing in my philosophy, or Tom's, that says "Don't punish the guilty", but there is no guilt here.' He looked at Janet, my ward, I suppose, to use an old-fashioned term. 'Agreed?' he asked.

She allowed him a quick smile, and nodded. 'Yes, Liam. Sorry I was rude.'

'You weren't, you were upset. What does he like, wee Jonathan? What really floats his boat?'

'Magnum ice creams,' she replied instantly. 'The white chocolate kind.'

'Then how about you and Tom going and getting him one, hell on, two, and sticking them in the freezer for when he gets back?'

Tom looked at me for confirmation; I nodded. They left, Charlie following behind, heading for the nearest supply of ice-cream treats on sticks. I turned to Liam. 'You gorgeous man,' I murmured. I took his hand and tugged it. There was no doubt about what I had in mind, but he shook his head.

'No,' he said, softly. 'I want you too, but this is not the time. You're worth more than the half-hour we'd have before the cops get here with wee Jonathan. When he does there's going to be a lot of emotion in here, and you're the best person to handle it.'

'Then afterwards.'

He grinned. 'Sure. And what time do you have to be at the airport tomorrow?'

'Early,' I admitted.

'What I thought. So you and Tom get up and bugger off, leaving me to share an awkward breakfast with Conrad, the kids and Charlie.'

I laughed, then gasped. 'Charlie,' I exclaimed. 'I'd forgotten, we have to give him to Ben Simmers this evening, and he'll be closing his shop soon.'

'You make my case,' he said. 'Primavera, tough as it may be to tear myself away from you, and your remarkable body . . . don't think I didn't take a good look . . . I'm going to kiss you farewell now and then I'm going back to the hotel. When you come back, you'll have had almost a week to think about me. If you haven't thought better of everything we both have in mind right now, we'll see where that takes us.'

I wanted to tell him, no way was he going anywhere, but I'd learned even in only a couple of days' re-acquaintance that he had an annoying tendency to be right all the time. So we kissed each other farewell, I gave him a quick squeeze for luck, hard enough to make his eyes widen, and I let him go on his way.

Eleven

I took Charlie down to Ben's as soon as Liam had gone. An hour later I'd have been glad of his distracting presence, for it was pretty emotional when the Mossos people, a man and a woman, arrived with wee runaway Jonathan.

They parked their car outside the village and wore plain clothes when they walked him up to the door. They may have been under orders from Alex, but whether they were or not, I was grateful to them for their sensitivity. The square was Sunday busy and being hauled out of a police car in full view would have dissolved what was left of the kid's self-esteem.

As it was, he was the picture of misery when I opened the front door to them, and he wrapped himself around me, tight as a small python. He was wearing what I can best describe as a long shirt, stretching down past his knees. The female officer explained that he had wet himself in the back of the truck and that his beach clothes were in his little bag, which he still carried slung over his shoulder. If he'd been planning to run away, I knew what I'd find in there when I looked: his favourite toy, a stuffed green dinosaur that he's had from infancy, and a copy of *Harry Potter and the Chamber of Secrets*, in French.

When I asked her if she could give me the names and address of the couple who'd been his unwitting taxi drivers, she shot me a look full of alarm and shook her head. I explained that I only wanted to apologise to them, and to thank them for doing the right thing when they'd found the wee chap, but still she said that she couldn't do that, or her bosses would hand her her head as a plaything. I didn't press her further. I decided instead that if Philippe and Theresa knew them, as almost certainly they would, I would give them a five-hundred euro tab at Vaive to work their way through, and that's a lot of chicken pigs.

Janet and Tom were waiting in the hall when I said goodbye to the cops and peeled wee Jonathan from round my legs. He looked at them fearfully, then saw what his sister was holding in her hand and burst into tears.

'It's all right,' Tom told him, as he took the white chocolate Magnum from his sister. The kid gave him an awkward, cracked smile. We took him into the kitchen, where Conrad joined us, and I sat him at the table, while I tossed his damp and smelly beach clothes into the washing machine, along with my reprieved bikini and a couple of towels, all I had left to boost the load after my earlier burst of laundry mania.

He was halfway through his ice cream when I came back from the utility room. I let him finish before I asked the question that we all knew had to be put. 'Why did you run away, son? You need to tell us, so we understand and can help you.'

His eyes became hard; they were scary in such a small child. 'I don't want Duncan as a daddy,' he whispered.

'Neither do I,' Janet exclaimed. 'But it's not going to happen. Mum doesn't like him any more, remember.'

'But she does,' wee Jonathan wailed. 'She's in America and they've got married.'

'No they haven't,' Janet protested. 'Jonathan, Mum's in America because she's been ill, but she's better now and she's on her way home.'

Fuck it, Susie! I thought. *You couldn't trust your daughter with the whole truth, and now I'm stuck with it.*

'They are so married,' the wee fellow insisted. 'I heard Auntie Primavera talking to Mum on the phone and that's what they were talking about.' He looked at me warily. 'I couldn't help it, Auntie Primavera. I was going to the toilet and the door was open.' That was a small lie, the toilet being one floor above the room where I'd spoken to Susie, but I wasn't going to pick up on it. 'I heard you say it.'

Janet was struck dumb. She turned to me, and I nodded. It was all I could do. 'Mum never told me,' she said, sounding more bitter than a twelve-year-old ever should. 'When I spoke to her she told me about her illness, but she didn't say anything about that.'

I reached out and ruffled wee Jonathan's hair. 'Maybe you can see why,' I suggested. 'I am sure she felt, and still does, that it was something she had to tell you in person.'

'She can tell me any way she likes,' she protested. 'I agree with Jonathan. I don't want her to be married to that man. He's not nice. He tried to bully the boys, and I don't like the way he looks at me either.'

That was a new element, although it didn't take me completely by surprise. 'What do you mean by that, Janet?' I asked her.

She hesitated. 'It's just . . . not nice. There was one time at home last year when I'd just got out of the pool and I'd taken my bikini off. I thought I was alone, but there's a glass door and it was like a mirror and I could see Duncan there and he was looking at me, with no clothes on. When he realised I'd seen him, he just smiled. He's a bad man, Auntie Primavera.'

Too bloody right he is, I thought, as alarmed by the revelation as she must have been by the experience. 'Then you must tell your mother that story,' I insisted.

'I can't,' the girl whispered.

'Then I will,' said Conrad. 'And I'll be asking Mr Culshaw about it as well.'

Janet took her brother's hand. 'We don't want to live with him, Auntie Primavera. We don't have to, do we? Can we stay here tomorrow?'

'I'd love to say yes, Janet. But you know I can't; your mother wants you home. You might not like her choice of a husband; hell, I don't, as you must realise, but it was hers to make.'

'But you don't always need to have a man,' she pointed out.

'True,' I admitted. 'I haven't had a partner, not since your dad and I split up thirteen years ago. That's been my choice . . .' I felt Liam's presence in the room, '. . . but I'm free to change my mind about it, just as your mum's free to . . . make her own mistakes. Duncan will know, or be told by me if necessary, that as your stepfather, he has to care for you two as if you were his own. Let's not condemn him out of hand. The fact that he's back with your mother means surely that he knows he could have been better last time, and that he'll be a good stepdad.'

Her expression told me that she didn't believe a word of that. I couldn't complain; neither did I.

Wee Jonathan slept with his sister that night. It was Tom's idea; maybe he was considerate, or maybe he didn't want to have to listen to the wee man crying.

We were all up at sparrowfart next morning; quarter to seven, to be exact. Tom and I had to be on the road by eight to reach Barcelona Airport comfortably for our eleven thirty flight to Heathrow, and Conrad wanted to get the kids back to Monaco for midday, which meant that he had to leave around the same time. As I got myself ready, I reflected that Liam had been right to go back to the hotel. First morning with a new man, one, I would not have wanted to rush off and leave him, and two, I'd have preferred less company. There was a third factor too, that I hadn't taken into account the evening before, not until Susie's example had been laid out for us all. It was a potentially life-changing step for Tom, and I needed to prepare him for it in a way she certainly hadn't done with her two.

I almost rang Liam to tell him we were off, but I didn't reckon the Riomar was geared for early morning calls, so instead I sent a text to the mobile number he'd given me. All it said was, 'Hasta Sabado. Pxxx'; he could work that out for himself. I confess that I was anxious when I said goodbye to the kids and Conrad, worried about what awaited them and also, naggingly, how he might react to Janet's story of Culshaw's sneak peek at her undressing, once he was face to face with the guy.

I would have liked to go with them, and I believe they'd have preferred that too, but the promise I'd made to Susie had made that impossible, and so I could do nothing but trust that she and the Kents would make the situation as easy as possible for them.

We took our other car down to the airport. The jeep is a few years old now, and much as I love it, Tom reached the age a while ago at which his head started to be turned by rather flashier motors. There was gentle nagging, about a BMW, or maybe one of those cute little Mercedes sports cars with the folding roof, or maybe an Audi. I resisted them all, but then the Mini Coupé was launched, and I was as hooked as he was. We bought a nice blue one, the Cooper S model, with all the toys they had on offer thrown in by way of a discount, and that's become our treat car. The jeep still does most of the mileage, but when we're going somewhere special it's in that flash little bugger.

It goes like that off a shovel, but I rarely allow it to express itself. Still, we made good time down the autopista. Tom didn't say a word until we were south of Girona, but eventually he came out with the question I'd been expecting, the one he could only ask when we were alone.

'Do you like Liam, Mum?'

'I rather think I do,' I admitted. 'Do you have a problem with that?'

'No, I like him too. I want to train with him. He told me he's a sixth dan black belt in karate. That's serious, Mum. Our instructor's only third dan himself. I can learn a lot from him; so could wee Jonathan.'

That surprised me. 'You think?'

'Yes. Wee Jonathan needs somebody to teach him things. He's frightened of everything. I try my best to make him not scared, but I'm not with him all the time.'

'We're a long way from Monaco,' I pointed out. 'And besides, Liam's only visiting; he's on holiday, like most of the people who come here.'

'He'll still be here when we get back, won't he?' he asked, anxiously.

'Yes,' I said, 'unless he gets bored and goes back to Toronto. That's where he lives.'

'He wouldn't do that, would he?'

'I don't think so. I'm sure he won't. I hope he doesn't.' All of a sudden, I was less sure of myself. He wouldn't. Would he?

As if in answer to my question, my phone rang, loud in the car through the speakers. 'Yes,' I said, to accept the call.

'Hi.' I was getting to like the sound of his voice,

well-travelled Irish. 'I got your text; received and understood. Did you get on the road okay?'

'We did, thanks.' I stressed the plural, hoping he would realise that he wasn't speaking to me alone. 'We are, in fact; about halfway there. We were just talking about you. Now I'm gone, Tom reckons you'll bugger off with the first blonde you see.'

'I do not,' he protested, loudly. 'I never said that, Liam. It's Mum kidding. Do you really live in Toronto?'

'I do. I have a nice big duplex down on Harbourfront, with a view over Lake Ontario, right across to America, if you could see that far. When you come back, I'll show you some of my photographs.'

'We will hold you to that,' I told him. 'I'll call you when we get to our hotel in Glasgow.'

'Which one? Some of those can be dodgy.'

'The Malmaison; it's fairly new, very chic, from what I saw on its website. Bye for now.'

I hit the button on the steering wheel that cancels the call and drove on. 'I'd like to go to Toronto, Mum,' Tom said, dreamily.

We had reached the airport, five minutes before our target arrival time of ten o'clock, and I was reversing into a parking space in the multi-storey when the phone rang again. I switched off the engine, killing the Bluetooth, and took it from my pocket. I checked the number, imagining it would be Liam, calling again to wish us a safe flight. I was wrong: 'Audrey mobile' showed on screen. I thumbed the icon to accept her call.

'Hi,' I began. 'Where are you calling from? You should be almost home by now. Conrad and the kids will be well into France by now.'

'I'm at the airport, Nice Airport,' she replied. I knew from her voice . . . it was shaky and she sounded scared . . . that something was wrong, very wrong, and felt a sudden surge of relief that I wasn't on hands free and that Tom couldn't hear her. He was engaged in taking out bags from the boot; I left him to it and took a few steps away.

'What's happened?' I asked.

'It's Susie. Primavera, she's died.'

Looking back, I shouldn't have been as shocked as I was. I knew how ill Susie was; I knew that her chances of long-term survival were practically nil. I knew the complications of the chemotherapy regime she'd been on. I knew why they'd pumped platelets into her bloodstream, and what the implications of that were. And yet, when Audrey told me, I was as stunned as she was; even with all that knowledge, there is still an inbuilt refusal to accept that someone close to you is approaching the point of death.

I was speechless for a few seconds. A sound came from behind me: Tom closing the boot lid. Then another, a loud click as he locked the car. Then a third, the wheels of our cases as he pushed them in my direction.

'Tell me,' I murmured, back in command of my voice.

'She died during the flight from Charles de Gaulle to Nice. Looking back, she was a bit hazy in the lounge before we boarded, but she said she was just tired from the transatlantic flight. We got on board, Duncan grabbed the window seat, I took the middle and Susie was on the outside. She didn't mind that; she said it would make it easier for her if she had to go to the toilet.'

She paused; I imagined she was finding it difficult to hold herself together.

'As it happened, nobody did. It's a relatively short flight. We took off on time, and we were still climbing when Susie said to me that she was going to try and sleep all the way, so she'd be bright when she met the kids. And she did, she nodded right off.'

'Did she waken at all?' By that time Tom had reached me with the cases; he was standing beside me frowning. I took one case from him, and gestured towards the lift; he headed in that direction.

'I don't think so,' Audrey replied. 'They brought the bar trolley, but I don't think she was aware of it, not even when the steward reached over us to give Duncan the two bottles of white wine that he'd asked for.' She sobbed; I said nothing, but let her get it out.

'We touched down in Nice at nine twenty. It was quite a hard landing; everyone else on the plane was shaken up, but Susie didn't stir, not at all. At first I thought it was just because she'd been so tired. I didn't try to waken her until we'd taxied in and were on stand, and then I couldn't. I tried, very gently at first, then I shook her a little bit harder. It was only when I took my seat belt off and turned round to take a good look at her, I saw . . . the way her mouth was hanging open . . . Primavera . . .'

'I understand,' I said gently. Tom was at the lift; the doors were open, but I waved for him to wait, knowing that if I stepped inside I'd lose the signal.

'I called the flight attendants,' she continued. 'They're all first-aiders, and they could see right away it was serious. They asked if there was a doctor on board and a woman came up from the back of the plane. She had ID that showed she worked in a hospital in Paris. She couldn't find a pulse, she held a mirror under her nose, and I could see there wasn't the faintest sign of breath on it. Then she shone a penlight in her eye and said the pupils were completely non-reactive. They had oxygen on board, and those shock pads, but the doctor said she was beyond resuscitation, and she pronounced her dead, at nine twenty-nine local time. The captain was there; he made a note of it, and got her to sign a declaration.'

'Did she suggest a cause of death?'

'No. The pilot asked her, but she said she wasn't prepared to guess, that there'll have to be an autopsy.'

'What happened then?'

'They put a sheet over her, and got everyone off the plane through the back exit. We had to clamber over her, Duncan and I.'

'How did he react?' I asked.

'You know, Primavera, I can't answer that, not properly. He didn't burst into floods of tears or anything, put it that way. He was very quiet. That's until the captain asked me who was the next of kin. I said it was Janet, just automatically, without even thinking, and Duncan shouted, "No, she's fucking not! I am!" The crew probably just thought he was hysterical, but he wasn't. He was making a point, if you ask me.'

'I don't have to,' I told her. 'I can see that. What are you doing now? Where are you?'

'I'm in the VIP lounge; they've asked us to wait here to talk to the ambulance crew that are coming to take Susie's body to the morgue. They're going to take her to the hospital in Nice. I want her to go to Monaco, but that might not be possible, a jurisdictional thing, the airport manager says, since she died in France. Duncan's outside, having a cigarette . . . to calm his nerves, he said . . . but I can see him from where I'm sitting. He's standing in the forecourt and he's not smoking; he's on his phone. He switched it on when we got in here, and got a text right away.'

'I'll bet,' I muttered. 'Audrey,' I continued, 'I have to think about all of this, and I have Tom with me. I can't kid him on about this. I will call you back as soon as we're through security and I've had a chance to talk to him.'

'You're still going to catch your flight?'

The thought of not catching it hadn't even occurred to me. 'Oh yes,' I said. 'It's even more important now that I do. I'll speak to you again shortly; meantime, hang in there.'

'What's wrong?' Tom asked, as soon as I'd joined him at the lift. We weren't alone; a fat bloke with a suit bag and a briefcase was waiting beside us, and I didn't want to be breaking any news in his earshot.

'Not now, love,' I said. 'Be patient, until we're inside the building.'

He nodded, but his face was set in a look that wasn't fearful exactly, but told me he wasn't expecting to be hearing any good news. I'd called Audrey by name and if he'd heard me . . . He said nothing, though; instead he fussed me through the fast bag drop, which wasn't, and security, putting his carry-on bag and mine on to the X-ray conveyor and reminding me to take off my belt and watch. I set the damn gate off, of course, thanks to the metal button on my bloody trousers, and had to endure a pat-down, no, a feel-up, from a clumsy woman who was so thorough in her search that I asked her if she was enjoying it, for I sure as hell wasn't. She threatened to call her supervisor. I threatened to call the police. I must have been better at threatening than her, for she backed off.

I was still steaming mad with her by the time I'd reclaimed my stuff, but my son's presence, and the knowledge of what I was about to tell him, helped me control myself. We went straight to the business class lounge. I've known those to be busier than the concourse at some airports, but Barcelona's was quiet that morning. I checked the board as we walked in, letting Tom show our tickets. Our flight was showing a ten-minute delay; that meant we had more than half an hour to boarding time, enough for what had to be done.

I fetched a soft drink and some biscuits for him and a coffee for me, then steered us to the quietest corner I could see. His patience finally ran out as soon as I sat down.

'It's Susie, Mum, isn't it?' he said, his face tense.

All I could do was nod.

'She's dead. I can tell by your face.'

'Yes. She died on board the flight to Nice, about an hour ago. It was very sudden, Tom. Audrey said she died in her sleep.'

I'd thought he might shed a tear. After all, for that part of his early childhood when I was away, in various places, and Oz had custody, he'd been brought up by Susie, hence the name by which he always called her. But he didn't, he sat there stoically and it was I who felt my eyes go moist. *Twice in two days, Ice Maiden,* I thought. *What's happening?*

'She was very ill, wasn't she? Janet told me,' he added, 'after she'd spoken to her.'

'Yes, she was. She was very frail, and in her condition, many things could have gone wrong any time. From what Audrey told me, I'd guess she had a brain haemorrhage, and died pretty much instantly.'

'Was Duncan there?'

'Yes, apparently so.'

'What's going to happen now? Does that mean that Duncan's going to be Janet and wee Jonathan's stepfather?'

'I suppose it does.'

He glared at me. 'Mum, we can't let that happen. He's not a good man. They have to live with us.'

'Tom,' I sighed, 'that's easier said than achieved. It's never that simple. Like it or not, Duncan and Susie were married when she died. You're their half-brother, but I have no relationship to them at all. I suppose I could petition the court.'

'You could, Mum,' he insisted. 'Duncan won't want two kids. Why shouldn't he let them live with us?'

'These are not two ordinary kids,' I pointed out, 'any more than you are, given that your father was a famous man, and still is. Christ, there have been as many sightings of Oz Blackstone as there were of Elvis after he died! Tom, you are all wealthy kids and Susie's will is going to make you even wealthier. If I can speak to you as if you were all grown up, not just two-thirds of the way there, I think Duncan Culshaw is a greedy, grasping son-of-a-bitch, and he's unlikely to give up control of Janet and Jonathan's wealth. Understand?'

He nodded. 'Maybe Uncle Harvey could fix it. He's a lawyer.'

'Yes, but he's not that sort of lawyer any longer. He's a judge. We couldn't take a case to him, because he knows us.'

'Okay, maybe he could get one of his pals to fix it!'

I smiled at his remaining innocence . . . or was I the innocent, and was he right? Do the courts really work on the old pals principle? It didn't fucking help me when I was in the dock, that's for sure.

'We have to wait and see what happens, but I promise, I won't let anything bad happen to those kids. And nor,' I reminded him, 'will Conrad Kent. Speaking of whom,' I concluded, 'I must call Audrey again, like I promised I would.' I picked up my coffee and took a sip, but it was cold, and anyway, I didn't fancy it any longer.

'Be a love,' I asked him. 'Go and get me a drink. White wine; biggest glass they've got.'

He looked at his watch, raised an eyebrow.

'Hey,' I exclaimed, 'gimme a break.'

As he walked over to the self-service bar, I called Audrey back. 'How are things?' I asked. A damn silly question, looking back on it; unless Susie had suddenly stopped being dead, 'things' were not going to be any better.

'I'm still in the VIP lounge. They've taken Susie's body away to a hospital in Nice. A police officer came with the ambulance crew. I tried to persuade him to let me take her to Monaco, but no way. I've just spoken to the British Embassy in Paris, and told them what's happened. They're going to get involved, and send a consular observer to the autopsy. It's a judicial procedure; the authorities have to satisfy themselves that the death was natural. Once they've done that, they'll release the body.'

'Who'll organise the funeral?'

'Me, if I'm still around. I've just had a blazing row with Duncan. He knows about our being appointed to the board. It went public as scheduled; the text that he had must have tipped him off. As soon as he finished that phone call I told you about earlier he came storming in here and started yelling at me, even though I was in the middle of talking to the police officer. What the hell did I think I was playing at, I'd manipulated a dying woman, and it was all that witch Primavera's doing; nasty, furious, threatening stuff. Eventually the policeman intervened, and told him to have some respect. Duncan didn't understand him, of course, so he just carried on. He might have been arrested if the airport manager hadn't intervened and explained who he was, and that he'd just lost his wife. He quietened down after that, and walked out again.

I don't know where he is now. And I don't know what to do.'

'That's obvious, Audrey. You get yourself back to Monaco as fast as you can; it's essential that you're there when Conrad gets back with the kids. Have you called him?'

'Not yet. It's not easy; the children will be in the car with him.'

Tom appeared at my side with a large glass of yellow-hued wine. 'Don't say anything about what's happened,' I suggested. 'Just ask him what time he expects to arrive, and tell him that things have changed with Susie, and that you're not going to Scotland any more.'

'But I have to, Primavera; the board meeting.'

'There will be a quorum without you, trust me. You're needed in Monaco; things have happened over the last couple of days to make that essential, now that Susie's gone. Listen,' I said, 'Susie's intention in appointing us to the board was to protect the children's interests. That was when she was alive, and it's all the more important now that she isn't; you have to be with them. I will handle the board meeting on my own, don't worry.'

'What about the other things she asked you to do for her? Setting up the trust, her will?'

'I don't know. She gave me a very clear written mandate, and her signed authority to implement it. It's clear that while she accepted Duncan as her husband, she didn't want him controlling her kids' inheritance in the event of her death.'

'Maybe we've got him wrong,' Audrey said. 'Perhaps he'll agree to what Susie wanted.'

'Can you see the sky where you are?' I asked.

'Yes,' she replied, puzzled.

'Are there any pigs up there? Audrey, don't be naive; all the peaches have fallen off the tree at once and landed in bloody Duncan's lap. Damn it!' I snapped. 'Why the hell did she have to fly so soon? Didn't she know how fragile she was?'

'Yes, she did. Her doctor spelled it out for her the last time she saw him. He was okay with the Vegas trip, but told her she should stay in Arizona for another two weeks at least, preferably a month, with her platelet levels being monitored, before even thinking about flying transcontinental. He said her blood chemistry was still too unstable.'

'Was Duncan aware of that?'

'Yes, we both sat in on the meeting.'

'And he let her fly?'

'Yes, but so did I, Primavera, so did I. I didn't want her to, but she insisted; she told me that she knew she was going to die soon anyway, and wanted to see her kids before she did. I suggested that we could fly Janet and wee Jonathan out to Arizona, but she said the trip would be too tough for them, since they would know why they were going, or at least Janet would, for sure. Duncan backed her up; he said that if I didn't book the flights, he would.'

'God,' I snapped. 'You're making it sound as if he wanted her to die.' I'd forgotten completely that Tom was sitting alongside me. At the edge of my vision I saw him stiffen in his chair, glanced at him and saw his eyes ablaze with a fury that his wing chun master definitely would not have liked.

'I'm only telling you how it was,' she replied. 'Do you know what her last words were? After she said she was going to sleep on the flight to be alert when she met the kids, she said, "I'm not looking forward to telling them what I've done." Now I'll have to tell them, unless Duncan gets to them first.'

'You won't,' I said. 'They know already. And they're not happy.'

'In that case, I've got to go, now. I've just seen, literally a couple of seconds ago, Duncan getting into a taxi, and you can bet he's heading for Susie's. The swine's even left me to take care of the baggage.'

'Then get off your mark and call me later, in Glasgow.'

I ended the call. 'What did you mean?' Tom asked, immediately. 'About him wanting Susie Mum to die?'

'Nothing. Forget I said it. I was angry, like you're always telling me not to be.'

'If Dad was alive, he'd be angry,' he countered.

'If your dad was alive, Duncan wouldn't be there, would he?'

I sighed, feeling suddenly tired myself. I thought of Susie on her last flight and had a moment of panic. What if I wasn't here either? None of us know the moment when it will end.

I needed comfort. I called Liam.

'Hey,' he said, cheerily. 'Are you not on board yet?'

I told him what had happened, and put an end to his happy morning. 'Oh shit,' he murmured. 'That's terrible. I am so sorry. Those poor kids.'

'Yup.'

'What are you going to do? Go to Monaco or come back here?'

'Neither. Audrey's staying at home, but I still have to go to Glasgow; there will be a board meeting in the morning and I will be in the chair, as Susie wanted it.'

'How's that going to go down?'

'With the bereaved widower? Spectacularly badly. With the rest of the board? I have no idea. But I have to do it.'

'Wish I could help,' he murmured.

'You just did. Be there when I get back, okay?'

He chuckled. 'I will, I will, honest.'

I ended the call and went to check the flight status. It showed 'Boarding'. We didn't rush to get there, as we were fast-track category, and by the time we did, most of the passengers were in place. I let Tom have the window place. He shoved his man-bag under the seat in front, once he'd retrieved his iPad (a Christmas present from Grandpa Mac; Janet had the same) and the Bose in-ear phones he'd had from me, and held them in his lap, obedient to the regulations, until we were in the air and the seat-belt sign was off, when he disappeared into a combination of Beyoncé and a Spanish e-novel called *The Sun over Breda*, one of the adventures of Arturo Pérez-Reverte's swashbuckling swordsman, Captain Alatriste.

He didn't say much during the flight, even declining the meal, and I left him to his thoughts. He'd been introduced to death far too young to understand it fully . . . 'Who does?' you might ask . . . and I wondered whether the latest encounter would make him revisit the first.

Once we touched down in Heathrow, however, he was his usual self. Just as well, for I didn't need any hassle. I'm one of those people who will take any alternative to flying through Heathrow, particularly when I have to change terminals, and my pawing in Barcelona had made me even less enthusiastic as I approached the transfer process. But we got lucky. The bus left as soon as we stepped on and our business class status speeded us through security. The lounge was packed, in complete contrast to the other one, so busy that we went for a Starbuck's instead, and a sandwich, since Tom had decided that finally he was hungry. Looking back, the journey and its complexities formed a bubble around us both, one that isolated us from the awful thing that had happened earlier. It would come back to haunt us later, I knew, but at that moment, the presence of so much bustling life around us kept the dead at bay.

The London-Edinburgh leg was more crowded, and with only a single class of travel in that flight, less comfortable. We were in the third row, seats A and B. C was already occupied when we arrived, by a guy who looked as if he'd been a rugby prop forward in his youth, and had put on a lot of weight since. Tom gave him one glance and pushed me towards the window seat.

We arrived on time, and amazingly, so did our luggage. We wheeled it to the Hertz desk . . . quite a long wheel in Edinburgh these days, and soon we were on our way. It had been a while since I was last in Glasgow, so I was grateful for the satnav that Audrey had specified when she'd booked the car. It's not that I don't know how to find the city, but road systems change all the time, and in some it's possible to see your destination without being able to get anywhere near it, if you don't know exactly how. I needn't have worried, though; West George Street still ran in the same direction as it had the last time I was there. We came off the M8 and more or less drove straight to the door.

I let the door crew take care of the luggage and of parking the car, and led Tom through the imposing entrance into the foyer of a building that had once been an episcopal church.

There have been times in my life, very few of them, when I've refused to believe the evidence of my own eyes. That was one of them. There was a guy standing beside reception, and for a moment I thought it was Liam, but I dismissed the silly notion and marched on without giving him a second glance, until Tom exclaimed, 'Hey, how did you get here? You were in St Martí when we were at Barcelona Airport.'

'That is true, buddy,' he conceded, 'but what's the point of being a GWA superhero if you don't exercise your superpowers from time to time?'

I stared at him, still in denial. 'But . . .' was all I could say, and then he smiled and I more or less melted into him. 'But,' I sighed, 'I am so fucking glad you're here. I don't know why, for I am a forceful and independent woman . . . "My Way" could have been written for me . . . but I am. Now, how the hell did you manage it?'

'You can thank my ex,' he said, as I released him from my grasp. 'After you called, I was sitting there worrying about you two. I reckoned a little back-up wouldn't do any harm even if I couldn't get to you till tomorrow. So I went online and saw there was a flight from Girona to Prestwick, today, with a couple of hours to departure. It was showing "Full" but I took a wild chance and phoned Erin. Miracle of miracles, her husband was the pilot; she called him and he got me a jump seat. I made it to the airport just in time. Honest, I'll never say another bad word about the guy, or about his airline.'

'When did you get here?'

'About two minutes ago. I was just in the process of booking myself a room when you walked through the door.'

'You don't need to do that,' Tom volunteered. 'We've got a room spare, now that Audrey isn't coming.'

That was true, but it wasn't how I wanted things to work out. I looked at Liam. 'Wait there and do nothing,' I ordered.

I took my son across to the window to the right of the door. 'It's big boy time,' I said. 'How would you feel if Liam and I shared a room?'

'Would it be forever?' he asked.

'I have no idea. But he's a good man, I like him and I want to be with him just now. Could you handle that?'

He looked up at me, but only up by a couple of inches. 'In my English class,' he began, 'we've been doing a poem called "The Lady of Shallot". Do you know it?'

I nodded. 'Yes, by Alfred, Lord Tennyson. I love it. It's how our language is supposed to be. Do you like it?'

'No,' he replied. 'Because when I read the words, they make me think of you, and that's sad. Dad's dead, Mum, he's not coming back, and it's time you had a loyal knight and true, not just a pageboy like me. I don't want you to wind up like the Lady did.'

Profound? All parents think we know our kids, and what their capabilities are, but mostly we're wrong. Our expectations are usually over the top, or we take the gloomy view, that they'll get by and that'll be enough. I've always tried to expect nothing of Tom, other than decency, honesty and integrity, and he's shown me every one of those. But when he said that to me, I was plain flat out astonished.

'How long have you thought that way?' I asked.

'For a while now. I want you to be happy. I wouldn't want you to be with a *culo* like Duncan Culshaw, but you're too sensible ever to pick anyone like him. I like Liam, so if you want to live *en pareja* with him, I won't mind.'

'I'll still be your best pal, you know,' I said.

'You'll still be my mum and that's the important thing.'

I gave him a quick kiss on the forehead and then returned to reception, where I did a deal. Two minutes later, Liam and I had what they called a Rock 'n' Roll suite, for a reason that still escapes me, and Tom had a room along the corridor. It had just gone six thirty; I booked a table in the brasserie for half past eight and told Tom that we'd knock on his door on the way down.

You probably imagine that we put those two hours to good use. You'd be quite right, but you may continue to imagine the details, for I'm not planning to describe them. There was a moment when it did seem a little weird to be in bed with a man on the day that a long-standing friend had died, but it didn't take me longer than another moment to realise that if our roles in the day's drama had been reversed, Susie would have done exactly the same thing.

The only things I will say are that it was good, and that having a man's seed sown deep inside me . . . don't worry, I was nowhere near ovulation, although I made a mental note to go back on the pill for as long as I needed it . . . put my Barcelona bunny friend in its proper perspective. I made a mental note to attend the next Estartit car boot sale and slip it into someone's car, in a box labelled 'Ten euro' when they weren't looking. I had the very lady in mind for the nice surprise.

We didn't talk much, Liam and I, not for a while at any rate, not until we were soaping each other in the suite's enormous shower . . . you could have fitted the whole Rock 'n' Roll band in there. 'Tom okay?' he asked me, finally.

'Tom is fine. He sees you as Lancelot . . . and I want no lewd cracks about that name,' I added, as I explained what he'd said about Tennyson's poem.

'Bloody hell!' Liam exclaimed. 'I assume he takes his sensitivity from his mother's side of the family, for it was never evident in his old man, not that I could see.' As he spoke, he felt his nose, checking that it was intact.

I smiled. 'As a matter of fact, he does. My mother was an author, and my dad, whom I plan for you to meet later this week, is a craftsman, in wood. That's if you're willing, of course. I'll understand if you don't want to get involved with families yet.'

'Given the disaster that mine was?'

'No! I didn't mean that at all. The thought never occurred to me. We've only known each other . . . or been reacquainted . . . for three days. This could be just a fling for both of us. I'm not naive; I understand that. Christ, man, we live on different continents.'

'One day at a time, sweet Jesus,' he sang softly, in a rather nice tenor voice. 'Primavera, my love,' I smiled, a little coyly no doubt, at his use of the 'L' word, 'I can't wait to meet your old man. You're forgetting, he's the only member of your family I haven't met yet, given that I've worked for your brother-in-law a couple of times, and met your sister in the process.'

'In that case, prepare yourself for a gentle interrogation in Auchterarder, and for being taken to the pub. My father's not a big boozer, but he does like an occasional pint of Guinness . . . don't worry, though, he won't force it on you.'

We stepped out of the shower and towelled ourselves dry, then I shooed him from the bathroom. 'I've got to do my hair and put my face on,' I told him. 'For that I need space and privacy.' I checked the time. 'Go on, get dressed, we're running late.'

I was also running on empty. I'd had a long, eventful, and inevitably tiring day. I needed refuelling, for I had to prepare for the board meeting next morning and that would mean another early start. It took me less than five minutes to make myself reasonably presentable; my hair is never a problem and I restricted myself to what I call a half face, that being more make-up than I usually wear but not the full works.

I was in the Rock 'n' Roll bedroom of our Rock 'n' Roll suite, dressing for dinner, when the phone rang. Liam . . . why are men always ready first? . . . picked it up.

'Yes?' The inevitable pause. 'No, reception was correct,' he continued. 'This is Primavera's room. Hold on a second, and I'll pass you across to her.'

I stepped round the bed and took the handset from him. 'Woman,' he mouthed silently.

'Hi,' I began, as he read my mind and moved behind me to finish the job of fastening my bra. 'Primavera.'

'Who the hell was that?' Audrey gasped. 'And don't tell me it was Tom. I know his voice is changing, but that one belongs to somebody else.'

'Ask Conrad,' I told her. 'He'll be able to work it out. Or ask Janet; so will she.'

'I will, don't worry. Whoever he is, he sounds, mmm, interesting.'

'You got that right,' I agreed. 'How are the children?'

'As you'd expect,' she replied. 'They were both stunned when we told them. Wee Jonathan's in pieces. I've left Janet to look after him. She's done her crying, for now at least, and she's in control of herself.'

'What about Duncan?'

'Not a problem, as yet. He tried to . . . let's say, assert himself as the new head of the house before they arrived, when it was just the two of us there and the housekeeper. "I'm the children's daddy now," he said. We had a bit of a confrontation; I told him that might be so, but they barely knew him, and that if he ever wanted to have any sort of a relationship with either of them it shouldn't begin by him telling them their mother was dead, and that he had to leave that to me. I'd already sent Conrad a text, letting him know what had happened. Duncan got the message. He was there when they arrived, but backed off as soon as he'd said hello . . . or tried to. Wee Jonathan spat at him as soon as he saw him. Now he's staying away from them. To be honest, Primavera, I don't believe he's interested in them. He's been on the phone for half the day, but I don't know to whom.'

'Uncle Phil?' I suggested.

'That's a real possibility. I had a call from him a few hours ago. He said that he'd been advised by the company secretary of my appointment to the board and asked if I'd be at the meeting tomorrow. I told him that, in the circumstances, I couldn't attend. Then he said, "In those same circumstances, we should cancel it, shouldn't we?" I replied that that would need the approval of the chair. He asked how he could contact you, and I told him you were in transit, bound for Edinburgh. I lied a little; I said you probably wouldn't be contactable this evening. Mind you, maybe it wasn't a porky after all, given who answered the phone.'

'Whatever,' I said, 'you did the right thing. Does Phil Culshaw know I'm here?'

'Yes. He asked for the name of the hotel and I couldn't not tell him. But I said that you probably wouldn't be there until the evening.'

'Even at that,' I pointed out, 'it's nearly half past eight. I'd have thought he'd have called by now.'

'Will you cancel the meeting if he asks?'

'No way. This is a listed company, and we must give the impression of business as usual. I have to get my arse firmly planted in that chair, right away.'

'But who'll control it, Primavera, who'll really control it?'

'That's the question. You go and look after those kids and leave me to work that out. I'll keep you informed of what's happening here. Bye.'

I hung up, frowning as I pulled my top over my head . . . carefully, not disturbing my hair.

'How are they?' Liam asked, quietly, from the bedroom doorway.

'Bereft,' was the only word I could find to reply as I moved to join him. 'It makes me shudder, to think of what they must be feeling right now. Tom too, to an extent; he and Susie were close. She was his stepmother, remember.'

'Of course.' He took my hand, and I leaned against him for a couple of seconds, enjoying the sheer, long-forgotten luxury of having someone with whom I could do that.

'Okay, Lance,' I said. 'Let's go and knock on his door. He must be hungry and I am thirsty. In fact I feel like getting pissed, an option that a single mother has very rarely; so please, honey, make sure I don't.'

'That'll be easy. Drink the same as Tom and me, and you'll be fine.'

I smiled as I remembered our first dinner together, forty-eight hours before, when I'd somehow got, or felt, half cut on sparkling water, as my protective barriers began to collapse. 'I should be wearing the Versace, shouldn't I?' I chuckled.

'Yeah, you should. You'd have had to pack one fewer flimsy if you'd brought it.'

I gazed at him. 'You knew I wasn't wearing any?' I exclaimed. 'Is it cut so low you could see my minge?'

'Not quite, but it is tight. When we went into the restaurant and I was walking behind you, well, let's just say there was something in the way you moved.'

'Oh no! Then most of the people in the square that night . . . and all the women, trust me . . . will know that Primavera was out with a man, *sin bragas*.'

'*Si*,' he agreed. 'Y *por qué no?*'

'You speak Spanish?' I gasped.

'*Solo pocito*. But as a global-travelling single man you'd expect me to know the word for knickers, surely.'

Twelve

We knocked on Tom's door a minute after the promised time. He must have been waiting behind it, for it opened in one second flat. It was clear he saw it as a special occasion, for the boy who would normally dine with his mother on a June evening wearing shorts and a cap-sleeved T that showed off his thickening biceps was dressed in creased, dark, long trousers, a conventional pale blue shirt and his black soft leather jerkin. I glanced at his feet. My God, he was wearing black shoes . . . and socks!

He looked different, a boy who'd taken a firm step up the ladder to manhood. Having reclaimed my womanhood, I wondered whether he saw a change in me.

He had his iPad tucked under his arm. 'Do we need that?' I asked. He nodded, frowning slightly, and so I didn't take it further.

He waited until we were seated at our table, before flipping back the tablet's blue cover, and handing it to me. 'I thought you'd want to see that, Mum,' he said.

Tom's a regular trawler of news sites, among them the BBC. The page he showed me was from its Scottish section, a report headed, 'Oz Blackstone widow dies'.

Immediately below was a photograph of Susie, taken some years ago, with Oz; around ten, I reckoned, for she was pregnant with wee Jonathan and they were on the red carpet at a movie premiere. I read the story.

Scottish business is today mourning the death of Susie Gantry (40) who passed away this morning at Nice Airport, after touching down on a flight from Paris, the last leg of a journey from Arizona, where it is understood she had been receiving treatment for leukaemia.

Her death came minutes after the company she controlled, The Gantry Group PLC, announced that she was stepping down temporarily as chairman, to be replaced by her friend Mrs Primavera Blackstone, the Scottish film legend's second wife, and mother of their son, Tom. Tragically, Ms Gantry, three times winner of the Scottish Businesswoman of the Year award, was accompanied on her last journey by her second husband, the Scottish writer Mr Duncan Culshaw. The couple were married in a whirlwind ceremony in Las Vegas only last week.

This afternoon Mr Culshaw was unavailable for comment at the family home in Monaco, where he was understood to be comforting his two stepchildren, Janet and John.

His uncle, Mr Philip Culshaw, the chief executive officer of the Gantry Group, said, 'We are all devastated by this tragedy. The company has a board meeting scheduled for tomorrow, but it is questionable whether it can proceed. In the meantime, shareholders can be assured that its business will continue as usual, in their best interests.'

Sources close to Duncan Culshaw added that he was overcome by the tragedy, but that he would protect his stepchildren's interests as their new guardian.

I was steaming mad as I handed the iPad to Liam, but I kept quiet until he'd finished reading, and handed it back to Tom. 'Two points,' I said, when he had. 'Phil Culshaw is not the CEO of the Gantry Group, and he never has been. Susie always had executive control, until this morning. I'm the new chair, and I will have a part to play in deciding who the new chief executive will be. Second, he can question all he likes, but the board meeting is going ahead. If he thinks I can be brushed aside . . .'

Liam touched my arm. 'Darlin',' he murmured. 'Be cool. This man worked with Susie for years. He'll be as shocked as the rest of us, so it's best not to make judgements on what he says in the immediate aftermath, based on quotes in a report that can't even get the kids' names right.'

I frowned. 'Granted. But surely to God he's not so dazed and confused that he isn't making a point of getting in touch with me. He knows where I am. Audrey told him.'

'Oh.' Tom's voice was a murmur but it carried across the table.

'What?' I asked.

'I had a phone call,' he said, 'in my room. I picked it up and I answered.'

'How did you answer?'

'I said *Digue* at first, then I remembered where I was and said, "Yes?" the way you tell me to answer the phone in English.' It's true; I taught him to give nothing away before the caller's identified himself. 'There was a silence and then a man said, "Is that . . . ?" then he stopped and said, "No, that's absurd, it can't be. I'm sorry, I must have the wrong room," and then he hung up.'

'The voice,' I asked. 'What can you remember about it? Young or old? What accent?'

'Older. And he was Scottish, a bit like Grandpa Blackstone, but it definitely wasn't him.'

I looked at Liam. 'Culshaw?'

'Probably.'

'But why was he put through to Tom's room?'

My new partner beamed, and his eyes twinkled behind the specs. 'Because I signed for our room. As far as reception's concerned, you're Mrs Matthews. If Culshaw asked, "Do you have a guest named Blackstone?" they'd put him through to Tom automatically.'

'Okay, I can see that, but when he picked up, why should he ring off like that?'

'The only thing I can imagine,' Liam replied, 'is that he

thought he was talking to a ghost. When Tom used his telephone voice just now, it dropped an octave, and went right down to where it's headed full-time. It even gave me a start and I'm sitting across the table from him. Culshaw must have known Oz well. To hear his son, out of the blue, without knowing who it was . . .'

Of course. I remembered I'd warned Susie about that very thing, in one of our last conversations. And that made me think of her, and realise that we'd never speak again, and that she would never have the shock of hearing her stepson answer the phone in his father's voice.

And that made me whisper, 'Poor Susie,' lay my head on Liam's solid, comforting shoulder and shed a few tears.

He slipped an arm around me, with Tom, my young man, looking on. When I was okay and had dried my eyes, thankful that I hadn't given myself the full treatment and wasn't in need of repair, I was aware that there was a waitress hovering, ready to take our orders. I hadn't even looked at the menu, so I told Liam that fish of the day would be fine by me, if that's what he fancied; he did. Tom is still a full-on carnivore; he opted for steak and chips.

I went with Liam's suggestion and joined the guys in the fizzy water. 'Should you call Culshaw?' he asked as we waited for the bowl of green salad that he'd ordered as our starter.

'Hell, no. If I did, we'd probably get into an argument about whether the meeting should go ahead or not. I don't need that right now . . . nor is there any need for it. The company secretary had his instructions. It's been convened. End of story.'

'What's the agenda?'

'The usual; minutes of previous meeting, chair's remarks, review of current activities, finance director's report, any other competent business.'

'Will there be?'

'Other business? Almost certainly, but I'll decide whether it's competent or not.'

Liam smiled. 'You're looking forward to it, aren't you?'

'No,' I protested. 'It's the last thing I wanted to be doing.'

'But you are. Susie's destiny has affected yours. Yes, you could walk away and decline the chair. You could still do that with a one-page letter. But you won't because it's not in your nature. Your blood's up, you're seeing enemies in the shadows, and you're spoiling for a fight.'

I raised an eyebrow. 'You reckon?'

'I do. When I was in the GWA, we all played characters, and that was mine. For a while it was me for real, too, until I got straightened out.'

'But my enemy isn't in the shadows. He's Duncan Culshaw. We've clashed before, and he threatened me again a couple of days ago. He told me he was out to destroy Oz's memory.'

Tom straightened in his seat, his face darkening; he hadn't known that.

'That was before Susie's death, and it was bluster,' Liam said. 'I won't ever let that happen, I promise you. If you ask me, Culshaw was only ever out to make a fast buck for himself. That's what his extortion attempt was about. As Susie's widower, he's achieved that, so why should he bother with you any longer?'

'Because it's personal between us?' I suggested.

'If so, he's made a big mistake and he'll discover that. As of now it isn't just between you two,' he nodded in Tom's direction, 'and him. A threat to either of you is a threat to me, and I'll deal with it.'

'How?' I asked.

'Simple. I'll visit him and tell him to stop.'

'When you do,' Tom murmured, 'can I come?'

'As long as you promise not to get angry with him.'

'I promise. I know, Liam,' he added. 'Anger weakens me.'

'In that case I'll barely be able to lift that fork in front of me,' I told them both. 'For what I feel about the man goes way beyond anger.'

'Which is why you must put him out of your mind,' my man declared. 'He won't be in the room at your meeting tomorrow, and you mustn't give him access through your thoughts.'

As he spoke, the salad bowl arrived. One of us had been wrong, for not only had I the strength to lift the cutlery, I wolfed my way through half of it.

Dinner was over by nine fifty-five. There were a few people in the bar, but Liam and I didn't even think about joining them. Instead we went upstairs with Tom, and straight to our rooms. I warned him not to stay up late watching television, realising at the same time that his own hotel room was effectively his own household, and that he could bloody well do what he chose.

I switched on the *Ten O'Clock News* on BBC as soon as the door closed behind us. *Still thinking like a single person, Primavera*. 'I'm sorry,' I said. 'Did you have other ideas?'

'Maybe,' Liam grinned, 'but watching the TV news shouldn't knock them on the head.'

We sat on the couch in the Rock 'n' Roll sitting room, and watched as the day's events unfolded. I hadn't expected Susie's death to make the national news, but it was second lead in the Scottish segment that followed. It was no more than a video version of the report I'd read, but with some library footage of Susie with Oz and a clip of Phil Culshaw being interviewed. I'd seen a still picture, but you can never be quite sure when those were taken, and a good photographer can be a really accomplished liar. I tried to picture Duncan in his late sixties, but couldn't see much of a family resemblance. I hoped that extended to his character as well, noting the truth that it was the BBC who'd described him as CEO, and not a title he'd claimed for himself.

I turned the telly off as the end credits ran. 'You want first shot in the bathroom?' Liam asked.

'No,' I replied. 'You go ahead. I've got one thing left to do.'

I'd put my phone to sleep during dinner, so I wakened it and checked to see if I'd missed any calls or texts. I hadn't so I used it to call the landline number in St Martí, and punched in a code to interrogate my voicemail there.

I had two messages. The first was from Miles, my brother-in-law.

'Hi, Primavera,' he began. There's virtually no Australian left in his accent; today it's nearly all Californian. 'I just had a call from your father, telling me about Susie. That'll be bad news for Tom even more than for you, but I guess you parted on good terms, since David said she's made you chairman of her company. If there's any help I can give you, or any advice on your new role, you just have to pick up the phone. Say hi to our nephew, from us and his cousin.' I thought he was done, but he carried on. 'By the way, I spoke to an old acquaintance of yours a while back, Liam Matthews. He's at a bit of a crossroads in his life. His partner left him for somebody else a while back, and he's been on a bit of a downer ever since. He told me he was going travelling, and it struck me that you two might be good for each other, so, I hope you don't mind, I took a big chance and suggested he looked you up. Don't be surprised if he does.'

Miles's offer made me feel good, although I'd always been confident that he'd be there for me if needed. So did the second part of his message.

The other call was much more disturbing. It was from Oz's father, Grandpa Mac, and he was far from cool and composed.

'Primavera,' he barked. 'I've just heard about Susie. I didn't even know she was ill. You think somebody would have told me since she's the mother of two of my grandchildren. But maybe not, since she and I were never the best of friends after the way she split you and Oz up. Anyway, what's this about her having married again? Did you know about it? And how does it affect Janet and wee Jonathan? I've called Monaco, of course. I spoke to Janet . . . Hardly recognised her. God, she's grown up . . . and I asked to speak to this man Culshaw, but Audrey said he wouldn't take my call. Then I remembered the guy. He came to see me last year, to interview me for a book he claimed to be writing based on Oz's life. I didn't take to him, so I didn't tell him much. I've heard neither hide nor hair of him since, or of the book, and now he shows up married to Susie and claiming to be my grandchildren's guardian! What the fuck's going on, Primavera? Call me as soon as you get this, please.'

Mac is normally a placid guy, as laid-back as Oz was until Jan died and everything started to change. But when he goes off on one, he goes, and you see the side of him that Ellie's inherited. I'd decided that it was too late to phone him back and that I'd do it in the morning, when I realised that my suite-mate was standing in the doorway, leaning casually against the jamb, barefoot and shirtless but still in his jeans.

'Everything okay?' he asked.

'Just hold that pose,' I ordered.

I took a photograph with my phone and sent it straight to Miles, with a message that read, 'At a crossroads, did U say? Gone travelling? We'll see about that.'

And then I took him to bed, and gave him good cause to stay put for a while.

I'd hoped to sleep until seven thirty, giving me time to be completely ready for the meeting but my sister knocked that on the head by calling my mobile at six forty-five. My ringtone is Bruce Springsteen's 'Born to Run'. But I'm usually awake when it goes off.

I woke and sat bolt upright within a couple of seconds, and for a few more I was very disorientated. Christ, there was a man lying beside me and we were both naked! Then everything fell into place, and I snatched the phone from the bedside table much too late to prevent Liam from stirring.

I swiped the screen to take the call, rolling out of bed as I did so. 'Do you know what fucking time it is, Dawn?' I mumbled.

'Quarter to ten here,' she replied cheerfully. 'You're lucky I didn't call you straight away, after you sent Miles that photo. What have you been up to? Or were you still up to it? Did I *interruptus* the *coitus*?' Those are the only two Latin words that ever stuck in Dawn's head. The rest passed all the way through, largely unimpeded.

'No, you did not,' I told her, firmly.

'Prove it, then. Put me on video. Ever since you and Oz caught Miles and me on the job in your flat I've been waiting for a chance to get even.'

'Bugger off!'

'How did it happen?' she laughed. 'Did he drug you? I thought you were off men forever.'

'So did I, but I'm glad to say I was wrong. Now go away. I have some serious business to do this morning. We're in Glasgow and I have to chair a board meeting later.'

'Yes, of course.' Her tone changed completely. 'Tragic

about Susie.' 'Tragic' is another Dawnism, but for once it was accurate. 'Call me later and we can have a longer chat.'

'I will do,' I promised. 'In six or seven hours.' I ended the call, leaving her to do the sum on her fingers. (Actually my sister isn't that dumb; that's just a game we've played since she was a kid.)

I put the phone down and got back into bed. 'Does that happen every morning in your life?' Liam asked.

I slid up against him, and my eyes widened. 'No,' I replied, 'but I hope that does in yours.'

By the time we'd done something about it, I was on the schedule I'd set for myself. I showered and did all the other morning stuff, then dug my laptop from its bag and logged on to the hotel's wireless network. Audrey had promised to send me a briefing for the meeting, most importantly the minutes of the last two . . . they were usually held quarterly . . . and the latest set of management accounts, that Susie received on a monthly basis.

Once I'd downloaded them, I called Tom. He was awake and I could hear *Daybreak* in the background. His interest in the female presenter seems to be growing; it's a toss-up between her and the witch in Merlin as to who's his top girl. A sign of the times. I asked him to join us for room service breakfast at eight thirty, then called to order it. With all that done, I began to study Audrey's documents.

The minutes didn't tell me anything that I didn't know in broad terms already. As Tom's guardian I had oversight of the equity in the company that he'd inherited from Oz, and so I received all the company's shareholder communications, and was aware of its business. The Gantry Group was split into divisions: property management, leisure and development. It owned a large portfolio of economic rent housing, commercial offices, retail parks and a chain of pubs and boutique hotels; they made up the first two divisions. The development side held its construction interests, in private housing for owner-occupation, factories and commercial buildings.

Given that knowledge, what was in the minutes was mostly old news, apart from one reference to a projected golf course-cum-country club down in Ayrshire: that, I hadn't heard of. (Yes, I know, 'they' say you shouldn't end a sentence with a preposition, but I have news for 'them': language evolves.)

No, it was the management accounts that would give me a detailed insight into how the group was actually running, and how sound its trading position really was. I scanned through them; the information was detailed and it showed that while the group was sound, across the board, it was no more recession-proof than any other company. The rental houses were fine, but there were a number of voids . . . empty units . . . in the office and retail holdings that were pulling down the profits of those sectors. The pubs and hotels were washing their face, but their profit contribution was way below what it should have been, given the value of the assets.

Still, given the economic situation, those two divisions were okay, yet the company's bottom line wasn't. I'd brought the last annual report with me; I dug it out and compared the last year-end figures with the accounts I had on my computer screen, then did some simple calculations in my head. A healthy profit had been reported for the previous year, but I was looking at a future projection of break-even at best, and a chunky loss at worst. The company's year-end was September; just about the time when Susie's illness was diagnosed. She'd been more affected by it than she'd admitted in our conversations, but there was more to it than that. Someone beneath her in the group's hierarchy hadn't been doing his job. I went back into the management accounts and spotted the devil in the detail at once. Construction of private housing and commercial stock had stopped; there were a few high-value houses left unsold but they weren't suicidal. No, it was that damn golf course that was the money pit. Over the previous six months, twenty million pounds had been transferred to the subsidiary company that was executing the venue. Without that, the business would have been far healthier, and obviously its indebtedness would have been that much smaller.

Liam came out of the bedroom as I was looking at the figures. 'Do me a favour, lover,' I asked him. 'Give Tom a call and ask him to get along here now, if he's ready, and to bring his iPad with him.'

'Sure.' He noted what I was doing. 'Trouble at mill?'

'I hope not.'

Rather than call, he walked along the corridor, and returned a couple of minutes later, with my son, who was dressed more like himself, in pirate pants and a T-shirt that he'd blagged from a friend of ours in the village, who combines running a restaurant with a music career. Monoceros, his alter ego, might not have been a household name in Glasgow, but my son was doing his bit to change that. I was pleased that he seemed completely relaxed in Liam's company, and that they were chatting like a couple of old mates.

'When we get back to St Martí, Mum,' he said, 'Liam and I are going to do yoga on the beach in the morning. You can come too, if you like.'

'Maybe I'll just watch,' I replied. Liam and I had been too busy with other things to discuss what was going to happen when we did return home. I was taking nothing for granted. Our three days and one night together had been great, but I was making no assumptions . . . of either of us.

'What do you want me to do with this?' Tom asked, holding up his tablet.

'Can you log on to the BBC website and find out what the Gantry Group share price is doing?'

'Sure, but I can log on to the Stock Exchange as well. That would be quicker. Susie Mum showed me how last time I was in Monaco.'

'Then do it, please,' I asked. It was something I should have done the day before; I'd been asleep at the wheel . . . or maybe the previous day's events had simply overwhelmed me a little.

He nodded and set to work, with a certainty in every step he took and every page he called up. 'The share price fell by twenty-eight per cent yesterday,' he announced, after only a couple of minutes, 'and it's fallen by another twelve per cent this morning.'

I looked at Liam. 'A forty per cent drop,' I exclaimed. 'On the basis of what I've been looking at here it's been overvalued lately, but by nothing like that much. That needs investigating.' I picked up the annual report and looked through the list of the company's professional advisers: auditors, solicitors, stockbrokers, all blue chip, and last of all, financial public relations, a consultancy called Groynes deVelt.

There were contact details for each one; I called the PR people, knowing that if they were any good at all they'd be open during stock exchange hours and beyond. They were; I was answered almost instantly, by an androgynous voice, youngish and pronouncing the firm's name very carefully in a voice that made me wonder if Mick Jagger had sent one of his many kids out on work experience.

'My name is Primavera Blackstone,' I told him/her. 'I'm the new chair of the Gantry Group PLC and I'd like to speak to the person who handles our affairs.'

'Mmmm, let me see, mmm, that would be Cressida Oldham. I'll see if she's available.'

As I waited, patiently, there was a knock at the door. Tom opened it and admitted the room service waiter with breakfast for three on a tray, thanked him and bunged him a couple of coins that I hoped were sterling and not euro.

'Mrs Blackstone,' a decidedly female voice boomed into my ear. 'Cress Oldham here. Look, I hope you don't mind, but since we don't know each other would you mind answering a standard verification question?'

'Depends what it is.'

'Your mother's maiden name?'

I told her and she relaxed. 'How can I help you?'

'You can give me some insight into the company's share price. It's heading groundwards like a skydiver in lead boots. What the hell's going on?'

'Well . . .' she began, giving the impression that she was struggling to come up with a good answer, '. . . Ms Gantry was a strong and prominent company chair, highly regarded by the City. It's quite natural that the share price should have fallen as a reaction to her death. I have to say it might have been wiser to prepare the market for it.'

'As in Susie releasing a statement,' I retorted, 'that her street-smart twelve-year-old daughter might have read, announcing that she was terminally ill? That sort of preparation?'

'Well,' she conceded, 'maybe not.'

'In any event, Ms Oldham,' I continued, 'forty per cent is a hell of a strong reaction.'

'Yes, but . . . Can I be blunt?'

'As blunt as you like. The way I see it, advice only comes in two categories, good and bad. Sugar-coating always leads to the latter, so don't do that with me.'

'Okay. First, the analysts don't know you; you don't have a track record with them. So when you suddenly pop up as the last act of a dying woman, they're likely to see you as a desperation gambit, someone chosen in haste because there was nobody of quality available.'

'I was chosen in haste,' I conceded, 'but Susie could just as easily have appointed someone from the board. She anticipated market reaction; a small initial fall, but nothing to worry about.'

'Yes, but then she died.'

'And three or four per cent suddenly became forty? I might be a novice, but I'm not a fool. There are other factors involved. I want to know what they are. I might have been appointed as non-exec chair, but as you say, Susie's death changes things. I'm forced to be hands on, to protect the shareholders, one of whom is my own son. So trust me, Cress, if you don't spill everything you know and I find out you've held back on me, your firm will be history as far as the Gantry Group is concerned.'

The guys were watching me. Liam was smiling; Tom was looking as if he'd never seen me before, as I laid it on the line for the PR lady.

My message was absorbed. 'Very well,' she said. 'I've been told by a couple of analysts I spoke to in the fifteen or so minutes before you called that someone's been briefing against you. They're saying that you have a criminal conviction for deception, and that you've been in prison.'

'That's true,' I admitted, 'but it was a long time ago and it had nothing to do with any sort of business activity, as Susie Gantry was well aware. You can brief in return that I'm happy to talk to anyone about it and to give them a Nigella-style critique on the standard of catering in HMP Cornton Vale. And you can add, as robustly, and publicly, as you like that anyone who suggests that it makes me an unfit person to hold the chair of a public company will be hit so hard by the ensuing writ that they will be knocked flat on their back. Now please get that message out there, and put a stop to this selling stampede.'

'I will do, I promise,' she replied, 'but there's more. I am reliably informed, although nobody will give me a source, that someone has leaked extracts from the company's recent confidential management accounts. That more than anything else has made the institutional shareholders run for cover.'

That, I hadn't expected. 'Oh shit,' I murmured. 'Now that is trouble. I've just been looking at those, and there's a great big twenty-million pound hole in them. But it's not life-threatening and it's a hole that I intend to plug. Would it help if you put that word around as well?'

'Yes, it would. It would show that the new chairman is firmly in charge, and aware of the company's position.'

'Then do that too. Anything else,' I asked, 'that would turn this around fast?'

'Buying,' she shot back, without any pause for thought. 'At the moment it's all one way, but if a serious investor came in, that would stop it, at the very least.'

'How much?'

'About five million.'

'Ouch! Too rich for me, in cash terms. Some of my personal wealth is in a private investment trust in Canada. I could move some stock around, but it would take time.'

'Maybe the briefing I'm about to do will stimulate some new investors. At the very least it should stop the slide.'

'Let's hope so, but leave it with me anyway.'

'What's up?' Liam asked as I ended the call. 'Come on,' he grinned. 'Tom and I have a right to know. Remember, we're both shareholders.'

'And your shareholdings are under attack,' I retorted. 'We have an enemy.' Breakfast came first, though; there was plenty of it. The trolley was continental rather than the notorious 'full Scottish', which can have pretty much anything on it, including black pudding, fried dumpling and, for all I know, for I'm out of touch, pakora.

Tom started with muesli, with a couple of vanilla yoghurts stirred into it instead of milk, while Liam and I went straight for the fruit. It took us less than ten minutes to demolish everything, down to the last piece of melon and the last slice of toast. Liam's a fairly big guy, Tom's fuelling his growth, and I was unusually hungry. Whether that was because I was nervy in advance of the meeting, or because of my unaccustomed nocturnal exercise I knew not, but whatever the cause I wired in as if I'd been a jungle celebrity and they'd just got me out of there.

Once we were left with nothing but slightly stewed tea, I gave them both a rundown on my discussion with Cressida. Tom stiffened in his chair when I told them that my brief run-in with the law was being used against me. It's a part of my life that he knows about but we don't discuss it.

I tried to tell him once that I did something wrong and that I paid for it, but he asked me, 'Did you think it was wrong?' I told him that at the time, I didn't, but that sometimes the law takes a view that's different from a person's. 'I don't care,' he declared. 'If you thought that what you did was right, then it was. I don't care what the law said.' Ever since then, 'lawyer' has never featured among the future careers included in his list of possibles.

Liam agreed with me that my ball and chain time was ancient history and therefore irrelevant. 'You never did anything remotely as serious as crashing a bank, honey,' he commented, 'and all those guys walked away scot-free. As for whoever's leaking confidential information, in what has to be an attempt to sabotage the company, I'd like to see him thrown in clink. In fact I'd even volunteer to guard the key.'

'What are you going to do, Mum?' Tom asked. Before I had a chance to answer he put a second question. 'Do I have enough money to buy shares?'

Tom knows he's wealthy, but that's about it. Unlike Susie, his father kept his will up to date. In it, he expressed the view that since his wife had a plenty in her own right, she didn't need any of the fortune he left behind him. Therefore, apart from a substantial bequest to a charity established to provide for hard-up actors and actresses, it was divided among his three children to be held in trust until they reached the age of eighteen, in the care of, the will specified, 'their legal guardians'. In Tom's case that's me. His seven-figure inheritance is invested by the same people who look after me, and thanks to the earnings that still accrue to the estate from DVD sales, it's completely recession proof.

And it was going to stay that way. 'Yes,' I told him, 'but

you're not going to. If I let you do that, I'd be gambling with it and I'm not going to do that. Besides, you already own six per cent of the company, and when Susie's affairs are settled, you, your sister and your brother will own a lot more. But your shares will be equal, and I don't believe it would be right to upset that balance.'

'There's nothing to stop me investing, though,' Liam murmured. 'I'm not minted, but I'm comfortable. I have some spare capital, and I was planning to sell my Dublin apartment. I only ever bought that for tax reasons anyway.'

'Five million?'

'No,' he admitted. 'Nowhere near.'

'In which case, boys, I have to look elsewhere. Tom,' I said, 'wheel that trolley out into the corridor, then go and sort out what you're going to need for the day.'

'What am I going to do today, Mum?' he asked.

'Well, you can't come into the meeting,' I said, 'nor can Liam, even though the two of you are both shareholders. So I thought that you might spend the morning getting acquainted with Glasgow and with each other.' I looked at them both. 'How does that sound?'

'Good to me,' my partner agreed. 'There's some new stuff been opened down by the river since the last time I was here. You up for checking that out, Tom?'

He nodded, picked up his iPad and headed for the door, pushing the trolley as requested.

'I'm not rushing you, am I?' I asked Liam, once he'd left. 'If you feel uncomfortable, just say so.'

'About what? I don't see myself as a child-minder. He's a bright, mature kid, and I enjoy his company, just as I enjoyed his father's. If you're worried that I might put myself forward as a replacement, then don't. I'm happy to be his mate and his mentor, but never his dad.'

I hugged him to me. After years with nobody to hug whose head came past my shoulder, I was enjoying the novelty. 'You're a sweet man. I'm going to miss you when you go back to Toronto.'

'It'll be quite a little while before I think of that. You've promised to show me Catalunya, remember. I have a book to do. This morning might help towards that. I brought my camera with me.' He kissed me on the forehead. 'Once the smoke clears, babe, we'll be able to see the future better.'

'Agreed,' I said. 'But one thing I can see already; when we do get back to Spain, you are moving out of that hotel and in with me.'

'What was that you were saying a minute ago, about rushing me?' He laughed.

'I'm sorry,' I murmured, my crest a little fallen. 'Too big a step?'

'Hey, I'm kidding. That would be great, this is great. If Tom's happy with it, let's take our thing for a test drive.'

'Good. Now that's sorted, let me get on with clearing the way so we can go back. I have a call to make.'

Liam went through to the Rock 'n' Roll bedroom and left me to it. I dialled the number, straight from my contacts list. Miles answered, straight away.

'Primavera!' he exclaimed. 'Hussy! I knew you and Liam would get on, but not that well. Your sister has been smirking like the cat that got the cream ever since I showed her that image. Go carefully, both of you, but have fun.'

'Don't worry, Miles. We're both grown-ups; and we like each other. Listen, in your message you said I could come to you for advice.'

'Of course. Shoot.'

I thanked him, and I did.

'I see,' he said slowly, when I was done. 'Someone has got it in for you, in a big way. You reckon it's Susie's new husband, do you?'

'Yes, I do. Who else would it be?'

'I have no idea,' he admitted, 'but why would it be Culshaw? Doesn't he stand to inherit?'

'That's another story. Susie's will was out of date. She never changed it after Oz died. When I showed her the implications of marrying Culshaw, she asked me to do some things to ring-fence the children's interests, and gave me legal authority to act for her. But you're right, even in the absence of a relevant will he's likely to be entitled to a good chunk of her assets.'

'So, I ask again; why would he want to diminish those?'

'To get at me, by hurting Tom. There's something else you don't know.' I hadn't told him about Culshaw's crude attempt to extort two million from me the year before, so I updated him and told him of the get-even threat the shit had made in our last exchange.

240

'Indeed?' Miles growled when I was done. 'Yeah, the guy is a nasty piece of work. But from the sound of things he isn't exactly stupid either. He made that threat while Susie was still alive. You're small beer to him now, Primavera. Still, I don't like the idea of him having any hold over those other two kids of Oz's.'

'How do you think they feel about it?' I said.

'I know, I know.'

'And what can I do about it?' I moaned.

'Could the marriage be declared invalid?' he murmured, more to himself than to me. 'It happened in Vegas, you said?'

'Yes, but that doesn't make it any less valid. Audrey Kent was the witness. I don't imagine there's any doubt about it.'

'No,' he conceded, 'as long as all the legal requirements have been met, and as long as the person who performed the ceremony is fully licensed. Leave it with me. I'll have that checked out. Now, about your problems in the City. If someone in the US accessed, without authority, information that's confidential to the management of a quoted company, and used it in any way, that would break a whole raft of laws. I'm sure it will be the same in the UK. You might want to get back on to your PR people and get a list of anyone they know to have been shown this information. They won't have any sort of privilege; you could go to court to force them to reveal the source.'

'I can do the first part of that in two minutes and instruct the second in not much longer,' I told him.

'Yes but, and there is always a but . . . what if the information hasn't been stolen? Who's on the circulation list?'

'I don't know.'

'Normally it would be the directors and maybe also the
company secretary if he isn't on the board.'

'He isn't.'

'Okay, then if I were you, before I took any action I would
report what you know to the directors and ask them point
blank whether one of them has been leaking information.
They'll scream bloody murder, but you can tell them it's your
duty to ask the question, and they'll have to live with it.'

'What if one of them admits it?' I asked.

'Then you push a pad and a pen across the table and ask
for a resignation letter there and then.'

'It could get messy, Miles.'

'From what you've told me, Primavera, it's messy already.
Your PR lady was right, you need some public support, and
you need it fast.' He paused for a few seconds. 'This golf
course development; what do you know about it?'

'Very little. There's no reference in last year's annual
report, and only a couple of brief items in minutes since then.'

'In that case, you ask the managing director for a full
report, and to account for every penny that's gone into the
development so far. Then you veto any further spend.'

'Can I do that?'

'You're the chair; you can do what you like till the
shareholders stop you.'

'It's my first meeting,' I pointed out. 'I'm a new girl.'

'By the time the meeting begins, you'll be a very powerful new girl.' He laughed.

'How, for God's sake?'

'Sister-in-law,' he drawled, 'I could invest five million in Gantry shares with one call to my London broker. Problem is, if I did that, the city would see through it; it would be me doing a family member a favour. However . . . I have friends, seriously wealthy friends, that I've made even wealthier by giving them crazy returns on their investments in my movie projects. When does your meeting begin?'

I checked my watch. 'An hour and a quarter.'

'In that case, check the company's share price fifteen minutes before, and look for recent acquisitions. When you get in there, lay the information you get on the table, and look around as you do it. If your enemy's in that boardroom, he'll be the one who looks sick.'

My conversation with Miles boosted my confidence for the meeting. I'd had no clear plan of action before, but he'd more or less drafted my agenda. I'd packed a business suit for the occasion, the kind that Susie would have worn, but on impulse, I left it in the case and opted instead for my casual Catalan look, Cardin jeans, a flowery shirt, tucked in, a wide black belt and black moccasins. I wanted to make a statement. I wanted to say to them, 'This isn't someone sent along to play a part and nod her head when required. This is a new broom and watch it, or you will be swept away.'

'You sure?' Liam asked, when I revealed myself.

'Absolutely.'

'Then God help whoever's been making mischief,' he chuckled.

The guys decided that they were going to visit Glasgow's still relatively new Riverside Museum. Tom had done the planning on his iPad and had decided that the best way to get there was by using the dedicated bus service, which runs from the city centre. I let them go on their way, and then called a taxi to take me to the Gantry Group head office. While I waited in the lobby, I went online via my laptop (I'd asked Tom to use his iPad earlier because it's instant, and takes no time to boot up), found the Stock Exchange site, and looked up the Gantry listing. The share price hadn't recovered fully from its slump since Susie's death, but the loss had been halved. As Miles had told me to, I checked recent acquisitions and found an eight million pound purchase by an American corporate buyer. Eight million! Bloody hell, Miles had called in a big favour. I managed to link up to the hotel's printer and ran off a copy, just as my black cab arrived.

Actually they weren't that far away from the hotel, in a modern block on the intersection of Waterloo Street and Wellington Street, nice military names that helped boost my combative mood.

The noticeboard in the foyer told me that the company occupied the third floor. I took the lift up and stepped out, at five minutes to ten.

The first thing I saw was a framed photo of Susie, on a table in front of the reception desk. It was draped in black ribbon and there was a condolence book in front, with a ballpoint pen in a stand. I signed it, glancing at some of the other names; there were many. I recognised a couple of footballers, a musician, and a comedian; three others had added the word 'Councillor' after their names, as a form of underlining.

If I'd been expecting the managing director to be waiting to greet the new chair, I'd have been disappointed. There was no welcoming group in reception. The immaculately dressed woman behind the desk wasn't too effusive either, but I made allowances for that. She'd have known Susie well, no doubt, and had no reason to be cheerful.

She had done her homework, though. She knew who I was. 'Mrs Blackstone,' she said, rising from her chair and coming round from behind the barrier. 'Cathy Black, office manager.' We shook hands, and she ushered me into a corridor to my left. 'Mr Culshaw and the other directors are here already. They're waiting in the boardroom. I'm sorry, I should have said two of the other directors. There's been a formal apology for absence from Mrs Kent.'

I nodded. 'I'm aware of that,' I said. 'She advised me.' I didn't bother to add that she'd also faxed me a proxy form allowing me to vote on her behalf in any division, as I thought fit.

Mrs Black . . . I assumed from the weight on her left-hand ring finger . . . opened a door halfway along the corridor, then followed me into the long room behind. 'I take the minutes of the meetings,' she explained quietly.

My new colleagues were gathered at the far end of the board table, coffee cups and saucers in hand. I'd seen Culshaw on TV the night before of course, and I knew who the others were, since the annual report had included directors' photographs, and the odd one out had to be the company secretary, Wylie Smith, a plump little guy in his forties, who had the air of someone who's always slightly out of breath, a man running for a bus who's never going to catch it.

The other woman in the room, Gillian Harvey, was all smiles in the report mugshot, but not in real life. I'd read up on her; she was a banker, which may have helped explain her cheerless expression as she eyed me up and down, making me feel glad that I'd dressed the way I had. There had been a period in the company's history when its bank had felt it necessary to insist on having someone on the board, and she'd been put in place then. Those days were long gone, but somehow she'd managed to hang around.

Gerry Meek, the finance director, middle-aged, balding and bespectacled, hadn't been foisted on Susie by anyone. He'd been her choice when she had taken complete control of the company from her old man, to replace his less efficient predecessor. He'd been around as she'd rebuilt the group from the mess she'd inherited, so he must have been competent to say the least. Whether he'd also been compliant in recent months, I planned to find out.

Phil Culshaw came towards me, hand outstretched, white-haired, tanned, with the weathered complexion of a sailor. That's what he had been, mostly, easing out of his accountancy firm when Oz had recruited him and brought him in on a temporary basis that had become permanent when he and

Susie had moved offshore. He was smiling, but I eyeballed him and didn't see it reflected there.

'Primavera,' he exclaimed, 'welcome to the Gantry Group. You've met Cathy, let me introduced the rest of my colleagues.' He did the rounds; the two men were pleasant, if diffident, but the grey-haired lady banker gazed at me as if I was a member of a parliamentary select committee.

'Can we have a word in private?' the managing director murmured.

I beamed at him. 'Once I have a coffee in my hand, Mr Culshaw, certainly,' I replied. I used his surname deliberately and spoke loudly enough for the rest to hear.

Wylie Smith rushed to the coffee pot, poured me a cup and handed it to me. I thanked him, declined the Belgian chocolate biscuits, then walked to the other end of the table, leaving Culshaw to follow behind.

'Yes?' I said sweetly, being a bitch and revelling in it. Fucking man had annoyed me, twice, first by using my given name without invitation and second when he'd said 'my colleagues' rather than 'our'. I'd gone in there with the intention of building a high wall in my mind between him and his nephew, but I was having trouble.

'I'm sorry I wasn't able to get hold of you yesterday,' he murmured, dispensing with the smile.

'You got close, though. I assume that was you who spoke to my son in the hotel last night.'

His jaw dropped. 'That was . . . ? My God, I don't mind telling you . . .'

I cut him off. 'You don't have to. I know what you thought. If you hadn't hung up on him, we'd have made contact then. If we had,' I asked, 'what would you have said to me?'

'More or less what I said in my television interview. I'd have asked you about the advisability of continuing with this meeting.'

'That's what I assumed. And I'd have told you then what I'm telling you now, that there is not one good business reason for cancelling it, and several valid ones for pressing ahead, as I intend to do.'

'Then I have to tell you that in my opinion, your taking the chair of this company, unless it's so you can resign immediately, isn't in its best interests.'

I pursed my lips. 'In that case,' I murmured, as I sipped the worst coffee I'd tasted since I left prison, 'we'd better bring the meeting to order, and we'll see what I do.'

I sat myself down in the big chair at the head of the table, that I just knew had been Susie's, and I called along to Wylie Smith, 'Mr Secretary, I'd be grateful if we could convene the meeting now. It's gone ten a.m.'

'Of course, Madam Chairman,' he replied, picking up his papers as I took out my meeting folder and laid my bag on the floor. The other two directors followed suit, although Harvey shot me a glare that made me wonder if she'd gobbed in my coffee when no one was looking.

When everyone was in place, I kicked off.

'The first thing I want to do as your chair,' I began, 'is to call for two minutes' contemplative silence in memory of my friend Susie. I've known her, I believe, for longer than any of you have, so do not any of you think for a second that I feel any lightness in my heart as I sit in her chair. I wish that she was in it, and not me, but she isn't, and so I promise you as I promised her that I will preserve and protect the company that bears her name.'

I fell silent, and so did the others. When the two minutes were up, Wylie Smith signalled the fact by shuffling in his seat and distributing agendas. 'Since this is an unscheduled meeting of the board,' he explained, 'this is a very short list of business. As always it begins with minutes of the last meeting. You have all received them, yes?'

'Taken as read,' Culshaw grunted.

'Was that a motion?' I asked him, calmly.

'Yes,' he replied, 'of course, I'm sorry.'

'Seconded,' Harvey snapped.

I looked at Meek; he nodded approval. 'Agreed,' I declared, glancing at Cathy Black, who was taking what I guessed was old-fashioned shorthand, in a pad.

'Second item on the agenda is chair's remarks,' I noted. 'That's as well, because I have a few.'

'Before we proceed,' Gillian Harvey interrupted, 'I would like to ask you to explain to us your qualifications for chairing this company. Your background calls them into question.'

'What do you mean by that?' I asked her, evenly.

'You have a rather colourful past, if you don't mind me saying so. Is it not the case that you have a criminal conviction?'

I laughed. 'Isn't that funny,' I exclaimed. 'There were

people running around in the City yesterday asking every sector analyst they could find that selfsame question, and here you go and bring it up at a board meeting. Your bank, Miss Harvey; it employs people to run around in the City of London, doesn't it, spreading information and asking questions?'

'Oh, really, that's—'

'True or false?'

'True, but—'

'Stop,' I snapped. 'I have another question. Were any of those people involved in spreading the word about me? But think before you answer. I spoke to Cress Oldham, the company's financial PR adviser, this morning and instructed her to find out who they were. I could receive a text from her at any moment. So once again, were your people out there spreading the poison to undermine me as chair, and severely damaging the company's share price in the process?'

She stared at the table. 'They could have been.'

'I'll take that as a "yes". On whose instructions?'

'Pardon?'

'Don't prevaricate, Miss Harvey. If I phone the chief executive of your bank right now, and ask him if it's his policy to brief against the chair of a client company, in any circumstances, he's going to do his nut and launch an investigation. When the bank's messengers are put up against the wall, who are they going to name as the person who sent them out there?'

She sighed. 'They're going to blame me,' she confessed. And then she shot me a look that was nothing but pure envy.

'Because you expected to be chair yourself,' I said, 'and that's not a question; I can see it.' I looked at the company secretary. 'Mr Smith, please give Miss Harvey a notepad and a pen, if she needs one.'

He did as I instructed. She stared at the items as they were put before her. 'What are these for?' she asked.

'Jesus!' I exclaimed. 'Would you prefer a pearl-handled revolver? Write your resignation, please, with immediate effect. Otherwise I will put a motion of no confidence, it will be passed and all this will be minuted and reported to the bank, your employer, when the company's business is moved to its rival.'

She looked at Culshaw, and then at Gerry Meek. Neither would meet her eyes. She picked up the pen and scribbled a few words, tossed the pad back at Smith, and started to rise.

'Hold on,' I told her. 'Before you go, will you confirm also that your people have been leaking information from our confidential management accounts, also on your say-so? If they have, I'll find that out too, one way or another, easy or hard.'

'No!' she protested. 'Certainly not! That would be outright dishonesty.'

I shrugged. 'As I say, I'll find out, but actually, I believe you. Goodbye.'

The remaining five of us sat in silence until the door closed behind her.

'I never did get round to answering her question,' I remarked, once she'd gone, 'but I don't think I need to as it's a matter of record. What's also a matter of public record is that

I'm a director of another company, in Spain, and that I have operated successfully in a commercial role for the UK government. Privately, I manage personal wealth, accrued through my association with my late former husband, that runs into seven zeroes and has grown significantly since it came to me. Susie knew all that; it's why she appointed me to the chair.'

'Non-executive chair,' Culshaw murmured.

'She didn't, actually. She appointed me chair and that was it. When she did it, she envisaged that she'd still be around, still pulling the strings. Sadly, she isn't, so I intend to assume an executive role.'

The managing director leaned across the table. 'The shareholders may have something to say about that, given what's happened to the company's share price since your appointment was announced. I don't condone what Gillian did, but we can't hide from the reaction to the information she circulated.'

'Your problem, Phil,' I countered, 'seems to be that you don't keep up to date. This is what's happened in the last hour.' I took the sheets I'd printed in the hotel from my folder and slid them across to him, then watched his face change as he read it. 'Seems there's a significant new shareholder on my side, who now owns, by my calculation, around one-eighth of the equity, based on the buying price. Before you ask, it certainly is not me and no, I don't have clue who it is.' I looked at Wylie Smith. 'Would you call the PR people, please, and find out what the current share price is?'

'Certainly, Madam Chair,' he replied, with a look in his

eye that suggested he was enjoying the show, then rushed from the room.

'While he does that,' I continued, 'I want to come back to the so-called confidential information that's been used to undermine the company. I've had a day to study the accounts, that's all, but even I can see that there's a question needing answered. This golf course project; what the hell is it and why are we involved?'

'It's a joint venture with a partner,' Culshaw replied, 'a company called Monsoon Holdings Limited.'

'How big a piece do we have?'

'The Gantry Group owns fifty per cent of the vehicle company. It's called Babylon Links Country Club PLC.'

'Fifty,' I repeated. 'Not fifty-one?'

'No, exactly fifty. It's a true joint venture.'

'Where's the minute recording board approval? I can't see it and I've checked.'

'The late executive chairman signed off on it, last October. I can show you her instruction.'

'That would be around the time she was diagnosed with a very aggressive type of leukaemia.'

He nodded. 'It was, but what does that have to do with it?'

'It suggests to me that Susie's eye might not have been too firmly on the ball. Did she also sign off on the twenty million pound contribution that we've made to the new company?'

'Effectively; she gave me permission to proceed as I saw fit.'

I eyeballed Gerry Meek. 'Is that correct?'

He nodded.

'Do you know anywhere I can hire a set of golf clubs?' I asked Culshaw, casually. 'I'd like to try the course out for myself.' I smiled. 'In fact, why don't we have a board outing?'

'That won't be possible for a while,' he murmured. 'Construction hasn't begun yet.'

'No? Then where's the twenty million gone?'

'Nowhere yet. The planning authority needed assurances that the company was properly capitalised before they would give consent.'

'And has it? Given consent?'

'Not yet, but my project team assure me that it's close.'

'So meanwhile the company's sitting there with forty million in the bank, uninvested and earning nothing.'

We were interrupted by Wylie Smith as he came back into the room. 'The company's share price has stabilised,' he announced. 'The wave of selling has stopped, but our market value is still twenty per cent below its closing level on Friday.'

It wasn't the greatest news, but still I was pleased to hear it. It strengthened my hand as I turned back to Culshaw.

'Not forty million,' he said. 'Twenty.'

I stared at him. 'Are you telling me we've only got fifty per cent of the shares, yet we're putting up all the money?'

'Yes,' he snapped impatiently, 'but it's not as cut and dried as that. Monsoon Holdings are putting up the land; they own that.'

'How much land?'

'Three hundred and ten acres.'

'Of what? Agricultural?'

'No. There's a little woodland, but mostly it's just grass.'

'Not residential, though?'

'No, it's green belt, but that's not an issue. There are golf courses on similar land all along that coast.'

I did some sums in my head. 'I'm a country girl, Phil. I'm not up to date with current land values in Scotland, but I do know that if you can't build homes or factories on it or grow things or graze things, then it isn't worth a hell of a lot. Let's say on a good day, three to four grand an acre. That would value it, tops, at one and a quarter million, against the Gantry contribution of twenty.'

'Yes, but . . . When permission is granted and the course is built it will be worth much more.'

'So where's the business plan?'

'There . . .' He stopped, and glared at me, fiercely. 'Look here,' he barked, 'enough of this! I haven't come here to be cross-examined by some bloody woman who's just walked in the door!'

'Then resign.' I eyeballed him back. 'I could have another managing director in here by the end of today. Gerry,' I snapped at Meek, 'as finance director do you believe that the company has got itself a good deal here?'

As I looked at him I thought I saw an honest man, and he proved me right. 'Frankly, Mrs Blackstone, I don't. Phil is right that when the project is up and running, value will have been added to the property, but to give us a decent return on investment it would have to be showing an operating profit of at least seven million a year and have a capital value of fifty. In my opinion, those are high expectations, and no way will they be achieved overnight.'

'Were you consulted over the commitment of this sort of investment?'

'No,' the FD replied. 'I was simply told. I did consider going to Ms Gantry about it, but she was uncontactable.'

'Where's the business plan?' I asked Culshaw, again. 'The one you showed the bank.'

'There is none,' he admitted. 'We funded it from within our own resources.'

'Added to by a certain amount of borrowing from the bank,' Meek chipped in.

'All well within our agreed limit,' Culshaw shouted, 'as Gillian would have told you if she'd still been here.'

'Boys, boys, boys,' I said. 'Let's be calm, please. Phil, I have a duty to ask these questions, to try to get a handle on substantial spending that I don't understand.'

'Investment,' he hissed.

'Twenty million out of our coffers any way you look at it,' I shot back. 'Who are the directors of Babylon Links?'

'Must we dwell on this?' he protested.

'Yes, until I'm reassured about this project.'

He threw his hands up in exasperation, and turned to the company secretary. 'Wylie, tell her.'

Smith nodded. 'There two. Mr Culshaw, and Mr Diego Fabricant.'

I frowned. 'Diego Fabricant?' I repeated. 'Never heard of him. Who the hell is he?'

'He's a member of the board of Monsoon Holdings Ltd. Its only director, in fact.'

'So he owns the land?'

'Not personally, no. The company owns the land.'

'Okay, but he owns the company, so same thing.'

'Actually, he doesn't,' Smith said, a little diffidently. 'He's an appointed director, but it's unlikely that he's actually a shareholder.'

I almost blew up, almost but not quite. 'So . . .' I murmured.

'All one hundred issued shares of Monsoon Holdings Limited,' he continued, 'are held by a company registered in Jersey, where there's no requirement to disclose the beneficial owner. Nominee shareholders can be used; that's what Fabricant is.'

'Fucking hell!' I glanced at Cathy Black. 'You can minute that if you like. Wylie, you're telling me that the Gantry Group has a business partner and we don't know who he is?'

'Effectively, yes.'

I turned on Culshaw. 'Who brought you this deal, Phil? Let me guess. It wasn't your bloody nephew, was it?'

There followed one of the most eloquent silences I've ever not heard. I felt like someone who'd just fired a rifle straight up in the air, and hit my target on the way down. The managing director's jaw fell a couple of inches 'How the h . . .' he began.

I laughed out loud. 'I didn't know. I wasn't even serious. I think you're done here. Mr Smith, I need advice on the legal implications of this.'

'Enough,' Culshaw shouted. 'I've had enough of this interference. Mrs Black, please minute my withdrawal from this meeting. Note also my request for a general meeting of the company to be held as soon as possible, to consider and pass a vote of no confidence in Mrs Blackstone as chair, and requiring her resignation.' He pushed himself out of his seat, and leaned over me, right in my face. 'In case you've forgotten, a majority of the shares in this company are now held by two young people who are by marriage my great-niece and great-nephew. How do you think their stepfather is going to vote on their behalf?'

'Phil,' I asked him quietly. 'Did you leak the contents of the management accounts?'

'No, of course not,' he blustered. 'I'm a shareholder in this company myself.'

'Then who the hell did? It wasn't Gillian Harvey, it wasn't Gerry or Audrey Kent, it wasn't Wylie and it wasn't me. So who the hell did it and why? Ask yourself that as you plan my downfall.'

Thirteen

After he'd left, I had to ask myself the same question, but I couldn't come up with a good answer.

There was one prime suspect, of course. As soon as I'd closed the meeting, formally, I called Audrey Kent in Monaco.

'How did things go?' she asked, at once.

'Combustibly,' I replied. 'Gillian Harvey resigned and Phil Culshaw's just walked out in the huff, vowing to have my head in a basket. He's called for an extraordinary general meeting, as soon as possible.'

'Can he do that?'

'Technically, no; Wylie Smith says he doesn't have enough shares to force it. But I'm going to allow it. This golf course scam that he's committed us to is a resignation issue; he's more or less gambled company money with no guarantee of a return. No chair could let that go unchallenged: one of us has to go. I've suspended him from his employment pending the meeting, and Gerry Meek will be acting managing director till the EGM takes place.'

'But will you win?' Audrey asked, nervously.

'I don't know. It'll depend on who votes Janet and wee Jonathan's shares and how. My next meeting will be with Greg McPhillips, Susie's lawyer. I'm going to show him my power of attorney and instruct him to put the trust in place, the one she asked me to set up.'

'Can it be done in time?'

'Time shouldn't be a problem. I can delay the meeting, to an extent. The key question is whether I'll be able to do it at all; right now I just don't know what the position is. But to other things. First, how are the kids?'

'Calmer this morning. Janet's still a bit tearful; I'm staying close to her and wee Jonathan's hardly let Conrad out of his sight. At least Mr Murdstone isn't around . . .'

'Who?' I asked.

'David Copperfield's wicked stepfather,' she replied, chuckling. 'You should read Dickens, Primavera; it's full of analogies.'

'Where's he gone?'

'I have no idea. When Conrad and I got up this morning he'd left, without as much as a note on the kitchen table. Is it too much to hope that he won't be back?'

'Probably,' I suggested. 'As for your Dickensian image, I'd be surprised if he's at all interested in the kids.'

'In that case, what'll happen to them? There's no role for me here without Susie, and you can forget what Duncan said last week about keeping Conrad on. The two of them had a big argument last night. Conrad tried to speak to him about the children's needs, and how he should be considerate with them in the wake of their mother's death, but Duncan blew up at him, told him to mind his own so-and-so business.'

'What did Conrad say to that?'

'He got specific, and said that if he ever caught him looking at Janet inappropriately again, or if he frightened the wee chap any more than he does already, he would have to take action to protect them. Duncan yelled at him that from now on he was to have nothing more to do with them, but Conrad replied, very quietly, that he takes his orders from the chair of the Gantry Group, and that isn't him. Primavera,' she murmured, 'I'm glad he's gone too. You don't push Conrad one inch.'

'I wouldn't worry about that,' I suggested. 'Bravery isn't the man's trademark. Duplicity is, though. Audrey,' I went on, 'do you know if Duncan's had access to Susie's private papers?'

'Physically, no,' she said, at once, then knocked me back by adding, 'but he doesn't need to. He's had access to her laptop, and I think he's taken it with him. Everything's on there, and if he has the password . . .'

'Would she have given it to him?'

'Susie was so erratic in her final days that she might have; or he could simply have watched her key it in. I'm an idiot, Primavera; I knew what it was and I could have changed it after she died. Dammit, I should have. But why do you ask?'

I updated her on what had happened in the Stock Exchange community, and the briefing that had been going on. 'Gillian Harvey put the boot in me, and got caught, but she wouldn't have done the other stuff. That golf course information, that's done real damage; I've recovered some of it, but we're still vulnerable.'

'Do you reckon Duncan might have done that?'

'I'd like to pin it on him,' I admitted. 'But I'm having trouble working out why he would. After all, it was him that brought the dodgy golf course deal to his Uncle Phil. So why would he want to undermine it? There's no sense in that. But somebody's using it to shaft the Gantry Group, that's for sure.'

I left Audrey to think on that and turned to Wylie Smith. I'd asked him to wait in the boardroom after Gerry Meek and Cathy Black had returned to their offices.

'Diego Fabricant,' I fired at him, 'our partner in Babylon Links. You're that company's secretary as well, so tell me about him.'

'I wish I could, Madam Chair, but . . .'

'For God's sake, call me Primavera. What's stopping you?'

'I've never met him.'

I frowned. 'But don't you attend all the board meetings?'

'There haven't been any, after the first, when the company was started. Mr Fabricant recorded an apology; the articles allow a meeting in those circumstances, so a minute was taken, but there have been none since.'

'No formal record of progress?' I asked.

'There hasn't been any progress, Primavera. The company

has lodged an application for planning permission in principle for a golf course, clubhouse and associated buildings; no more than that, just in principle. The requirement that it be formally capitalised was Mr Culshaw's instruction; it's never been put to me by anyone else, and I've submitted all the paperwork.'

'Where is our money now?'

'In a high interest account, offshore.'

'How far offshore, Wylie?' I growled.

'The Isle of Man.'

'Okay,' I declared. 'Get it back.'

He winced, hunching his shoulders as if he thought I was about to aim an axe at his neck. 'I can't do that, Primavera, not on my own initiative, or on yours for that matter. Technically you can now appoint yourself a director of Babylon, since Mr Culshaw held office as a representative of the Gantry Group, but even then you couldn't simply take the money back. All expenditure above a certain level must be approved by both directors.'

'Then the sooner I sit down with Mr Fabricant, the better. Where can I find him? Jersey, I suppose.'

'No, Edinburgh,' he replied.

I raised an eyebrow. 'Can you be a little more specific?' I asked.

'No I can't. Mr Fabricant's address is a post office box.'

'So we don't know what our partner looks like,' I said, 'and we don't know where he lives, or works. That's what our Phil got this company into?'

Wylie nodded. 'Yes. Gerry and I did point out that it was an unusual, possibly even an unsafe, situation, but he said he had private assurances that everything was all right. That may be the case, Primavera; after all, the money Gantry put into Babylon Links hasn't gone anywhere.'

'It might as well have,' I suggested, 'if we can't get it back without Fabricant signing for it, and we don't know where he is. Come on, let's find him.'

'How?'

'We'll ask Mr Google to look for him.' I took my laptop from my bag and booted it up, then went online through the company's network.

'What if it's an assumed name?' Wylie asked.

'Would it be legal to be a director under a pseudonym?'

'If it was an act of deliberate deception, no.'

'Then I'd love that to be the case, but I'll bet it isn't.' I keyed 'Diego Fabricant Edinburgh' into the address bar and pressed the return key.

The response was instant; there were six hits, of which five led to newspaper articles. The other was for the Law Society of Scotland. I scanned the digital cuttings first, four of them were from the business sections of the *Scotsman* or the *Herald*, and each referred to corporate mergers of acquisitions in which our man had been a player. Two of them described him as 'dealmaker', a term I'd never come across before.

'What does it mean?' I asked Wylie.

'More or less what it says,' he replied. 'Let's say you want to sell your business, or make an acquisition, but don't have a specific buyer or target in mind. You'd go to a man like Fabricant seems to be, and he'd put you together with someone.'

'What does he get out of it?'

'A fee, equity or both.'

There were no accompanying photographs, but the fifth item was coverage of an awards dinner, complete with an accompanying picture of a group of ten men in evening dress, lined up and cheesing for the camera. Fabricant was listed as second from the left; the image was that of a tall man, bulky, with a prominent nose and a forehead so high that it was beyond rescue by any hair clinic.

'So far so good,' I murmured. 'Now let's get more specific.' I clicked the link on my search page that led me to the Law Society. I'd expected it to be 'members only', but in fact it turned out to be publicly accessible and very helpful, with a section that invited me to 'Find a solicitor'.

I keyed in the surname, the only line I could complete, hit the button, and had only a single response: 'D. Fabricant, Suite three, eighth floor, Cousland Tower, Lothian Road, Edinburgh.'

'No phone number,' I murmured. I noted the address then went on to the BT site, and keyed in Fabricant's details. It told me that the subscriber number was unavailable.

'Very discreet,' Wylie observed. 'Ex-directory.'

'I wasn't thinking about phoning him anyway. I think you and I should pay him a surprise visit. Is the rest of your day clear?'

'I can make it so.'

'Good. We're going to Edinburgh. But first, I have to call on someone else, your partner, Greg McPhillips. I need to talk to him, urgently.'

'Do you have an appointment?'

'I made one for four o'clock,' I replied, 'but I'll need to bring it forward now.'

He pursed his lips. 'Oh, I don't know. Greg always has a very full diary. He may not be able to reschedule, not for today.'

'He'll see me, Wylie, don't you worry. Greg and I go back more than ten years.'

I gave Gerry Meek and Cathy Black my mobile number and my room number at the hotel, then Wylie and I grabbed a taxi and headed for Greg McPhillips' office.

The McPhillips practice had gone up in the world since I'd last had reason to consult it. From a small office just off Sauchiehall Street, it had moved into a top-floor suite in a new build block at the top of Renfield Street. Wylie had wanted to call ahead, but I'd decided that I wasn't giving anyone advance notice of anything else that day. He paid the cab and led me towards the lift. 'I really don't know about this,' he murmured. That didn't surprise me; the Greg McPhillips I'd known was Wylie's exact opposite, outgoing, full of himself and, when it suited him, overbearing.

'I'm sorry, Mr Smith,' his secretary said when he asked her if he was in. 'You've just missed him. He's gone for lunch with a client.'

'Where?' I asked.

She stared at me. 'I don't know if I could . . .'

I stared back. 'You do, trust me.'

She glanced at Wylie; he nodded. 'La Bonne Auberge,' she said. The name was fresh on my mind; it was across the street from the building in which we stood and we'd just passed it in the taxi.

'Then call his mobile number, please,' I requested, politely, 'and tell him that Mrs Blackstone can't do four o'clock as arranged previously, but needs five minutes now.'

'Of course, if you insist, but . . .' I waited as she made the call and relayed the message, watching as she pursed her lips and nodded. 'I'm sorry,' she murmured, the phone still held to her ear, 'he says it's impossible.'

I signed to her to pass me the handset; she was so surprised that she did. 'Greg,' I chirped, amiably, 'Primavera here. Are you still shagging that actress? Remember, the girl who was your bit on the side about twelve years ago when Oz and I were in business together in Glasgow, and we were all pals? She had a part in a TV soap and knew my sister. Did Mrs McPhillips ever find out about her?'

His sigh could have carried across the street from the restaurant without the amplification of the phone. 'Okay,' he said, 'five minutes; meet me in the reception area just inside the entrance.'

Wylie wouldn't come into La Bonne Auberge with me. He said that since it was obviously personal business I was going to discuss, he had to keep well clear of it as company secretary. I could see the logic in that, but I couldn't help feeling that after hearing what I'd said to his senior partner, he didn't want to be within earshot of the discussion that followed.

Before I go any further, understand one thing: I didn't, and don't, harbour any ill feeling towards Greg. He was a good friend to Oz, and me, back in the days of our private enquiry business, and he put some nice work our way. Oz's links with him went even further back, and one job he'd sent to him had been the start of all the fame and fortune that came his way. With that history between us, I didn't crash his lunch date out of malice, only necessity.

He understood that too, for he was smiling as I walked through the door. 'Christ, Primavera,' he chuckled. 'You haven't changed a bit, and before you ask again, the answers are, no, I'm not, and no, the wife never did find out. Look,' he continued, 'I'm sorry I can't walk away from this engagement, but I can't and that's an end of it. What is it, quickly?'

I took from my bag the documents that Susie had sent me, the one specifying the changes she wanted to make to her will, and the other instructing that the children's trust be set up. Finally, I let him see my power of attorney.

He scanned them for a couple of minutes, then looked up. 'Fuck it,' he murmured.

'I take it that does not mean good news,' I said.

'No, it doesn't.' He handed me back the will paper. 'Susie's wishes are quite clear in there; there's no doubt about what she wanted to do. The wasp in the embrocation is that she's no longer alive, so she can't enact them.' He looked at me, and I could see sympathy in his eyes. 'Susie wasn't herself when she did that, I can tell.'

'She meant every word of it, Greg,' I protested.

'I know that. I just acknowledged that, didn't I? What I meant was that she must have been confused, or drugged or whatever, for the Susie I knew would have realised that if she'd just got Audrey Kent, or anyone else, to date and witness what's written there, then I would have accepted it as a codicil to her existing will. But she didn't, and so I can't. That will must stand as it was written. It would survive any challenge in court. And if you did try to overturn it, I'd be the guy who had to defend against you, for the moment that Susie died, I became her executor.'

I frowned. 'Understood.' I couldn't argue, for I could see that he was right. 'Greg, Susie told me some of what was in the will, so my next question is how do you interpret it, given that Oz is named in it, and he's dead?'

'But you're wrong,' he exclaimed, 'she didn't name him. The will refers to "my surviving spouse" as the children's guardian. When she died, she was married to Duncan Culshaw; I've seen the marriage certificate and it's legal. I know this for sure because a guy I know got hitched in Vegas, and he made very sure of that before he did.'

That was a blow, but I pressed on. 'She also told me who would inherit her shares in the company: all three kids, Tom included. Are you telling me that my son is now under the guardianship of that man Culshaw?'

He shook his head, firmly. 'No, I'm not. Susie drafted her

will at a time when Oz had custody of young Tom, but clearly she anticipated a situation in which that might change, for the will specifies that during his minority, his interests will be under the curatorship of his legal guardian at the time of her death. That will give you some relief.'

I did a very quick piece of mental arithmetic. 'A little,' I agreed, 'but it doesn't remove my concern. Susie owned sixty per cent of the Gantry Group shares, meaning twenty per cent goes to each child. But have you forgotten Oz's will? He owned eighteen per cent, and that is also split three ways. So that gives Janet and wee Jonathan a total of twenty-six per cent each. Twenty-six times two equals fifty-two per cent, and that equals a controlling shareholding when under the guidance of one person. Susie might have been addled over the will changes, but when she instructed me to set up the children's trust, she knew exactly what she was doing and why. Can I go ahead with that, even though she's dead?'

Greg let out another industrial-strength sigh. 'You might be able to,' he said. 'I could see an outside possibility that you might, but you'd have to go to court to do it. And it would take time,' he added.

'Longer than it would take to hold a company EGM?'

He frowned. 'That's not a hypothetical question, is it?'

'No.'

'Then it would take much longer, and until the court said otherwise Culshaw would be able to vote the children's shares as he chose. To be honest, I don't really believe the court would say otherwise, but you can only try.'

'Could you represent me?'

'Not a hope, chum. Susie's surviving spouse, i.e. Culshaw, would most certainly contest you. As the executor I have to be neutral, so you'd need to get yourself another lawyer.'

'How about Wylie Smith?'

'He's good enough, but he's too close. He's a partner in my firm, and there's the greater complication for him that he's company secretary of the Gantry Group. He'd probably have to give up that position if he acted for you in such a matter, and frankly, that's not business I'd want my firm to lose.'

'I see,' I murmured. 'Any ideas?'

'Sure, but if I gave you a couple and things went against you, you could wind up blaming me, and I wouldn't want that to happen.' He paused. 'You really don't like this man Culshaw, do you?'

'That obvious, eh?'

'Rather.'

'I have good reason to dislike him. What I can't understand is why he's been targeting me so specifically, and Tom for that matter. I'm in no doubt that he'll kick me out as chair, given the chance. His uncle seems to be my enemy on the board. He's calling the EGM and he'll have his nephew's support.'

He shook his head. 'I can't help you there either, for I don't know. I can see why you would hate his guts, but . . . let me give you one single piece of legal advice.'

'What?'

'If you do take this to court, don't make it personal.'

'I'll do my best, Greg. Thanks for being so frank.' We shook hands, and he turned to return to the restaurant. 'Hey,' I called after him. 'Who's your lunch date, by the way?'

'I can't tell you that, honestly,' he replied.

But he didn't have to. I couldn't see all the restaurant's dining area from where I stood but did have a view of a wall mirror, halfway along. As I took a single step to my left, the reflection changed, and I saw, sitting along at a table set for two, a profile that I recognised: that of Duncan Culshaw.

I stepped outside to rejoin Wylie and did some thinking. Culshaw must have caught the first flight out of Nice to get to Glasgow in time for a meeting with Greg, but was he going straight back there? I doubted that; there's no direct route between the two cities and four flights in a day would have been pushing it. I'd have loved to follow him, just out of interest, to see whether he and Uncle Phil met up, but that wasn't possible; Fabricant was my priority. But . . .

I dug out my mobile and called Liam. When he answered after a few seconds, his voice sounded different from the one I'd come to know. 'Where are you?' I asked.

'Burger King,' he replied, more clearly. 'You caught me mid-bite.'

'Burger King,' I repeated. 'You?'

'Mine's a veggie; Tom's reducing the animal population.'

'Are you almost finished? If so, I've got a game the two of you might like to play.'

'Sounds good. What does it involve?'

'A little sleuthing.' I explained where I was, and who was

inside the restaurant. 'How would you and Tom like to tail him when he leaves?'

He laughed. 'That sounds like fun, but how exactly?'

'I've got a hire car parked at the hotel; you can pick it up and park outside. You'll need it, for I can't see him walking anywhere.'

'Are you sure you want Tom involved in this?'

'As long as he's with you, what's the problem? Besides, you'll need him; he knows what Culshaw looks like, you don't.'

'True,' he conceded. 'But why can't you do it?'

'Frying other fish,' I told him. 'My company secretary and I have to go to Edinburgh to corner somebody else. We'll take the train.'

'Okay,' Liam said, cheerfully. 'Hey, Tom,' I heard him call, 'd'you fancy playing detective, like your old man used to?' I head a muffled reply. 'He says yes. Bad guys beware: the A Team is mobilised and coming to getcha.'

'Don't let him spot you, mind.'

'No chance. I've always wanted to do this sort of stuff. I'll pick my camera up when we collect the car.'

'Good idea. If you could get a picture of him with his fucking uncle that would be useful.'

'You and old Phil didn't hit it off, then?' he surmised.

'That would be an understatement, my darling. If he wasn't a boring old accountant at heart, I might be watching my back right now.'

'You're not serious, are you?' he exclaimed ''Cos if you are, the only place I'm going to be is by your side.'

'That is noble of you, but I have seen off much, much tougher guys than him. Don't you worry about me, Sherlock, you just get into position opposite La Bonne Auberge, soon as you can.'

I hung up on him and left him to it. I was under no illusions about Liam's tracking ability; he could find his way around a woman pretty well, but he was so laid-back generally that I was sure he'd either get lost or give himself away. Regardless of that, though, he was the only show in town as far as I was concerned, and if he could come up with a snap of Duncan and Phil Culshaw deep in conversation, it might do me some good. After my conversation with Greg, I understood the depth of the shit that I was in, and any stick that might haul me out had to be clutched at.

It's a very short walk from where we were to Queen Street railway station; past the concert hall, down Buchanan Street, turn left and you're there. We caught the one fifteen train with a couple of minutes to spare and less than an hour later we were in the nation's capital. In past times Edinburgh was called the 'Athens of the North'; today the comparisons are with Barcelona, but since that city is four times as large, and its urban sprawl contains as many people as the whole of Scotland, they don't really bear much scrutiny.

We jumped from one of Scotland's most expensive trains into one of Britain's most expensive taxis and asked the driver to take us to Fabricant's address. He must have read Wylie as a Glaswegian, for he took us for a ride, and no mistake. Sixteen quid fifty later he pulled up outside a building that was less than a mile from the station. He blamed the Princes Street closure, but the chancer hadn't needed to cross it. I gave him the exact fare, and smiled as I told him in Catalan that he was a chiselling son-of-a-bitch.

Cousland Tower turned out to be one of those blocks that were chucked up towards the end of the last century as Edinburgh business moved out of its traditional Georgian offices into premises that were deemed to be more IT friendly. There was no reception in the lobby, so we rode a glass-walled lift up to the eighth floor and stepped out, into another area with no welcome mat but with a wall board listing the occupants by suite number.

Fabricant's was to the left, round a corner; the door was solid, with no name, only the number, Three. Wylie rapped on it, gently, and we waited. I was about to give it a more solid thump when it was opened by a tall woman in a hip-hugging dress, with supermodel looks. Her dark hair was piled on her head, her cheekbones were high, and her lips were naturally full, without the aid of collagen or any other agent. Bitch.

If she was surprised, she didn't look it. 'Yes,' she purred, 'can I help you?'

'I, I, I,' Wylie stammered; he still hadn't got past the hips.

'Is this Diego Fabricant's office?' I asked.

'Yes, it is,' the cover girl replied. 'I'm Kim Coates, his secretary.'

'Good. We'd like to see him. My name is Primavera Blackstone, and this is my colleague, Wylie Smith.'

'Mmm,' she murmured. 'I'm afraid that Mr Fabricant doesn't see anyone without an appointment.'

'Then make one for us.' I checked my watch; it showed two twenty-eight. 'Half past two will suit us nicely.'

Her smile was patronising; the Queen couldn't do that to me and get away with it, and Ms Coates had to be at least ten years my junior. 'I'm afraid you'll have to tell me a little more than that,' she laughed.

'Okay. Try this. Your boss is a director of a company that's trousered twenty million of my company's money. My colleague here is secretary of both of them, and he doesn't know what's happening to it. So, Tootsie, unless you back off and put me together with your boss, I'm going to stand here shouting so loud and so long that eventually the police will come to see what the fuss is about. Or maybe I'll give my voice a break and go and fetch them myself. Go speak to him, now!'

She took half a pace back and that was enough. I stepped past her into the suite, with Wylie following, muttering a nervous, 'Excuse me,' as he did, but ogling her nonetheless as she sashayed towards the door behind her desk. I could understand why. I guessed that when he'd employed her, Diego hadn't asked about her doorkeeping abilities. With that body, a wink, a smile and a crooked finger would get her through most situations.

I scanned the office as we waited. The furniture was a strange mix of modern and antique, as if some of it had come from Charlotte Square or some other former base. There was a bloody awful painting of a hunting scene on the wall beside the entrance door, and next to that an honours board, headed 'Client companies', with a couple of dozen corporate entities listed below.

I was halfway through scanning them when Ms Coates returned. I'd found Monsoon Holdings Ltd, and was still looking for Babylon Links Country Club PLC. 'Mr Fabricant will see you,' she announced, managing to make it sound as if it was an honour and one that had been granted against her advice.

'Thank you,' I said, moving towards her boss's sanctum. 'By the way,' I murmured as I passed her, 'a word of advice. In a dress like that, a woman can always tell when another woman isn't wearing any.'

'I imagine you know from experience,' she hissed.

'Yes indeed,' I replied, 'I surely do, but I never go without in the office.'

I let Wylie go into Fabricant's room ahead of me . . . and almost had to catch him. The man was holding a shotgun, its stock pressed to his shoulder and he was sighting it almost straight at us. I was startled too, but I wasn't going to let him see it.

He held the pose for a second, then broke the breech and laid the weapon on his desk. 'Shooting party this evening,' he said, in a public school accent that could have originated anywhere. 'Just getting the feel for it again.'

'You should relax a little more,' I suggested, as we all took seats. 'You looked a bit stiff.'

He peered at me, over his substantial nose. 'Indeed? I'll bear that in mind. Do you shoot?'

'Not for a while.' No, not for over fifteen years in fact, and then it had been a pistol.

'Well, shoot now, Mrs Blackstone, in another way. What can I do for you?'

I held up my left hand; occasionally I wear a wedding ring, but not that day. 'How did you know it's Mrs?' I asked. The window behind him offered a view of the Usher Hall, and also a reflection of the computer monitor on his desk. I could see that it was switched off, and there hadn't been time for him to look me up and then power it down.

'I read the business press,' he replied, without pausing for as much as a beat. 'You're in it this morning, quite prominently, if I may say so.'

'That's more than I can say about you, Mr Fabricant. Not quite a man of mystery, but you keep a low profile, particularly when it comes to our joint venture, Babylon Links. Mr Smith, here, has never met you, and your name isn't listed as present at any meeting. Don't you have a duty to the shareholders of the company you represent, Monsoon Holdings?'

'My dear lady, I am the sole shareholder of Monsoon.'

'But you're not the beneficial owner,' Wylie pointed out. 'You're listed in Jersey as a nominee.'

Fabricant laughed. 'You have indeed been doing your homework.'

'It's not too difficult,' he countered. 'My assistant established that on day one. I don't suppose you'd care to disclose the name of the actual owner of the company, and through that of the land that seems to be its sole asset?'

'No, I do not care. If that person wished to be known, there would have been no point in using a nominee. Mr Smith, you're not suggesting there's anything illegal in what's been done, are you?'

'No, I'm not,' Wylie admitted; he'd been thrown on to the back foot.

'Me neither,' I said, 'but as the chair of your partner I want to know the process that's led to the Gantry Group being exposed in this way.'

'Then hadn't you better ask your managing director?' Fabricant suggested. The man was confident, annoyingly so.

'I did,' I told him. 'My former managing director, currently suspended from his position. From that, you might gather I wasn't given a satisfactory answer, so now I'm asking you. Who initiated this deal?'

'I'll throw you one bone, Mrs Blackstone. I'm prepared to tell you that Mr Culshaw was approached by a representative of Monsoon. The proposition was that we own a piece of land in Ayrshire that's ripe for leisure development, and that we needed a fifty-fifty partner to fund the operation.'

'And how's our investment going to be recouped?'

'Entry to membership will be through the purchase of bonds or debentures. These will be marketed internationally. It's quite a common model; there are many examples.'

'And how many are currently active,' I asked him, 'with the global economy hiding somewhere up its own arse. Man, I don't live in Scotland, but even I know that the Ayrshire coast is lined with golf courses, and that the current insolvency rate among ventures like this is scarily high.'

'You have to take a long-term view, Mrs Blackstone,' he countered.

'No, I don't,' I shot back at him. 'First and foremost I have to protect the interests of the Gantry Group, and this deal is undermining them. Leaked information about it is being used against us in the City, and it's very damaging. I'm pulling our company out of this thing and I want our money back, pronto.'

He shook his head, still wearing that annoyingly assured smirk. 'It's not as easy as that,' he said. 'Babylon Links can only be wound up by agreement between the parties, and I have very firm instructions from my principal that we are not going to agree to that. The same goes for the Gantry Group's investment; it won't be returned either.'

I was contemplating how long I'd get for battering dear Diego to death with his own Purdy when my mobile sounded. I looked at the number, recognised it as Cress Oldham's, and took the call.

'I've got a certain amount of information,' she announced. 'It's strange. Two different consultancies have been active against us. One of them is Seventh Financial; its people have been spreading the personal stuff about you, but I'm sorry, they won't tell me who's instructed them.'

'Don't worry about that,' I told her. 'I know who it was, and I've dealt with it. What about the others?'

'According to my tame analyst, the leaked information is being put about by a firm called Greentree Stanley City. I know a couple of their people and I nobbled one at lunchtime. He admitted it but didn't give me the faintest hint of the source.'

'Any chance of progress on that front?' I asked, cryptically, because Fabricant was making no pretence of not listening to my end of the conversation.

'I'd have to go through their entire client list, and when I did I'd still be guessing. I'll try, though.'

'You do that, and respond soonest.'

'I will, but . . . there's something else happening, Mrs Blackstone, and I don't know what it is. The share price is heading south again; that tells me there's new information out there, and it's not good.'

'Then get digging. Cheers.' I pocketed my phone.

'Not bad news, I hope,' Fabricant oozed.

'Only for whoever it is that's trying to undermine me. I will find them, and I will get even. When that happens, mate, it will be cataclysmic.'

'That may be,' he said. 'But I would suggest you do it quickly. From what I hear your tenure of office may be rather short.'

'That's been said at other times and in other places, but I'm still here.' I started to rise. 'I'll give your principal forty-eight hours to authorise the release of our funds.'

'Actually, I had the opposite in mind.' There was something in his tone that made me sit down again, as he took a document from his desk and slid it across the desk. 'This is a copy of the agreement signed by Mr Culshaw when we set up our joint venture. If you read it, you'll see that it commits Gantry to providing funding of up to fifty million, not merely the twenty that's been lodged so far.'

I scanned the document, then passed it to Wylie. He read it and winced. 'What he says is the case, Mada . . . Primavera.'

'And we're calling for the balance to be subscribed immediately,' Fabricant announced. That was Cress's new information, I realised at once; it was out there in the public domain and it was screwing us already.

'And I'm telling you to fuck off,' I retorted. 'Come on, Wylie, we're out of here.'

As we stood, he stayed seated, grinning at my anger. 'We'll sue,' he warned.

'You do that,' I snapped. 'See if you can arrange for the case to be heard by Lord January. He's my son's uncle. I'll be telling him all about you, Diego, and he'll be telling all his friends.'

It was a crap threat and we both knew it, but it was all I had, other than the satisfaction of shaking his office door on its hinges as I closed it behind me. I'd expected to see Kim Coates beaming behind her desk, but she was gone.

I headed for the exit, then paused. I took out my phone and photographed Fabricant's client board, then stepped into the corridor. Outside I sent the image to Cress Oldham, with a text message.

'Check this against the enemy's client list. See if it sets anything off. P.'

'We're in trouble, aren't we?' Wylie sighed as we stepped into the glass lift.

'That's a fair analysis,' I chuckled.

'You must be regretting letting yourself get involved in this.'

The chuckle became a full-out laugh. 'Are you kidding?' I exclaimed. 'I haven't felt so alive in years.' He probably thought I was crazy, and if he did, quite possibly he was right.

Finally, I had to admit to the truth, that I'd been hiding from myself, and that, apart from watching Tom grow towards manhood, the challenge of risk and danger, be it financial or physical, is the only thing that really floats my boat.

Fourteen

Wylie and I had quite a bit to take in. I didn't want to do it on the move, or in a pub, and so at his suggestion we went for afternoon tea in the Caley Hotel. Expensive yes, but compared with that taxi trip, good value for money.

'What do we do, Mr Company Secretary?' I asked him as we surveyed a three-tier stand laden with the kind of items that I'd been warning Tom since infancy were bad for his teeth.

He didn't reply immediately. Instead he took Diego Fabricant's document from the pocket to which he'd consigned it, and reread it, slowly and carefully.

When he was finished he passed it to me. 'That's watertight,' he decreed. 'Phil did have the authority to commit the company to providing that level of finance, when called upon by our partner. We are liable.' He paused. 'Look, you'd need to ask Gerry Meek to confirm this, but I don't believe it would bankrupt the company. You could cover it, but it would mean selling assets in a down market for much less than their potential worth, or borrowing against them at rates that would make your eyes water. It won't bust you, but it will devalue your shares.'

'And that's what's happening already,' I murmured.

'So it appears. Did you mean it when you said that you wouldn't meet your obligation?' he asked.

'Christ, Wylie!' I exclaimed. 'Don't put it that way. You don't need to be that blunt.'

'I'm sorry, but Monsoon's QC will be even more direct than that if this gets to court.'

I called Cress Oldham. 'What's happened since we spoke last?' I asked her.

'The opposition is suggesting that Gantry's due to funnel another thirty million into this development,' she replied. 'Tell me it's not true, please.'

'Sorry, it is. I've just found that out.'

'In that case we can't hide from it.' I was getting to like Cressida, for her frankness and the honesty of her advice. 'We have to advise the Stock Exchange of the position . . . as gently as we can, but we have to do it.'

'I can see that. I'll authorise you to issue a statement by me, confirming that we are committed to providing up to fifty million to finance the development. You should add that it is the upper limit of our involvement, and that the plan is for the investment to be recovered by the sale of tradable bonds to future members of the club. Finish up by saying that pending an extraordinary general meeting, Mr Philip Culshaw has been suspended as managing director, and succeeded temporarily by the finance director. How does all that sound?'

'Strong,' she said. 'It doesn't hide from the company's weekened position, but it does show that you're firmly in charge. The market will approve of that; they're getting to like you already.'

'Hopefully it isn't going to turn into a long-term romance,' I told her, 'and I'll be able to hand over to a permanent chair.'

She whistled, softly. 'If you don't mind, Mrs Blackstone, I'm not even going to hint at that. They've worked out who your brother-in-law is.'

'His name is not to be mentioned,' I warned her.

'And it hasn't been, by me, but it's a fact and if it helps us, so be it.'

'It won't help us when it counts, though: at the EGM. Culshaw's called it and he's threatened to bring me down.'

'But he can't, can he? He doesn't have the shares.'

'No,' I agreed, 'but two people can, even if neither of them would. Two children, kids I love and who love me. The way things stand, they'll be my undoing. And probably yours too,' I warned, 'if it goes that way.'

'Is there anything you can do about it?'

'Change the rules of the game,' I responded, 'but right now I don't have a clue how to do that.' I didn't want to depress her further so I changed tack. 'Did you get the image I sent you?'

'Yes I did, and it's legible. I've put my assistant on it. If there's anything there he'll find it.'

'Soon?'

'Yes. Meanwhile, I'll issue your statement, and brief as hard as I can in your support.'

I let her get on with it, and turned back to the tea table to find that Wylie had eaten all the sandwiches. I picked up an éclair and was halfway through it when he asked me, 'How many members do we have to recruit to get our money back?'

I made him wait until I'd finished the pastry and picked up another. 'If income is split evenly between the partners . . . a safe assumption given the stupidity of everything else Phil did . . . there will have to be a thousand before we break even. But that depends on the bonds actually being sellable at a hundred grand.'

'Is that realistic?'

'I doubt it. I'd need to ask Jonny, Oz's nephew. He's a pro, and he has a very efficient manager called Brush Donnelly. He might be able to advise us. My gut, though, says that if we were marketing aggressively and internationally, quoting a hundred thousand US dollars, not sterling, it might be doable, but it would take a long time.'

'If we could persuade Monsoon to hold off on demanding the extra thirty million?'

'And finish the course with what we've put in so far? The number needed would drop to four hundred. But you saw Fabricant. Did he look negotiable? No, Wylie, it's a set-up and old Phil's taken us right into it, with his fucking nephew, if I read his reaction right. But what does Duncan have to gain if he is involved with it? Unless,' a conspiracy revealed itself to me, 'it's a complete scam, the course never gets built and the money disappears. What about that?'

'Then Farbricant would be party to a fraud,' Wylie countered, 'and there are no shooting parties in jail.'

'True,' I conceded. 'So what else is up? Why do I feel there's another game being played, right under my nose, only I can't see the action?'

As I demolished my second éclair, my companion shook his head. 'I have no idea, Primavera,' he murmured. 'I'm only a humble solicitor.'

I had to laugh. 'That makes you unique in your profession, chum. Let's go back to Glasgow,' I said, 'and find out what my boys have been up to.'

I let Wylie pay the bill . . . as an unspoken punishment for scoffing all the sandwiches . . . and we left the hotel. We headed along the tram-ravaged Princes Street, towards Waverley Station, and had almost reached the Mound junction when my phone sounded once again. I took it out and was surprised to see that the caller was Tom.

'Hi, love,' I answered. 'Where are you?'

He shot my question back at me. 'Where are you?'

'I'm in Edinburgh with a colleague,' I told him. 'Now it's your turn.'

'So are we.'

'You are? How come?'

'We waited for Duncan,' he began, 'like you asked, outside. He had a car parked on a meter just around the corner. He didn't see us and we were able to follow him. He went on to the motorway then came all the way through here and stopped at a house in a street called Farmer's Way.'

'When did he arrive?'

'About ten minutes ago.'

'What's Liam doing? Why are you making the call?'

'He's busy, taking photographs of the house. It's a big place, but we can see up the driveway. Duncan went right up the driveway and parked in front of the garage, then he went into the house. What's he doing here, Mum?' he asks. 'He should be in Monaco, with Janet and wee Jonathan, if he's going to be their stepfather. Shouldn't he?'

'You might think so,' I murmured. 'What happened when he got there? Who answered the door? Did you see?'

'Nobody. He used a key and went in. He didn't ring the bell or anything.'

'Do you know if there's anyone else in the house?'

'That's what Liam's trying to see.'

'What number is it?' I asked. 'Are you close enough to see that?'

'I don't think it's got a number, Mum. But it does have a name. "Springs Eternal", it says on the sign at the entrance.'

'Somebody's got a sense of humour. Let me see if I can find out anything about it. Tell Liam I'll call you back.'

As we crossed the junction I explained to Wylie what had happened. 'How easy is it to find out who owns the place?'

'Simple. Let me call my secretary.'

I gave him the details. He phoned his office, snapped out clear crisp instructions, then suggested that we wait for a reply.

We sat on one of the benches that look down into the eastern side of Princes Street Gardens. It was a warm afternoon, although not hot by my standards. Yet people were sunbathing, possibly getting themselves a base tan for the holiday season.

'Is it as easy as that?' I murmured.

'Sure. The land and property registers are public documents; we can access them online, and get a pretty much instant return.'

And it was. It took less than three minutes for his very efficient secretary to call him back. As he listened, I saw him smile. 'Thanks, Rita,' he said, then turned to me. 'You're going to love this. The property is owned by a corporate entity.'

'Monsoon Holdings Limited?'

'Bullseye.'

I rang Tom back, on his phone. As he answered, I could hear road noise. 'We've had to go, Mum,' he told me. 'Liam was worried that Duncan would see us if we waited any longer.'

'I understand. Look, come into Edinburgh and pick us up. Tell Liam we'll wait across the road from the station.'

We headed for Waverley Bridge. I'd been tired before we'd eaten, but all that sugar had refuelled me; as we passed it I was ready to run up the Scott Monument. When my mobile sounded yet again, as we stood waiting, across from the station access roads, I snatched my phone from my pocket like a gunfighter.

'Yes!' I exclaimed, so assertively that I think Cress Oldham was taken aback, for she paused for a second or two before replying.

'I've issued your statement,' she told me, 'and it's gone down well, so far. The analysts I've spoken to appreciate that you're not a pushover, and that the Monsoon people aren't going to have it all their own way. Also, we've got a hit, from that image you sent me. The one name on Fabricant's board that's common to the Greentree Stanley client list is a company called Torrent PLC. I can't confirm that it's behind the briefing but . . .'

'That name's familiar,' I told her, 'but right now I can't place it.' It was too, it had been mentioned recently, but I had so much information swirling around inside my head that I couldn't bring it to the surface.

'I'm in the process of finding out as much as I can about them,' she replied. 'But it could be a coincidence; I repeat, nobody at Greentree Stanley will confirm the source of leaked information . . . unless they're forced to in court. I'll —'

'Yes, do that, get back to me. Got to go now.' I cut her off because I could see our car turn down from Princes Street on to Waverley Bridge, with Liam at the wheel. Wylie and I ran across the road through a gap in the traffic and climbed into the back seat as he drew to a halt.

'Starsky and Hutch,' I laughed as he pulled away again. I could see him grin in the rear-view.

'Who?' Tom asked, twisting round to look at me.

'Blasts from my past,' I said. 'What have you got?'

'I don't know,' Liam replied, as he turned right into Market Street, as our taxi driver could have done, but didn't. 'A few shots of Culshaw getting out of his car and going into the house. Whether he's identifiable, that's something else again. He's in profile in one of them, but in the rest he's mostly got his back to the lens. There are others, though. For a very short time, I could see him through an upstairs window, and there was someone else there. I got off a couple of frames, very fast. That was when we decided we'd better get the hell out of there. If we had a clear view of him, then vice versa.'

'How good are the images?'

'I've no idea. I haven't had a chance to look at them. Even if I did, I'll probably need to load them on to a computer screen for them to be big enough to be legible.'

'Can I have a look?' I asked, reaching out a hand to Tom, who was holding the camera.

'Better not, Mum,' he said. 'You might delete them by accident.'

'Thanks for your touching faith in my high-tech skills,' I muttered, but he had a point. Push the wrong button and the memory card could have been wiped.

'How do I get out of here and back to Glasgow?' Liam called out from the driver's seat. I hadn't been in Edinburgh for years, but my trip up Lothian Road had reminded me of one route, and I was able to give him directions to and along the Western Approach Road, past Murrayfield Stadium, on to Gorgie Road, and eventually to the motorway.

Once we were headed westward, moving steadily through heavy traffic, I asked Tom about his morning. 'What did you see in the museum?'

He shrugged. 'Old stuff. Cars, trams, a steam train; like the motor museum in Monaco, only much bigger. There are a couple of streets too, like they used to be.' He grinned, then switched into Catalan. 'I liked it well enough,' he said, 'but Liam, he was like a dog with two cocks in a forest.'

I came within a breath of asking him why a dog would go on a woodland walk with poultry, when I realised that wasn't what he'd meant at all.

'Tell her about the ship,' Liam chipped in, blissfully unaware that his tackle had been mentioned in despatches, and that I was still coming to terms with the mental image.

'There's a tall ship moored there as well,' my son explained. 'It has three masts, and it was built on the Glasgow river. It's quite big, seventy-five metres long, but it doesn't sail any more. I've seen bigger in L'Escala, and been on a couple.'

Tom's more into surfing these days, but he's been to the local sailing school, and over the last year or so he's crewed for a few people.

'Have you?' Liam exclaimed, clearly impressed. 'Could you fix it for me to do that?'

Tom nodded. 'Sure, as long as you know what you're doing.'

Jesus, I thought, smiling, *this man I'm involved with, he's a schoolboy at heart.*

Suddenly, Cress Oldham's last called forced its way back into my mind. I turned to Wylie. 'Does the name Torrent PLC mean anything to you?' I asked him.

He swivelled round to face me in his seat. 'Are you kidding?' he gasped. In our admittedly short acquaintance, I'd never seen him so animated.

'Hey,' Liam called from the front, 'even I've heard of them. Last time I was in Edinburgh, got to be ten years ago, making my first movie for Miles Grayson, after Oz got me the gig, he . . . Oz that is, got involved in this thing. It was a big scandal at the time. It involved a company and that was its name. There was this chick, too.' He twisted as if he was trying to look at Wylie in the rear-view. 'Isn't that right . . . I'm sorry, I don't . . .'

I realised that they hadn't been introduced, and did the honours.

'So I believe,' Wylie told him. 'I wasn't involved in that in any way, but there was another incident later on, and I was party to that. Torrent PLC tried to take over the Gantry Group, even though it wasn't really big enough to do so. Oz was involved again, very much, since Susie was expecting her second child at the time, and he dealt with the crisis. I'm not entirely sure how he did it, but the bid was withdrawn.'

Of course; and it was Harvey who had mentioned it by name.

I knew how Oz had seen off the threat, because years later, he'd told me. It was one of the secrets that I had not wanted Duncan Culshaw to explore; it was well buried and it had to stay that way.

'Torrent PLC is owned by a woman called Natalie Morgan,' Wylie continued, 'one hundred per cent. She inherited it from her uncle whose name it bears.'

'That's right,' Liam exclaimed, again. 'She was involved in that thing. The actor . . . Ewan Capperauld was his name . . .

who was supposed to play the cop in our movie, it turned out he was banging her. His wife found out, the whole thing blew up in his face and hers, big time, and he had to pull out of the movie.'

A few days before, I might have been concerned about his choice of words for Tom to hear, but after that crack about dogs and trees, my last delusions of innocence were in pieces.

'If that's the case,' Wylie said, 'she came out of the experience with a grudge against Oz, because the failed takeover bid was personally motivated, most certainly. But Primavera, why are you asking about Torrent?'

'Because that's who's been using those leaked management accounts against us. The name jumped off Diego Fabricant's client list.'

'Can we prove they're doing it?'

'I doubt it, going by the advice I'm getting.'

'But I don't get it,' the lawyer murmured. 'Why?'

I was pretty sure that I'd got it, but I was keeping it to myself for the time being.

We were silent for most of the remainder of the journey. As we came off the motorway, Wylie asked Liam if he wanted to use his office computer to study the images he had shot, but I vetoed that. 'It's Greg McPhillips' office as well, and he's involved with the dark side. I'm not saying he'd spy on us, but let's not put him in a situation where he might feel he had to.'

With that decided, we went back to the hotel, returned the car to the parking valet and went up to my, our, suite. I booted up my laptop and handed it to Liam. He connected his camera through a USB socket, then waited while the machine recognised its software. Initially every image on the memory stick was displayed, but he soon isolated those in which we had an interest.

He began by looking at the shots of Duncan leaving his car; yes, I could tell it was him, because that profile shot was recognisable. Another of those shots interested me. It showed him with a key in the Yale lock of the front door. He looked completely at ease and sure of his circumstances, not glancing over his shoulder, nothing furtive about him. He'd been there before, many times. Even in a still image, his body language was that of a man going home.

Liam moved on to the last two pictures that he had snatched, before he began to feel exposed and split from there. The first was blurred beyond redemption, but the other showed two figures. It was a telephoto shot, though, and their faces were indistinct. By the clothes he wore Duncan was one; by the clothes she wasn't wearing the other was female, very obviously female. Long dark hair fell on to her shoulders, but didn't hide any assets.

'Tom,' I began.

'Forget it, Mum,' he said. I didn't argue, but I made a mental note to monitor his computer usage from that point on.

'Liam,' I asked, 'can you make that any clearer?'

'Sure,' he replied. 'It's a high-resolution image, the sharpest the camera can do. Let me zoom it up, and make it as sharp as I can.'

He leaned over the laptop, two fingers moving gently, almost sensually, over the track pad, then when he was ready, clocking the return key with his thumb. 'There,' he announced, turning the computer so that Wylie and I could see what he had done.

Wylie's mouth fell open 'That's . . .' he gasped.

So did mine. 'That's Kim Coates,' I exclaimed.

Liam chuckled. 'You two can call her anything you like, but trust a man who never forgets a face, especially if it's above a rack like that: that is Natalie Morgan.'

Why was I not surprised? She'd played me for a mug in Fabricant's office, and she must have loved it.

'I am professionally embarrassed,' Wylie Smith said. 'I should have known who she was, given her past history with the Gantry Group.'

'Forget it,' I told him. 'You're a man; you never got as high as her face when we met her. What I want to know is, what's her past history with Duncan Culshaw? Do you keep company annual reports in your office?'

'Only those of client companies,' he replied, 'but if Torrent has a website, you might find its reports available there. That's if they publish them at all, beyond what they have to list with Companies House, by statute. It doesn't have any shareholders to impress, other than Natalie herself.'

'What does the company do?'

'It's always majored in office equipment. When Natalie's uncle, James Torrent, was alive, they called him the photo-copier king. When that market started to die, Natalie was smart enough to spot the symptoms early and diversified into information technology. She sells, installs and updates computer systems to companies of pretty much any size. In fact, when I think about it, I recall that Torrent provided a new set-up for us a couple of years ago. Let me call our IT manager; she may have some information about it.'

I left him to do that, and phoned Cress Oldham. 'I've got the low-down on Torrent,' I told her, then explained what I knew of the company and its owner.

'How did Torrent get the leaked information? Do you have any idea about that?'

'From very early on. The source was Susie Gantry's second husband, now pretty much ecstatic widower, Duncan Culshaw. He stole it off her computer, although I'm sure he'll argue that he had every right to do so. This is the same guy who brought the Babylon Links project to his uncle, and got him to commit fifty mil of Gantry money to the project.'

'So why's he feeding information to this Morgan woman?'

'He's feeding her more than information,' I snorted, then had a particularly vicious brainwave. 'I'm going to email you an image. You might be a little shocked by it. I don't want you to do anything with it, until you hear from me, just keep it and think about where you would put it if you wanted to do the maximum damage to an individual's reputation. I do believe I can answer your question, but I'd prefer not to, until I've sorted a couple of things out in my head.'

'Okay to all of that,' she said. 'But help me out here. We've got Culshaw setting up the Babylon Links project with his uncle for Monsoon Holdings, then going to Torrent with information that's designed to shaft it and Phil. That right?'

'Spot on.'

'So who's Monsoon really?' she asked. 'Who's Fabricant fronting for?'

'Natalie Morgan, who else?'

'I don't get it.'

'If I'm right, you will, very soon.'

'It's funny you should say that,' Cress exclaimed. 'I've just been tipped off that there's a press briefing tomorrow morning, nine thirty, in Greentree Stanley's office in Canary Wharf. I have a contact there and he told me I should keep an eye on it.'

'No,' I contradicted her. 'It's not funny at all. It's the beginning of the end.'

'Of what?'

'Your client, Cressida; your client.'

Wylie was standing beside my chair as I ended the call. 'My IT lady has some Torrent corporate brochures,' he said. 'I've asked her to send them here.'

'Fine,' I acknowledged. 'Don't wait for them, though. You've done a lot for me today. Get yourself home.' The reports wouldn't add anything to my knowledge base, but he was pleased with himself, so I didn't tell him that.

After he'd gone, and after I'd attached Liam's candid camera shot to an email to Cress, I called Audrey. 'What news?' I asked.

'The French police have released Susie's body,' she told

me. 'The cause of death was a massive cerebral haemorrhage. The pathologist agreed with you, and with the consultant in Arizona. She should never have flown that far.'

'What about the funeral?'

'I don't know, Primavera.' She sighed. 'Like him or not, Duncan's her husband. I can't do anything until he gets back, and that won't be until tomorrow afternoon. He called Conrad to tell him that, and to say that he's got about a week to find a new job. He didn't say where he was though.'

'He's in Scotland,' I told her. 'He got in quick to check on Susie's will.'

'Where does it put him?'

'In the driving seat, from the looks of things. I'm going to try to set up the children's trust that Susie wanted, but even if I can, it'll probably be too late.'

'You sound really down, Primavera,' she said. 'You shouldn't; however this turns out, nobody could have done more than you.'

'Oz would have,' I sighed. 'He'd have killed that fucker Duncan by now.' It slipped out. I looked around for Tom, but he wasn't there. He must have gone back to his own room while I was on the phone to Cress. 'Don't tell Conrad I said that, please.'

'The mood he's in, I wouldn't dare.'

I decided to keep to myself the titbit about Culshaw shagging Natalie Morgan. That might have tipped both Kents over the edge. And then I realised . . . Tom had seen the image.

I jumped up, ran down the corridor to his room and

knocked on the door, hard. He didn't answer at first, not till I thumped it a second time. When he did, his expression was grimmer than I'd thought I would ever see it. His young face was set hard, full of rage.

'How could he do that, Mum?' he growled, as he stepped aside to let me in. 'He was Susie Mum's husband, she's only just died, and he was with another woman. You know what? When I see him, I hope he tries to hit me again. If he does, he won't get up this time.'

'Tom!' I exclaimed. I was genuinely frightened by him. I'd been half joking with Audrey about Oz and Conrad, yet here was my son making the same lethal threat, and serious, deadly serious, even if he was probably still too small to make good on it. I held him, but he was stiff in my arms. 'Please, love,' I begged him. 'Don't ever think like that. Remember what Liam said about anger being your enemy.'

'I don't care,' he snapped. 'I'm that man's enemy.'

'Cool it, boy,' I said. 'Cool it. Do you think your father would have wanted to see you like this?'

'Maybe he would. Maybe he'd have been proud of me if I did something to Culshaw.'

'No, my love,' I replied, 'he wouldn't. I promise you that, on my life. Why do you think I've brought you up to be good, kind and gentle? It wasn't his fault, but he wasn't always like that, he knew it, and he would never have wanted me to raise you in that image. That would have been his worst nightmare.'

I stayed with him until he was something like his normal self again, then I went back to the suite. I was still shaken;

Liam realised that straight away, so I told him what had happened. 'I'll take care of him,' he promised. 'I'll talk him down, clear his mind.'

I called the office; Cathy Black was still there. I told her that I expected the next day to be a busy one and that I'd be in by nine, at the latest. That was a long time away. I was restless; I still had some energy to burn, and an idea came to me, of how to use some of it up. I called Cathy again, and asked her for the suspended managing director's home address. He didn't live too far away, in Bearsden, an upmarket suburb on the western outskirts of Glasgow.

'I'm going out,' I told Liam. 'I'm going to see Phil Culshaw.'

'Want me to come?'

'Thanks for the offer, but no. I won't need a minder. Anyway, I'd rather you stayed with Tom.'

He nodded. 'Sure. How about I take him to the gym, let him show me his stuff, let him kick the crap out of me, if that's what he needs?'

I kissed him in the middle of the forehead. 'You're a doll, you really are. You do that, but listen, don't let him wear you out too much. You're forty-something, after all, and you're going to need some strength later on.'

I put my laptop in my bag and headed down to the lobby. The staff recovered my car from the park and I entered Culshaw's address into the satnav. It took me out of the city along Maryhill Road. I remembered that as being busy, but the worst of the evening traffic was over, so it was quiet. I hadn't been driving for much more than twenty minutes before my guide told me that I'd arrived at my destination.

I could have called ahead but I didn't want to give any advance warning. I realised there was a good chance he'd slam the door in my face, assuming he was in, but I was prepared to risk that.

His house was a big stone villa; there was a Range Rover parked in the driveway, almost hiding the Mini behind it from sight. I rang the bell, and heard an old-fashioned clanging from inside.

Phil was in. His eyebrows rose when he saw me standing there, and I reckon he did consider the slamming option, before deciding against it.

'Mrs Blackstone,' he exclaimed, then peered theatrically at my hands. 'Sorry,' he chuckled, 'I thought you might have been carrying an olive branch, but no such luck. I take it you want to talk, though?'

I nodded. 'I do.'

'Then you'd better come in.' He stood aside and ushered me into a dark hallway, then through to the back of the house. The place had a lonely feel to it. I looked around for any clues suggesting the presence of another person, but there were none, no lady's coat on the stand in the hall, only a well-worn Barbour jacket and a flat cap.

'You live alone?' I asked.

'Yes,' he murmured. 'Beth passed away four years ago. I know, you'll be thinking this place is far too big for an old guy on his own, but I can't be bothered to do anything about it. I haven't even sold her car.'

'No,' I replied, 'I wasn't thinking that, honestly. My house is as big as this and there's only my son and me to rattle about in it.' The guy was lonely, I realised. By unseating him, I'd probably taken the best part of his life away from him.

He led me through to the inevitable conservatory; in Britain every home should have one, it seems. It took up a good chunk of the back garden. We took seats facing each other across a low table. He offered me coffee, 'or something stronger', but I declined either. 'In that case, Mrs Blackstone,' he continued, 'what have you come for?'

'Let's cut the formalities, please. I want to show you something, Phil. It could go public and it involves a member of your family. That's one reason why I want to give you advance warning, but it's not the only one.'

I took my computer from my shoulder bag, and pushed the start button. I'd left it in sleep mode, so when it woke up, the image that had been there sprang instantly to life. It was Liam's candid camera shot, taken in Barnton through the bedroom window. I put it on the table and turned it around so he could see it.

He looked at it, frowned, then put on a pair of reading specs and looked closer. As he did, I heard a soft gasp.

'You know who she is?' I asked.

'Do I ever. That's Natalie Morgan.'

'So I'm told, although she called herself something else when we met in Diego Fabricant's office this afternoon.'

'Fabricant's office,' he repeated. 'What the hell was she doing there? Unless . . .' A sockful of pennies dropped, with the force of a thump round the ear. He stared at me. 'She's Monsoon Holdings? She owns the bloody land?'

'The way it's set up, we'll never prove that she's the beneficial owner, but that's the way I'd bet. Monsoon owns her house as well.'

He buried his face in his hands for a second or two then ran his fingers through his grey thatch. 'God damn it,' he sighed. 'And him too! Sleeping with the bloody enemy. Bugger it, bugger it, bugger it! I am sorry, Primavera; I had no idea.'

'I believe you, Phil. But tell me, please: how was the deal brought to you?'

He stood up, abruptly. 'Yes, I will tell you,' he began, walking over to a cabinet that stood against the wall. 'But first, I need something to help me absorb this.' He took out a heavy-based glass, a bottle of Isle of Jura malt and poured himself a sizeable slug. He waved it in my direction. 'Sure you won't?'

'No thanks.'

I waited, while he came back to his seat. He swallowed about a third of the whisky, then took another look at the image. 'I'll send you a copy,' I offered.

He shot me a sour grin. 'Better not. Bad for my blood pressure. The deal,' he continued. 'It was Duncan, of course, but you know that. He approached me last year. He said that he had an associate who owned a piece of land that was ripe for development as a posh golf course, aimed at a high-roller international membership. He explained that his colleague had done some research and had the vision, that all he needed was a funding partner to make it fly. I asked him how much, he said the whole thing could probably be built for under ten million, but it should appear that the developer company, which would be a fifty-fifty joint venture, had access to much more than that. This, he said, was because we'd be looking to recruit billionaires as members, Russian oligarchs, American hedge fund managers, German industrialists, et cetera, and that they would be more likely to be attracted by something that could demonstrate substantial resources. The proposition was that Gantry would agree to underwrite development costs of up to fifty million, with a verbal agreement that we'd only ever contribute less than twenty per cent of that.'

'Did you ever put this to Susie?' I asked.

'Yes, but not straight away. She had just gone to America for her first round of chemotherapy. Incidentally, Primavera, she told me at the very start of her illness that she was a long shot to make it, and that while she fought this thing she'd have to delegate much more than usual to me. So I signed up to the formation of Babylon Links PLC, and I only told her about it when the deal was done. She didn't question it at all.'

'Did you ever meet Fabricant?'

'That's the damnable thing; I didn't. Duncan was the intermediary all the way through. It was him who came to me and said that the planners had asked Fabricant to show a bank deposit of twenty million as a condition of their consent. I baulked at that, but Duncan told me not to worry, that Fabricant would agree to return most of it as soon as we'd been given the planning green light. Bastard stalled me on it, but I had, still have, hopes that he'd come through soon.'

'You can forget that, Phil.' I dropped the bombshell, that our partner was calling in the other thirty million. 'I'll resist it, but we're on a loser in court.'

'Couldn't we show that it's a conspiracy?' he suggested.

'They're not doing anything wrong; all they're doing is implementing a binding agreement which we signed.'

'That I signed,' he corrected me.

'In good faith, as I now acknowledge,' I added for him. 'Whatever, my advice is that under Jersey law we'll never prove that Natalie Morgan is the beneficial owner of Monsoon Holdings. Sure, I could leak that image to the tabloids and embarrass her and Duncan, the grieving widower . . . not . . . but if I did, she'd probably get court bans on publication within hours. My worry is, Duncan's involvement might damage the Gantry Group even further, given the power he can now exercise using the children's shares.'

Phil nodded. 'I apologise for my rudeness this morning, Primavera, and for my threat. Of course I'll withdraw my request for an EGM.'

'I'm sure it would be followed by a new one . . . if it's even necessary.'

'What do you mean?' he murmured, cautiously.

'You know what I mean,' I said. 'You know what'll happen next.'

He sighed. 'I fear I do. And there's no way of stopping it?'

'Not that I can see.'

'Then good luck. Primavera, I'm going to resign. I'll

announce it formally first thing in the morning and throw my full support behind you as executive chair. That might help.'

'It won't, but thanks for the gesture. Anyway, I don't want to be executive chair. I want to take my kid back home, as soon as I can.'

I left him in his big empty house and headed back to the hotel. The Rock 'n' Roll suite was empty too, when I stepped inside. That took my mind back to Phil Culshaw, and what I'd said to him; I really did want to be back home as soon as possible, for Tom's sake, for my sake, and for the sake of my new relationship. But I had other responsibilities, to Janet and wee Jonathan, and to the company, and if I was wrong about the outcome I envisaged, I couldn't walk away from them. Yes, Phil would carry on as managing director if asked, but honestly I wasn't sure that was the right move. He was beyond for what most people would be retirement age, and the ease with which he'd been suckered by his arsehole of a nephew cast doubt on whether he still had what it takes to run a hundred million pound company.

Of course, I was kidding myself there. It wasn't worth a hundred million any more, or anything like it. I switched the laptop back on to check the share price and shuddered when I saw it. The latest leak had done us in; my earlier bounce-back had been swept aside and it had gone back into free fall, down to forty per cent of where it had been at close on the previous Friday.

I was absorbing the news when the door opened and Liam came in, wearing one of the hotel's white dressing gowns that we had found in the wardrobe. He was slicked with sweat, and his face was flushed.

'I didn't realise till just now, but I am out of shape,' he announced. 'Tom and I ran on treadmills, side by side, same speed, same programme. He'd still be going if I hadn't called it quits.'

I smiled at him. 'Are you going to blame me for that? "Women weaken legs." Wasn't that what Rocky's trainer said in the movie?'

'No, I was just busted. I got him to show me his stuff, though. He's good, way in advance of his age, and very, very fast with his hands and feet.'

'Did you get the anger out of him?' I asked, still anxious about the way he had been.

'I tried to show him that his outrage was over Culshaw's behaviour,' he replied, 'and that his feelings had no place within the discipline he's studying. What I told him was that he should feel pity, not anger, for somebody as morally bankrupt as that, and that he needs to have patience, for sure as hell our sins and our guilt catch up with all of us eventually.'

'I can't think of Tom as having sins,' I confessed, 'or guilt.'

'He has pretty low counts in both, I'll grant you,' Liam chuckled, 'but we all have sins. I've told you my great sin. I took it upon myself to condemn my old man to death. Although he may have deserved it, the decision wasn't mine to make, and I'll do penance for it every day of my life. As for guilt, you never know when that's going to find you. For example, I feel slightly and irrationally guilty over sleeping with you.'

'Why?' I asked. 'Is your nose hurting?'

He felt it. 'No, not a bit. I know how Oz felt about you, that's all.'

'The late Oz,' I pointed out.

'Sure. I told you, it's irrational. Don't you feel some of it?'

'Maybe the first time we did it,' I admitted, 'there was a pang. Then I remembered how he felt about you, and since then I've been able to believe that if he'd had to choose someone for me to get together with, it would have been you.'

'But do you really? Deep down? Believe it?'

I nodded. 'Yes, I do.'

'But what about you? Suppose I'd never met Oz and we'd never met before and there were no associations with the past? Would you have chosen me?'

I took hold of the lapels of his robe, pulled him close, and kissed him. 'When I saw you last Friday,' I told him, 'then when we met on the beach, when I had no idea who you were, the truth is, I chose you then. It took me a day or so to realise it, that's all.'

'When we get back,' he whispered, 'back to Spain, can I stay for a while?'

'Honey,' I replied, 'you can stay for as long as you like. I know you didn't set off on your travels looking for a ready-made family, and if you decide it's not for you, I'll understand that, but I'll help you find out, for as long as it takes.'

Fifteen

The bomb was dropped next morning, as I'd known it would be. Cress rang me in the office at five to ten, but I knew all about it by then, for I'd been monitoring the Stock Exchange website on the computer in what had been Susie's office and was now, however reluctantly on my part, mine, and had read the announcement at the moment it was made.

A takeover bid had been lodged by Torrent PLC for the Gantry Group PLC. It valued the company at thirty-five million pounds, a couple of million above its quoted valuation based in the morning's share price, but around a third of its real worth. Fifteen million of the offer price came from Torrent's own cash pile; the other twenty mil would be funded by a new share issue, already underwritten by a consortium headed by, you guessed it, Mr Diego Fabricant.

'The bastards!' I shouted, as I took Cress's call. 'They're going to use our own money to buy us. You can bet that the twenty million will be diverted from the Babylon Links account.'

Of course, there was even worse. The announcement had concluded by saying that Torrent PLC had already secured acceptance of its offer by a representative of holders of more than fifty per cent of the Gantry equity. Duncan Culshaw, Mr fucking Murdstone, had committed Janet and wee Jonathan's inherited shareholding to seal the deal.

'What you said yesterday, Primavera,' Cress sighed, 'you were right. It is the end. But why?'

'I believe it's the culmination of a vendetta, but I won't know until I've talked to the bitch who's behind it.'

'Does it relate to that image you sent me yesterday?'

'Indeed,' I snorted. 'Very much so.'

'Who were those people? How did you get it? Who took it?'

'She's Natalie Morgan and he's Duncan Culshaw. It looks like they've met before, doesn't it? My boyfriend took it. Duncan visited Susie's lawyer yesterday, to confirm his position under the will as the children's guardian and administrator. I found out about it and asked Liam to follow him to see where he went. That's where he led us.'

'Do you want me to leak it? The trouble is, it wouldn't mean anything outside Scotland, and even there . . .'

'I know,' I said. 'Investors don't read the sort of paper that would publish it. No, don't do anything with it. Common sense tells me this is the time to stay on the moral high ground, even if it means smiling as we mount the scaffold.'

'What are you going to do?' she asked.

I'd been giving that some thought. 'I believe that I have a duty to call an emergency board meeting. I can do that right away, and I will. Gerry Meek's here, I can ask Phil Culshaw to come in, and Audrey can sit in on the internet. We'll have to consider the offer formally and make a recommendation . . . not that it'll make any difference, by the looks of it. What about the minority shareholders? Given your experience, how do you think they'll react?'

'Normally I'd expect them to cut their losses and accept. But you'll have a decision to make yourself, won't you, for your son?'

'No I won't,' I replied, firmly. 'I'll explain the situation to him. With what Susie left him, he now owns twenty-six per cent of the Gantry shares. He can't be forced to sell, and if he doesn't want to, I won't make him. Liam, my partner, has a few shares as well; I can see him staying in there if only to make a nuisance of himself at the annual meeting. Thanks, Cress,' I concluded. 'I'll be back in touch after the board meeting. We'll have to issue a formal reaction. Cheers for now.'

I hung up, then called Phil. He was up to speed with the news and he hadn't been surprised either. He knew what had to be done as well as, if not better, than I did. I set the meeting for eleven, giving him plenty of time to get to the office, then had a similar discussion with Gerry Meek, and asked Wylie to join us as well.

When I returned to my room, I had a call waiting. It was from a man I'd never heard of, but that didn't stop him being rather pissed off.

'Mrs Blackstone,' he began, in an accent that could have come straight from the oil barons' club in Houston, 'my name is Buddy Beaujean. I used to be a friend of Miles Grayson, until he persuaded me yesterday to invest eight million sterling in your company. I did that on his say-so, because he said you were a chance worth taking and now I find that my stake's worth five million and I've pretty much got to settle for that. I've tried to contact Miles to thank him personally for his helpful advice, but he's gone to ground, or maybe to Mexico, which is much the same thing. So you hear from him, you tell him, Buddy says thanks, but don't be givin' me any more hot stock tips.'

'I thought you Texans had balls,' I retorted.

'Say what?' he exclaimed.

'You heard me. You haven't even asked what I have to say about it, yet you're in the bloody lifeboat rowing for shore as hard as you can.'

'Indeed?' he drawled. 'So tell me, ma'am. What are you going to do to make forty-eight per cent worth more than fifty-two?'

'I don't know yet, but I'm working on it.' The guy had riled me; I let him have it. 'Fuck it,' I snapped. 'Guys like you don't invest money they can't afford to lose, not at the sort of notice you did yesterday. Okay, run out on me and you'll only lose three million; stay and you'll either find you lose most of what's left, or you'll make a decent profit at the end of the day.'

'Do you have any idea how you're going to bring that about?' He was curious, and his accent was suddenly less cowboy.

'At this moment,' I replied, 'not a single one, but there's this. The guy I was married to for a while, and whose name I still use, we had several things in common, but the greatest was this. We were both inexplicably, but invariably, blessed with the most extraordinarily good luck. You're a gambler, or you wouldn't have invested in me. So, Buddy, stick with me now.'

I didn't give him a chance to come back. Instead I slammed the phone down and left him to think about it.

Pure bravado, pure bullshit, ancient history. I didn't have a single card in my hand and I knew it. Well, no, maybe I had one. I would find the best family lawyer I could and instruct the implementation of Susie's wishes about the children's trust. I was sure that my power of attorney had ended with Susie's death and Greg McPhillips becoming her executor, but my talk with him had left me with a candle flame of hope that the court might respect her clear wish.

It took one phone call to blow it out. I caught Harvey January on his mobile, in a break between court sessions, and explained the situation. He was appalled by what had happened, and outraged that his niece and nephew were being manipulated, but that didn't override his legal instincts.

'You could try it,' he said, 'but if it came before me, I'd probably rule against you. Even if you did win a couple of rounds, it would be appealed all the way up to the Supreme Court in London, and meantime the existing guardian's rights would continue to be exercised.'

'Even if there's been fraud?'

'If you could prove fraud, that would affect the situation, but you're right. These people have been clever, so you never will, or not unless the law of Jersey is changed, and don't look for that to happen in a hurry. Sorry, Primavera. Barring miracles, we've had it. I say "we", because I'm as angry about this as you are, but if no law's been broken . . . well, we're down to Divine intervention.'

I thanked him, hung up, leaned back in Susie's chair and stared at the ceiling. That's what I was doing when God walked into the room.

'Miles,' I gasped, amazed, as he stepped through the doorway. 'What the hell are you doing here, and how did you get here?'

'On my jet, of course. This couldn't wait for normal scheduled.' He grinned from ear to ear. 'Sister-in-law,' he laughed, 'some things are so good that they have to be done face to face.'

Sixteen

Once we reached the Edinburgh Park office complex, the headquarters of Torrent PLC was pretty easy to spot. It wasn't the four-storey building itself, although it was classier than most of its neighbours in that it was faced in stone; no, it was the towering pole in front of it, with a bloody great 'T' on top, visible from a mile away.

We parked in the visitors' area and my driver and I went inside, into a square atrium, with glass walls looking down on it from the floors above. The reception desk was set in the middle; I announced myself to the young man who was stationed there.

He nodded. 'Miss Morgan is expecting you. If you'd sign yourselves in, please . . .'

I signed for both of us. The lad tore slips from each form and fitted them into plastic cases, then handed them to us. 'We like you to wear these all the time you're in the building. Health and Safety, you understand.' I didn't, but I nodded anyway. He handed me a key card. 'You'll find the lifts behind the desk. Take the one on the left, it goes all the way up. Put the card in the slot you'll find there, then press the button.'

I wondered why they both didn't go all the way up, but found out pretty soon. Natalie Morgan's office suite was on the roof of the building, out of sight of the car park, built around the glass ceiling of the atrium. Another young man met us as the lift opened. 'Mrs Blackstone.' He frowned. 'Miss Morgan is only expecting one visitor.'

I smiled, sweetly. 'And my driver is expecting to wait in an anteroom. It's what drivers do, isn't it?'

'Of course.' He chuckled. 'If you'll follow me, please.'

We did, along a corridor with a door at the end, facing us, and a low sofa outside. 'If you'll just take a wee seat there, sir,' our escort said, as he opened the heavy wooden door for me. It seemed to be the only upright surface that wasn't made of glass. (I must explain that it's a Scottish peculiarity, that in my home nation you are never simply offered a seat. It's always 'a wee seat'. It doesn't matter how small you are, or how large, or on the dimensions of the furniture in question; it's always 'a wee seat'.)

Natalie didn't stand as I entered. She leaned back in her very big seat and smiled at me, a look of triumph as naked as she had been last time I'd looked at her. And yet there was something else there too, a question that she couldn't quite pin down.

'Come to hand over the keys to the kingdom?' she asked.

I didn't wait to be offered a chair, I sat down facing her. 'I thought we should meet,' I replied. 'Imagine my surprise when I found that we had already.'

'Indeed. Maybe you think I should apologise for my small deception in Diego's office. If so, tough; apology is not my style.'

I shrugged. 'I don't give a toss,' I said. 'I would like a drink, though. It's going on lunchtime.' I glanced at a wine fridge in the corner. 'White wine, slightly dry, that would be nice.'

Natalie gazed down her nose at me. 'If you wish. I might even join you.'

She rose, walked across to the cooler and took out a bottle; Fransola, by Torres, I saw from the damp label. It had been opened but it was kept fresh by a pressure cap. She poured two glasses, and handed me one. The bitch had legs to die for, and clearly she was committed to figure-hugging clothes.

She eased herself back into her swivelling seat. 'You must be pretty close to setting a record,' she murmured, 'for the shortest period of office of a company chair.'

'I'll be there until my successor is appointed,' I pointed out. 'That can't happen overnight. You still have minority shareholders to buy out.'

'I take it the Gantry board will recommend against acceptance.'

'We've still to reach a consensus on that. I'm against, of course, and so is Audrey Kent, but my colleagues are still considering their position. Have you had any other acceptances yet?'

'It's a little early for that.' She frowned, very briefly, but it was her first sign of anything short of total confidence.

'You're still working on it, aren't you?' I said.

'Working? On what?'

'On how I knew before I walked in here that Kim Coates was actually you, given that you seem to be very camera-shy. Your face doesn't appear in any of Torrent's corporate brochures, and when I trawled the internet I couldn't find a single photograph.' I reached into my bag, took out a print of Liam's image and tossed it across to her. 'That's how.'

She picked up the image, and as she realised what it was, her eyes widened then she frowned again, full force, for real. 'What the hell is this?' she hissed.

'What does it bloody look like? What I don't understand, Natalie, is . . . why the hell didn't the idiot bother to close the curtains? Do you like it in the daylight, is that it? Can you fake it either way?'

'You cow! I could go to the police with this.'

'What makes you think I haven't?' I shot back. 'You and Culshaw, with the aid of his ageing and gullible uncle, have conspired to cheat the majority shareholders of the Gantry Group into accepting an offer for the business that undervalues it ridiculously. And he's gone further; the people he's cheated are my son's sister and brother, by committing their controlling interest to you at that price.'

'Oh really,' she blustered. 'Don't be so fanciful.'

'Don't give me that!' I shouted at her. 'I bloody know, okay! And what makes me even angrier is that I also know I'll never be able to prove it! I'm angry because I've spent some time as a guest of Her Majesty, and I would so enjoy sending you to do the same. So think on that, madam chair-in-waiting, as you're running the merged company with not much more than the percentage you have already. My guys and I haven't reached a recommendation to minority shareholders, because that's pretty much us now. My partner has an investment, Phil Culshaw and Gerry Meek have private holdings, Buddy Beaujean, my Texan support, he has a sizeable chunk. When you add them to my son's twenty-six per cent . . . and he has said, Natalie, without my coercion that he'd rather stick hot needles in my eyes than sell to you . . . we will have a block that's big enough to be a fucking spear in your side, never mind a thorn.'

'And I don't care,' she yelled back, 'because I've got it. Susie Gantry's business, bloody Oz Blackstone's business is under my control; my only regret is that they're not here to see it! I'd have loved that even more. I don't care about the company; all I want to do is wipe it off the face of the earth. I hated Oz for what he did to me, when I was with Ewan Capperauld! But for him, nobody would ever have known about it, but he spilled the beans and caused the chaos that followed. Then when I tried to get even with my first takeover bid, he got in the way of that too.'

She had so lost it that I thought for a second she was going to spit at me. 'As for Susie,' she hissed, 'little miss perfect? Businesswoman of the Year three times? Sure, thanks to her sucking every dick in Glasgow to get the votes! Well, let them fucking rot, the pair of them, because finally I've had a day of my own against them!'

She was out of her seat, leaning across the desk, glaring at me, eyes like organ stops.

'Sit down, Natalie,' I told her quietly. 'You've made your points; some of them might even be the truth. Now just tell me, how long have you been using Duncan to hatch these plots of yours? Because they weren't his alone, that's for sure. He's not the sharpest tack in the box. The exposé book about Oz for example; I'll bet that was your idea all along.'

'Okay, I'll give you that one,' she conceded. 'You want to know? Is your mobile switched off?' she asked. 'I don't want to fall for that one the way he did.' I took it out of my bag, showed it to her, then laid it on her desk. 'Good,' she said, 'then I'll tell you, for it isn't going to do you any good. Duncan and I have been a couple for a few years, but we kept it quiet.'

'How did you get together?' I asked.

'He did some writing for me. I fancied him, and it went on from there. He is a bit of a stud, I must tell you; his sword is mightier than his pen, and no mistake. We didn't make a noise about it, though, because I didn't want old Phil to know. The last time I tried to take over the Gantry Group, when Oz got in the way, Phil helped him stop me.'

'Are you telling me you were using the guy as a weapon all along?'

She shook her head. 'No. I didn't have that in mind at the start. But when Phil introduced him to Susie, and he told me that she'd made a flat-out play for him, I thought, "why the hell not?" so I told him what I wanted him to do. At first, all I'd thought about was getting some revenge in general. Yes, the book was my idea; I know that Oz was no lily-white, and don't you try to deny it, Primavera, so do you. But it was meant to embarrass Susie, that was all. Using it to extort cash from you, that was all Duncan's stupid idea. I don't know why, but Duncan hates your kid; that's where it came from, why he did it.'

She paused for a couple of seconds. 'Yes, I know, it was stupid; I went ballistic when he told me, I almost chucked him out, I was so mad. He backed off from Susie, thinking you'd be bound to tell her, then, just a couple of weeks later, Phil told him that she was ill, very seriously ill, maybe even terminally, and that he'd be pretty much running Gantry for a while.'

'Was that when you came up with the Babylon Links scheme?'

Natalie smiled, her self-confidence and self-satisfaction restored. She nodded. 'I'd owned the land for years. My Uncle James bought it for a song from a friend who needed some cash. He was a secretive sod, was old James; in particular he wasn't a big fan of inheritance tax, and did everything he could to avoid it. He salted away all sorts of assets in offshore companies, mainly Monsoon, using a nominee shareholder, usually Diego Fabricant. They all came to me when he died. Some I disposed of, but the Monsoon Holdings land was pretty much useless, so I was stuck with it.'

She sipped some wine and gazed at me, across her desk. 'There are some big advantages in looking like me,' she said.

'Probably the biggest is that people focus on one's body without even considering one's mind. But in business that can work against you, especially when you find yourself running a major company in your twenties as I did. That's why you didn't find my image on any of my corporate literature: I don't want it to affect perceptions of Torrent PLC. You must know this, Primavera; you've probably experienced it yourself. Little Susie, on the other hand, not being quite so gifted in the looks department, found it much more easy to be taken seriously as a businesswoman. You with me?'

I nodded; I couldn't disagree with her.

'What I'm saying is that I really am very bright. I think even you will concede that Babylon Links was a masterstroke. When I heard of Susie's illness, I knew that Gantry had to be vulnerable. But it was still too big for me to swallow without conceding a substantial slice of the ownership of Torrent. In other words, I couldn't do the deal for cash alone, there would have had to be shares involved, diluting my one hundred per cent ownership. So I wondered, "With Susie gone for a while at least, can I find a way to destabilise Gantry's share price?" and that's when the golf development was born, a joint venture, my land, their cash, and great wedges of it, without anyone ever knowing that I was involved because the true ownership of Monsoon is untraceable. Brilliant, yes?'

'Clearly so,' I conceded. 'It's worked, even if that owes a lot to poor old Phil being suckered by his nephew.'

'He was one of Susie's bigger mistakes,' she said. 'I knew from Duncan that the old man has never got over his wife's death. He goes home every night, gets drunk and talks to her across the dinner table, as if she was still there. Do you ever do that with Oz?' she asked, suddenly. 'Did Susie?' She laughed. 'Did the two of you ever get the ouija board out and try to summon up his shade?'

There's something hypnotic about Natalie Morgan. As I'd listened to her, I'd been drawn into what she was saying, seeing the sense and logic of it. With that last vindictive taunt she blew it all. But I bided my time.

'Still,' I countered, 'it was a long shot, was it not?'

'Not at all,' she insisted. 'The way it was set up, once Phil had taken the Gantry Group in he couldn't get it out. The damage was done. Then Duncan had a message from Susie, via Phil. She said that she didn't have long to go, that she didn't know why he'd left her . . . that was the first time we knew that you hadn't shopped him . . . and that she wanted him back. So I told him to go to her. I saw the way to complete control and now I have it.'

'The marriage was your idea?' I asked.

'Of course. It was really handy being so close to Nevada, where you can do the deed in a couple of hours if you really want to. Viva Las Vegas, eh? As it turned out, Duncan made it work just in time. To be honest, I didn't think Susie would be silly enough to defy the medical advice and fly all that way.'

'No. You'd have thought the loving husband would have put his foot down and forbidden her.'

She shot me the archest of looks. 'Oh, please,' she chuckled. Then she winked at me. 'You weren't anticipated, I admit. I was astonished when you popped out of the woodwork on Monday as the new chair. You of all people, the woman whose husband the little slapper stole.'

I laughed, so heartily that she was taken aback. 'Yes, she was good at that, wasn't she?' I rose from my chair, and headed for the door. 'I think it's time my driver joined us,' I told her, over my shoulder.

'What the hell are you doing?' she called after me.

I ignored her and opened the door; my driver stepped through it and into the room. As he did, he took off the grey German officer cap he'd been wearing, and the big Vuarnet sunglasses that had covered half his face. 'I don't think you've met my brother-in-law,' I said, 'but you may know him by sight. He's not as reticent as you are when it comes to cameras. Did you get that, Miles?' I asked.

'Every word of it,' he replied. 'Good quality.'

'I'll call security,' Natalie threatened.

Miles hook his head. 'Don't do that. There's a guy downstairs in the lobby by now; he won't let them anywhere near here . . . unless you have half a dozen or so, in which case he'll only delay them for a while.'

I resumed my seat, picked up my wine glass, and took my first sip. 'Ouch,' I murmured. 'It's a shame to treat a fine wine like that. You should use nitrogen storage; prevents oxidisation.'

Natalie stared at me; she'd run out of words, temporarily.

I nodded. 'Yes, you really are very bright, aren't you? Sixty watt at least.' I picked up my mobile from the desk. 'Yes, this is my phone,' I said, 'and it really is switched off.' Then I produced another from my bag. 'This is my boyfriend's, and it isn't.'

Miles produced a third from his jacket. 'This is my nephew Tom's phone.' And a fourth. 'This is mine; your entire conversation is recorded on it.'

She sat there, pale but fierce. 'And what are you going to do with it?' she challenged.

'Are you kidding?' he laughed. 'I'm going to see the friendly local police force, honey, and I'm going to play it to them.'

'And what exactly will they do?' she snorted. 'Tell me what law I've broken.'

'Well,' he said, 'there's this one. It's rare, I'm sure, so rare they've probably never had a case before, but it sure as hell has to be illegal somewhere.'

He grinned as he eased himself into a chair, beside mine. 'When Primavera told me yesterday morning what had gone down with Susie, and what she guessed was going to happen, she asked me to confirm that she and Duncan had actually been married, legally and above board. So I had an employee call the Clark Country marriage registration office and run a check. The person there did a computer search for the name Duncan Culshaw, and sure enough, there it was, he and Susie Gantry, Mr and Mrs.'

He gazed at her. When it comes to hypnotic looks, Natalie was an amateur compared to him; she couldn't break away.

'Trouble was,' he continued softly, 'the name was coughed out twice. Same man, same blood group, same nationality, same passport number, married in Las Vegas four years three months and five days ago to Miss Natalie Morgan, of Edinburgh, Scotland. Legally recorded, and never annulled in the great state of Nevada, nor, I will bet you, anywhere else. You didn't have time, did you? Susie was so ill that you took the chance and let Duncan go ahead and tie the double knot.'

She shrunk, visibly, into the big chair. When she looked at me, she wasn't super-confident, arrogant Natalie any more, she was just a scared lady.

'I have all the paperwork, copies of every document,' Miles told her. 'There's a warrant out in Vegas for Culshaw even now. I've got no doubt the Edinburgh police will issue one for you as soon as we've seen them, for conspiracy, by encouraging your lawful husband to commit bigamy. After that, they'll see how many other laws you've broken.'

'And as for your takeover bid,' I added, 'that is royally fucked, if you'll excuse my Catalan. Since Duncan and Susie's marriage was never legal, he can never have been Janet and wee Jonathan's stepfather, so he can't have committed their shares in your support. We've already been to see Susie's executor. He'll have called the cops himself by now, Natalie, and set them on your husband. You're next, just one phone call away.'

She picked up her wine and drained it. I pushed the rest of mine across the desk, and she did that in too. She looked out of the window for a while, then back at me. 'What's the way out?' she asked.

'What makes you think there is one, lady?' Miles drawled.

'There's always a way out,' she replied, 'if you look for it.'

'Why should we want to?' I asked.

'But you do,' she countered, 'otherwise you'd have made that one phone call by now. What do you want?'

I looked at Miles; he nodded. 'Okay,' I said. 'Here it is. You make the phone call; not to the police but to Diego Fabricant, instructing him to agree to the winding up of Babylon Links PLC and to return the Gantry Group's cash. Next, you announce this afternoon that you've dropped your takeover bid. All this happens before we leave this building. Agreed?'

She nodded. 'Yes. Relatively cheap at the price, I suppose.'

'Ah,' I continued, 'but I'm not done yet. Tomorrow morning you'll receive a counter-offer for Torrent PLC from an American venture capital fund. Its owner is a significant shareholder in Gantry, who'll be very happy by then, since he'll have made a tidy gain on his investment yesterday. You were out to pick up our company for about one-third of its real value. This offer will be generous by comparison. It'll offer you fifty per cent of yours.'

'What?' she gasped. 'Do you expect me to accept that?'

'Yes,' Miles said. 'Absolutely. I've looked at your accounts. I pulled them from Companies House before we drove through here. They're wide open; Torrent PLC is significantly overvalued, and its assets are a lot less than people think they are. It doesn't even own this building; that belongs to the same offshore company that owns your house, and you own that, so you're out of sympathy. Fifty per cent is okay, so when my friend Buddy's offer is on the table, if you don't accept it, we walk away, you go to jail, your client base evaporates, you go bust and the liquidator comes after you for your private wealth. You're not as smart as you thought you were, Miss Morgan, but you ain't stupid either. You'll still be left with a few million. I think it's crazy to let you go, but it's what's Primavera wants; I'd have turned you in without a second thought. Deal or no deal? You have five seconds.'

'Deal,' she sighed. She looked shell-shocked.

So, why had I asked Miles to let her off lightly? Let's just say I'm a kind person at heart. Within limits. 'One final condition,' I told her. 'When we leave here, you do not get in touch with Duncan. I know where he is, or at least where he's going, and the pleasure of breaking the great news to him has to be all mine.'

I poured the last of the tainted Fransola into one of the glasses and we left her there, to dwell at length upon the speed with which the world can be turned upside down by a single reckless act driven by over-confidence.

'What she said, about Susie,' Miles murmured as we walked towards the lift. 'About how she got those business awards. That wasn't true, was it?'

'Nah!' I replied. 'Maybe one or two in her time, but not all of them.'

Seventeen

Liam was waiting in the lobby downstairs. He looked at me as I stepped out of the lift and I nodded.

'All of it?' he asked.

'The works; she's a pragmatist. She had this irrational hatred of Oz and Susie,' I told him. 'Hopefully she's worked it out of her system now.'

'Let's hope so,' he agreed. 'To be honest, I didn't think she'd agree to sell out, even though the Buddy guy's offer was fair. To be even more honest, I don't understand why he made it. He's a US investor, this is Britain.'

Liam hadn't been there when Miles had spoken with his pal; he and Tom had still been on the Hampden Park Stadium tour. (Tom wasn't impressed, he confessed afterwards, having done the Camp Nou equivalent in Barcelona.) 'There's more to it,' I said. 'I'll tell you about it later.'

We'd done a lot of planning, Miles and I, in a very short time. The first part of our scheme for dealing with Natalie and

Duncan had gone as well as I'd dared hope. The second part lay ahead, and it was going to be made a hell of a lot easier by the luxury of having my brother-in-law's plane at our disposal.

He's been married to my sister for about fifteen years now. We've been close, he and I, for all that time, but I don't believe I've ever seen him as up for anything as he was that day. He's a guy who's made it big in his career; because of that, inevitably he'd become used to doing everything at arms' length. The search of the Las Vegas marriage records, for example: he'd told somebody to do it, and it had gotten done. Being involved in the aftermath, hands-on, had turned him into a kid at a lock-in in a sweetshop.

He, Liam and I joined Tom in the car, where he'd just eliminated the last Zombie Gunship on his iPad, and headed for Edinburgh Airport. On the way, I called the office and told Wylie to put the short-notice board meeting that we'd arranged on hold. I turned in the hire car, then we took a short taxi ride to the general aviation terminal, where the plane and its crew were waiting. It occurred to me as I got on board that the last time I'd been on a private aircraft the journey hadn't ended where it was supposed to, but I pushed that thought to the back of my mind and trusted in the singularity of lightning strikes.

Miles's pride and joy was the newest Beechcraft passenger jet, the aviation equivalent of a Roller. It isn't very big, but it can do Los Angeles to Scotland in one jump with a couple of thousand miles left in the tank, so the journey we were about to take was a short hop in its terms. I slept for most of it. The last couple of days had taken more out of me than I'd realised, and I'd nodded off before we reached cruise height.

When Liam roused me, we were a hundred miles short of Nice, our destination airport, and it was six forty-five, Central European Time. Immediately, I thought of Susie, who'd been on the same flight path, and who would never waken again.

We were hoping that Duncan had caught the Easyjet Edinburgh–Nice flight; that would have landed mid-afternoon, according to the timetable, and he'd have arrived in Monaco ahead of us. A guess, but well-founded; he had no other option.

I thought we might have been held in immigration for a while, but Miles has been there so often for the Cannes Film Festival that they treated him like a local, and we were waved through. The car that I'd booked was waiting for us on the rank. I could have called Audrey and asked Conrad to come for us, but I didn't want to let even them in on the surprise that was coming. It was going to be too good to spoil for anyone . . . most of all Duncan.

It's no distance at all from Nice to Monaco, autoroute all the way until you descend into the principality . . . but not all the way into it in our case, for the family home that Susie and Oz had shared looked down on to the famous harbour and the Formula One Grand Prix street circuit. It was just short of eight o'clock when our chauffeur pulled up at the gate.

As always, it was closed. Normally visitors announced

themselves into a video camera, but there was a keypad beneath for those who knew the entry code, as Tom and I did. I let him punch it in, and the gate slid aside.

There was nobody in sight as the four of us walked up to the front door. It's on the landward side of the property, and it doesn't have a keypad, and not even a doorbell, since by the time visitors get that far, the household knows they're coming. There's a door knocker, though, an ornamental thing that's never used. Tom gave it three loud raps, and then we waited. Liam and Miles were standing to one side, so they wouldn't be seen through the spyhole, should it be Duncan who came to see who was making the noise.

But it wasn't. Nobody answered, not until Tom had knocked again, harder the second time around. When it did open, Audrey stood behind it, chubby, friendly, bright-eyed little Audrey . . . only she looked none of those things. She seemed to have shrunk, her cheeks were gaunt and there was fear in her eyes. They told me as clearly as words that something dreadful had happened.

'Primavera,' she exclaimed, then stopped as she saw the two guys. 'Who are . . .' she began.

'Miles and Liam,' I replied. 'We bring tidings of great joy . . . but . . . what the hell's up? And where is that bastard Culshaw?'

'The kitchen,' she whispered, as if she had to force the words out.

'This way,' I said, heading for it. The three guys made to follow me, but Audrey grabbed Tom.

'No, not you, son. You stay here with me.'

'Audrey!' he protested. He could have freed himself from her grasp, easily, but I shook my head.

'No, Tom. If Audrey says you stay with her, you stay.'

The kitchen door was ajar when we reached it. At first I thought the floor had been relaid. Susie had never liked the Roman-style white tiles, trimmed with brown, and had been threatening for years to do something about them, but red, Susie, no, not red, much too garish.

At first I thought . . . then I stepped through the door, felt the stickiness beneath my feet, moved past the island work surface in the middle of the room and saw, behind it, Duncan Culshaw, lying on his back, mouth wide open, eyes wide open, staring at the ceiling, his face a waxy off-white, looking as dead as anyone I'd ever seen. He was wearing nothing but a pair of Speedo budgie-smugglers. It wouldn't take a detailed autopsy to determine what had killed him. There was a great gaping wound on the inside of his right thigh, and both of his legs were covered in his blood.

Conrad stood beyond him; he was holding wee Jonathan in his arms. The kid's face was pressed hard against his chest, and his body heaved with silent sobs.

'Gimme him,' I demanded, walking around the other side of the work unit, to avoid the great crimson pool. Conrad handed him over, without a word.

'Why did you do it?' I asked him. 'Did he threaten the children? Or did he just push you too far?'

'Let's just say I'd had enough of him,' he replied.

'It wasn't Conrad,' wee Jonathan mumbled into my belly. 'It was me, Auntie Primavera, it was me.' The sobs began again, with full sound effects.

Why did I have no trouble believing him? You might wonder that, but the answer's quite simple. If Conrad Kent had decided to kill Duncan, he'd have done it in a very quiet place with no witnesses, no mess and no fuss.

'How?' I didn't say the word, I mouthed it.

'Duncan got back three hours ago,' Conrad began. 'He told Audrey and me, in front of the two kids, that we were fired, then he went for a swim. He had a few beers by the poolside, then he came into the kitchen. Audrey was here; she'd started to make dinner for the children. Duncan said something to her along the lines of, "Are you trying out for a job as a chef?" Little Jonathan was standing beside her. He started to protest, but Culshaw said to him, "Shut up, you, and learn some fucking respect. I'm your daddy now!" The little chap picked up the knife that Audrey had been using to cut the veg, and lashed out at him. He didn't think about it, he just did it. He'd have grabbed anything, a carrot, a courgette, a handful of spaghetti, whatever was nearest. It happened to be the knife, and it happened to be as sharp as a razor, as all good chef's knives are. I was in the children's day room with Janet when the screaming started. And there was a lot of it, from Audrey, from little Jonathan, and most of all from Culshaw. As soon as I got here, I knew he didn't have a prayer. You can see that for yourself, Primavera.'

I nodded agreement; the wound was very high on the inner

thigh and the whole femoral arterial structure seemed to have been severed. A tourniquet wouldn't have done much good.

'He bled out in a couple of minutes,' Conrad concluded.

'When?'

'Less than a quarter of an hour ago.'

'Where's Janet now?' I asked.

'Where I left her, I hope. I asked Audrey to stay with her.'

I assumed she'd taken Tom there too. 'Have you done anything?'

'No,' he replied. 'Not yet. There hasn't been time. I suppose we should call the police.'

'And have this little boy stigmatised for the rest of his life?' I retorted. 'He might be below the age of criminal responsibility, but I don't care. I'm not having him mauled by the media.' Wee Jonathan made a snuffling sound, which I took to be agreement. 'He's just lost his mother. What's happened here stays here, just like Vegas. You're the fixer, Conrad; so fix it.'

'Primavera.' Liam spoke from the doorway. 'Miles can't be involved in this.'

'The hell I can't,' my brother-in-law protested.

'No,' I said, firmly. 'He's right. It's best all round for you to leave. You've got too much to lose. Whatever we do to clean this up it's going to be stupid, and it's going to be illegal. Our Dawn would kill both of us if I let you get involved then we got caught.'

'Nonetheless,' he insisted, 'I have to do something to help.'

'Then take the kids, Tom as well, and get them out of here on your posh new plane. Take Susie's car, leave it in a car park at the airport and once you've got where you're going, text me the bay number and I'll have it collected.'

'Okay,' he agreed, 'but where? I'd head for California, but the kids would need visas.'

'Then go back to Scotland. Take them to Mac Blackstone. Better him than my dad, since he's only Tom's grandfather, and the two Js have nothing to do with him, and don't know him. I promised Tom he'd see his granddads this week, and Mac hasn't seen the other two in a long time. Then you go home; I'll let you know later how this all pans out.'

'I'll do that,' he agreed. 'But hold on a minute. What about the chauffeur who brought us here? Won't he talk?'

'Miles,' I sighed. 'This is the south of France. As far as black car companies are concerned, we were invisible.'

'In that case, it sounds like a plan,' he conceded. 'But what about the little guy?' He nodded in the general direction of my bundle, who had quietened down. 'Isn't he going to need looking after?'

'There's nobody better to do that than Janet and Tom.'

Miles came with me as I took wee Jonathan to join his siblings. The other two were quiet, knowing that some serious shit had hit the fan but not quite what. 'There's been an accident,' I began, 'and Duncan's dead.' Janet and Tom were both impassive. At least they didn't whoop with glee.

Then I told them the rest as Conrad had explained it. 'We need you all to go away with Miles, to Grandpa Mac in

Anstruther. The rest of us have things to do here, then Liam and I will join you. But one thing,' I stressed. 'You don't talk to anyone else about what happened here. Wee Jonathan needs to try to forget about it and you have to help him.'

They both nodded. *Another year of childhood's gone in a single day*, I thought, and it almost broke my heart.

'What about Mum's funeral?' Janet asked, solemnly.

I looked back at her. 'Where would you like it to be? Here or in Scotland? It's your decision, yours and wee Jonathan's.'

She considered the question for a while, then replied, 'Scotland. It's where she was from.' Her brother nodded agreement.

'Then so it shall be,' I promised.

'Won't someone come looking for Duncan?' Audrey whispered as I left.

'The Nevada State police might,' I replied, 'and possibly Strathclyde. Shame he was never here. I doubt if anyone else will, though.'

Miles and the three children were gone in less than half an hour. Meanwhile, when I got back to the kitchen, the blood was almost all gone. Liam and Conrad had stripped off their clothes, all of them, to avoid contamination, hosed the bulk of it into a drain in the floor, and were cleaning the remnants with what smelled like industrial-strength bleach.

Duncan was still there, but he was wrapped in what looked to me like a sail.

It was. 'I have a boat,' Conrad said. 'I keep it in the marina at Fontvieille. Sometimes I do a bit of night fishing, and tonight's going to be one of those nights. Once it gets fully dark, I'll load him,' he jerked a thumb at the body, 'into the car and take him down.'

'We will,' Liam murmured.

'No, just me.'

'All due respect, Conrad, but there are bound to be cameras down there. You might be fit, but looking at what I can see right now tells me that carrying that thing on board, you ain't going to be able to make it look like it's nothing more than a sail.'

'But it won't look any more right with two of us carrying it.'

Liam grinned, and flexed his musculature for a second. 'There won't be two of us carrying it.'

'When you two naked men have finished your pose-down contest,' I barked at them, 'get used to the idea that there will be a woman on board.' Liam opened his mouth but I shut it for him. 'You guys are not risking everything on your own,' I decreed. 'No arguments.'

And that's how it was. We were able to park a few metres away from Conrad's mooring. Liam lifted the sail and its contents out of the trunk and hefted it on board as if it weighed ten kilos or so. On deck the three of us unrolled it so that the body fell into the footwell out of sight of everything, even the sharpest-eyed owl, and we fixed the sail to the mast, as if it had been taken away for maintenance, and returned renewed. Obviously there were no bloodstains on it, since Duncan didn't have any left.

We left the small port under the engine, but once we were clear, Conrad went on to wind power. It was a nice night for a sail, less humid on the Med than it had been on land. We headed away from shore until the lowest of the lights of Menton started to disappear below the horizon, when our skipper deemed we had gone far enough.

Duncan Culshaw didn't have a coffin, or even a shroud, just the boat's massive anchor and a few other heavy weights that we had found on board. Liam had never met the man alive, so he said a couple of words as we tipped him over the side. 'So long, mate.'

He'll be well into the aquatic food chain by now.

Conrad and I shared a bottle of red on the way back. Liam stuck to fizzy water; not even a nautical burial could shake his resolve.

Conrad was on his second glass when he glanced towards the horizon. 'It's funny how life works out, isn't it?'

I raised an eyebrow. 'Bloody hilarious,' I snorted.

'No, seriously,' he insisted. 'I had a plan for dealing with Culshaw and that was it, what we've just done, only my version was that I was going to persuade him to come night fishing for real, go as far out as we went, then tip him over the side. He couldn't swim a stroke; never left the shallow end of the pool. I was going to give it ten minutes then make a distress call to the marine patrol. They'd have found him floating somewhere, and a neat line would have been drawn under him.'

'Couldn't we still do that?' Liam asked.

He shook his head. 'Hardly. We'd have a tough job explaining why three of us couldn't have managed to save him. Also, the cops would wonder why he didn't come to the surface. But we couldn't have that happen, could we, not with that fucking great hole in his leg.'

As he spoke, my mind went back a few days, to the evening when we'd found out about Susie and Duncan being married. 'Friday, in my house,' I said to him, 'that tune you started whistling, when we were having a drink and talking about it; I know what it was now. It was "Sailing", wasn't it?'

He grinned, but said nothing.

As we neared port, and the lights grew brighter and Conrad had to concentrate on steering, I leaned against Liam. 'What happens next?' he asked.

'You mean apart from me fucking your brains out when we get home?'

'Yeah,' he murmured. 'I was thinking a little beyond that.'

'As far as the company's concerned, that will be sold; Buddy Beaujean's the likely buyer. He says he wants to expand his involvement in Britain and Europe. Obviously I have to talk to the kids about it, but I'll try to persuade them that they need to make lives for themselves and that it would only be an encumbrance to them.'

'That makes sense,' he agreed. 'Now go further still.'

I knew what he meant, and I had an answer ready, one that had been forming since Susie's death, and maybe even before. 'Janet and wee Jonathan have no one,' I said. 'No blood relatives other than Mac Blackstone, who's an old man, and Oz's sister Ellen, who's a great woman but who hated their mother, and couldn't hide it from them forever. They're orphans, Liam. Worse, they're rich orphans, and at least one of them is bound to be traumatised by what happened tonight. So what do you think happens next?'

'You'll adopt them,' he murmured.

'Absolutely. It's only right that they're brought up with their half-brother.' I paused. 'And that would be a hell of a lot for a lifelong bachelor to take on, more than I could ever ask.'

'Will you live here?'

'Hell no! With the memories of tonight, and Oz haunting the bloody place? No, it gets sold, and the two Js move to St Martí. They'll be fine with that. They like it there. I'll try and persuade Conrad and Audrey to come with us. If I can, we'll buy them a house near mine.'

He nodded. 'Sounds good,' he agreed. 'So why are you freezing me out?'

'I'm not,' I protested. 'I just assumed . . .'

He kissed me. 'Assume nothing about me, lover,' he whispered, 'other than the best.'

'In that case,' I sighed, with a smile, 'let's just try it on for a while and see if it fits.'

Eighteen

That night, when, finally, I fell asleep, I had the strangest dream.

We were still full of light, Liam and I, when Conrad parked in the garage beneath the house. The two of us climbed the single stair that led to the hall and stepped out.

Audrey was there, and still she looked anxious, even more than she had a few hours before, if that was possible. 'It's okay,' I reassured her. 'Deed done, everything fixed.'

'No,' she whispered. Her eyes flickered to her right. I looked over her shoulder and saw a figure, a tall male figure, the garden lights lending him an aura as he stood in the doorway that led to the deck around the pool, silhouetted against the night sky.

I moved towards him, frowning. He couldn't be the police, surely.

Then he stepped into the light; and his aura seemed to come with him.

He wasn't the police.

He was wearing jeans and cowboy boots, and a check shirt with no sleeves, so that you could see every one of the hard muscles on his arms. In a pose-down with this guy, Liam was a loser.

We moved closer to each other. His skin was tanned, but not like that of a northern European on holiday; instead, like that of a man who lived and worked under a harder sun.

He didn't look like Keanu Reeves any more, that was for sure. His hair was mostly grey, military-style, in what they call a buzz cut, as neatly trimmed as the beard that defined his features. His nose was a little broader than I remembered Keanu's having been, his cheekbones a little higher, his eyebrows a shade further apart.

Then he spoke, in an accent that might well have been Scottish in origin but which had become imbued with other influences, mostly west coast American.

'Okay,' he growled, 'where is the bastard who's trying to cheat my kids?'

And that's when I fainted in my dream, and in the same moment sprang into full wakefulness, my eyes searching the room in vain then filling with tears as I realised that however good, and true and loyal the sleeping man beside me might prove to be, he would always take second place to a ghost, one that would never let me alone.